"*The Last Shade Tree* ... takes readers on an enlightening journey across time and around the world. With vivid descriptive prose and engaging dialogue, Panofsky treats her readers to a novel infused with intimacy and adventure, at times humorous, and often deeply serious. The profound narrative, expressive writing, and wholly original concept are sure to intrigue and please a vast audience." ~Alex McIe

The Last Shade Tree

Margaret Panofsky

ALL THINGS

THAT MATTER

PRESS

To my brother Richard

Acknowledgments

I warmly thank my daughter Jessica Underwood Varma and Charles Waddington, and Ann Abruzzo, Catherine Sullivan, and Mary McGann, for reading versions of the manuscript and making valuable comments. I am also grateful to friends, family, and students who corrected the foreign language snippets: Mirjam Frank, Steven Freygood, Jeremy Lin, Trinidad Montalva, Jack Peisach, and André Wilson. I also convey special thanks to Stephen Kaldon for creating the stunning cover art, Alex McIe for writing the pre-publication review, Tatiana Daubek, photographer, and especially Harry Ossahwee for help with the Cherokee.

I am eternally grateful to Deb and Phil Harris of All Things That Matter Press for ushering me into their family of authors. As my editor, Phil remained ever gracious and patient as he prepared *The Last Shade Tree* for publication.

Saving the best for last, I extend heartfelt thanks to my friend Steven Freygood for his editing suggestions and for providing inspiration and continual encouragement. The help my twin brother Richard Panofsky has given me leaves me speechless—which is why I have dedicated *The Last Shade Tree* to him.

Chapter 1 Aleta in Trouble

Aleta gazed all around the airless room, trying not to seem too obvious about it. To relieve the institutional sameness of the walls, someone had decorated them to appeal to little kids. Along the top of the doorframe and just below the ceiling a foot-high border of gray hippopotamuses with pouting red lips and long curly eyelashes bounced on big balloons. She noticed that every fourth hippo wept mawkish tears over a balloon that had popped under its rotund, pink-tinged bottom.

Aleta squirmed from right to left, trying to rearrange herself to fit the confines of a bright orange plastic children's chair that was too tight even for her slender frame.

She couldn't help thinking, Why did they stick me in a room meant for six-year-olds? This chair is an insult, I have real hips now. It's so humiliating. I'm fifteen years old!

Then she sneaked a glance from under her eyelashes at Dr. Agonopoulos, the court-appointed child psychologist, and she couldn't help resenting the word "child" that came before psychologist. He towered over her lowly orange chair from behind his oversized army-green metal desk.

She wondered, Is this on purpose? He looks so authoritative and scary—and I suppose he should—because I broke the law!

Or at least she had caused her parents to call the police, bringing out half the force of Alameda County—not once, but twice—when she'd gone on some terrifying trips she couldn't explain. And that was her problem. Because Dr. Agonopoulos was going to ask her just that. Explain them.

Aleta took a second glance. Now she was pretty sure he wouldn't be mean to her; he was working hard enough to arrange his facial muscles into an expression of fatherly concern. His face, along with his absurd name that sounded like *Agony* and a mustache that looked like a hedge, brought her perilously close to laughing out loud. But at the same time she was so nervous about the ad-lib performance she'd have to give that she feared she might pee in her pants.

***

Dr. Agonopoulos nodded in her direction, the signal for her to begin. She barged ahead, hardly able to believe what was coming out of her mouth.

"The first time I left home—I know it sounds so, so stupid—a Greyhound bus with lots of flashing lights flew right into my bedroom, and I just had to get on it. The thing took off and in about—I don't know—half a minute, it came down in a town called Tahlequah. That's what the sign at the city limits said. There was something wrong with all the cars on the road. They looked, old-timey, you know, like from a gangster movie."

She averted her eyes from the intentional blankness of Dr. Agonopoulos's face. *What can he possibly be thinking about me? That I'm crazier than a bedbug?*

The doctor was thinking something a little less clinical. *Hmm, doesn't look the type, but does this fresh-faced young lady really read trashy science fiction? Or watch* The Twilight Zone *when she should be doing her homework?*

He tapped the top end of his fountain pen three times on his desk blotter, then asked with a studied indifference, "Is there anything more about your journey that you feel like sharing with me?"

Aleta felt squashed by the orange plastic chair arms.

"Yes, there's a lot more, but it gets really weird, and sad, too."

With a little groan, she shifted her weight to her other hip. "The bus stopped in front of a bunch of buildings that looked like a school. These four big white rocks all in a row were lying on the ground at the entrance and had initials painted on them: S-O-T-S, but I didn't know what they stood for. A cloth banner hanging in front said, Congratulations Class of '45.

"At first, I was scared. I thought maybe it was a really far-away transfer school my mom and dad had picked out for me because they were mad about something I did. But the date was way too early."

Aleta hesitated, her voice catching. "Here's the sad part. There was this little boy standing by those rocks. He was really small, maybe four years old, and … and so *sweet*. He wasn't doing anything. He just stood there alone in the dark. He had huge black eyes and all his hair was shaved off.

"Someone in a uniform came running out of one of the buildings. She grabbed his shoulder, and she was so big and tough, I could tell she was hurting him on purpose. She started shaking him and yelling in his face, 'Sequoyah, you can't do this every night. No one is coming for you, not tonight, not *ever*. You've earned a punishment.' Then she turned fast and walked away. She expected him to follow her, but I don't think he understood anything she said."

Suddenly Aleta's self-control deserted her. Ashamed, she hastily dried off her tears with a big wad of Kleenex that the seasoned Dr. Agonopoulos handed to her.

"Dr. Agon … Agonopoulos, you have to believe me, this upsets me so much, and I don't know why. The little boy started stretching out his arms to me—to *me*. And he was crying, so I held his hands tight. He was saying over and over, '*Diquenvsv aquenvsdi aquadulia!*'"

Dr. Agonopoulos paused to write down an approximation. "Do you know what those words mean, Miss Rosenthal?"

Aleta shook her head. "No, no. The words were in a foreign language that sounded like music. And his face, he had eyes kind of like … like I don't know what. A place where you could drown yourself if you were sad enough. I just didn't know what to do, and besides, I had to get back on the bus. So I left him."

Just then her throat constricted, throttling the spate of words she never could have said out loud. *That language the little boy spoke tore right through me. And just then I did something horrible to him. It was because he held my fingers too tight. I had to pry them off—one by one. With each finger I loosened, I felt a part of him crumble, and his tears just gushed out. Then his hand slipped out of mine like he'd given up. How can I forgive myself? Me, a big huge girl, I ran away from a little child.*

Aleta returned from her reverie. "Pretty soon I was home. There were tons of police running all over the lawn. My mother must've checked my bedroom and thought I'd been abducted. So she called the cops even though she hates being embarrassed, which I seem to do to her all the time. And just in case you hadn't guessed, she gets upset easily. But she's not half as bad as my father. He's—"

Dr. Agonopoulos interrupted her by standing up. The hour was over. But as he tried to escort her from the room by her elbows, she froze in place, lowering her head. She pushed her long red-gold hair aside to wipe two fresh tears off her cheeks with her sweater sleeve.

God, I wish I didn't have to go home. I'm in so, sooo much trouble. My parents won't talk to me they're so mad, and how will I get into college if I have a police record?

Dr. Agonopoulos gave her shoulder a comforting pat. She assumed by the way he did it that he understood her, at least a little. But what came out of his mouth was not encouraging. He said some things she would categorize as clichés.

"Don't be too hard on your parents, Miss Rosenthal. They're just worried about you, that's all. We'll sort this out, never fear. See you next week."

***

Once the door was safely closed, Dr. Orestes Agonopoulos sighed as he plopped back down on the hard-as-Hades desk chair with the aerated fiberboard seat—purchased with tax dollars collected from the good folk of Alameda County, California. Truth be told, his anatomy was not so different from the hippos on that abominable border that defiled his office walls.

He took off his coat jacket and loosened his muted steel-blue tie before taking one tiny nip from the flask in his desk drawer, just one, to prepare himself to write up notes on the bizarre Aleta Gaia Rosenthal. Then he tapped his pen three times on the blotter.

To begin with, why couldn't she be an ordinary juvenile delinquent like Teresa Birdweed who threw a brick through the window of Lacy Lady to steal a prom dress? Or Harry Tapfuss who just last week tried to run over a cow on Highway 80? And what's in a name, anyway? Aleta Gaia? Did her Jewish parents consummate the first night of their honeymoon in a drunken stupor on the steps of the Parthenon?

He took one more tiny nip before looking at Aleta's grades for sophomore year, the top sheet of a packet sent over from Alameda High. *Good Lord, straight A's, should have guessed.* He skimmed the page labeled "Special Notes." *And what's this? She's a commended art student and a violin prodigy? At her age, I just played baseball at the field next to the municipal garbage dump and lusted after Agrippina Papadakas.*

He took a third nip before reading Miss Rosenthal's police reports. They were housed in two brown paper envelopes with bright red stickers to hold the flaps shut. And across the fronts, diagonally stamped dates about three inches high read June 4, 1959, and June 19, 1959. *The poor kid. She has two informal citations pending at the Juvenile Court, and it's up to me. Either I recommend dropping the whole damn mess to let her go live her screwball life or I don't.*

So I'll just take another really tiny nip, or maybe two, and then I'm off to the library to look up "Tahlequah" in the atlas. Also the initials "S-O-T-S." He glanced at his notes. *Oh, right. And those mysterious words,* Diquen-*something, something,* Aquen-*something, something,* Aquadulia, *that came out of the mouth of the little foreign boy who upset her so much.*

He shook his head in wonder. *What I wouldn't give for half her imagination.*

Dr. Agonopoulos readjusted his tie and reached for his coat jacket and briefcase.

***

Aleta had one more appointment with Dr. Agonopoulos. As she folded herself into the orange chair, she wondered what he'd think about the second trip—when she happened to meet an older man who said his name was Ethan Marcus. And not just any man, but someone she was having trouble putting out of her mind.

"The next time I was taken somewhere, getting there was awful, like being sucked into a drain. I ended up in Frobisher Bay, Canada. I happen to know because the man I met there gave me his sweatshirt which says *Frobisher Bay 1974* with a big polar bear on the front. I still have it."

She added as an afterthought, "I looked Frobisher Bay up in the atlas, and it's really a horrid place, almost at the North Pole."

Dr. Agonopoulos perked up. They were getting into new territory. "You met a man?"

"Well, yes," said Aleta. "I landed flat on my face on some concrete, luckily with soft snow on it, but it hurt something awful. I was at an airport; I could tell from the planes sitting there. This man picked me up. He looked old—well, not old exactly—maybe thirty and kind of handsome if you didn't look close. He stood me on my feet, but I sort of crumpled."

Aleta wasn't sure how the psychologist would take the next part. "I was shaking, it was freezing, and I was scared because the Northern Lights were so bright. So he held me inside his parka."

Dr. Agonopoulos's bushy eyebrows seemed to be crawling up his forehead. "He did? *Inside?*"

Aleta was glad the doctor couldn't read her private thoughts. *Well, I really hated everything about it. How his hairy chest looked. And how it was covered with goosebumps like an uncooked chicken breast. I was so cold he gave me his ugly sweatshirt right off his back. When I looked up at his face, the inside of his nose could've been a double train tunnel. I tried to run, but he was talking to me, trying to keep me calm. And it kind of worked as long as I didn't focus on his bald head and his big stomach.*

"And then?"

"You mean, what happened next? He told me not to be scared of the Lights because he knew how they worked, that he was a scientist employed at a laboratory near the airport—doing something-or-other. Oh, the '1974 Geophysical Arctic Studies Project.'"

"Well, after that I wasn't so scared, but that '74 date was way off, like fifteen years from now. I didn't know what to think."

Then came a typical question from someone like Dr. Agony. "How'd that make you feel?"

Aleta hesitated. "You mean him? It's just so hard to put into words. When we were together there was this special warm place in the back of my brain like we had the same feelings. I felt butterflies in my stomach. And he knew my name. It slipped out by mistake, but I could tell he'd met me before."

Actually, it was terrifying. How'd he know my name, anyway? And I was feeling all shaky inside like I might throw up any minute. Is that what romance is supposed to be about?

"Next thing I know, I'm lying on the grass under my bedroom window surrounded by cops. I said out loud, 'Not again!'"

Aleta noticed that the doctor's eyebrows had crawled back down, forming a frown. "Er, Miss Rosenthal, you're not seeing an older man who lives in your neighborhood … at 2:00 a.m.?"

The question and all it implied made Aleta bolt out of the tortuous orange chair. "Oh, no. No sir! I … I've never even been on a date."

***

It was over, and Aleta wouldn't miss the stuffy, artificially cheerful office and certainly not the orange chair or the parade of hippopotamuses. But she had one regret; she had grown to like the well-meaning Dr. Agonopoulos, whom she was pretty sure she'd never see again. At least for now, he knew more about her than anyone else, but then, she knew one of his secrets, too. The brandy. She could smell it on his breath.

Thank goodness he said he'd recommend a clean slate for her with the Alameda County Sheriff's Department. But the talk they had next didn't clear up any of her confusion or worries. He said that she had an "out-of-control" imagination, and suggested that she stop reading trashy science fiction—but frankly, she never touched the stuff because she thought it was lowbrow. Then he mumbled something that she didn't quite catch about far-fetched adolescent fantasies. Finally, he strongly advised her not to take neighborhood walks at 2:00 a.m. in a shortie nightgown, even on nice June nights.

As Aleta rose to leave, Dr. Agonopoulos admitted, way too sheepishly for a psychologist, that some things were inexplicable, for example, the Frobisher Bay sweatshirt now in her possession and the sentence she remembered in the Cherokee language. That was most likely what the little boy had been speaking.

Once again Dr. Agonopoulos patted her shoulder as he escorted her to the door. "And I can even tell you where he was, Miss Rosenthal. He was standing in front of the Sequoyah Orphan Training School in Tahlequah, Oklahoma. At least that's what it was called back when there were 'old-timey' cars on the road."

Aleta's heart went into her throat as she turned towards him. "Did you find out what the little boy was saying?"

Dr. Agonopoulos shook his head. "No, but I expect that someday you will."

***

Aleta couldn't shake the notion that she had special gifts that defied the laws of nature and not just her taking those disturbing trips. She had also seen something really crazy. In fact, she couldn't describe it to anyone, not even to a psychologist like Dr. Agonopoulos. How come all the cops swarming around hadn't seen it? Because both nights after she got back from those places, an extra moon hung in the sky. That meant two moons were up there, and the new moon made the one she was used to look tiny and sick.

Chapter 2 Ethan and Aleta

Three robins perched on the sill outside Aleta's bedroom window, peering through the glass. Their black heads twitched and bobbed above puffy orange chests as their bright eyes popped with excitement. Aleta was practicing her violin, or rather experimenting with strange noises. She loved playing the violin. In fact, she loved it so much that her parents were afraid she might want to be a professional musician.

Aleta thought bitterly, It's their own fault. They made me play in the first place so I could be more perfect than that midget with the runny nose, Judith Rachel Steinberger from second grade, and what's-his-name, I forget, but Nathan something, the other Jewish kid down the street.

Aleta was an intuitive musician with unusual gifts. She knew how to improvise with sensual abandon, creating jarring dissonances and eerie harmonics that she dreamed up on the spot. She could go on all night, either making up her own music or playing Bach, although she adored later music, too. She had another talent up her sleeve—she could pick up almost any tune after hearing it once.

She mused, flexing her left hand to give it a rest, *Catching on to other people's music so fast; that's copying. I'm kind of like a parrot or a mynah bird if you think about it. Hey, hold on—weird.*

She kept her eyes on the windowsill. When the robins didn't fly away but continued to peer into her bedroom with shiny round eyes, she wondered if she had just stumbled into the uncharted territory of avian hypnotism.

Indeed, she had. Particular note patterns would bring different species—more robins, sparrows, pigeons, mockingbirds, and at dusk, even owls. If she really concentrated, the birds would stay on the sill after she had stopped playing. She would then quietly lay down her violin on the bed and pick up her watercolors. She painted them either realistically or in fantastical close-ups. By looking straight through their little eyes and into their minds, she could extract their true natures. Her portfolio grew. She figured that she would save the paintings to show her art teacher, or submit separate pages with those college applications that would be coming up in a few months. She had no idea that her art was almost as haunting as her music.

What really fascinated her was feeling like some kind of god. Play and the birds came flocking. Paint them, and they belonged to you, sort of.

She thought, What if, what if I could bring the man from Frobisher Bay the same way? Play with my whole heart, and there he'd be, just dying to love no one else but me?

The idea made her feel uncomfortable. She acknowledged that any sensible girl would have put the bizarre excursions from more than a year ago behind her. And seriously, the little boy from Tahlequah with tears running down his cheeks and eyes you could fall into had moved her far more than the old guy from Frobisher Bay who was a little bit creepy. But a four-year-old kid doesn't fit all that perfectly into a romantic daydream about the perils frustrated lovers go through to reach, well, something—having sex, maybe?

***

Aleta had been summoned to the living room by Queen Nefertiti and Dr. Germ. She noticed that her mother's pose with one arm outstretched along the grand piano displayed to full advantage a dove-gray suit with smart black velvet-covered buttons. This was a sure sign that the ever-appreciative Mrs. Lola Gonzales was coming to clean today.

Her father glowered as he stared anxiously at his watch. In addition to being late for work, he was annoyed. He barked in his daughter's general direction as he surveyed his wrist, "Aleta, what the hell's wrong with Berkeley? Thanks to me and a few of my colleagues it has the finest microbiology department in the world. Not that the self-absorbed *artiste* would care."

Aleta had an argument ready to support her dream school, but she shelved it as he raised his voice to an impressive boom. "Do you seriously expect me to pay out a fortune for tuition, room, and board to some inferior spa-by-the-sea when you can go to the best university in the state for *practically nothing?*"

Her mother interrupted him, taking Aleta's side, for once. Looking her husband in the eye, she did something mysterious with her mouth, a cross between a kiss and a pout, and yes, Aleta had practiced it in front of the mirror for years without being able to master its sexy allure.

"For goodness sake, Joseph, she'll be almost eighteen. Let her go where she wants. Santa Margarita has a marvelous music school and high-class students—not your usual riffraff who run around barefoot and pee in the Sproul Plaza fountain."

He mumbled to himself, "Talk about riffraff, my daughter will be a stone's throw from the Santa Cruz boardwalk." But under her sway, Dr. Germ's reasoned arguments collapsed.

"I'll think about it, Diana, as long as she joins a sorority."

Queen Nefertiti tossed her head in triumph before turning toward Aleta. "Darling, are you *seriously* planning to wear that burlap bag to school?"

***

A week before the beginning of the semester at Santa Margarita, Aleta visited the Housing Office since she had lost out in the dormitory lottery. She stared at the bulletin board covered with note cards. Here was a possibility: *Geraldine Watson, 20, looking for female student to share large sunny apt., 2 br. close to campus.*

***

From the first, Geraldine and Aleta eyed each other warily, summing up their differences, because in every way that counted, they were opposites. Geraldine was big, with flamboyant breasts that overflowed her red sundress; Aleta's modest bosom was hidden demurely beneath the gathers of her white cotton peasant blouse. Geraldine introduced herself with a trumpet's raucous blast; Aleta barely managed the peep of a newly hatched chick. Most important, Geraldine showed up at the door with a muscle-bound ape slobbering into her neck; Aleta had *virgin* written all over her.

The new freshman had a sober discussion with herself. *Geraldine's fat, but she's way sexier than me. That is seriously undermining. Can I take it?*

Aleta watched with a mix of envy and derision as Geraldine brought home a different man almost every night for the first week, and then the second and third. Maybe they were the same five or ten, recycled, she wasn't sure since they were all football players. As confused as Aleta was by such behavior, she hung on to her roommate's every word about sexual exploits. Geraldine had it all figured out, mainly just how far to go to keep them coming back, hoping for more. *If only* Aleta had half the confidence around men as her saucy new friend who could laugh uproariously at stupid jokes, even as she rolled her eyes and stuck out her tongue behind her date's back. At these moments, timorous Aleta thrilled with admiration. Would she ever feel at ease around these alien creatures?

***

Not surprisingly, Aleta had not met a single male interested in her—but she refused to panic *quite* yet. As all solitary people try to convince themselves, quality is more important than quantity. Besides, the semester had just started and the very air at Santa Margarita seemed charged with unknown possibilities. The early-morning fog, the brilliant sunshine at midday, the cool nights smelling of the sea—all held romantic promise for Aleta. She was sure something wonderful would happen any day now.

***

Ethan Marcus left his rooming house a few minutes earlier than usual. He felt an odd sensation rubbing in the back of his brain, a feeling sweeter than anything in his experience, of warm silk and the perfume of roses. He found himself wandering off his usual route towards a street of high-rent student apartments. Oh, the intensity! It was close to unbearable. The sound of a violin reached him—music by Bach coming from a second-floor window. His knees started to tremble and he panicked. *Please, no! Don't tell me I'm catching the flu so early in the semester.* He leaned his forehead on a lamppost to recover.

The music ceased and when he looked up a shadow appeared behind a lace curtain. And then, the most beautiful girl he had ever seen lifted it aside.

Ethan tried to pull himself together. *No wonder I feel sick. She looks pretty damned unattainable.*

Aleta stared at the boy by the lamppost for a long moment as her heart skipped a beat. How had she known that he would be standing there? Why else would she have put down her violin to pull aside the curtain? She couldn't fathom the trick her mind was playing on her because she recognized him. It wasn't possible. She felt suddenly brazen. She had been conjuring up her secret romantic lover from Frobisher Bay just now through her playing. In her imagination, she had desired this for more than a year.

Only something was wrong; this one appeared much younger. The youthful version was not handsome in the conventional sense, but he was a vast improvement over the older one. He was kind of cute, actually, although he wasn't very tall and was way too skinny. But he had a nice straight nose and friendly, brown eyes. Anyway, he was much cuter than anything Geraldine had dragged in.

She called out the window in an uncertain voice, marveling at her boldness, "If you wait just a minute, I'll walk to the campus with you."

Aleta and Ethan froze on the sidewalk, staring at each other. The wind, scented with late-blooming summer flowers, whistled past their ears as shafts of sunlight momentarily blinded them. But they came down to earth soon enough. They were, after all, two freshmen walking to their respective classes carrying piles of books. And they were nervous. Each felt obliged to say something, but the ideas wouldn't come.

Sometimes Ethan hated himself. As the campus drew closer and he struggled to find the words, he grew increasingly frustrated. *Holy shit,* he admonished himself. *Just ask her out, moron.* But he hadn't a clue what a girl who could play the violin like that would enjoy doing, especially on his crapped-out budget.

Aleta solved the problem for him.

"Ethan, I'm playing in the first concert of the semester tonight. My new violin teacher kind of said I have to." She peeked at him shyly from beneath her lashes. "My parents won't be there and my roommate hates classical music. Would you ...?"

Ethan's heart sang. He'd miss Engineering 101, but it didn't matter, not if it was only one time. No pull of conscience would keep him from going.

***

The concert hall was in the music building up on a hill, its high-arched windows glowing orange in the sunset. Ethan arrived early, carrying a single rose wrapped in paper; it had cost enough to put him on a diet of cornflakes for a week. He walked around on the lawn in front to calm his nerves. Was he dressed properly? Would he find anything to say afterward, and how could he take her out on $1.50? He tried to comb his unruly thatch of dark brown hair with the fingers of his free hand.

The audience inside the hall seemed to be mostly parents and music students holding instrument cases. Ethan had been too tongue-tied in the morning to tell Aleta that he loved classical music, especially Bach. He desperately wanted to hear the same Bach that had drawn him to her window, bewitched him, turned his knees to water.

According to the program, Aleta would play last. When she walked onto the stage in concert black, she fixed her eyes on him and smiled. But it wasn't possible. She couldn't see past the stage lights. And yet, he felt the same warmth in the back of his brain as in the morning. Ethan recognized the piece, and it *was* the Bach that had snared his heart. He was overcome with adoration, and admittedly, some lust. For a very long moment, even as she was playing, Aleta looked directly at him from eyes seductively half-closed. He was conquered.

Ethan went backstage clutching the rose in a sweaty hand. When she saw him, Aleta abandoned her admirers and hurried to his side.

She whispered, "Quick, get me out of here! This is the worst part."

Ethan picked up her violin case and pushed ahead, making sure that she was right behind him.

Out of earshot on the other side of the music building, Aleta doubled over with laughter. "I *hate* talking to them. I don't believe them, anyway."

Ethan was amazed. "But Aleta, your fans want to compliment you. They think you're really good."

"Do you really think so—from the bottom of your heart? I made so many mistakes." Tears filled her eyes.

He hadn't heard any. "Aleta, what if I said you sound better than my LP?" Embarrassed by his outburst, he awkwardly shoved the rose at her.

Aleta took it with a tremulous smile. She bent her head to bury her nose in the petals, breathing in the hothouse scent. Then she shoved aside a lock of red-gold hair that had fallen across her face. "Can I take you out for coffee since you saved a damsel in distress?"

"Coffee? Me? Oh, sure, right, coffee. I'd love that." His voice trailed off. Her asking first was contrary to the rules of conventional etiquette, but she had saved him from an explanation about his bank account, depleted from buying textbooks at prices bordering on extortion.

***

Aleta chose the comfortably grubby Momus Cafe. There were poetry readings most nights and hanging on the wood-paneled walls were amateur paintings that would never sell. As she and Ethan sidled between the tightly packed customers, a guitarist on a small stage strummed aimless chords while staring mournfully into space.

Aleta and Ethan faced each other across a tiny marble-topped table that was sticky with spilled sugar and ringed with wet circles. Silence reigned. Both of them were relieved when the waiter shambled over to take their order, looking even more hangdog than the guitarist. Ethan waited for Aleta to make up her mind. He was famished but was determined to choose the same thing since she had offered to pay. Following her lead, he selected a shake in a different flavor and when the waiter left, they were on their own.

More silence and suddenly Aleta found herself chattering about her hilarious parents, her absurd English professor, her nymphomaniac roommate. Then she stopped, her face red with embarrassment. She looked down at her own tense fingers clasped in her lap. "I'm so sorry. I did all the talking. What are you studying, Ethan? I should have asked."

He jumped. "Me? I'm … well, I'm only a freshman like you, so I'm not supposed to know this yet, but I plan to do a double major in engineering and physics."

As a look of disappointment crossed her face, he panicked. He hastened to add, "I'm not totally stuck on science. I've read tons of books about, about almost *everything,* and I played oboe a long time ago. I even played Bach once." He stopped, feeling ridiculous after the naked self-promotion, but he saw her eyes light up once more.

"Let me show you something wonderful." Ethan tore off the edge of his paper napkin, made a half twist in the long strip, and joined it together with his thumb and forefinger. "This is a road to … let's say, the fourth dimension. Follow your finger along it; it's called a Möbius Strip."

Aleta bent her head close to his to run her finger along the flimsy paper; after many turns on the outer and inner surfaces, she returned to the starting point. Her eyes sparkled. "It's a loop with two sides, no, with one side that was two sides before it got turned over. You can move forever without going anywhere. It's kind of frustrating, but that's how life is." She amended her statement, "If you're old."

The waiter returned with their order—a banana shake for Aleta and a coffee shake for Ethan. She tried a sip of his and wrinkled her nose.

"I hate the taste of coffee. It reminds me of my parents glaring over their newspapers at the breakfast table." She hesitated, then lowered her voice because she liked the drama of it. As she'd hoped would happen, Ethan leaned forward expectantly.

"I'll tell you a secret I never told anyone ever, not even my roommate, Geraldine. I call my parents Queen Nefertiti and Dr. Germ." As Ethan smothered a laugh, she went on, "If you ever have the pleasure of meeting them, you'll know why."

She was about to ask him about his parents but hesitated. By his expression, she could tell that he didn't want to talk about them.

Eventually, he mentioned off-handedly, "My father isn't living with my mother anymore, and she hasn't been feeling too well lately." He clammed up with his mouth in a straight line.

After that, they sipped their shakes in silence.

Then Aleta stared at the boy across from her, and she could not stop herself. She decided to try touching the back of his mind just like the man at Frobisher Bay had done to her. That was when Ethan felt it, a soft nudge, a gentle finger in his head. It was like the warm silk from the morning, only much more intense.

"What did you just do?" he asked in a dry whisper, his voice shaking. He also turned beet-red, thoroughly aroused. He wondered if she knew what the hell she was up to.

Aleta pulled back. That face; perhaps she'd gone too far. No, he was trying the same thing on her. She closed her eyes and took a ragged breath as the warm silk curled around inside her brain. When she looked directly at him again, she saw the adoration in his eyes. She was certain now. It made no sense at all, but she had found the stranger from Frobisher Bay, and he was just her age, too.

Ethan walked Aleta home and carried her violin, but he wouldn't hold her hand the way dates are supposed to. They felt shy suddenly and didn't have much to say. Aleta twisted her fingers straining the knuckles, hoping Ethan couldn't see how nervous she was.

She wondered, How do you get them to act affectionate if they're scared of you? Should she ask Geraldine? And a tiny thought kept nagging at the back of her mind. He wasn't *quite* everything she'd hoped for. He looked kind of handsome in an eager, unkempt sort of way, like Sal Mineo in *Rebel Without a Cause*—a tiny bit like him, anyway.

Something else pretty important was missing, though. He wasn't an artist, a writer, a poet, an actor, or a musician. It really didn't matter all that much how excited he felt about the miraculous physical world they inhabited, he would always be, well, a scientist, like her father. And he didn't display enough angst. Yeah, she knew she was still kind of immature, but that's what she loved in men: angst. The man from her weird trip to Frobisher Bay had plenty of it because she'd put it there. Every night, sobbing in convincing agony, she'd woven it into all their heartbreaking adventures—her arms wrapped around her wadded-up pillow.

Aleta stopped in her tracks as Ethan stared at her. *Oh, please, please, please don't let him know what I'm thinking. I'd simply die of embarrassment. I do love him. I do, I do. Sort of, I guess.* But one thing was certain; even if she had doubts, the ball had been set in motion. She had a real boyfriend now, and he was way better than any of Geraldine's parade of numbskulls.

*** *

The apartment's kitchen was about the size of a closet, but the girls weren't that interested in cooking beyond the basics. It was Aleta's night to make dinner for herself and for Geraldine and her latest boyfriend, Jack, Jock, or Jake—she couldn't quite remember which. The hefty pair were wedged together like sardines on the narrow sofa as he tried to explain football downs. Geraldine yawned and stood up. Jake— last week's boyfriend had been Jack, and Jock was the one from the week before—didn't notice her absence but just droned on like a stuck record.

Geraldine poked her head into the kitchen. "So what's cooking tonight, Ali?"

Aleta prepared herself for the inevitable fight. "Nothing really special, a mushroom omelet and a salad."

Geraldine made a gagging noise. "Jesus Christ, Miss Snob, don't you ever learn? My men like steak and fries, not this-*this sorry*, powder puff haute cuisine.*"

Aleta waved her paring knife and glared. "Yeah? Well, maybe you should cook. He's your boyfriend."

Geraldine hissed, "Pipe down, you bitch. He'll hear you."

So Aleta talked louder. "Let me think. Is that *hog* busting the sofa springs your fifth this month? No. Your sixth."

Geraldine shook her fist, her overstuffed sweater jiggling in accompaniment. "He's not a hog. Well, at least he's a *genuine* hog, not some ninety-seven pound weakling with no balls."

"Ethan is *not* a weakling. And he's just as equipped as—"

"So how would *you* know, Snow White?"

Geraldine had won the round, and Aleta felt her face grow hot with anger, and even shame. She slammed the paring knife down on a mushroom but missed, slicing deep into her thumb. "Goddammit," she yelped as blood began to spurt.

Geraldine blanched. "Hey, Ali, shouldn't you get a band-aid or something?" She hated the sight of blood and shut her eyes, backing into the stove.

Jake lumbered into the kitchen, but stopped in his tracks, eyes bulging. Aleta stared at them and panicked. She wailed theatrically, "My career. It's *over*." She thrust her thumb under cold water as blood ran down the sink drain.

The doorbell rang, followed by hammering fists. Ah, a diversion for the lily-livered spectators and none too soon. Looking relieved, Jake made a four-yard dash to the front door, followed by Geraldine.

Now blood was pooling in the sink. Soap, Aleta remembered, you were supposed to use soap. She screamed as she plunged her thumb into the bar; pain tore through the wound like fire.

Ethan slid past the halfback into the kitchen with Geraldine right behind him, grabbing at his shirt. "Hey, Superman, who called *you*, anyway?"

Without hesitation, Ethan wrapped Aleta's thumb in a dishtowel and applied pressure, holding her hand up in the air.

How ironic, she thought through her tears. This is the first time he's ever touched me. It felt strange and wonderful, like pins and needles all up and down her arm.

"Come on, you fucking assholes," Ethan shouted. "Call a fucking ambulance."

A flash of criticism momentarily blocked her pain. *Two fucks in two sentences. His choice of words could be more imaginative.*

In the end, Aleta and Ethan took a taxi to Student Health Services where a bored intern stitched and bandaged the wound. Afterward, they walked home because it was such a nice night. Aleta was still trembling a little, mainly from relief because the injury to her precious digit hadn't been worse.

She tried to make a joke. "Well Ethan, you saved me from certain death." As usual, she'd exaggerated and he didn't quite understand what she meant.

He tried to explain the facts. "I took a detour past your apartment, and I could just tell something was wrong." But a thought nagged at him. *How did I know? It defies science; I hate that.*

They walked side-by-side in silence. The scent of orange blossoms and jasmine mingled with the salt air blowing in from the west.

Aleta was puzzled. *What a romantic set-up. Why doesn't he do something like at least hold the hand without the bandage? Maybe Geraldine's right, and there really is something wrong with him.*

***

The following week Ethan and Aleta made a second trip to Health Services where the same bored intern took out the stitches. The wound had healed just as it should, but Aleta's thumb looked pale and puffy like an oversized slug.

On the way back, they decided to go to the top of Santa Margarita's bell tower, the school's oldest structure nestled among the other original buildings with their whitewashed stucco walls and red-tiled roofs. The pair took an ancient elevator to the top where the carillon's bells hung beneath squat arches.

Aleta and Ethan sank down by the balustrade that enclosed the four sides to gaze upward at the massive bells. As their shoulders touched, a wave of heat radiated between them. Aleta felt a flame run down her arms and into her stomach, hips, and groin.

Although his longing had often seemed unbearable, Ethan had never dared touch Aleta before, at least not in a romantic way, not even the tips of her fingers. But now he couldn't stop himself even though he had no idea what he was doing. He slid one hand all the way down her spine and the other deep into the silky hair at the nape of her neck. How was it possible to feel so enervated and inflamed at the same time?

Aleta felt her hands reaching into all sorts of places she had seen on him but never thought she'd touch. There was no kiss, just a sudden paralysis that Aleta later described triumphantly to Geraldine as first-time lovers' lockjaw.

Aleta and Ethan dropped onto one of the benches at the tower's entrance. They found themselves grasping each other's hands.

Ethan spoke huskily, the first words uttered by either of them since they'd gone up the tower. "Something happened up there, but I can't explain it."

Aleta had a ready reply, only mildly acerbic, "Then Ethan, don't try."

He embraced her, boldly murmuring into her hair, "I want to be alone with you. We'll find a place."

Aleta nodded her head uncertainly.

***

After Aleta's nervous consent at the tower, she had second thoughts. *I'll never be the same person after I do this, and I'm not sure I love him as much as he loves me. He's sweet, but what if I'm doing it more because he wants me to or to go further than Geraldine thinks I can? Oh, God no, I wouldn't fall that low.*

She and Ethan planned a hike in the hills behind the campus. They chose the popular Cove Crest Trail that wound among oak and eucalyptus for several miles before reaching the top, high above the bay's white-capped waves and rocky shoreline.

Aleta was an experienced hiker who left nothing to chance. But she wasn't perfect, and although she put their daypacks together like a pro, she didn't think to turn on the radio. If she had, they would've delayed the trip; the morning weather report predicted a freak thunderstorm and a torrential downpour. Not surprisingly, the trail was deserted as storm clouds built towers in the leaden sky.

Aleta walked in front. At every step, her expensive leather boots from Switzerland landed with a sure grace. Ethan hadn't seen her in jeans before; the curve of her spine and the sway of her hips nearly drove him into an adolescent frenzy.

The pair dallied over a picnic lunch packed by Ethan and when they thought to glance up, the sky had turned black—the storm was already upon them. Within minutes they were soaked to the skin, the thunder and lightning coming in close bursts.

Aleta screamed something about getting off the exposed trail. They ran willy-nilly along the crest of the hill and by sheerest luck, Ethan stumbled on a protruding rock. He inspected the outcropping impatiently before moving on, but instead saw a gaping blackness so huge that he knew a cave lay beneath. Scrub oak blocked the entrance, protecting the interior from the pelting rain. He turned back to show Aleta his discovery, to pull her inside with him, but she was gone.

Ethan ran in frantic circles, howling her name at the top of his lungs, ignoring the rain, the noise, the blinding flashes. And then he found her, lying in the soaking grass, face-down.

Oh God, don't let it be true. He turned her over ever so gently and pulled her limp form close, cradling her to his chest. He felt her stir, struggling against him.

Aleta sat up, looking deathly pale, but otherwise unharmed, although a burnt odor rose from her streaming wet hair. She was shaking from shock and exposure. He stroked her face and neck until she recovered her voice.

"Oh, Ethan, I got hit by lightning. Why am I even alive?"

He didn't reply so she continued in an awestruck whisper, "I saw something inside the light and it spoke to me, but not in words."

She sounded delirious, and Ethan didn't know what to do. If he went for help, he'd have to leave her alone. Instead, he half-carried, half-dragged her into the rock shelter.

Their new home was barely big enough to stand in, but that didn't matter. They sank to the stone floor, shaking from cold. Aleta was coming around, regaining her composure.

She tried to reassert her lost authority and mountain-climbing expertise. "We'd better take off our wet clothes before we freeze to death. I brought both of us sweatshirts. I hope they stayed dry."

First, they removed their sopping shoes and the socks that stuck to their feet. Then with chattering teeth, they stripped hastily and with some embarrassment. They didn't dare look at each other in the half-light that filtered through the bushes at the cave's mouth.

Aleta pulled two sweatshirts from her daypack. She slipped on the Bach sweatshirt that she had bought the very first day at the Student Union store, pulling it well down over her thighs. It was white, with Bach's giant-sized lithographed portrait across the front. She had loved that shirt the moment she saw it, delighting in its silliness. She wore it every day for a week until Geraldine remarked that Bach's eyes winked obscenely across her chest as she walked. For this trip, she had rescued it from the back of her dresser drawer. Thanks to her mother's elegant taste in clothing, it was the only sweatshirt she owned.

The shirt she handed Ethan was bright red. Emblazoned across it in tall white letters were the words, **FROBISHER BAY 1974.** A cartoon polar bear covered the whole front, completing a garment of unspeakable ugliness.

Bach and Frobisher Bay sat shoulder-to-shoulder, clasping knees drawn up to their chests under the oversized garments. Neither spoke because both felt ridiculous encased in thick fleece with nothing on underneath.

Aleta hated the way her brain kept reeling out thoughts that detracted from the romance she'd hoped to feel. *This may be the freakiest first-time sex anyone's ever had, and I won't tell Geraldine the details 'cause she'll accuse me of making everything up.*

Finally, Ethan cleared his throat; some things were just so hard to say. "Well, I thought maybe we'd find a place today, so this morning I bought a Trojan at the drugstore." Aleta seemed relieved that the subject had been broached, so he went on. "I was standing in a long line, and when I got to the cash register, the saleswoman waved it around and said in a loud voice, 'Fat chance.' She repeated it twice. Well, I'm not all that handsome, you know, and everybody in the line laughed at me."

Tears of empathy glistened in her eyes. "People just like to hurt each other, it makes no sense."

Then she sucked in her breath. *It could be worse. At least it's not a violin audition.* She lifted his hand carefully and slid it beneath the Bach sweatshirt up to one tiny breast. He caressed it, feeling the nipple go hard under his fingers. Then she slid his hand across to the other.

"That's all there is. Geraldine says they're way too—"

He stopped her words with something resembling kisses all over her face, for his mind was going fuzzy, he was hot all over, his heart was bursting beneath the Frobisher Bay sweatshirt. Aleta ran her fingers down Ethan's neck, kissing it, too, but she was shy to touch him. He trailed his fingers along her inner thighs, her belly, and across her hipbones that sloped down to the quick of her. When he touched *that* spot, a blinding light went off in her brain. She opened to him, fumbling to help him enter her, but he sensed her sudden fear and horrible pain. He tried to pull out, but she clasped his buttocks, forcing him deep inside. His mind, his body, his very being exploded like some kind of crazy supernova.

It was over, much faster than either of them had ever imagined it could happen. They lay stiffly side-by-side, hardly daring to look at each other. And although Aleta could sense a singing happiness throughout Ethan's body, his mind seemed uneasy.

He whispered finally, "I didn't get the rubber on."

"That was my fault, I wouldn't let you."

"Why did you do that? I was hurting you."

"Ever since Eve was thrown out of Eden—figuratively, that is— women have been meant to suffer." Aleta thought to herself, That was one dumb answer. I don't know why I did it. It certainly wasn't too smart.

He went on, "And this is really trivial, but we never took the sweatshirts off, I mean, your first time is such a big deal and all."

He stopped because she had turned solemn, even grave. "My shirt doesn't matter, but yours is really *important.* Never lose it, take it everywhere with you. I can't explain."

Aleta sat up suddenly. She continued in a hushed voice, revealing more private thoughts close to her heart. "You know that our feelings kind of touch. Do you remember when Jane Eyre heard Mr. Rochester calling out to her during the fire that burnt down his house? She was miles away and she heard."

Ethan hugged her and smoothed her singed hair. "I'm not saying we can't do it a little bit, but it isn't logical, and besides, what happened to Jane Eyre isn't real life! It comes from a book."

Aleta grasped his arm. "Ethan, at least *try* to understand what I'm saying. Some things you can't explain by trying to be logical or anything else."

She lowered her voice, not for effect, but from fright. "I've been to terrifying places. Twice in high school, I got taken someplace else. And today that, that *thing* in the lightning showed me another place. A beach with no end and two moons in the sky."

Ethan sounded impatient and scared at the same time. "My God, Aleta. You were hit by a thunderbolt!"

"No, Ethan, I know I saw something."

Ethan tried to clear his head. He wanted to love everything about her, but he'd never understand a mind so remote from his own.

***

Aleta wondered if the cave lay just beneath the top of the hill on the side facing the ocean. She led him to the front where they sat somewhat uncomfortably on the hard stone. She parted the overhanging branches; a few night birds sang and the moist air smelled of earth. She was right. They had reached the other side because now Aleta could see the bay below, with two moons above it.

No, not the two moons of her journeys, but the one everybody saw—the real moon a stark yellow as it hung low on the horizon, and its reflection, crystal-clear on the water. They held hands and let their shoulders touch, but Aleta averted her face as two great tears slid down her cheeks. She tried out a new word fresh from English class, *Well, it was kind of okay, I guess, but it wasn't Transcendent.*

Chapter 3 Aleta Gone

Aleta became increasingly annoyed by the little flaws she perceived in Ethan, especially his clumsy approach to sex. Except for his unintentional bull's-eye the first time, he hadn't figured out her anatomy where it mattered, he finished too soon, he ran off to study the minute the sex was over. *Was it his lack of imagination?* This was certainly a worrisome question, but she refused to give up on him. Deep down, she was sure that someday he would miraculously become the man of her dreams. Because hadn't they met under the most unusual circumstances in 1974 on a snow-covered airport runway near the Arctic Circle?

Ethan didn't seem unhappy with her. He especially loved the way their feelings touched with a gentle humming sound deep inside his head—something he'd never experienced with anyone before. He wanted to make love as often as possible, which actually pleased Aleta, if perhaps for the wrong reasons. It certainly placed her in favorable competition with Geraldine, and it also gave the two girls plenty to giggle about.

Accomplishing the feat of meeting in private meant breaking the rules at both their residences. The separation of the sexes was a rental policy designed to please parents by helping to preserve youthful morality, although each apartment house worked differently. Aleta's landlord was seldom around to enforce the rules, unlike the perceptively nicknamed Slime, ever-present and vigilant owner of Ethan's substandard building.

Ethan's apartment building was far away—a thirty-minute walk from campus. It wasn't very clean, it had flimsy walls and peeling paint, and it had only one smelly bathroom on each floor. Aleta had to sneak in, ducking her head as she slipped by Slime's office door with the frosted glass window. Then she raced up the stairs on tiptoe with her heart pounding in her throat.

From her point of view, the only good reason for going there was to visit Fuck, the gorgeous Sports Education major who lived across the hall from Ethan. She thought the world of Fuck. Five minutes with him made her love being alive, and maybe she loved him, too. Because a truly odd, even terrifying sensation took over her body whenever she stood next to him. Her veins would catch on fire, her face would turn bright red, and her stomach would tie itself into a knot.

Sometimes Ethan felt a stab of pure jealousy when he watched the two of them together. They had a way of looking so directly into each other's eyes that he wondered just what they could be seeing.

Shit no, he thought. She can't like him in that way. She's always insulting what I study, so how can she go for someone majoring in Sports Ed? Fuck's not dumb exactly, but he's slow, and he's big and looks different.

Besides, Ethan didn't want to share him. Fuck was his closest male friend, a rock-solid confidante, generous with his things, and he even lent Ethan money when the guy obviously didn't have a whole lot for himself. And Fuck didn't blab on and on about his own problems. There was something else. Fuck was the only human being in the history of their apartment building who truly terrified Slime. When Slime headed up the stairs for the third floor, everyone hid in their rooms and let Fuck deal with the asshole.

There were a few weird things about Fuck, though. For one, he wouldn't say where he was from. And he didn't like his real name and never said what it was to any of them—which is why everyone ended up calling him Fuck.

The nickname was pretty appropriate, actually. Fuck was a man of few words. He could use "fuck" to express almost any emotion, from anger to sympathy to delight. In a verbose moment, Fuck told Ethan that the name hurt his feelings, but it stuck, partly because he hadn't offered an alternative. Fuck was the oldest student on the floor. His lack of language proved cruelly limiting; he was taking English and European History for the third time. One evening when he wasn't around, Ethan and the other guys had heartlessly mocked his English papers as multiple sheets containing nothing but strings of fucks, his most-used word.

Only Aleta enjoyed the challenge of getting Fuck to talk freely, which no one else had ever tried to do. And no way would she use that repulsive name. She alone called him by his real name, Sequoyah, which he'd finally slipped to her written on a piece of paper as if he were revealing a state secret. It had taken her three days to pry it out of him. Aleta had heard that name before, and it belonged to a four-year-old boy crying in front of his school in Oklahoma. At night she rolled the name around on her tongue. She had never mulled over a more beautiful word—colossal, sunlit, and dusky-green like the redwoods in the valley behind Santa Margarita.

***

The major obstacle facing Ethan and Aleta at Geraldine's place was Geraldine herself because she had no concept of boundaries. She and her succession of male friends flopped about everywhere except Aleta's room, which Geraldine would invade day or night without regard for Ethan's presence. Locking the door was no help. She simply pounded on it until she received a response.

On a rare occasion when Geraldine was "at the library," a phrase implying a more intriguing activity, Aleta and Ethan had the apartment to themselves. Relishing the sudden opportunity that a library night offered, the pair leaped on the bed, throwing their clothes right and left. But foreplay was more desultory than usual since Aleta obviously had something else on her mind. At first passionately eager, Ethan found his sexual desire waning. He gave up, but not without a grumpy twist to the opposite side of the bed.

"Ethan." Aleta sounded earnest. "I don't know anything about your parents."

Ethan was still nursing the rejection. "So? I don't know anything about yours, either, except your nasty names for them and I'm not sure I care."

Aleta persisted, "You *should* care. If this is going to last, sooner or later, you'll have to meet them."

Ethan acknowledged reluctantly that she had a point. "Okay, describe away, I'm all ears."

"Well," it was harder than she'd thought, "my mother grew up in New York City. She wanted to be a fashion model, but her parents were first-generation Jews from Alsace and they just had a cow. They sent her to City College where she majored in Classics." Aleta giggled. "Do you want to know my full name? It's Greek, Aleta Gaia Rosenthal. Me, 'wanderer, earth-mother.' Then she met my father. End of story."

Ethan was impressed. "She must look good."

Aleta hesitated before answering. "Well, she does, I guess, in a weird sort of way. She talks all sultry like Zsa Zsa Gabor, but she acts as cold as an ice cube. One thing's for sure, she hates how *I* look."

By now, Aleta had captured Ethan's full attention. "My father is famous, actually, a microbiologist at UC. You know, at Berkeley. He was born in Hungary but left with his parents when he was a teenager because they had to escape the Nazis. It was easy. His father was some kind of big-wig, a friend of Churchill's or something." After a minute she burst out laughing. "Not really. I made that last part up."

After her flippant recital, Aleta was not prepared for the stricken look on Ethan's face. He didn't speak for a long time, and when he did, his voice sounded different, tight, and even angry.

"My last name wasn't Marcus, it was Marcowitz. My father died just after the Nazis got him in Treblinka, April 1943. But first, he managed to smuggle my mother to Romania. She didn't know it, but she was already pregnant with me."

Aleta put a hand on his shoulder, but he struck it off roughly. "Just let me try and tell this."

He waited so long that Aleta panicked. *God, what will I do if he starts crying?*

Ethan scrunched up his eyes before going on. "Matka, that's what I call her, brought me to this country after I was born, and we ended up in California in a town not too far from Monterey called Puerto Seguro. When I was younger, she was sweet, gentle, beautiful. She wanted everything for me, and I, uh, loved her so much. Now she's crazy. From the strain, I guess. She's in a mental hospital pretty close to here. It's called Agnews."

Aleta held him as he mumbled into her shoulder. "Even when I was little she called me Prometheus because of the *e-t-h* in my name. That's because she wanted me to bring fire, make the world better for people." He was crying, finally.

***

It was the middle of November and Aleta waited with diminishing hope for her period to arrive. She stared at her calendar for the hundredth time. No matter how often she counted the days that followed the X's representing her last period, the numbers didn't lie; she'd had a lot of sex around the worst possible days of her cycle. She added up the months on her fingers over and over. She could expect a baby sometime next August.

She saw Ethan almost every day but refused to make love and eventually avoided any physical contact. Her rejection of him was not entirely without cause. Her breasts had expanded and were painful to even the lightest touch. She could feel his hurt and longing and also his bafflement. When the morning sickness started, at any hour of the day or night, she had an excuse to not see him at all. She missed half her classes and rehearsals, telling her professors that she had the flu, which she almost believed during more optimistic moments.

It was Geraldine who finally took charge. The two of them sat at the foldout table in the kitchen as Aleta choked down a few bites of toast and took a sip of tea. She fled to the bathroom, turned on the water in the washbowl to block the sound, and vomited. Then she lay on her rumpled bed, exhausted. Like yesterday and the day before, she would not be attending morning classes.

Geraldine strode into Aleta's room, not bothering to knock. She sat on the bed, placing a wet washcloth on Aleta's forehead. "Ali, we both know what's wrong with you. Have you told Ethan yet?"

Aleta mumbled something indistinct that Geraldine interpreted as a no.

Then Aleta wailed, "I can't tell him, he'll be so angry. I can't go to Health Services, they'll call my parents."

Geraldine turned over the washcloth to the cool side. "Ethan is weird, but he won't take off. Jesus, Ali, the kid is half his." She paused for emphasis. "You need to get a pregnancy test now, and no, not at Health Services. My sister is married to a doctor. I'll take you, but you better lie on the written form and say you're eighteen."

She stood up to leave. "The test doesn't hurt, although the rabbit won't like it. You just pee in a cup."

"The rabbit?"

"Yes, they have to kill a cute little bunny rabbit to get the results. You'll know in a few days. But don't get your hopes up for a negative."

In forty-eight hours Geraldine's brother-in-law called with a positive result. Two hours later half the apartment's occupants knew thanks to Geraldine's broadcasting of a really good story.

Aleta called Ethan a few days later. They met that evening at the bench by the bell tower, a place they already recalled with nostalgia. Ethan looked drawn and thinner than she had remembered and his anxiety was palpable. But nothing had prepared him for her appearance and underlying terror. She was gaunt, her hair was tangled, and her whole face was puffy from crying. She didn't touch him and with downcast eyes whispered that she was "expecting."

Ethan responded with a gasp of sobbing relief. "You were sick and crying all the time, I could hardly touch you, your thoughts were miles away, and then you disappeared." His throat felt so tight that he couldn't go on.

Aleta mumbled through sobs, "I made sure, I got a test."

Ethan tried to hold her, but she brushed him off. He was hurt but nonetheless, he whispered affectionately into her ear, "We'll figure everything out, don't worry. It's our baby. Yours and mine."

His enthusiasm alarmed Aleta even though she knew she should be feeling reassured—not trapped as she now did. She was absolutely positive he loved her, which was good. But raising a kid when both of them were so young could be kind of awful.

Things had changed. She was not the same person she had been so long ago when they first embraced at the bell tower. There was someone else now pulling her in two. Did she love Ethan at all?

Ethan felt drowsy. The thermostat was set too high, the lecture hall was stuffy, and the history professor droned on about the Constitutional Convention. He stopped taking notes, his eyes were so heavy.

An alarm went off inside his brain—a cry of anguish from Aleta. It obliterated the gentle humming that he'd come to expect, that he loved so much. This was a cry of physical pain, of fear. He left by the side exit and started running toward the source, which seemed to come from the direction of his apartment house. As suddenly as the alarm had started, it ceased. Now Ethan was truly terrified. He had not experienced silence like this since before they'd met on that September morning.

Where was she? Probably in his room. He flung the door open and rushed inside but Aleta wasn't there. It took him almost a minute to make sense of a small note on the floor, torn from a piece of binder paper. He knew it was from her; even this token of Aleta seemed to radiate a kind of silky sweetness. For nearly another minute he just stared down at it lying on his worn-out Turkish rug with the missing fringe on one edge. Surely it was just a harmless looking piece of paper. It wouldn't bite, or anything. Finally, he picked it up.

Goodbye Mom and Dad love Ali, and that was it.

Fuck was standing at the door watching Ethan. It crossed Ethan's mind that Fuck looked seriously fucked up. His knees were shaking and he was wringing his hands.

"Fuck, did you let her in?"

Fuck nodded and said nothing, but now Ethan was sure there was more to it. He'd never seen Fuck so upset, as if he wanted to cry. But the big guy just bit his lip and pointed mutely at Ethan's desk. There was another note on the same binder paper only this one was almost illegible. It also made no sense.

The yellow moon. I love you

Then, ever so slowly and painfully it began to sink in. He remembered something vague she'd said about terrifying places. Could she have left him, just like that? Gone for no reason? He looked at the note again. It still said what it said, and nothing more. And yet that nothing was ... something black and empty. Ethan touched the note to his lips as tears began to slide down his cheeks. He thrust it into the bottom of his pants pocket and gripped his head in both hands. Someone was screaming. He realized that he was the one screaming only after Fuck laid a hand on his shoulder. He squirmed free and started to run.

Hours later Ethan found himself half way up the hiking trail to the cave where they had first made love. The sun was setting, Ethan was cold, and he was undone by the total lack of sound in his head. He wandered back to the benches in front of the bell tower and dropped down on the closest one. Fuck was waiting for him by the tower entrance to take him home.

During the saddest night of his life, Ethan clung to one idea to keep from falling apart—his hope that the cave would help him recall Aleta's vision in the lightning. As impossible as it seemed, maybe there was some truth in those stories.

At sunrise, he rushed out to hike the trail that he'd started up the evening before. He found the spot easily, but the romantic bedchamber was more a dank hole under a huge rock. He couldn't make himself enter it and sat disconsolately at the opening. He did remember some of Aleta's vision. She said she was taken to a beach with two moons in the sky. Then she had shown him the real moon and its reflection over the bay. Ethan sat by the scrubby bushes sobbing over his own helplessness. His head felt thick. He would try to put it all together. But for now, it was far easier to just let himself hurt.

Ethan returned to his bench in front of the bell tower. He had given up on studying or going to class, sunk as he was in misery. He had plenty of time to think. His conclusion about her disappearance made no sense, but it was the best he could do. Aleta had been terrified of something irrational that had seemed very real to her. Something about those moons. Before she vanished into thin air, she wrote a note just for him about a yellow moon, and it was all that was left of her.

***

For two nights Fuck brought Ethan home from the tower and made him eat something, shower, and sleep. On the third day, he returned to his old bench and that was where the police found him. There were two of them in plain clothes hiding behind dark glasses. The squad car was parked nearby, and curiously, the door on the passenger side hung open. The cops towered over him while he was stuck sitting on the bench. He was trying to figure out why they were there at all.

The tall, thin officer introduced himself. "I'm Detective Patrick Healy, Fifth Precinct." He waved a badge, and then removed his dark glasses, revealing weary hazel eyes in a lined, but not unfriendly face.

Ethan thought that for a guy who wasn't old he looked pretty exhausted for 9:00 o'clock in the morning. For just a second, Ethan felt sorry for him, but then it occurred to him that he was guilty of something or the cops wouldn't be standing in front of him. Ethan felt confused and nervous. What *had* he done besides mourn for three days?

Detective Healy gestured toward the second officer who was shorter and heavily muscled. "This is my partner, Anthony Virgilio."

This cop was more vigorous, but looked angry, although Ethan had no idea why. As things progressed he noticed that Detective Healy ordered poor Virgilio around a lot, which maybe he didn't appreciate.

The officers sat down on either side of Ethan on the bench. Now he felt trapped on top of being nervous, sandwiched between two authoritarian men, both bigger than he was. Detective Healy, the skinny one, cleared his throat, and Detective Virgilio, the muscle-bound one, flipped open his notebook. When Virgilio started waving around a sharpened yellow pencil, Ethan felt like screaming. Perhaps he was going crazy like his mother. After all he'd been through, he kind of expected it to happen sooner or later.

"Are you Ethan Marcus? I'm going to ask you a few questions."

The officer certainly had a strange way of speaking, in a kind of monotone. One minute into the questioning and he already sounded tired and bored.

"Aleta Gaia Rosenthal was reported missing by her roommate. Don't you think you should have notified us?"

Ethan was floored. Why hadn't he? He'd been too wrapped up in himself. So he *was* already guilty of a crime. And he hadn't even realized it.

His answer came out sounding inane and stupid. "Sir, I-I had no idea I was supposed to. I didn't think, I guess."

Detective Healy looked at Ethan's miserable, drawn face and swollen eyes. Poor, dumb kid, he thought to himself. It's amazing any of 'em grow up.

"When did you last see her, Mr. Marcus?"

"Sir, I left her apartment … on Monday. Yes, Monday night. She was fine, fine. Happy, in fact …." His voice died out.

"A simple answer will do. Did you know your girlfriend was pregnant?"

"I know, that's why I'm so …." He wanted to say fucked up but didn't.

"So did you have plans?"

"Well, no, not really, but we were talking about what to do."

"Did you and your girlfriend want the baby?"

"Oh yes, I wanted the baby, and Aleta, well, she never said she didn't. I mean, yes. Want it, I mean."

Ethan was twisting his hands, chewing his lip. Detective Healy hated this kind of case. It was tough on the boys, that is, if they cared. The ones that did, like this kid, looked all broken up and sometimes cried. But it was a hundred times worse for the girls. He should know, he'd seen enough suicides. He wished he could grab a cigarette, but it was against regulations.

Detective Healy was tired and his voice came out with a hard edge. "Mr. Marcus, did you argue with Miss Rosenthal about the pregnancy?"

"What? Oh, no. No sir!"

"How was her mental health? Was she depressed?"

Ethan hesitated before answering. "No. *No.* She was, she was scared about having a baby, but no. We had each other."

"Mr. Marcus, try to be specific. Just why would Miss Rosenthal leave you?"

Ethan was pretty sure that Aleta had not left voluntarily, but he couldn't say that. "She left me for ... for no reason."

Detective Healy frowned. The kid was hiding something, but he couldn't put a finger on it. "Mr. Marcus, we saw the note in your room. It is just to her parents and not to you. Does that make sense if you were getting along as well as you say?"

Ethan shook his head. No, it didn't make sense as long as he kept *his* note hidden in his pocket. He knew he was withholding evidence, to be technical, like on *Perry Mason,* but he'd never part with the last reminder of Aleta. It was also the only clue to her disappearance.

"Do you like to hike, Mr. Marcus?" Ethan nodded, wondering why this question had popped out of the blue.

"We found hiking boots in Miss Rosenthal's room. Did you and Miss Rosenthal hike together—have a special place where you would go?"

"We hiked the Cove Crest Trail to the top. There's a cave. It's just off the trail where you can see the bay."

"And when did you last go there, Mr. Marcus?"

"Sir, I think ... I think it was two days ago."

"After her disappearance?"

Suddenly Ethan's stomach knotted. He nodded, barely.

Detective Healy turned to his partner and spoke in an undertone. "Call for a detail to check it out." Detective Virgilio walked to the squad car.

Oh God, *no,* thought Ethan. He asked in a tiny voice, "Do you think she's *there?* That she's ...? That I—"

The detective looked sad and resigned. "Mr. Marcus, I ask the questions, you answer them."

There were many more questions and repetitions of previous ones, but Ethan answered like an automaton. Although the winter sun's slanting rays warmed the bench, he couldn't stop shivering. Detective Virgilio offered him coffee from a thermos. He didn't drink it, but stared into the murky liquid, gripping the cup tightly so the officers wouldn't see his hands trembling.

Even as Ethan answered the questions, he repeated the same thought over and over in his head, *Please, please, please, let me go home now.*

At last Detective Healy concluded, "Where were you on Tuesday afternoon?"

"Huh? Oh, in American History at the History Building."

Then both officers shook hands with him and Detective Healy offered a few parting words in a flat, sorrow-tinged voice, "Son, go back to school and keep your nose clean. This investigation isn't over."

The carillon bells rang eleven. It was still early, but Ethan felt like fifty years had passed. First of all, he was embarrassed. All his answers had been stupid, so stupid. These cops, they knew what they were doing. He might have a high IQ, but it had been pretty much useless. Yes, he would go back to his classes, yes, he would. He was being watched, so he must act normal from now on. Yes, act normal. He must toe the line. But today, just today, he'd go back to his room. Shut the door. Not let anyone see him except maybe Fuck if it got too bad. He'd try to digest the horrors that the cops had revealed—what they thought about him.

***

Someone was pounding on Ethan's door. "Holy shit," he murmured, squinting an eye at his clock. "6:45 a.m."

The voice outside the door yelled, "It's me, Fuck. Phone."

Ethan staggered out of bed and into the hall in his drooping pajamas.

The man on the other end of the line identified himself as Aleta's father, Dr. Joseph Rosenthal. He talked in a hurry, his voice lightly accented, and he certainly sounded superior, like he was playing Sherlock Holmes in a Basil Rathbone movie.

"Ethan, we're overdue for a discussion. Diana and I will visit you a week from today at three-thirty. The police provided me with your phone number and address as well as other information. I hope you are prepared to enlighten us."

He hung up without a goodbye. The call made Ethan's blood boil. He grumbled at the mute receiver, "Demanding bastard didn't leave me much of a choice."

To prepare for the visit, Ethan cleaned his room thoroughly, did his laundry, and baked oatmeal cookies in the communal kitchen. He bought imported tea for his Brown Betty pot, colored paper napkins, and a set of matching cups, saucers, and plates—draining his bank account for the entire month. The final touch was a madras tablecloth, purchased to cover the table he'd assembled out of rickety orange crates rescued from behind the grocery store. He remembered to borrow an extra chair from Fuck to supplement his own chairs with their splitting plastic cushions.

Lastly, he lay the laundered and carefully folded Frobisher Bay sweatshirt, words uppermost, on the green velvet arm of his sagging Victorian sofa, just in case Aleta's parents could explain her fixation on that particular place. He surveyed the tiny room with a combination of pride and apprehension, *It's not exactly Versailles, but I'm sure Aleta would approve.*

***

Aleta's parents arrived punctually. Her father—tall, with a full head of black hair and oversized horn-rimmed glasses—wore a pressed suit and a big garish tie with purple amoebas swimming all over it. To Ethan, its width was the sure sign of a bloated ego.

At first, Aleta's elegant mother terrified him. She had swept her dark hair into elaborate swirls on top of her arrogantly tilted head and had accentuated a Jackie Kennedy dress with knobby gray pearls draped along her collar bones and a skinny silver belt cinched around her wasp waist. Even though he'd been briefed, Ethan could hardly believe that this pair had either conceived or nurtured his gentle Aleta of the red-gold hair.

Both parents checked out the room, examining the sofa, his threadbare Turkish rug, his LPs, his bricks-and-boards bookcase.

When Dr. Rosenthal spotted Ethan's texts and papers, he turned around. "Well, Ethan, you appear to be studying both engineering and physics. You *do* know you should not take on too much at once; only the most gifted should attempt more than one scientific discipline. If I were your advisor—"

Diana placed a hand on her husband's arm to steer him toward the improvised table. Her voice was suave. "Joseph, I'm sure Ethan would like to offer us tea."

Dr. Rosenthal drank his own tea in three gulps. He began to pace around the room, intimidating Ethan with his booming voice and stature. "I've been informed by the police that Aleta left a farewell note, expressly for us. If she was so enamored of you, why weren't you included?"

He smiled unpleasantly to rub in his point before going on, "They also told us that she was expecting a baby. They received that information from her roommate, who identified you as the father." He paused in disgust. "The two of you were damned stupid, Ethan—damned, unforgivably *stupid!*"

Ethan, feeling guilty and remorseful, looked down at his plate, just as Dr. Rosenthal had intended.

"Did you two *lovebirds* come up with any brainy plans for the future?"

Ethan replied with as much assurance as he could muster, "I thought we should get married in December as soon as I turned eighteen. Then I was going to get a summer job so we could rent an apartment before the baby—"

Aleta's mother interrupted, "Hogwash, you would have fallen flat on your behinds." Her mouth was pursed tight. "You *disgraced* her, Ethan. She worshiped romance, in fact, anything tastelessly tragic from literature, poetry, opera, movies. But she had never dated, not once. And for God's sake, why didn't she just tell us?"

The answer seemed obvious to Ethan, but he didn't say so.

Dr. Rosenthal sat down, straddling his chair to face Ethan, his head thrust forward aggressively. "So, Ethan, you must have an idea where she is?"

Ethan felt unnerved, tongue-tied. How could he explain what he didn't understand himself?

He began after a long pause. "This is what I think, but it's really hard to put into words." His voice shook. "When people are in a coma, their minds wander far away, we don't know where. I believe something like that happened to Aleta, but not just her mind, her whole body. Maybe she didn't have a choice. She could be anywhere, maybe in another time." He stopped and swallowed some tea.

Holy shit, he thought. From one scientist to another, that sounded like crap.

The three sat in frozen silence, both parents momentarily stunned.

Abruptly, Dr. Rosenthal leaped up and hammered his fists on the makeshift table. With the screech of wood against nails, three out of the four crates turned into rhomboids—dishes and cups flying, tea splashing, the tablecloth swinging by a few loose threads on an upended corner.

Dr. Rosenthal backed into the center of the room, looming to his full height. "Ethan, do you take me for some sort of idiot? I'm a famous microbiologist, and you patronize me with that comic-book *bullshit?* I came here to meet the fool who impregnated my daughter, and maybe, *just maybe*, to find out some facts. And what do I get?" He raised his voice an octave in a derisive imitation of Ethan. "Comas, time travel!"

To anyone but Ethan, his growing fury might have seemed amusing, like watching a play.

The self-promoting famous microbiologist wasn't finished. "Damn it, man, I'm surprised you had the *equipment* to ruin my child. And while we're at it, what kind of engineering student is so inept that he can't hammer four orange crates together?"

He turned on his wife, who had kneeled down delicately in the wreckage to search for surviving porcelain. "Stop groveling on the floor like some damn housewife, Diana. Get the coats. We're leaving."

Diana stood up, smoothing her mussed dress, and skewered her husband with a menacing whisper, "Joseph, you've gone one step too far, especially for someone without any ideas himself."

She raised her voice to summon Ethan, who had taken refuge by the window. "Stop staring at that parking lot and listen to *me*, for once."

She continued with self-righteous anger, "Just over two years ago, your little Aleta made our lives hell. She waltzed out of the house and disappeared, not once, but twice at two in the morning, dressed in a risqué nightgown—totally unsuitable except in the bridal chamber. We had to call the police, Ethan! Those boors pranced all over the lawn crushing my delphinium borders, and the Steinbergers are still gossiping about it every Saturday at Synagogue.

"Aleta didn't happen to mention these unflattering episodes to you, did she, Ethan? Your precious girlfriend has a *police record!*"

Diana paused for emphasis before going on, her tone strident. "If you'd care to know *why* I'm here and didn't just let my overly capable husband do all the talking, it's because I wanted to add *my own* deduction about this unfortunate disappearance. Listen carefully, Ethan. You too, Joseph."

Her eyes filled with unexpected tears. "Two years ago she told her psychiatrist that she'd kill herself someday in the High Sierras. That she'd walk deep into the snow where her body couldn't be found. There's lots of snow in this world, Ethan. Maybe even in the god-forsaken Frobisher Bay on that hideously ugly sweatshirt of yours. How long do you think she would have lasted out there?"

Diana sat on the sofa, dabbing at her face with a lace handkerchief as Dr. Rosenthal gathered up their coats from Ethan's bed. They departed without ceremony. Dr. Rosenthal said nothing, although he nodded curtly in Ethan's general direction.

Diana had regained her composure. She turned icy eyes on him and hissed, "Thank you for your hospitality."

***

Ethan took stock of his ugly sofa, his ugly rug, his ugly, bursting bookcase, the stupid orange crates protruding from the remnants of his dishes and tablecloth.

He whispered, "That was so fucked up." Then for emphasis, he yelled at the top of his lungs, *"Fucked u-u-up."* And in his head, *Stuff it, asshole, you're entertaining the whole fucking building.*

For a moment, Ethan wanted to laugh at his own wit but started crying instead, shedding tears of anger and shame. He knelt among the tea things as Diana had done but tackled the mess somewhat like Hercules cleaning the Augean stables. He swatted the tablecloth at the spilled tea, the crumbled cookies, and the glass splinters, throwing the big pieces in the middle of it. He swiped it around on the floor, then balled the whole thing up and threw it in his wastebasket.

In the process, he cut himself. Blood dripped from his fingers onto the rug as he kicked the crates, screaming, "You goddam pieces of *shit.*"

Ethan wasn't angry anymore, just broken, humiliated, in despair. He wiped the blood off his cut fingers with the hideously ugly Frobisher Bay sweatshirt and then threw it in his wastebasket on top of the tablecloth.

He fell to his knees in the center of the rug and cried hard, not caring if anyone heard him through the paper-thin walls. He even sobbed out loud, "Aleta, don't be de-e-e-ad."

Finally, Ethan looked up. Outside his window the sun had set, leaving a pink glow. He ordered himself to stop the bullshit, to stand up. He had to get to that fucking Engineering 101. His eyes were red and swollen, his heart was so oppressed that he felt like he was wading through glue, but he did get to his 7:00 o'clock class.

Chapter 4 Ito-San

Aleta had been warned. She hoped it would never happen to her again, but she'd felt it coming. She knew she would be pushed into an unknown place pretty soon now. And Sequoyah had told her as much that afternoon when they'd sneaked off together, hiking to the redwood forest that stood beyond the crest overlooking the bay.

Sequoyah had a sixth sense about such things. In a shy whisper, he told Aleta that he'd grown up with the Moon People talking to him inside his head. She didn't laugh at him. She remembered vividly what she'd been through two summers ago. She found herself gripping his hand tighter, touching every sinew in his thumb, every callous on his fingertips, even the fan of bones that formed the arch on the top. How she loved that hand, the arm to which it was attached, the shoulders, the chest, belly, legs, the whole body, and, yes, the soul of its owner.

The Moon People, so mysterious. God, something is happening to me that I can't explain. Now that she understood what she and Sequoyah shared, she grew weak with longing for him. They lay beneath a giant redwood deep in the valley behind Santa Margarita, kissing, touching, tightly bound in ecstasy. But she was Ethan's girlfriend, and they both knew it couldn't go on.

Twice during the next week, she saw the two moons on the horizon, one bigger and shinier than the other. Ethan had been walking her home the first time, but she would never have pointed it out to him. The second time Sequoyah was with her. As often happened, he had taken over for Ethan, who sat glued to his desk chair studying. Sequoyah noticed the extra moon first and nodded toward the sky. She took one look, then cowered, almost in tears.

"Why do I have to go if I don't want to—if I want to stay with you?" He opened his arms, and she knew she shouldn't do it, but she fell into them.

She murmured against his chest, listening to the sure heart pumping just beneath her ear. "Sequoyah, will you help me go when it happens?"

"You … you know I will." She heard his voice catch.

***

How had he known she was being taken away? It didn't matter really because he was there holding her tight, but her feet had penetrated right through the fibers of Ethan's worn Turkish rug. She was slipping, slipping from his grasp one piece at a time until all he held was an arm. She heard him sob with the effort of keeping her, but that last limb was stretching, growing brittle, turning to shards of glass in his hands.

She cried out, "My violin." And he had it ready for her, although she didn't actually feel her fingers grab the case. "The notes? I can't finish ...."

There was nothing left of her for him to hold onto, so she cried out in terror, first to him and then to Ethan. But it was too late. Ethan's tiny apartment was gone—the rug, the floor, the whole rooming house had snapped shut over her head. The first time this happened she had glided in a sleek Greyhound bus with more lights on it than a fire engine. Next, she had been swept through a nasty drain that smelled of frogs. But this time was different. The earth stood still as hundreds of blue and silver planets crashed all around her before they vanished—falling to their deaths beneath a night sky streaked with blood. What would Dr. Agonopoulos have thought?

***

Aleta landed uninjured but without dignity, her legs sprawled in front of her. And there was her violin lying a few feet away on a plot of crabgrass. A hazy winter sun bounced off the mica chips in the sidewalk, making her squint as she peered about. The view was hardly exotic. Across the street from her was a restaurant with a red swinging sign announcing the **CAFE CANTON**. Looking squat and boxy with exterior paint peeling in the acrid salt air, it was flanked by wind-blown cypresses. The owner had cheered it up with window boxes, and the arbor that stood over the two picnic tables out front was festooned with red and white paper lanterns.

As Aleta stood up shakily, she felt an asymmetrical lurch inside her belly. Surprised, she put her hand on the spot, thinking, A kick already? That's unexpected. I guess the baby made the trip just fine. Then she straightened her skirt. It's time to face my new world. I must still be in California, and I don't think I've gone very far away from Santa Margarita. She smiled to herself. The new place could have been a lot scarier, like Outer Mongolia or Timbuktu.

She had relaxed too soon. A great hulk of a man appeared right beside her, apparently out of nowhere. He wore a filthy military uniform of an ancient cut, which may once have given him an air of dignity. But that time had undoubtedly ended with his discharge.

From the Civil War? Aleta wondered. She hadn't a clue. But no matter when, or where he came from, he stank, he drooled, and he was so unsteady on his feet that Aleta was sure he'd fall on her. The nightmare creature thrust his scarred face toward her, lips puckered for a kiss. Out came filthy hands gnarled by arthritis.

He sang in a gravelly bass, "'K-k-k-Katy, beautiful Katy! You're the only g-g-g-girl that I adore!' Tha's what me 'n my mates sing for all the pretty'uns."

Aleta wanted to run, but not without her violin, which he was almost standing on. She could try pushing him, or screaming might work better.

Both of them heard heels clicking, coming closer across the street.

A towering redhead made her presence known. "Shame, shame, shame, Troll!" Then in a velvety voice with a peculiar Southern drawl, she purred, "Troll, dawling, go back to your bridge, Scarlett says so." And louder with the accent falling away, "I mean it. You leave my friend alone, or you don't get handouts behind the cafe no more."

Troll took the loss of his next meal seriously. He didn't argue, but turned tail and ran, perhaps in the direction of his bridge.

Aleta blinked, too overcome to thank Scarlett properly. But Scarlett didn't notice.

She looped her arm through Aleta's and picked up the violin—jabbering non-stop. "I'm asking you to tea at Cafe Canton where I work and don't mind him. He's typical Puerto Seguro scum. Great War veterans living like tramps. They're hopeless. Shell-shocked they call it." She added ruefully, "He's just like a scruffy stray you feed. Do it one time and they're back tomorrow. But don't tell Ma and Pa Ito. They'd *kill* me. Well not really, but they'd dock my pay."

Aleta hardly dared to open her mouth. She'd surely reveal herself as an amnesiac, or worse. People would think she was crazy like the shell-shocked Troll reliving World War I. But so far, Scarlett had talked far too much to notice how quiet Aleta was. She motioned Aleta to a table for two near the front door as she went to fetch the tea. Aleta sized up the room. In all, she counted four more small tables like hers and five family tables. All were covered with white cloths and silverware bundled in starched napkins.

The art on the walls was a study in contrasts. Across from her, she spotted a crisp new movie poster hung with Scotch tape displaying a grinning Bob Hope in uniform, his arms around Dorothy Lamour. The movie's title was *Caught in the Draft.* Hanging over the family tables in a heavy gilt frame was the *pièce de résistance:* an oversized rainbow-striped, sequined Chinese dragon with bulging pearly eyes and fiery nostrils. But in the back corner where it was almost invisible was Hokusai's "Great Wave."

Then something else caught her eye, *The Seguro Daily News* lying on the table next to hers. She reached for it. The date at the top was

November 30, 1941, and under that, the headlines: *Hull Note, Last Try*, and *Moscow Under Attack*. Her brain whirred back to history classes in high school. Yes, she had just located herself in Time: World War II, and Pearl Harbor in a week. Could she actually be in Puerto Seguro, Ethan's home town? What a terrifying idea, meeting him as a baby! She exhaled a long-held breath. *No, impossible! He was born in 1943.*

As Scarlett returned from the kitchen with two steaming cups, she almost tripped over Mrs. Ito who entered through the back door carrying a watering can. A collision would have been unfortunate; Scarlett was a foot taller than her tiny boss.

Plump-cheeked Mrs. Ito registered surprise, waving the watering can in the direction of the cups in Scarlett's hands. "Miss Siobhan need two tea, meet gentleman?" Then she noticed Aleta and craned her neck around Scarlett to size up the stranger.

Mrs. Ito's curiosity encouraged a tumble of words to burst from the talkative girl. "Ito-san, you won't believe. Outside on the sidewalk, I just ran into my best friend Alice from high school, well, really from Chicago where she moved when I was eight. She kind of dropped from the sky. Imagine! She's back home from The Juilliard School where she studied with the great Paganini."

Mrs. Ito sighed as she had long since given up separating Scarlett's fabrications from fact. "Okay, Miss Siobhan, five minutes you back to work."

Scarlett dropped down in the chair opposite Aleta's and removed her heels. She grumbled, "Damned uncomfortable, these. What's yours, sneakers? You wear them all day long?" She burst out laughing. "You, Miss Alice, are a brave one." Then she turned suddenly serious. "Okay, we got four minutes to figure lots out, so talk. Who the hell *are* you, 'cause I happen to know just about everyone in town."

Aleta opened her mouth to speak, and she had concocted a good story in the last few moments—something about dropping out of Juilliard to find her husband who had enlisted and was stationed nearby because she had to tell him she was expecting, and how her purse and her suitcase got stolen on the Greyhound somewhere in Kansas when she fell asleep. Instead, she burst into tears. She turned toward the wall so Mrs. Ito wouldn't see her, feeling both painfully stupid and utterly terrified. Right now, she was pretty sure she would end up under a bridge like Troll.

Scarlett patted Aleta's shoulder. She whispered discreetly, "I'm not a mind-reader, but close to it, just call me a student of human nature. And I knew the minute I saw you with those skinny legs and arms along with a little round belly that you're expecting." She shook her head violently for emphasis. "And no, no, no, you won't talk him into marrying you. He enlisted to *get away.* He's at Camp Ord, right?" She added almost with pride, "I'm an expert, honey, an *expert!* My mama's caring for mine right now."

Aleta turned in surprise, wiping her eyes on her sweater sleeve. She stammered through her first words, hardly believing how ridiculous they sounded. "M-my goodness, Scarlett, what did everybody say? I mean, the people in the town? Were you—"

Scarlett cut her off with a laugh. "Did they make me wear a scarlet letter to match my name? No, they didn't, but I tell you, when it comes to sex, we ladies get the short end of the stick."

As Scarlett lifted Aleta from her chair by the elbows, she whispered. "Smooth your hair and try to smile. And for goodness sake, pull your skirt down as far as it'll go. It's time to meet Motomi Ito. I call her Ito-san, you call her Mrs. Ito. And another thing. You are already Alice, so don't forget and make me look like a liar."

Aleta felt butterflies in her stomach. She thought, Scarlett has something up her sleeve, I can tell. She talks a blue streak, and then when you really need to know what she's up to, she clams up.

Mrs. Ito was busy writing figures on a notepad by the cash register but rose to make a slight bow when Scarlett and Aleta approached.

She shook hands and bowed a second time toward the abashed girl as Scarlett started in with the superlatives. "Alice, here, is the best. She can work for you because soon I'm leaving for Hollywood. And you know you were looking for someone since we get so many enlisted men now from Camp Ord. Furthermore, she's my best friend—"

Mrs. Ito interrupted, "I *not* say we need new waitress, and you *not* go to Hollywood. We are very, very small Ma and Pa business, we *not* big like China Palace in Fresno."

Scarlett acted like she had barely heard. "Alice will double your patrons, Ito-san. To begin with, she'll attract the men 'cause she's pretty like me." She raised her voice with enthusiasm, waving her hands in graceful arcs. "And Alice knows waitressing. It's a *fact* she served Mayor La Guardia lunch right in New York City. That is when she was studying with the great Paganini at Juilliard."

Scarlett clambered onto a chair. "And she can play anything. I've heard her. One beautiful song after another. Just think, Saturday nights, all those rich shipping magnates and their snooty wives eating your dumplings and dancing under the lanterns—"

Suddenly, Mrs. Ito's amused eyes turned to ice and her voice gained a steely edge. "I think Miss Siobhan stretch truth. And Alice, too, too quiet. Alice, you speak?"

Aleta jumped. "Who, me? Oh, yes, Mrs. Ito, I do play the violin really quite well."

Mrs. Ito's face looked pinched, even hostile. She grumbled, "Get off my chair with dirty shoes, Miss Siobhan. I think one more thing. You bring new stray with name Alice to front door like you bring Troll to back door."

Their uncomfortable silence was broken by Mr. Toshiro Ito who had heard the entire conversation from the storeroom where he had been taking inventory. The elegant man with graying hair at his temples introduced himself to Aleta, bowing low from the waist.

He gestured toward her violin case standing in the corner. "Do you play tango music, Miss Alice? After university in Tokyo, I began my graduate studies in Paris, but what I loved best were the classes every evening at the tango school."

He slid an arm around his wife's portly waist and gave it a little squeeze. "We were newlyweds. Paris was ...." He stopped, but in her mind, Aleta filled in the rest of the romance implied by his sentence.

As Mrs. Ito beamed, Scarlett grew red enough to match her name. Never before this minute had she noticed any affectionate gestures between Toshiro and Motomi Ito.

Aleta stepped forward, encouraged. "Mr. and Mrs. Ito, I can play tangos, and Bach. Anything you like. And I am strong and will learn from Scarlett how to wait tables."

***

By quitting time, Aleta was a casualty of waitressing. Her feet were swollen, her arms felt like they'd fall off any second, and to her embarrassment, she had dropped three plates full of food in front of a gawking family. She had poured coffee on the knee of an overly forgiving officer who then put a hand up her skirt when she bent close to apologize.

Aleta could barely drag her aching limbs as she listened with one ear to Scarlett, who hadn't stopped talking since they'd begun the long uphill walk to her mother's rooming house that Scarlett called The Living Hell Hotel.

Aleta mused to herself, *Carrying those heavy trays would be easy for Sequoyah, gorgeous man that he is, and just about now I'd be lying beside Ethan, or maybe even kissing Sequoyah if I could get away with it.*

Scarlett's voice cut through her reverie. "Why aren't you *listening* to me, Alice? There's some sad things you gotta know about the Itos 'cause their lives have been real hard. Twenty years ago they came to this country so Mr. Ito could get his PhD at Berkeley, but no one ever hired him for teaching because they didn't trust a Japanese man. But he and

Mrs. Ito, they had their little boy to take care of. That's why they opened the restaurant."

Growing pensive, Scarlett knelt on the sidewalk to loosen the straps on her painful shoes. "And here's the worst part. Their boy, his name was George, he was so cute, too. He signed up for the Army last year for flight training, you know, at Moffett Field in Sunnyvale. And right away he died in a plane wreck. He was only eighteen."

***

The boarding house at the crest of the hill was a three-story Victorian with fish scale shingles and looping scrollwork under the eaves. The scroll motif ran the length of the elevated porch with its swinging **Rooms for Rent** sign. The gray paint peeled in sinewy curls on the sides facing the ocean, giving it a derelict look of not so genteel decay.

Oh, God, thought Aleta. It's a house for witches and warlocks and I hope for me. Or maybe I don't want to live there. She had only just seen *Psycho* with Janet Leigh and Tony Perkins the week before, holding hands with Ethan on her right, and surreptitiously gripping Sequoyah's comforting hand on her left.

Scarlett pulled Aleta back around the corner. "Let's get our names straight before we go in, shall we? Mine is really Siobhan O'Hare, but who the hell can pronounce that first name anyway?"

Aleta was about to make a comment about pretty Irish names when Scarlett continued, "I took Scarlett last year after seeing *Gone with the Wind,* which was so dreamy. You want me to do some Southern drawl for you? It's my ticket to Hollywood."

Aleta was shivering and wanted to get inside. "Maybe tomorrow, Scarlett. Mine's Aleta Rosenthal."

Scarlett smacked her forehead with the palm of her hand. "Oh, Jesus, Alice—I mean Aleta. Mama *hates* Jews. You're really Jewish?"

Aleta turned in anger and started back down the hill, calling over her shoulder, "Yes, really."

She heard Scarlett's clattering footsteps behind her and her fury changed into sympathy thinking of the painful pinch of high heels on a downhill grade. The girls hugged quickly and when Scarlett broke the silence, she sounded teary.

"What my mother thinks doesn't mean a thing to me. You and me, we're so tired, we're about to bite our own heads off. Please be my best friend, we need each other."

***

The Living Hell Hotel seemed peaceful enough when Scarlett and Aleta entered on tiptoe. Scarlett's mother was curled up against the arm of a high-backed velvet sofa as shoddy as Ethan's prized piece of Victorian furniture. She had tucked her legs under a pink and blue crocheted afghan and while waiting for her daughter, had apparently fallen asleep with a six-month-old baby stretched across her lap. Aleta noticed a striking familial resemblance between mother and daughter, although the mother's last bloom had departed long ago, leaving an old woman with ashen cheeks. But her lanky gray hair still had a few remaining strands of the once glorious red. To Aleta's surprise, this homey scene was actually the backdrop for an oft-repeated epic battle.

Scarlett stomped across the rag rug, yelling, "Dammit, Mama, every night I come home to the same accident about to happen. Tommy's gonna slide off your lap, *you ... you drunk.*" To be sure, a few empty beer bottles stood precariously on the broad sofa arm draped with an embroidered antimacassar.

Scarlett snatched up the child, who screamed with fright.

Jarred from sleep, Scarlett's mother roared, "Is this the thanks I get for watching the bastard of a wayward whore, no better than any other Catholic girl dropping litters like a sow?"

She paused to prepare an attack on a new front. "You brought home anything for Tommy—booties, a rattle, a wee blanket? No, but you *will* throw cold cash at me, no doubt." She began a cruel imitation of her daughter's newly acquired Southern drawl, "Mama, *dawling*, please shop *for* me. Can't you see I'm *sooo* busy swinging my ass at the Ching-Chong Chinaman café?"

Mrs. O'Hare cocked an eye on Aleta. "And who the hell is that, Siobhan? Another stray?"

Scarlett rallied from the derisive scolding, wiping her eyes on Tommy's shirt. Her salesmanship from the morning had lost most of its vitality. "This is Aleta Rosenthal, my best friend from high school who moved to Chicago when I was eight. She's back home from The Juilliard School where she studied with the great Paganini."

Mrs. O'Hare frowned, running her fingers slowly through her hair to come up with a reply. "If she was eight when she moved to Chicago, how did you know her in high school?"

As Scarlett pondered her slip-up, her mother continued huffily, "I don't give a good god damn if she stays. Tell her to pay the rent every Friday and get used to the smell of bacon grease. And if a single *Oy vey* leaves her mouth, she's out."

Aleta stood by watching while Scarlett tucked her son in for the night. Tommy appeared to be remarkably serene with an ample supply of sunny smiles for his tearful mama. Perhaps he hadn't been damaged yet by Mrs. O'Hare, or more likely, the lonely old woman had saved up a day's worth of resentment for her daughter alone.

Then Scarlett led Aleta to a spartan room at the top of the house under the slanting roof. The exhausted young mother was barely herself. As they plodded up the final set of stairs, she managed to utter wistfully, "Aleta, maybe you and me could pool the money we make and rent a little apartment somewhere."

She had apparently forgotten about Tommy's daycare.

***

That night Aleta had an odd dream. She rolled herself in a tight ball in her borrowed nightgown with her arms wrapped around her knees because the room was full of old ghosts. True, she was warm enough under two wool blankets, and she reminded herself that at least she wasn't sleeping under a bridge. But the relentless wind from the sea whistled around the outside corners of her little tower room and the rain drummed dolefully on the roof. She was frightened and her heart raced. She tried to think about Ethan, but the consoling Sequoyah kept edging him out, calming her down, kissing her tight eyelids and trembling lips.

Then the water rose up. Soon the blood-streaked horizon was drowned by Hokusai's white-capped wave. It blotted out the sky, it drew back, it left an expanse of pocked gray sand. She looked up. What she saw over her head were two yellow moons, one larger than the other. She felt two men wrenching her in two by her two outstretched arms, and suddenly, she knew there were two babies swimming like twin seals inside her womb.

When she forced herself awake she saw World War II. Can you see a war waking from a dream? Yes, all the time if you are crazy like Troll. But she had only one question to ask, not two. Why was she here at all?

Chapter 5 Losing the Dream

It was semester break, or to most students, Christmas vacation. The third floor of Slime's rooming house emptied out all in one day leaving only Ethan and Fuck to keep each other company. The way Fuck held his shoulders hunched up all the time inside his big gray sweatshirt worried Ethan a little. His eyes looked kind of droopy, too. Maybe he was sad about something, or maybe he had a cold or a stomachache, but as usual, the man of few words didn't talk about it. Ethan shrugged; he had his own problems. He had to visit his mother.

First, he called the nurses' station at Agnews Insane Asylum to make an appointment. He even considered bringing a gift, but he had no idea what she liked anymore. The day Ethan picked was not propitious. He took a painfully slow local Greyhound bus to Santa Clara during a ferocious winter rainstorm that seemed hell-bent on devouring the coast.

***

Ethan's Matka had been incarcerated two years earlier while he was in high school, following a dreadful period in his young life. The first signs of her deterioration were subtle. She began to reminisce more often about Ethan's father Samuel, but she placed her memories in settings resembling country houses in Chekhov short stories rather than in Warsaw's Jewish Quarter where she'd grown up.

Soon Matka stopped caring for herself. Ethan hated the very sight of her. To begin with, her body was disgusting. Her thick wavy hair that used to flow about her like an opulent black river hung in matted wads. Every time he begged her to bathe she ran away from him, raving about the showers at Treblinka. If that weren't enough, she saw Samuel in any man of medium height, including Ethan. Without warning she'd throw herself on the unfortunate victim, covering him with embraces and kisses. At this point, Ethan had to lock her in the apartment when he left for school.

But worse, she had abandoned him. His grades slipped, he broke all the furniture in his bedroom, he even threw a rock through the living room's bay window. He didn't know what to do. She had long since quit her job at the city library, the savings account was depleted, and he hadn't paid rent or utilities for two months.

It was Matka herself who brought the crisis to an end. One afternoon when he was at the grocery store around the corner, she climbed out of a window into the apartment garden. There she drowned her nice neighbor's chihuahua in the fishpond, screaming, "I'll get you—you little fucking *pisior* with the Hitler mustache."

After Matka was taken away, Jewish Services stepped in. They found an elderly couple in the neighborhood who invited Ethan to live with them, actually welcoming his company during his last two years of high school. He received money from Jewish Services, Social Security, and the State of California—just enough to get by.

***

Ethan felt lost. An Agnews's nurse first led him to an empty visitors' room but then deserted him for a good ten minutes. He gazed around, taking in a sagging maroon couch and unopened olive-green drapes covered with bird-of-paradise flowers. A butt-filled ashtray sat too close to the edge of a card table, and a TV with the sound turned off winked down at him from a perch near the ceiling. Not much of a TV watcher, he stared in distress as a pert Tweety Bird twisted and squirmed, barely escaping Sylvester the Cat's snapping jaws.

Ethan was almost relieved when the nurse brought Matka in. At thirty-four she was still a beautiful woman, but her eyes had lost their fire. Immediately she started acting strange. As she hugged him, she turned her gaze away to focus on the empty air beside him.

"Aleta, such a pretty girl! All that long red-gold hair. Her eyes, so large and gentle. She could use a little meat on her bones. I'll fatten her up—"

"Matka, she isn't here."

"But she is, standing by Sammy." Matka threw her arms around Ethan. "Oh Sammy, I am so *happy*. She'll make a fine daughter-in-law. Do you remember, Sammy, how we played in the meadow when we were children, how we listened to the larks? Do you, Sammy? You kissed me the first time by the pear tree at the country house. The branches were heavy with fruit, so heavy."

Ethan wriggled out of her embrace; the conversation was veering into dangerous territory. "Matka, I'm not Samuel, I'm your son. Ethan."

"No! You are *Prometheus?*"

"Yes, Matka, Prometheus."

A nurse entered the room, signaling the end of the visit. It was only 5:00 o'clock, but she had brought his mother's tiny paper cups filled with pills and a glass of water. Dinner would follow soon after. Ethan kissed Matka stiffly as she held his hand. Her other hand clasped the air a few feet to his left.

"Prometheus and Aleta, you will never be parted. I bind you together forever with silken cords. I bless you."

***

Ethan leaned his forehead on the fogged bus window that streamed rain in broken diagonal lines. It hit him suddenly: he had inherited his heightened sensitivity toward Aleta from Matka, whose madness was a drastic exaggeration of his own puny ability. Oddly, Matka's vision of Aleta had been accurate, down to her name and the color of her hair. But it was far too rosy a picture, for where was his girlfriend now? And why had she started loving him a little less each day? Ethan concluded that Matka could indeed read his thoughts, but to save the little sanity she still possessed, she'd turned them into fairy tales.

He curled up over his knees and lowered his head into his hands. *God, how I hate seeing her, even if she is my mother. At least I won't have to go back until spring.*

Ethan felt very sleepy. *Aleta slid next to him on the seat and he sighed with happiness. He buried his face into her neck and collarbone, just above her right breast, breathing in the perfume of her.* But what he received in return was a sharp jab in the ribs.

"Lord, child, keep to your own side. I know I have more than my share of flesh, but move over. Oh, you are a skinny one. Don't your mama feed you? Now me, I coulda been a great singer—you know, blues and such in clubs—but I got The Cancer. And my man, he weren't no good. Just left me. My son, about your age, too. He's in the joint, a lifer an' he's innocent. Do you walk with Jesus?"

Ethan shrank into the corner of his seat. *Whoa, way too much information.* But the message was clear. The lady needed Ethan's attention, his affirmation. He turned on his brightest smile, and, to his surprise, he actually meant it. He also gave her an emphatic nod, then turned his head to watch the rain outside.

***

Ethan arrived back at Slime's by midnight. After the long walk from the bus station, he had to admit that he felt terrible—hot and sweaty, with a searing headache. He raced to the bathroom, making it just in time. He tore off his rain-soaked clothes and dropped onto his bed, pulling his knees up to his chest. He fell asleep instantly, but woke up over and over again, sweating and trembling, each time staggering to the bathroom before falling back on his bed.

By morning, someone was in the room with him, holding a bowl when he vomited and wiping his forehead with a washcloth. And he seemed to be dressed in pajamas now, with several blankets weighing down his shaking limbs.

"I'm dying."

"No, Ethan, you're not dying, but you're pretty fucking sick."

***

Ethan went out of his mind with fever. "I feel awful," he groaned, gripping his seasick stomach with both hands as his bed rocked like a boat.

The walls around him bulged like wind-filled sails, black and moldy. His floorboards rose up in wavy peaks.

Fuck loomed large and threatening over Ethan. "I should drown you. How about in the bathtub or even better, the toilet?"

"Oh, God, Fuck, why?"

"Did you forgive Matka for drowning the chihuahua in the fishpond?"

"Of course not, Fuck. What she did was horrible, and wrong."

"No, Ethan, what she did seemed wrong to you, her neighbor, the police, the judge, the State of California, the Agnews' staff, the psychiatrists, but to her, she killed the Treblinka Nazi who murdered her husband."

The rotten ceiling was falling, shedding large chunks of plaster.

Fuck dragged Ethan toward the door. "I'm drowning you now, for smallness of mind, lack of compassion, an unforgiving, puny, dried-up heart."

"Fuck, don't hurt me. She's crazy. Most of the time she thinks I'm him."

"Ethan, you ungrateful prodigal son, you dumb-ass. She loves you, but through him. Forgive her. Learn to love her again, or you won't love Aleta. Maybe Aleta's little breasts and cute rear end, but not her soul."

Ethan began to wail aloud, "Oh please, Fuck, I beg you on my knees, don't drown me."

He clung to the black walls, his face and nose buried in the reeking mold. But the walls were receding now, leaving him stranded as they bleached to a stark white. He tried embracing the peaks of his broken floor even as it flattened into a linoleum checkerboard. He had nothing to hang on to; he shrank into a corner of this new place, Matka's cell at the asylum. But Fuck was still dragging him by the ankle.

"Dammit," Ethan mumbled. "I have no traction." He was sliding inexorably across the icy-cold squares.

"There's a really big fishpond on the Agnews' grounds, Ethan."

"*Fuck, please don't drown me. I'll try to love Matka, but I don't know how.*"

"*Stop blubbering, Ethan. It's unmanly. Start by accepting her. Marry Aleta according to Matka's wishes.*"

At first, Ethan couldn't see Aleta at all. As Matka clasped their hands in hers, Ethan tentatively stretched out his other hand to touch Aleta's invisible fingers. A female form materialized, but it wasn't Aleta. A woman with a face like a harvest moon and a winsome smile held his hand in a bone-crushing grip.

Ethan pulled his hand out of hers, massaging his hurt fingers. He hissed at the apparition, "Where's Aleta?"

The moon-faced woman replied, "She's out sick today; I'm the substitute. Will I do?"

Ethan glimpsed Moon-face's open smile and glossy black hair just as fat raindrops began to fall from Matka's ceiling. He reconsidered her offer and reached for her hand, but she wasn't there. Both she and Matka had dissolved into a sheet of rain.

Ethan didn't ask why the bus station's lights twinkled through the downpour. Even though Moon-face had intrigued him, he was glad to have escaped drowning in the fishpond on the asylum's grounds. But to actually board the unlikely Greyhound that stood in front of him now with its sleek lines and huge windows didn't seem too smart. But he wasn't given much of a choice; Fuck, all muscles and frowns, yanked his arm half out of its socket chucking him into a plush seat. Ethan clambered out in a fury, only to fall on his knees, cowering in front of the wrap-around window.

"Holy shit, Fuck. What's going on?" A shocking blood-red sky shot through with silver streaks devoured a thousand multi-hued moons in two well-timed gulps.

Fuck stood silent, so Ethan elbowed him, imploring, "Where the hell are we going?"

"What's written on your ticket, Ethan?"

"To the End of Time. Where is that?"

"How the hell should I know? You bought the ticket." Fuck was fading, losing shape.

"Fuck, don't leave. Tell me why I'm here."

"On another bus ride, you offered a gift to a certain lady—a stranger. It was a smile, the gift of a compassionate heart."

***

Fuck pushed open Ethan's door and entered on tiptoe, displaying unusual grace for such a large man. He was carrying a beat-up tray borrowed from the communal kitchen.

"Oh, fuck, man, I'm glad you're awake. You had the flu, real bad, for three days. I took care of you."

Ethan struggled to a sitting position as Fuck moved a kitchen chair next to Ethan's bed and placed the tray on it.

"I made some chicken soup, but it's out of a can."

"Aw, Fuck. I—"

"Hey, you woulda done the same for me."

Ethan looked doubtfully at the pale noodles and pink cubes circling listlessly in the broth. But it smelled wonderful, and once he tasted it, he realized that he was famished.

"Y'know, Ethan, it's Christmas. Your people are Jews and probably wouldn't—"

"How'd you know that, Fuck?"

"You talked a lot when you were sick, even about, um, the gas chambers. That's how I know. So, same deal. Mine are Cherokee."

Ethan almost dropped his spoon. "Cherokee? You're an Indian? Do you have a name like Sitting Bull or Hiawatha?"

Fuck shook his head and looked down, mumbling, "I hate my name. But you gotta hear it someday." He hesitated for a long time, at last blurting out, "It's Sequoyah."

Ethan countered, "It's an okay name. No, it's really nice. Like the redwoods. You don't let anyone call you that?"

Fuck bit his lip. "Yeah, sometimes."

He changed the subject. "Now you know why English is tough for me. It's because I went to a terrible school, and …." He broke off, as usual, unwilling to speak of his past.

Fuck could feel his courage slipping and his mouth going dry. But he had to get out the next sentences. "Ethan, I have a Christmas present for you, only it's Words."

"But Fuck, what is a present of Words?"

"I … I heard from Aleta, from where she is now."

Ethan started shaking; he couldn't help it. "Fuck, you are messing with my mind. What are you saying?"

Fuck put his huge hand on Ethan's shoulder to steady him. "That's what I'm trying to tell you. I … well, I can feel what other people are feeling." Ethan's jaw dropped as Fuck went on. "And I can hear what they're thinking." He flinched and trailed off.

Ethan turned white and gasped. "My God, Fuck, where the fuck did you learn to do that? Is it some weird Indian thing?"

Fuck tried to defend himself. "No, I … I didn't *learn* it, it just—" Poor Fuck. He had created something of a sensation without meaning to. "What? Well, do you want to hear them, or, I mean …."

Ethan twisted out from under Fuck's hand. He wasn't sure he did. "Fuck, listen to me. This flips me out because Aleta doesn't do words. I should know."

Fuck turned to leave, mumbling, "They're good Words. She said them to me last night."

Ethan frowned. He was jealous. "Okay, tell me, but stay out of my girlfriend's head from now on."

Fuck looked at his feet. At first, his voice wouldn't cooperate, his throat felt so tight thinking of her. At last, he got them out. "Aleta said, 'Tell Ethan I'm fine and I love him.'"

***

The week before the break ended, Slime started heading up the stairs. Fuck and Ethan leaned over the third-floor banister to watch the slow ascent from his ground floor office. His bald pate shone beneath the meager wattage of the electric bulbs suspended at each landing, and the clomp of his dark brown Sears and Roebuck oxfords reverberated in the stairwell. For once, neither of them had any contraband to hide in a hurry—no marijuana, no cigarettes, no alcohol, no forbidden food. As they waited for the huffing and puffing to reach the third floor, Fuck flexed his biceps a few times and stood in front of Ethan to shield him.

He twisted his head around, whispering, "Fuck. I mean, what the fuck?"

Ethan whispered back, "Holy shit, Fuck, how should I know?"

Neither of them knew for sure what Slime's real name was, but the letters on his door read **D'Angelo Assoc. Housing Men Only**. He could have been a boxer before he got too old because he had a giant set of shoulders.

Slime grunted rather than spoke, "I'm fixin' up this floor, workmen comin' in on Thursday, gettin' in a spiffier class of people. I don't need no Jew-boys and Redskins in my house."

From the corner of his eye, Ethan saw Fuck's fists clench, unclench, and clench again. Slime noticed the hands, too. The Indian was a scary customer, the first renter ever to intimidate him. He didn't wish to find himself rolling down the stairs beaten to a bloody pulp.

Slime opened his own hands placatingly. "Hummingbird, it ain't so much about you, you're clean."

He turned to Ethan. "It's *you*, Marcus, an' all them cops. In, out, slammin' my front door, runnin' up and down my stairs, searchin' my place. I gotta keep my reputation."

No one moved for a solid minute.

But Ethan's brain was active. *Holy shit, Hummingbird? That's Fuck's last name?*

Then Fuck leaped forward with an aggressive bound. "Okay, man, we go. We get back our deposits and —"

Ethan broke in as Fuck's fists continued to open and close. "Fine, Mr. D'Angelo, we'll go. But we sure as hell won't pay rent for this January."

Ethan despised apartment hunting and moving, but with Fuck being so strong, it wouldn't be all that bad. And he knew where to look, further away from campus in the slum neighborhoods where the poor Mexican families lived. They'd rent a place together with three rooms and a real kitchen and bathroom, maybe even a yard. His only worry was Aleta coming back to Slime's and not being able to find him.

Fuck must have read Ethan's mind. He announced reassuringly, "Fuck, man, Aleta will find us."

Ethan thought, Us? What does he mean by *us*? So what the fuck's been going on between those two?

***

Aleta and Scarlett began each morning at the Cafe Canton with breakfast in the kitchen—bowls of steamed rice and broiled fish with pickles on the side. On one cold rainy day, Mrs. Ito also served them piping hot miso soup, its surface thick with mysterious white cubes and some kind of green salty lettuce.

It took a while for Aleta to get used to Mrs. Ito's snappish answers, but nonetheless, she ventured forth courageously after tasting the grainy broth, "Mrs. Ito, I love Japanese breakfast. Why don't you and Mr. Ito serve Japanese food? You could be the first restaurant in California!"

Mrs. Ito smiled, but her eyes turned down a little at the corners. "Oh no, Miss Alice, no one like. Japanese food not *American* like Chinese food."

***

With each passing day, Aleta's waitressing improved. She learned how to write an order in shorthand, how to balance the heavy trays, how to please her customers without hovering, and how to avoid marauding males' roving hands.

On the sixth day, a Saturday, she played tangos on a makeshift stage constructed out of apricot drying flats from the San Joaquin Valley. When she took her breaks every half hour, Scarlett showed off her

Southern drawl, reciting from memory the famous "Frankly, my dear, I don't give a damn" scene from *Gone with the Wind.*

The Itos had a hit on their hands.

But first, Mr. Ito had put his degrees from the University of Tokyo and the University of California to use. He knew four languages besides his own, including German. The slogan he came up with for the show's star was derived from Aleta's last name, and Mrs. Ito spent all day Friday painting it on a wooden sandwich board for the front of the restaurant: MEET ALICE ROSE, TANGO QUEEN OF VIOLIN VALLEY, and in smaller letters at the bottom, Special Bonus: Siobhan O'Hare Plays Scarlett.

The restaurant finally closed about eleven. Even though Scarlett knew that her mother would throw a fit over the lateness of the hour, she skipped triumphantly up the hill to meet her fate head-on.

But Aleta dragged her feet. She wanted to celebrate along with Scarlett, but the weight of her knowledge oppressed her. After six days of trying to forget about Pearl Harbor, she had to accept that tomorrow morning on Sunday, December 7th, lots of people would die horribly when battleships and air bases would be bombed and torpedoed, and the United States would go to war.

At last, she asked timidly, "Scarlett, what would you do if you knew something terrible was going to happen and you couldn't even tell your best friend?"

Scarlett threw her a quizzical look. "Well, if it was me, which it isn't, and I didn't want my best friend to know, why the hell would I bring it up in the first place?"

***

The days that followed Pearl Harbor were almost too heartbreaking to bear. The restaurant stayed open even though the Itos never left their tiny apartment at the back during business hours. When Aleta and Scarlett arrived in the morning, all the vegetables for the day would be chopped. The menu was shortened, and Mr. Ito wrote out the recipes for the remaining dishes in a clear hand so the girls could both cook and serve. The clientele dropped precipitously. The military never appeared since most of them were deployed, although many customers from town remained loyal. They couldn't help themselves; they returned for the deliciously prepared food and the tango show that Aleta offered nightly in short bursts in between cooking, serving, and washing up.

***

On the first day of April when the emerald-green grass on the hills behind Puerto Seguro had reached its full height before turning a summer yellow, Toshiro and Motomi Ito summoned both girls into their tiny apartment at the back. Aleta and Scarlett had never seen it before, and they stood amazed. Where were the beds, the rugs, the sofa and chairs, and all the other ordinary trappings that cluttered an American house? Instead, they saw rush mats on the floor, screens to divide the room in half, and two bedrolls tucked away in a corner. Then they followed the Ito's example, first removing their shoes before kneeling around a low table set for tea.

Aleta announced in an awed whisper, "Mr. and Mrs. Ito, I love this room." She stopped abruptly, worried that she'd spoken out at the wrong time. The air suddenly seemed laden with tragedy.

Mr. Ito waited for his wife to pour the tea before he began to speak in the precise English that he had learned in his youth at the university.

"You understand, Miss Siobhan and Miss Alice, that we are Japanese. We have read the posters, we have talked to our friends. There is nothing we can do. All of us leave our homes on April 7th with only a few things."

As Mrs. Ito wept, he continued, "You see, we are considered dangerous, maybe we hide secrets. I myself am very dangerous. I learned German many years ago."

Aleta asked softly, "Where will you go?"

"We do not know, but we think we go to what is called a relocation center, and from there to a camp. We have heard rumors about barbed wire." Mr. Ito went on with an eerie serenity as he stared into the depths of his tea. "Miss Alice, it is best not to speculate."

Aleta frantically scoured her memory for what she'd learned in her high school American History class, but she could not recall a word in her textbook about this human catastrophe. A thought flashed through her mind, *Like the Jews, but I sure hope it will end better.*

Aleta noticed with surprise that Mrs. Ito had slipped an arm around Scarlett's waist as the poor girl tried to talk through tears.

"But Mr. and Mrs. Ito, this is the worst thing that could ever happen to me, worse than when my father died, worse than when my heart got broken."

With gentle fingers, Mrs. Ito smoothed Scarlett's hair. "No, Siobhan, very own child die—much, much worse. You and Alice, you make us happy, you our children now. We set up bank account for you."

Mr. Ito broke in, "My daughters, there will be no more Cafe Canton. It is rented to new tenants, and by next week, our existence in Puerto Seguro will be a part of the past. But you are fresh, young. Please make something of your lives just as we had wished for our son, George."

As the girls slipped on their shoes at the door, Mrs. Ito tucked a tiny gift into Aleta's palm—a brass wedding band from a Cracker Jack box. She whispered, "Is high time. You wear now, Miss Alice Rose, Tango Queen of Violin Valley."

***

Early in the morning of April 7th, a thick white fog rolled in from the ocean but would probably burn off by noon. Aleta threw on an itchy wool sweater to make the last trip to the Cafe Canton. She had planned to say goodbye to the Itos and wanted at least to help them carry their bags. But they were gone. As she made the climb back up the hill to The Living Hell Hotel, she met Scarlett half way, awkwardly juggling baby Tommy and a small suitcase.

Scarlett tried to sound brave, but her lips trembled. "I'm catching the bus to the Salinas train station. The Daylight leaves for L.A. in an hour." She added unconvincingly, "Hello Hollywood, are you ready for Scarlett O'Hare?"

With Scarlett gone, Aleta moved out of The Living Hell Hotel, leaving a shattered old woman keening for her daughter and cherubic grandson. Brokenhearted herself, Aleta settled into a small apartment at the corner of Main and Orchard, vowing to check the movie posters in front of the Paramount every week for her friend's name.

In her grief, she thought, If I were Otto Preminger or even Alfred Hitchcock, I'd choose the most beautiful, kindest girl in the whole world for every single movie I made. I mean my best friend Scarlett O'Hare— and I don't want this to sound like an epitaph.

***

By May, Aleta was too encumbered by her own belly to keep her waitressing job at the Seguro Hotel Restaurant. With extra time on her hands, she dedicated her life to fighting for, and finding the Itos by writing letters to President Roosevelt, to all nine Supreme Court justices, to every senator, to her congressman, and repeatedly to the newspapers. But she never received an answer from anyone or saw a single one of her letters in print.

At night as she counted the kicks of four sharp heels and the jab of an occasional sharp elbow, she thought up her *Theory of the Keystone*. When the Itos at the top of the arch were yanked out, all the other stones came tumbling down. She and Scarlett were snuggled tightest on either side of the Ito keystone. They fell the farthest and crashed the hardest. Mrs. O'Hare, the next stone over, fell almost as hard when her daughter left her. Tommy, on the other side, fell along with his beautiful mama. Aleta didn't forget Troll, already the casualty of another war. He fell, dying of starvation beneath his bridge. The Itos' customers fell, the man who sold the Itos his plump white harbor shrimp fell, and so did the men with the cabbages, mushrooms and string beans. The Itos' Japanese friends fell, bringing down their own arches. In Aleta's mind, even the tango fell because she would never play one again. The most romantic of all dances belonged solely to the gentle Itos from Tokyo who fell hardest of all, losing the American dream.

***

Nurse Isobel de Silva thrilled with anticipation. Newborn twins were coming up from the delivery room, underweight, but unusually strong. Isobel was the most unflappable nurse on the ward. Her parents had left Brazil in 1932 after the cattle ranch had failed, but Isobel had never cared about ranching and even less about cattle. Instead, she'd spent every waking hour since she was eleven years old helping out at the tiny mission-run infirmary for the Aché people. These saddest of human beings, driven deep into the interior, would walk miles to the coast when their own medical arts failed them. The gravely injured, the mortally ill with white men's infectious diseases, and the stick-thin dehydrated infants all arrived at the infirmary gates. When Isobel came to the United States, she learned English in record time, enrolled in nursing school, and ended up practicing her desired specialty at the neonatal ward in Santa Ynez Hospital.

Nurse Isobel was the first person to rock Aleta Rosenthal Marcus's tiny twins, Yacy and Kuaray. At least that's what the birth certificates said, but she had her doubts about the husband, Mr. Marcus. She had a practiced eye and a Cracker Jack prize did not look like a wedding ring. But how, and she crossed herself, had Miss Rosenthal come up with the names Yacy and Kuaray, names for the moon and sun gods straight from the Aché heathen religion?

Once Aleta had recovered enough to explain, she told Isobel that they had come to her in a dream. The good Catholic Isobel had seen and heard just about everything working in the maternity ward, but an eighteen-year-old Jewish girl giving her children Aché names seemed sacrilegious. And yet it could not be denied. Little Yacy was as pale and iridescent as the moon, with translucent skin shot through with delicate blue veins. Her brother appeared as ruddy and rich in coloring as the blazing hot sun. Although both children were healthy, Yacy's body temperature was a chilly 97 degrees, and Kuaray's held steady at 100 degrees. In one way the twins were identical. Both had staring almond eyes the color of polished amber. These unnatural babies rarely closed their eyes because they seldom slept.

The midnight shift was Isobel's favorite. With the daytime bustle at a standstill, she could hear the wind and the surf, the foghorn, and the hoot owls that perched on the cypress tree outside the window. Most of the babies made tiny gurgling, snoring sounds, punctuated by the occasional crying that demanded her attention.

Then she heard something else—bassinet wheels squeaking on the waxed floor. No, *impossible*. But there was the sound again, this time coming from two bassinets. She started with alarm, for Kuaray's and Yacy's little beds were now six inches closer together, disrupting the even rows. When she summoned up the nerve to look at the twins, they stared back at her with piercing amber eyes that glowed from expressionless infant faces. By morning, the bassinets' sides touched, and Yacy and Kuaray had fallen asleep at last.

***

Dr. Sullivan checked the babies every two weeks. They were growing rapidly and passed all their cognitive tests months too soon. The doctor should have been overjoyed, or at least enthusiastic.

Instead, he spoke coldly to Aleta. "The twins are doing splendidly, there is no doubt about that. They have more than made up for their low birth weight; you must have very rich milk. But there are oddities, like their basal temperatures. I'm planning to consult with a pediatrician in San Francisco. I don't want to see these children again."

Isobel caught up with Aleta in the hall. "Aleta, how can I say this, it hurts me so. There are certain important people in town who have heard things about what your babies can do, like move their toys with their eyes, and say 'Mama' already. It's almost like they copy the Aché gods they are named for. You should go somewhere else. It's hard to believe, but people are scared of your children."

Chapter 6 Miriam and Ariel

After Aleta was taken away, Fuck was so miserable that he considered dropping out of school. He couldn't talk to anyone about missing her, especially not Ethan. Even worse, he found himself in the unenviable role of consoling Ethan, whom he knew he had betrayed, all the while covering up his own feelings for her. He was also hiding forbidden knowledge about her disappearance that he couldn't reveal to anyone. Besides, as the Moon People had told him repeatedly, Aleta was never meant for him and he should have kept his hands off her. In his darkest moments he asked himself whether the Moon People had snatched her away to satisfy some diabolical plan of their own, or simply to separate the clandestine lovers.

He wanted to rip out his hair, cry his eyes out, and break all his dishes to smithereens. That's how much losing her radiant eyes, the key to his happiness, hurt him. Instead, he bit his lip and tried to forget her. Once the new semester started, he spent every afternoon pursuing the one comfort he knew. He worked out so hard at the school gym that he could no longer think coherently about Aleta or anything else and could barely drag himself home to the bug-ridden, moldy apartment he and Ethan had rented together in Little Mexico.

But then he would slip backward. First, he stared at the canned soup he didn't feel like heating up, and the Wonder Bread he couldn't swallow. For the rest of the evening, he missed her with a throbbing ache that penetrated his whole body. All the while, he sat at his desk, fiddling with his Venus #2 pencils and contemplating the unopened covers of his ratty second-hand textbooks.

***

Early in February, Fuck had a dream so vivid that he decided it must be a vision. He'd had similar dreams before, but never as intense as this one.

He asked himself if it was okay to complain from inside a dream because nothing felt right. The mountain path was made of lava, and the sand on it was cruelly sharp. He noticed his feet leaving bloody tracks that streaked the ground. And why was he shivering? He looked downward, taking in his clothes.

No wonder, I'm dressed in a ridiculous tunic straight off the Spartacus movie set.

He noticed a black-haired woman approaching him, the wind blowing a sheer white gown against her long thighs and full breasts. He sucked in his breath, trying to gather his courage. She's beautiful. Things are strange, but at least try to act normal.

When they met, she clasped his hands. "Ariel, leave the Trail of Tears and come with me." She led him to a tiny mountain lake nestled deep within weathered crags, slippery as ice. The lake was ruffled by the wind, but the water was so densely covered by opulent white lilies that the surface could hardly be seen.

Then he gazed down the length of the woman's lovely body. His eyes reached her feet. He noticed that they also bled, pierced by the path's tortuous sand.

"Ariel, I am Miriam. You know me already from my son Ethan's fever — from his delirium." She ran her hands up his arms to clasp the back of his neck as she kissed him full on the lips. He returned the kiss, all the while combing his fingers through her rich, wavy hair. Then she slid both hands from the nape of his neck to his face, letting her sensitive fingers brush across his eyelids. Their touch ignited a fire that raged inside the base of his brain.

She spoke her next words as Thought, right into the white-hot center of the flames. "Ariel, close your eyes. I want you to see."

Fuck woke up then, both aroused by the woman's body and terrified by her powerful mind. The searing fire she had lit still glowed deep inside him. The experience was new to him, beyond anything the Moon People had ever managed to do.

Once he had calmed down he asked himself, *I understand the trail, but why all the fancy trappings like the tunic and the mountain lake? Who made them up, me or her? And what can she mean by "Close your eyes, I want you to see?" It sounds crazy.* Nevertheless, the first thing he did was consult the Greyhound schedule to Santa Clara and the Agnews asylum that was tucked into Ethan's address book by the telephone.

***

Red tape at the nurses' desk was minimal because Miriam had already told the staff that Ariel, one of her dearest friends, was visiting today. He signed in, not forgetting to use the name she'd given him in the vision. No one seemed to notice when a plump round-faced nurse wearing a rustling uniform with "Miss Montag RN" written on her badge escorted him directly into Miriam's room at the end of the hall.

Fuck, newly named Ariel, was mystified. After Ethan had recovered from the flu, he mentioned seeing his mother in a depressing visitors' room where he had watched Tweety Bird almost get his head snapped off by Sylvester the Cat. So Ariel wondered why the rules had been changed, apparently just for him. Perhaps the whisper of Miss Montag's skirt and the disturbing yellow gleam of her panther eyes had hypnotized the whole staff into looking the other way. She smiled at him now as if they were already acquainted, which struck him as odd.

At a glance, Ariel took in the sparse furnishings of Miriam's little cell, the barred windows, the unadorned white walls, the white bed, and the black-and-white checkered linoleum floor.

But the *woman*. Ariel was instantly mesmerized by her arresting beauty, her half-closed black eyes with the sweeping lashes, her arched nose, her full lips and high cheekbones. She seemed to pulse and shimmer, almost as if she might vanish into her own thoughts and disappear even before she had met him. And yet her body could hardly have been more compelling. It alone could reel him in like a helpless fish, hooked by her black hair that hung loose, her breasts, her hips, her delicate slipper-clad feet. She may have been wearing hospital-issue clothing, but he doubted it since the cut of the diaphanous white fabric left little to the imagination.

He had the odd sensation that he was seeing himself in a mirror. Her eyes, cheekbones, nose and lips were almost identical to his own, although his were naturally far bolder. He noticed that he and Miriam offset each other, too. His skin was dark, especially compared to her pallor from spending her life inside a cell. Her abundant curls reached almost to her waist, while he kept his thick straight hair neatly trimmed, curving behind his ears and touching the nape of his neck.

Miriam stirred herself into full wakefulness as her eyes suddenly pierced through him. She took in his massive physical beauty with a boldness that he had never experienced before.

She spoke first. "Ariel, I called to you in a vision, but I did not think you would hear me. You did hear, and I am weeping. Yes, I am weeping for joy." Even though she had overstated the copiousness of her tears, her eyes glistened.

He also loved the name Ariel since he never would have imagined it for himself. He asked Miriam shyly why she had picked it. She told him to close his eyes. The fire in his brain burned to a white heat just as it had in his vision. *In the flames a lion pawed the earth, stretching one fiery limb skyward. A male sprite rode on the lion's back, but not in triumph. He was cruelly bound in heavy chains that choked his throat with each step the lion took.* Ariel kept his eyes closed, the fire still hot in his head.

Miriam spoke then. "Open your eyes, Ariel. You have seen your name. You are the mighty Hebrew Lion of God and the slave of Prospero from *The Tempest*, begging for your freedom." She smiled. "You can be either or both."

Miriam asked Ariel to sit beside her on her neatly made bed with its white waffle-weave cotton blanket and crisp sheets. He hesitated at first, but since there was no other furniture in the room, he joined her, sliding only as close to her as he thought was appropriate. She turned toward him, her sad black eyes drilling into him with such intensity that he let out an involuntary gasp.

Then she took his hands. When she finally spoke, she asked a question so personal that it was almost impossible for someone like him to answer; it went to the core of his being. "Ariel, tell me, please, who are you?"

Then he surprised himself. He started to talk, saying more words at a stretch than he had spoken to anyone in his entire life, except perhaps to Aleta. Miriam tightened her grip on his fingers as if she wished to absorb his words through her flesh. He felt his hands turn molten.

Ariel started slowly because he didn't entirely trust her. How could she exert such power by merely holding his hands? And why should she care about him?

He stumbled over his first words. "I-I never knew my mother. She died ... she died, well, just after I was born." He hung his head, his voice trailing off. Miriam sat perfectly still, waiting for him to go on.

"She had a name, Sunali. It's the Cherokee word for 'morning,' like when the day is new." He stopped again. *God, how can I do this?*

His throat hurt, but he took a deep breath. "Being a Cherokee in Oklahoma, well, you get ruined, from alcohol mostly. But my mother didn't die that way. She was so pretty, everyone said so. She worked in a white girls' fancy whorehouse."

The beautiful woman sitting next to him moved a few inches closer. She asked, "How do you know this, Ariel?"

He whispered, "Everybody knew it. At the school where I went, they said it, you know, behind my back." He squirmed, remembering the pain of being the butt of gossip. "They said everyone did heroin at the whorehouse. And that's how she died."

Ariel should have gotten used to his crushing childhood by now, but he always felt his throat close up when he recalled early memories.

"I was raised by her sisters, my aunties. But they didn't like me much—"

She broke in impulsively, "Ariel, you cannot be sure."

"But I am. They tried to make the man who probably was my father take me, but he wouldn't." His next sentence was all but inaudible, "He was ashamed of me, and I guess they were, too."

Miriam exclaimed, "I would have taken you into my heart and loved you."

He was moved by her outburst. Never before had he heard such kind words expressed just for him. From now on, his own words flowed a little easier.

"They sent me to this school where lots of the other Indian kids had to go. Some of them liked it—if they had families they could go home to during the summer, or brothers and sisters at the school. For kids like me, it was an orphanage and a school at the same time, all the way through high school. It was my residential school, the Sequoyah Orphan Training School, and later the name was changed to Sequoyah Vocational School. There are lots of schools like it for Indians, and they're all over the United States."

Miriam stared at him with her big sad eyes. "Ariel, it was better there than living with your aunts, yes?"

Ariel felt his throat tighten again. "Well, no. I cried a lot late at night and sometimes wet my bed. I tried to run away, I got punished. The kids beat me up almost every day because I was the smallest one there."

Miriam questioned him softly, "Did your aunts visit you sometimes?"

Ariel tried to sound calm and not reveal the anguish of being rejected. "Well, I waited for them every night, but they never came. I was four years old, I didn't know any English which was all they'd let us speak."

Tears filled Miriam's eyes. For a moment Ariel couldn't talk, but he would never let himself go, especially not out of self-pity.

"It took a couple of years, but I learned three things that made me who I am, I guess. Don't talk, because if you say something wrong, they'll hurt you. Don't get angry, because you'll have to fight. Don't ever cry in front of anyone because they'll laugh at you and rub your face in the dirt."

Miriam looked aghast. "You mean you never talked to anyone? You did not have friends?"

"It wasn't so bad. When I grew up big, the kids and teachers couldn't hurt me. But I was lonely."

"Well, that time is past. No longer will you be lonely." Miriam brushed her lips on his cheek and suddenly he felt hot all over as if he were standing too close to a stove.

Although he went on talking, his body was competing with his brain. He took a big breath. "I did well in school. Then I got a scholarship and government money to go to Santa Margarita. I wanted to get as far away from Oklahoma as I could, to forget being Cherokee, which the residential school made me do anyway."

Ariel tried to laugh as he began a sort of confession. "It's been hard for me. The school wasn't that good, more of a vocational school and a farm, and only going up to about eighth-grade level, and my English writing is terrible." He grimaced. "I don't really like sports, but it's all I can do because I can't write or talk. I'm still trying to pass my first-year English and history courses, and I'm twenty."

Then Miriam kissed him again, this time hard on his lips as if to emphasize her next words. "Well, sports make you beautiful, Ariel, more than you realize." She paused. "But what would you really like to do with your life?"

Ariel felt the room spin. In a passion-induced haze, he blurted out an answer without thinking. "I know there's poetry inside me, the words are in my head; they just can't come out. More than anything, I want to be a poet."

Miriam didn't seem surprised; perhaps she had known what his answer would be. Pulling him closer, she placed one hand over his eyes and the other on his thigh. She spoke to him in spontaneous poetry of her own, and maybe her words were silent, transported directly into his brain. Ariel couldn't tell for certain because her gently pressing fingers made white-hot sparks shoot through him, which stifled most of his conscious thought.

As Miriam spoke, he also felt the fire in his head behind her hand. *You are Ariel, a lion in limb and heart, beautiful as a god walking along the Trail of Tears. Leave it behind, turn away. Pierce the lilies in the black lake.*

It was Ariel's first experience speaking silent words, but his reply came easily. *You are Miriam walking the Trail of Tears, locks of hair blowing across your face, black eyes weeping. Leave the Trail with me. I rest my head on your breast, kiss your white neck, touch your bleeding feet.*

When his words ceased, her eyes fluttered open. They filled with tears, which he couldn't understand.

Ariel stood up in a panic. He had never held such an erotically charged conversation, and certainly not silently, with anyone. His whole body felt weak.

"Oh, God, Miriam, what are we doing? This just can't go on for a hundred reasons. And I have to leave or I'll miss the last bus."

Miriam kissed him deep into his mouth, and he thought his heart would burst from the intense arousal.

"Will you return?" Her tone was full of longing.

He allowed his fingers to comb through her thick dark hair and linger at the base of her neck just like in the vision. He was way beyond controlling himself.

"How can I not?"

***

Ariel tried to stay away from Miriam to figure out what to do. He lasted for barely half a week and even this short interim was torture. Her erotic presence remained so vivid that he was in physical agony most of the time. He had never been so confused by anyone. What could she possibly have done to end up in an insane asylum? Ethan was no help on that score. He had never said a word about his mother's illness, but during his fever and delirium, he had revealed a guilt-ridden filial relationship.

What filled Ariel with the most doubt was the way Miriam had led him on, not with practiced skill or artificial charm, but with utmost sincerity, and he didn't know why. All these facts should've scared him off, but instead, they filled him with such longing to comfort her and the desire to make love, that he trembled all over.

**

When Ariel entered Miriam's stark room on a rainy afternoon three days later, the pair embraced with fervor as if they hadn't seen each other for weeks. Miriam looked exquisite, again dressed in white, but with a blue sash that accentuated her tiny waist and curving hips. She couldn't contain her excitement, clasping his hands over and over, and kissing his lips, his face, his neck.

Finally, he held her at arms' length. "Miriam, I really want to keep going, but let's hold off for a little while longer. We should go slow, and I hardly know you. Tell me about yourself, like I told you about me."

Miriam grew pensive and slumped down on her bed. The powerful allure she had radiated at first was suddenly gone. She murmured, "Of course I'll tell you because you have to know. But then you might hate me."

Ariel burst out, "Even if you'd killed somebody, I'd still feel like I do now."

He instantly regretted his hasty words, perhaps inadvertently cruel, but she replied simply, "Ariel, I did kill somebody, but it was because I had to. And nobody knows except the people who were there."

"Not even Ethan?"

"Especially not Ethan."

Ariel didn't know what to expect, but he was sure that this would be very difficult for her. He sat down beside her on the bed and drew her close. She started off hesitantly, but soon her voice grew in confidence as if she were relieved to be making her confession.

"Ariel, I was a really beautiful girl and from a good family. All the Jewish boys in Warsaw were after me for my looks, and I was an excellent student, too. I danced, played piano, I was at the top of my class, I knew all the classics—Greek and Latin. We studied French, naturally, and English. But then came the war. Our lives fell apart when we were closed into the Ghetto."

She hesitated for the first time. "War does funny things to you, Ariel. I was crazy for a man named Samuel who didn't love me, but he was very romantic, a hero, fighting for our people. To him, I was nothing, and I was not the only one he took. I was sixteen, and he would not marry me even though I had his baby daughter Danya, a year old, and already Ethan on the way. Ariel, the Ghetto was choking us, all my people were dying. I had to get to Romania for the sake of my babies. I went on my own with five other people."

Miriam started crying softly, wiping her eyes on her sash. Ariel tightened one arm around her shoulders, all the while stroking her hair with his free hand.

"I carried Danya hidden in my coat. She was starving. We had no food and my milk had dried up. We walked in the middle of the night, but there were patrols everywhere looking for people like us, so we hid behind a farmer's house in a shed. We could hear the soldiers right outside the door. My little Danya started to cry. Her voice was so weak, but they heard her. They started to turn the handle, we held our breaths. Just then an owl made his noise—a great hoot. A soldier said, '*Nur eine Eule,*' only an owl."

The rest of Miriam's confession was nearly inaudible since she had buried her face against Ariel's neck. "Before the trip, I made a bargain with Pavel, our leader. He would take me only if my little girl made no sound. But she did. She cried from hunger. Pavel nudged me in the ribs; it was our sign. So I took her outside. I pinched her little nose and I held my other hand over her mouth. After she died, I buried her next to the shed under the tree where the owls slept. I begged them to watch over her grave because I could never come back."

Ariel rocked Miriam until the flood of tears stopped. He caressed her, kissing her lips, her eyes, even her fingertips. He had a great lump in his throat; he loved her so much, he wanted to cry, too. But at the same time, he felt superfluous in the face of such tragedy.

Miriam sat up, brushing her tangled hair out of her eyes with a trembling hand. "It was so terrible. I never told Ethan that he had a big sister once, a long, long time ago. How could I? He would not understand how I could have done what I did.

"And I told Ethan lies, and they are terrible, too. I told him I was married to Samuel, his father, and that it was Samuel who took me to Romania to save me."

When she went on, her voice was tinged with anger. "I told a third lie, much, much worse. I told him Samuel died in Treblinka—a true hero of our people. But I do not know what happened to that man. I only know he deserted me and my children. Sometimes, even now, I wish him dead."

Miriam took Ariel's hand. Her touch felt icy cold, not like the red-hot furnace of three days ago. "Oh, Ariel, I tried so hard. I held on for such a long time, it felt like years and years, but when Ethan grew up and started to look like the man who did not care for me at all, I did a crazy, evil thing and they took me away."

Ariel and Miriam left the bed and stood in front of the solitary window. They stared at their rippling reflections in the dark pane as rain washed against it through the sturdy iron bars.

Eventually, Miriam whispered, "Ariel, you say nothing, but I see inside your heart. Our stories are almost the same. We both lost so many of our people that we do not know what to do."

Ariel whispered, "The Trail of Tears. It is where my people died, but we saw the same place in our first vision."

Her reply was simple. "Yes, Ariel. It *is* the same place."

So she knew. She had looked inside him. She had seen past the great emptiness of his lost self, she had seen him walk the Trail of Tears every day of his life. Her experience was not so different. She had never stopped mourning for her girl-child and for six million other Jews whose bones lay scattered all over Europe.

***

Ariel was fully aware of the many risks, which he had reviewed over and over in his head: Ethan would never forgive him, Miriam was certainly still hovering on the verge of madness from killing her child, her deception toward her son, and from her sensitive morbidity. During wiser moments he was plagued by a recurring thought that should have given him pause but did not do so. In seventeenth-century Salem, one period in history that had stuck successfully in his mind, she would have been hung as a witch—a murderer who experienced hallucinations, and a formidable temptress proffering the apple of Eden to unwitting males. In this enlightened century, she had simply been locked up.

But Ariel loved Miriam enough to die for her. He loved the visions, the poetry, the talking without words, her hair, her eyes, her smile, her body, even her grief. By now, he was pretty sure that he was losing the battle with his saner self.

***

Ariel returned the following day because he couldn't stay away. When he entered Miriam's room, he planned to say something, anything, to slow himself down. He tried to form a coherent sentence just as she slipped out of her dress, the same simple white gown that she had worn in the vision. Naked, she radiated a combination of unearthly purity and the sweetest sensuality, utterly destroying his will and sense of reality. With clumsy, shaking fingers he clawed at his shirt buttons, his belt buckle, his pants zipper. What the hell was he doing, anyway?

Later Ariel couldn't recall the exact moment the vision had started. One minute he was in her room, and the next, on their Trail of Tears.

He kept asking himself, Why am I letting this happen?

He watched her approach through shimmering white-hot sunlight, her black hair blowing across her face and breasts. As if she'd learned from the first vision, she picked her steps carefully to avoid the windblown heaps of sharp sand, her perfectly molded hips swaying. They kissed for a very long time.

Even through his passion, he couldn't help whispering, "I'm breaking every rule in the book."

Ariel was frightened. He found himself teetering on the icy boulders high above the lake. He tried to break through the panic that imprisoned his reason but failed. He thought, I'll fall in, I know. Then what?

And he did, slipping off the narrow ledge that crumbled beneath him. On the way down, he caught a protruding tree root by one hand, but the harder he tried to pull himself upward, the further it bent. He groaned. His hand was tiring .... How he yearned to release his fingers, to let his long limbs, grown powerful and arrow straight, drop into the water. Suddenly one foot grew slimy-wet as it slipped under the white lilies that floated on the gleaming surface. He closed his eyes, trying not to think.

"Ariel." It was her voice from far away, yet next to his ear. "Ariel, open your hand, let go."

And so he did. His arched feet and taut legs, his huge erect penis, slim hips and flat belly, his giant body in all its beauty, shot deep into the lake, zooming past banks of white lilies, their bulbous roots trapping bright birds, snakes, tiny lizards. He felt the lake boil as fire consumed him. He let flames burn his brain right through, leaving nothing but glowing embers. All around him, flying moons, red, black, yellow, and silver, whistled past his ears only to tear apart in great molten globs.

But wait. If I, Ariel, must die, shield me from the End of Time; hide me, Miriam, deep within the lily's satin throat.

The sepals and petals closed tight around him, bending, twisting, sighing in the lake's current. He let himself go, shattering into a million, billion fiery shards.

***

Miriam shook Ariel awake. He returned from miles away to focus first on the high ceiling, and then on the tear-filled eyes of the woman he loved. She stood above him in a halo of white light. He reached up, running his hands downward over her breasts, waist, and hips to the place between her thighs—now temptingly hidden beneath the white gown.

"Miriam, I dreamed about you and me at the end of the world." He sounded sleepy.

"I know you did, Ariel. Put something on. Even Miss Montag can't keep the door closed much longer."

Then he looked down at his naked, newly erect self with one forlorn sock dangling from a toe. He sat up abruptly.

"My God, we didn't, it felt so … I thought it was a vision. Did I hurt you? You're crying."

She kissed him gently on the forehead. "No Ariel, you have made me very happy."

Miriam hurried him into his clothes, kissed him again, this time full on the lips. Then she shooed him out, all the while straightening the sheets and the blanket on her pretty white bed. Ariel sidled past the nurses' station, but no one looked up. Only Miss Montag who was walking in the hall gave him a bright smile. He may have imagined it, but he thought she winked at him.

As soon as the door swung shut, Miriam sank down onto the checkerboard tiles, weeping. *You Moon People! You fooled my son and Aleta, and now you've fooled my Ariel, but you don't fool me. You have forced me, twisted me, lied to me, but I know making god-babies kills. I will pay for this with my life. But I don't care, if you will only let me die in his arms.*

***

On the long bus ride home, Ariel marveled at the strange erotic sex that had driven him past ecstasy—more poetic and yet more terrifying than any he had experienced or even imagined in his wildest fantasies. Miriam's sweet presence remained vivid in the back of his brain, and he could hear her weeping. If only he could return to comfort her, to slip his hands over and under that white gown. When he glanced down, he noticed that in his haste he'd buttoned his shirt wrong, and he sure wished he could have washed up a bit.

Then he had a horrible thought; no wonder the poetry had flowed so copiously. His mind rushed back to the only information the boys at Sequoyah Orphan Training School had ever received about the opposite sex, delivered by the football coach who also served as the guidance counselor. This patient man dealt skillfully with the snickering, bragging boys who tried to act like the Lotharios they weren't. Meanwhile Ariel absorbed the advice, namely, *use a condom*. By now, he was plenty old enough to have put this wise dictum into practice. My God, what had he done? This was his second screw-up. He dropped his head into his hands.

Miriam knew that she had conceived during their consummation at the black lake. Ariel felt deeply ashamed of his negligence, but at the same time he was secretly elated, although he didn't think the news would please the Agnews staff. He thought it best to act responsibly by broaching the uneasy subject before she began to show. He was right to worry about the reaction, but at least he wasn't thrown in jail or forcibly removed from the premises. The reason was simple: Miriam's doctors had already noticed a remarkable improvement in her mental health and had petitioned the California Courts for her early release.

Besides, the happy pair were legally married in the Agnews chapel on a brilliantly sunny day in April. The chaplain concocted a service with a little bit of everything to cover the diverse religious and secular requirements, and Miss Montag, who had guarded Miriam's door from the beginning of the affair to prevent its discovery, served as maid of honor. The only shadow that marred a perfect wedding was Ethan's absence; the reluctant pair hadn't figured out how to tell him.

Something about Miriam's love released Ariel's amazing creative powers. It had actually started when he first told her about himself without inhibition. From then on, torrents of words flowed out of him. When the crisp blank paper wasn't sitting in front of him at his desk, he wrote on the backs of envelopes, on napkins, tablecloths, in the margins of newspapers, even on the back of his hand. He absorbed the world's music, history, literature, and art within a semester, amazing the Santa Margarita humanities professors. His English professors were dumbfounded by his brilliant essays, fiction, and especially by his unabashedly erotic poetry. All that was missing was the history of his own people. It was never taught at Santa Margarita, except in the most unflattering light.

Miriam and Ariel made love many times in the following weeks. Ariel often smoothed his hands over the tempting white gown and then reached under it to find the soft nest beneath as she touched his white-hot penis. They went much further, exploring the thousands of places, ripe and throbbing, that only true lovers know about. They never grew tired of lying in peace after the passion cooled, running gentle fingers over the bumps and hollows of their luminous flesh, lingering for a long time on her swelling belly. Finally, before sleeping, Miriam and Ariel intertwined their minds into a perfect harmony that permeated their dreams. But occasionally a dark thought plagued Ariel, tearing at the edge of his bliss. Such an exact match of telepathic minds was too powerful a union for mere humans to bear for long. There would be consequences.

Ariel's premonition proved to be true. If gods still reigned on Mount Olympus, perhaps they became jealous. Miriam and Ariel had challenged them by usurping divine rapture reserved for deities alone. Their vengeance was swift. About the fifth month into her pregnancy, Miriam began suffering from headaches, nausea, and blurred vision. Her left arm felt numb, and she could barely drag herself through an entire day. X-rays revealed the cause that her physicians had surmised from her symptoms. She had a brain tumor, already far advanced. They could have tried surgery, but she refused, fearing for the baby in her womb. Besides, it was probably too late. Hopes of release and a normal life were dashed. She was moved to San Jose Hospital where she received the best palliative care.

If possible, Ariel loved her even more passionately than he had before. To shield her, he refused to show his suffering, although Miriam could see it in his thoughts. She tried to reach out to him on the Trail of Tears where he walked with bleeding feet and dry, hollow eyes. They spent many hours in each other's arms as he fought to hold in the grief that threatened to tear him apart. He cried only once when she told him in meticulous detail the location of the Owl Tree where she wanted her ashes to lie with Danya's disintegrating bones.

"Ethan and our new baby must go, too. I know Aleta and the twins will be there in the thoughts of everyone." She paused for breath as Ariel tried to regain his control. "Go next summer when the berries on the elder tree are ripe, because that is where the owls sleep. Our family will be whole for the first time only when this is done."

Miriam delivered a healthy full-term baby girl on the last morning of her life, not in the maternity ward, but in her own hospital room because the doctors were afraid to move her. When her labor started, Ariel was sent away. No one noticed the solitary young man sitting for hours in the hall with his great shoulders hunched in misery as the hospital staff surged around him like worker bees, the nurses' white oxford shoes squeaking on the waxed linoleum.

At last, the ever-devoted Miss Montag, who had wangled a transfer from Agnews to San Jose Hospital, emerged from the room. She reported that Miriam was not in much pain and that everything was going smoothly. After the birth, Ariel glimpsed the baby girl all washed and bundled up as the attending pediatrician whisked her off to a bassinet in the neonatal ward. She looked unnaturally serene and alert, with huge glowing black eyes.

When Ariel was finally allowed back into the room, he clasped Miriam to his heart and kissed her over and over. She was terribly weak but fully conscious and ready to talk about her last hours on earth.

"I want to bring Ethan and Aleta together at the moment of my death when I go to where there is no Time. If you hold me up, I can make it happen. The Moon People will help me bring Aleta from wherever she is now." She stopped, gasping for air.

"Ethan is coming this afternoon; the doctors called him this morning. I will tell him about Danya, but not about you and me and the baby; that is what you must do after I am gone."

She went on, almost in a whisper, trying not to give orders, although she knew exactly what had to happen before her death. "Afterward, I shall send Ethan to the bus station where the Moon Bus is already waiting."

"The Moon Bus? Miriam—"

"It will fly for you. Take him from here to Seguro Beach where *it* will happen. But come right back to help me."

Then she slid her slender left hand into his massive one. "Ariel, take my wedding ring now. Miss Montag gave me a chain for it. It would never fit on any of your fingers."

Ariel eased the ring off with tenderness and placed it on the chain, which he then hung around his neck. Following this final ritual of parting, they embraced as tightly as any two people could, fusing their thoughts during the remaining hours allotted to them.

***

The time came for Ethan's visit, so Ariel left by the emergency stairs to avoid him. He assumed that Ethan and Miriam would have a lot to talk about since Ethan had shirked all his responsibilities and hadn't seen his mother for almost a year.

With a bowed head, Ariel dragged himself to the bus station where he located the Moon Bus parked next to the other Greyhounds. The blue and silver vehicle seemed to wink in and out of existence, but when it showed itself, the low-slung body was as streamlined as a bullet with huge windows that wrapped all the way around it. Ariel guessed correctly that something this peculiar must be invisible to most people.

When Ethan finally reached the station, it was obvious that he had been crying. Ariel felt utterly miserable himself, but right now wasn't the time to show it. Although Ethan remembered the bus from his delirium, he refused to board something that he'd seen only in his imagination.

"Fuck, you're nuts if you think I'm getting on that … that *spaceship*. And what's going on with you? You aren't even supposed to be here."

"Ethan, just get on the damn thing. Aleta and the kids will be meeting you."

"So Matka said. But just where, exactly, are we going?"

"Seguro Beach. And here's a piece of advice. When you see Aleta, don't try to touch her, because you can't. That's the way it is."

Ariel could hardly hide his resentment. *Why am I ferrying this snot-nosed brat all over the map when I need to be with her? There's no time left. She's dying.*

As soon as they reached Puerto Seguro, he dropped Ethan off and headed back toward the hospital. He kept biting his trembling lower lip to hold in the tears that would obscure his vision.

***

Aleta woke with a start from a very strange dream. She couldn't remember the details except that Sequoyah had been talking to her. "Go to the beach right now, take the babies."

She threw warm clothing on them and herself. Her first thought was, Would Sequoyah be there?

Then she hurried along the splintered boardwalk that led to Seguro Beach. She would have felt unsure of her footing in the dark if it weren't for the twins. The pram rolled along in front of her without her having to push it. The twins steered it efficiently, for even at five months they certainly had a way with wheels, at least when they were single-minded about the direction they wished to take, as they were now.

Amazed, she marveled at the unfamiliar horizon. *Why were two moons hanging low in the sky?* Immediately she recalled the ominous second moon that always accompanied her dire misadventures. Yes, something unprecedented was about to happen.

Aleta stopped on the sand, momentarily transfixed. There stood Ethan, about twenty feet in front of her, his back to the water. She couldn't help what she did next; she looked everywhere along the sand for Sequoyah, but he wasn't there. She was disappointed, but nonetheless proudly showed Ethan their babies—so plump and healthy. They both tried to talk, calling out above the surf. But it drowned out their voices, or maybe there was something else damping their greetings.

Ethan ran to embrace her, and his hand touched a barrier, not barbed wire, not iron bars, but a glittering liquid laced with silver streaks, malleable, but glassy-cold. He remembered Fuck's warning too late. Aleta and the babies were receding rapidly, shrinking until they were no bigger than grains of sand. Then he fell deeply asleep, stretched out full length on the gritty beach.

***

Supporting Miriam in his arms, Ariel tried to exert all his mental powers to help her sustain the wall because the gaping years that separated Ethan and Aleta could never mingle. But when Ethan touched the barrier, it collapsed. Time slid back, returning to where it had been, sweeping Aleta and her babies with it. When the wall broke, Miriam died without uttering a sound, her face peaceful and her eyes closed. Ariel held her body until it grew cold, his aching brain too numb to comprehend exactly what had happened.

Two doctors entered the room to declare the time of death. Ariel wandered away in no particular direction. Miss Montag found him in the hall, staring vacantly with tearless eyes, although his breathing sounded ragged, like sobs. She steered him to the exit, telling him that he must return in the morning to do many things, including picking up his child.

In this stunned condition, he drove back to Puerto Seguro where he pulled Ethan off the detritus on the sand—broken glass, old condoms, and cigarette butts. Ethan brushed the filth from his clothes while babbling on about the wonderful experience. He somehow failed to notice that Ariel was lurching all over the beach like a zombie.

Chapter 7 Luna's Fork 'n Spoon

Ethan wanted coffee. He and Ariel slid into a booth at **LUNA's FORK 'n SPOON**, a run-down place by the shore. It was the kind of place for fishermen who eked out a living from the almost depleted coastal waters, but at this early hour, the bedraggled pair were the only customers. The decor was listless: a fly-spotted mirror, draped with last December's tinsel, reflected a three-tiered display case on the counter that housed a single piece of lemon meringue pie. A gentle Spanish *balada* wafted from the jukebox, filling the narrow room with saccharine wistfulness.

Ethan stood up, searching his pockets for coins. "Give me a moment. I gotta call the hospital to see how Matka is."

At last, Ariel fell apart, bursting out crying in a torrent of grief and anger. He bolted up from the seat and clutched Ethan's shoulders, pushing him down hard onto the split upholstery.

"She's dead, *she's dead!* I dropped you off at the beach. I drove like crazy back to her in that flying thing. I've been visiting her for weeks because—*where the hell were you?*"

Ethan was furious and started crying, too. He clenched his fists, making a lunge at Ariel across the Formica tabletop. "Fuck you, stealing Matka away from me."

Ariel grabbed both Ethan's wrists before the fists could land in his face. "I held her up so she could make that wall. *For you.* He shook Ethan's wrists. "Afterwards, she died, Ethan, she *died!*" Another shake. "Then I came back to take *you* off that fucking beach." He gave a third shake that made Ethan howl from the pain. "I hate you. You don't know *shit* about love."

***

A big shadow loomed over Ethan and Ariel, as capable hands stretched forward, slamming the two down onto the banquette seats. The hands remained on their respective shoulders a little longer. Even though they seemed to comfort rather than coerce, Ethan and Ariel hardly dared to glance upwards.

"Brothers, I am Luz Luna, and I own this place." She drew up a ladder-backed Mexican chair with poppies and butterflies painted on the slats. It creaked as she sat down, because Luz was considerably larger than life, with shiny black hair and an open, friendly face as broad as the full moon. But right now, she wasn't smiling.

"The tears, that is natural. But cursing and fighting like *matones* when your mother just passed away? That is *sacrilegio*. And you are?"

Ethan regained his voice, although it quivered and broke. "I'm Ethan Marcus. My brother is, I can't tell you his name, it's rude, but anyway he's not really—"

"Well, Ethan, I know you from the *Seguro Daily News*. Your *mamá* upset many people in this town a couple of years back when she drowned that dog, but I always felt bad for her."

Luz gave Ethan a handful of paper napkins for his eyes and nose. "Listen, my boy, you are real, real lucky to have a brother, what with funeral plans coming up. You should be on your knees to him saying, *'Gracias mi hermano. Gracias* for staying with my *mamá* when I could not be there myself!'"

Luz turned toward Ariel with another handful of napkins. Then she reached for his hand and stared directly into his stricken eyes. "Ariel, stay with that *niño. Deja que San Cristóbal sea su inspiración.*" Even in his distraught state, he marveled that he had understood her. Perhaps she had spoken directly into his brain. He nodded through his tears, although he had no idea how St. Christopher could ever inspire him.

Luz rose up, straightening her pink uniform and smoothing out a minuscule ruffled apron with a pocket for her notepad and pencil.

"This is what you two will do now. I can tell you because I am your *mamacita* for today. Go left down the block to La Iglesia de la Paz. It is maybe, how do I say it, *no es apropiado* for Jewish brothers to walk into a Catholic church. But go in anyway, first light a tall white candle for your poor *mamá*. Then you talk to Padre Xavier, and say Luz Luna sent you. You grew up here in Puerto Seguro and I have eyes in my head, so I know you need help from the charity fund for your mother's funeral. Your religion does not matter and Padre Xavier will not ask you.

"Then turn around. I got leghorns out back just laid four extra eggs; must be a reason. Breakfast will be waiting."

A winsome smile lit up her face. *"Adiós muchachos, vayan con Dios."*

***

Ethan made Ariel light the candle because he felt horribly uncomfortable in the church. The interior was steeped in an odor of old incense, mouse droppings, and mold. The sun's early morning beams did not penetrate the high arched windows, and motes of dust swirled in the grainy half-light. There were morbid statues in every corner and huge, darkened paintings on the walls. Ethan wasn't used to any places of worship. He was also seething; Luz had failed to calm the awful fury that festered inside him. He waited impatiently for Padre Xavier, fidgeting and tapping his feet on the stone floor. Ariel sat next to him, his eyes fixed on Miriam's candle that shrank into waxy tears.

Suddenly Ethan's mouth flew open almost on its own, and the big question popped out. "So just what did you think you were doing visiting Matka, Fuck? Did you hope that she would magically become *your* mother, too?" Ariel bowed his head and squeezed his eyes tight shut.

"Just spit it out, goddammit. What the hell were you up to?" Ethan rudely shook Ariel's arm.

Ariel spoke then, but his words came out in jagged pieces. "I started visiting Miriam—"

Ethan waved his fist in Ariel's face, his own face red and contorted. "Don't you say her name, you *parasite.*"

Ariel absorbed the insult. "She was so lonely, so beautiful. We didn't need to talk. The same thoughts just happened inside our heads. I loved her and she loved me. We were together all the time, and then she got sick."

Ethan leaped up, his words suddenly virulent with hatred. "'We were together all the time.' What the hell does that mean, you fucking prick? You were screwing my mother in the nuthouse?" He bellowed, "Talk to Padre what's-his-name yourself, 'cause I don't care if she … *rots in the goddam morgue."*

Ethan fled all the way past the pews and out through the heavy wooden doors, turning around every few seconds to yell a "fuck you" in Ariel's direction.

Ariel stayed rooted where he sat as Miriam's candle flickered and went out. He rested his elbows on his knees so he could cradle his heavy head in his hands. He should get up, run after Ethan. But he couldn't stop sobbing.

Then he felt a gentle touch on his shoulder. "Ariel, it's Father Xavier. I know something about this; Luz called me. Also, I heard you and Ethan, and sorry for eavesdropping, but he was yelling loud enough to wake the dead under the floor. Your Ethan has a colorful way of expressing himself, and I must say, you are in a fine mess. Let's talk in my office."

Ariel felt ashamed to look up and tried to mop off his face with his sleeve. "What about Ethan? I'm responsible for him."

"Luz has collared him, and she's stuffing him with soggy pancakes and burnt toast. The chickens she's got out back have yet to lay a single egg. Just between the two of us, they look like roosters. If he survives her cooking, he'll live."

***

For thirteen long years, Ariel had unwillingly spent the better part of his Sundays in the residential school's whitewashed chapel, but he'd never been inside a lofty church like La Iglesia de la Paz. Any vague notions he had of such gigantic edifices he'd picked up from books and movies. He had assumed that Father Xavier would match his church in appearance, looking crabbed and ancient in a voluminous sackcloth robe girded by a rope and rosary, its hood draping from his shoulders to his waist. Instead, Ariel saw a cheerful, well-muscled man in his forties, about his own size, dressed in black slacks and a sweater. Except for a clerical collar and a silver cross hanging on a chain around his neck, Father Xavier looked quite ordinary.

The priest's office was bright with morning sunlight and crammed from top to bottom with papers and books. He moved a pile of folders to the floor and offered Ariel the chair they had occupied. Huge trailing plants ran riot on the windowsills and along the tops of two incongruously tiny end tables covered with crocheted doilies.

Father Xavier observed the direction of Ariel's gaze and chuckled. "Yup, the church ladies really have an eye for decor."

Father Xavier peered with concern at the distraught man sitting across from him, whom he guessed was around twenty or twenty-one. Unconsciously, Ariel's fingers sought out a delicate gold ring with one pearl that hung around his neck on a simple chain.

"Tell me about the ring, Ariel."

"This was Miriam's ring. It belonged to her mother. Miriam hid it in her coat lining when she got out of Warsaw. She was only sixteen. She had her baby girl with her, but the poor little thing died, and Miriam was pregnant with Ethan, so I thought he should have it."

Ariel twisted his own ring, a wide gold band on his left hand. "It didn't work out that way. I put Miriam's ring on her finger the day we were married. It was last April, in the Agnews chapel."

He could barely get the next sentence out, "She gave it back to me a little while before she died."

Father Xavier was stunned as much by Ariel's tragic story as by Ethan's obliviousness. *How could he not have noticed his roommate wearing a wedding ring for seven long months?*

Ariel was so close to tears that Father Xavier quickly changed the subject. "May I call you Ari? Ariel is too long, too formal."

"Ariel isn't my real name. You already heard what Ethan calls me and I have a Cherokee name I don't use. Miriam called me Ariel when I saw her the very first time. It means 'Lion of God.'"

Then he added softly, "We met in February. The minute I saw her, I knew. It sounds silly to say out loud, but for us both, it was love at first sight."

Father Xavier gently pressed Ariel for more information about the marriage, and Ariel answered with far-away eyes.

"Everyone was so happy about it. Her doctor, the nurses, they all thought she was well enough to be released. And we … we just looked at each other for hours, held hands, talked about our baby."

"There's a newborn then? Girl or boy?"

"Yes, Father. A little girl born yesterday morning."

"Do you have family to help you, your mother, or sisters?"

Ariel made no reply but twisted his fingers into a tight knot.

"Then will you be putting her up for adoption?"

"No, I would never do that."

Father Xavier had anticipated this answer, but went on, "You're still in school, how will you manage with an infant?"

With despair in his eyes, Ariel shook his head.

"Well then, since she is Ethan's half-sister, I'll put in something extra above burial expenses so that you can get started. Diapers, nighties, blankets, bottles—that sort of thing. But how can you explain all this to Ethan when he is so angry? You'll need his help, or at the very least, his understanding."

Ariel answered in a choked whisper, "I don't know what to do." He made his way to the back of the small office where he fell to his knees crying silently, his face hidden in his hands.

Father Xavier was at a loss how to help. An intuitive man, he usually counseled the bereaved quite successfully but never before had he run into such hollow despair, except perhaps his own. Twenty years ago when he was only slightly older than Ariel, he had lost his faith. He considered dropping out of the seminary, living a life of sin, or even killing himself. But in the end, he was inspired anew by Jesus' Passion. Ariel would never be so lucky; his passion had been temporal, and it was gone forever.

After a while, Father Xavier left his desk and stepped over the books stacked on the floor. He knelt down beside Ariel, who was essentially a youthful version of himself, and put an arm on his shoulder. He had an idea that at the very least would be a distraction, and it just might help the young man get through the worst day of his life.

"Ari. Let's do something different. We'll go on an art tour—a little pilgrimage. Most of the stuff is not great art, but it might explain a few things."

Father Xavier led Ariel to a dark corner in the main sanctuary. "Here is Saint Christopher. You know of him?"

Ariel gazed up at a gargantuan wooden statue, crudely carved. "A little, and Luz brought him up this morning. San Cristóbal."

"Right. The fishermen around here love him because life at sea is so dangerous. That wavy stuff around his feet is a river."

Ariel nodded, squinting through the gloom at the saint's burden, a somewhat misshapen child carrying a globe, the world's continents inscribed on its surface.

"So the story goes that Saint Christopher carried the kid across the roaring river, and about half way, he became monstrously heavy, almost killing the poor guy. They got across, of course, and there is a parable about it. But my message to you is, put Ethan down in the middle of the river and let him grow up. Keep him from drowning, but don't let his problems kill you. You are not Saint Christopher."

The next stop on the art tour was at a side-chapel off the sanctuary. Father Xavier pointed out a brightly glazed statue of the Virgin about two feet tall, dressed in a real satin gown covered with sequins. She held a chubby Jesus in her arms.

"This is the Virgin Mary all prettied up. Here she looks bland, but to Catholics, she is very powerful: the protective mother who is absolutely pure and fiercely loving."

Ariel was only half listening as he fixed his eyes on the glistening pink-cheeked terra cotta baby. The odor of incense and candle wax made his head swim. *Suddenly he saw his own child, her arms stretched towards him, her eyes black and shining.*

Somewhere in the distance, he could hear Father Xavier's soothing voice, "Miriam is gone now, Ari. You will have to be both father and mother to your child."

Ariel rubbed his eyes. He was trembling from the force of the vision.

They moved on to the sacristy where Father Xavier rummaged in a drawer, displacing clouds of dust.

"Here's an illuminated page that I found way in the back of this dresser, and I have no idea how long it's been here." Father Xavier held up a small vellum sheet. "Look, the words are in Latin, and it probably came from a fifteenth-century Spanish bible. You can touch the paper, it's tough. It is made of sheepskin."

Ariel stared at the miniature in wonder, marveling at the vibrant reds, greens, and browns, the gold leaf, the delicacy of the brushstrokes.

Father Xavier pointed to the margin on the left. "This is what I wanted to show you. Here are two vines wound together from the bottom to the top. When they reach the illuminated letter up here, they burst into huge flowers, showing the blossoming of divine love, or in your case, earthly love. Take it, it's yours. The vines will be there for you whenever you are feeling really down."

Ariel closed his eyes because he couldn't bear to look at them. It was only his imagination, but he felt the twisted stems cutting deep into his flesh.

***

On the way back to Luna's Fork 'n Spoon, Ariel dragged his feet at every step to delay the inevitable. He knew exactly what the well-meaning, even inspirational Father Xavier had been trying to do—prepare him for the rest of this terrible day. First, he would have to explain everything to Ethan, who despised him. Then say goodbye to the woman he loved and plan for her cremation. Finally, take their baby home. He'd have to drive the Moon Bus on that horrible Highway 17 for the fourth time in twenty-four hours.

I can't do it, it is too much, I just can't.

Instinctively Ariel searched for Miriam's gentle, comforting presence inside his head, but it wasn't there. The thoughts that swirled into the vast cavern of his skull that she'd left empty were about that little Cherokee boy, the one curled up under the bedcovers to hide his tears. Inside, he felt no older, his eyes burning like fire and a throat so tight he could barely breathe. His body had betrayed him, growing huge and virile, yanking him into an adulthood that was now crushing him.

Then his attention turned to *Romeo and Juliet*, the play he was studying in his English Drama class. Romeo is in the Capulets' tomb, intent on suicide. The words he speaks to Juliet are too full of poetry to issue from the mouth of an anguished seventeen-year-old. "O my love! My wife! Death that hath suck'd the honey of thy breath …."

Ariel stopped in his tracks. *God, I'm just like that poor kid, I loved Miriam so much. Dying only hurts for a minute, then it's like falling asleep.*

***

Luz was standing at the door of the diner, her hands on her hips, her round face lowering like a thundercloud.

She twisted her head toward the tables and hollered, "Go play in the sandbox, Ethan. I have to talk to your big brother." All traces of the homey Mexican accent were gone. She pushed Ariel into the storage room and locked the door.

"What the hell are you thinking about, 'dying is like falling asleep'?" Ariel shrank back.

"You look shocked. Of course, I can tell what you're thinking. We all can do it in different ways, you, too. You understood my Spanish this morning, didn't you?"

She added, "Come now, Ariel, you know they're manipulating us."

"They?"

Luz answered Ariel's question obliquely. "The Moon People, of course. They've been hanging around inside both our heads since we were little kids, although I'm not saying I understand why the hell they're in there. But we know something's up because they're so damn persistent. I bet they follow us into the bathroom."

She attempted to amuse him by rolling her eyes, but he barely managed a nod. He was not surprised that she knew the Moon People and in his present mood, he was way beyond humoring.

"And you know they set up this chain. We have to take *care* of each other. I have you. You have Ethan, and you had Aleta until she vamoosed down some rabbit hole. And poor Miss Montag tried her best to protect Miriam."

Hearing Miriam's name was too much for Ariel. He turned away as tears leaked down onto his cheeks. Then Luz did something unexpected. She drew him to her and hugged him, pulling his great muscled body onto her oversized chest.

She patted his back and rocked him gently, "There, there, I truly am your *mamacita* for today. Miriam wasn't supposed to die. You're crying for her, and all of us are crying for both of you. You have amazed us with your big beautiful heart. We don't want to lose you, too."

Luz gave him a gentle push. "Go on, now. Take care of Ethan, but remember what Father Xavier said about that river. Ethan has to be ready to make the trip. And you, too."

Ariel straightened up. "Luz, what trip? What's it for, and where are we supposed to go?"

"I haven't a clue, Ari. Oh, another thing. Your little one is a god-baby."

Luz unlocked the door to the storage room. "You don't recognize me? I taught ROTC at Santa Margarita along with those other military octogenarians until I took a leave of absence to rent this joint. Good thing I did. My assignment was to repair the emotional damage after that peepshow on the beach."

Ariel tried to smile at her wit, but his lips trembled and wouldn't cooperate.

Luz didn't notice; she was in a good mood. "I'm ditching this apron today. Can't cook worth a damn. Do you think I enjoy poisoning people? I'll see you on campus, but first I'm kicking the ass of the bastard who sold me those roosters."

***

Ariel stumbled through his longest day in a haze of grief. He didn't kill Ethan on Highway 17, although he wanted to. Ethan expressed his anger and sorrow by yelling insults and jostling Ariel's arm as he tried to navigate the treacherous curves. For some reason, the Moon Bus refused to rise off the ground. Its glory days as the airborne "Greyhound of the Future" were over; it had shrunk to the dimensions of a VW bus. It also burned gasoline in noxious fumes that obscured the road, all the while attracting the derision of fellow motorists with its automotive stench, squat ugliness, and lurid paint job.

Ariel had reached the limit of his endurance with Ethan. He swerved off the highway at Scotts Valley with a squealing of tires and screaming brakes. In the parking lot next to the reindeer pen at Santa's Village, he and Ethan held a shouting match punctuated by tears and shoving. Eventually, they reached a temporary pact that skirted the painful issue of the love affair. If Ethan would stop insulting Ariel by calling him Fuck, Ariel promised to never mention Miriam by name.

***

After Ariel's distracted departure from the hospital the night before, Miss Montag had arranged the transferal of Miriam's body to the mortuary chapel next door, since no autopsy was required. When Ariel first saw Miriam, his knees buckled. Miss Montag was at his side, holding a cool cloth to his forehead.

Ariel tried to reorient himself. Was he in a tomb? He stood up, trembling all over, then reached his hand past the coffin's unvarnished pine rim to tenderly touch Miriam's cheek and smooth her hair. To him, she still looked unbearably beautiful, although she appeared sealed up, the secrets of the universe locked forever behind her sunken eyes.

Ariel gave up any attempt to control himself. He wept out loud, flailing his arms about and falling down. Miss Montag had the good sense not to intervene, but when it was time for him to leave, she had to pry his fingers loose from the coffin. Finally, she shut him out of the grieving room and sat him down in a chair in the office to sign the papers authorizing Miriam's cremation.

Early on Miss Montag had gotten rid of Ethan, sending him on a bizarre errand that he didn't understand at all, although he dutifully accepted the shopping list and her blank check. His destination was an odd establishment with a pink and blue striped and scalloped awning in front named **THE STORKY STORE**. There he bought newborn baby nighties, bottles, diapers, safety pins, and blankets.

About four that afternoon, Miss Montag led Ethan and Ariel up three flights of chipped concrete stairs reeking of old cigarettes to the hospital's maternity ward. She wanted to avoid curious stares in the elevator; Ariel, whose eyes were red and swollen, looked ready to collapse. Ethan was exhausted, too. He complained non-stop in an irksome monotone about carrying the bulky Storky Store package. Unbelievably, he had been lugging baby clothes around for half a day without figuring out why.

But the moment Ethan held his new half-sister in his arms, his life changed. It was love at first sight, for Svnoyi, bearing the Cherokee name that Ariel had chosen, captivated him with her huge black eyes and soothing nature. She was indeed a god-baby, and Ethan forgave Ariel for almost everything, except the sex with his mother, which was just too embarrassing an idea for him to dwell on. He also found it difficult to think of Ariel as his stepfather.

**

Ariel drove the sputtering carcass of the Moon Bus directly to a Santa Clara junkyard where the proprietor eyed it with pleasure, thinking of the resounding chomp it would make inside the metal crusher's jaws. Little did the man know he would be finishing off the Greyhound of the Future that had once hovered aloft, pulsing and winking.

Late that night after the three of them reached home in a pathetically slow Greyhound of the Present, Ethan helped tuck Svnoyi into a temporary bed in a dresser drawer placed on Ariel's desk. After he had kissed her and reluctantly left, Svnoyi talked to Ariel in silence, her poetic thoughts penetrating directly into his brain. She had inherited his and Miriam's telepathy as well as the cognition of an adult.

I am Svnoyi, my name is Night. In the womb, I soothed my mother's terrible pain. I cannot comfort you, my father. You are beyond my help, drowning in a black lake choked by the Lilies of Death. My eyes do not know tears, but someday I will weep for you. I am Darkness, I am Sleep.

**

When Ariel was seven, some kind-hearted librarians had visited the orphanage. One of them gathered the children in a circle to read the fairy tale *The Tinder Box* by Hans Christian Andersen. The kids were restive and rude. Most of them squirmed and made noise, but the little Cherokee boy, who had no idea what a tinder box was, listened with fascination.

The pretty lady opened the brightly illustrated book with creamy pages and began reading in a lilting voice that issued from glossy red lips that looked like pillows.

"There came a soldier marching down the high road—one, two! one, two! He had his knapsack on his back and his sword at his side as he came home from the wars. On the road he met a witch, an ugly old witch, a witch whose lower lip dangled right down on her chest."

The story grew ever more convoluted, but at the point where the soldier entered the room containing the first dog with eyes as big as saucers, Ariel's mind froze in place. *How could a dog have eyes larger than its face? If I had eyes like that I could see the whole world. I could even see inside people.*

Ariel's daughter was hardly a canine, but a child who had inherited the transcendent beauty of her parents. Nonetheless, she possessed the very same saucer eyes that had haunted Ariel's dreams ever since he had heard that story. Her eyes were as big as they could possibly be while still fitting on her face, and they were as black as the lake where she had been conceived in his and Miriam's vision. Even at birth, Svnoyi absorbed the darkness in other people's hearts through her eyes, replacing it with tranquility.

But she could not alleviate her father's all-consuming grief that had never eased since her mother's death. When she looked through him with her saucer eyes, she saw a great suppurating wound, as if he had been brutally ripped in half from head to toe.

***

Soon after Svnoyi's birth, Ethan and Ariel began planning the trip to Poland to deposit Miriam's ashes. The simple wooden box with its sad contents was tucked in the back of Ariel's clothes closet, wrenching his heart every time he opened the door. Both of them had gotten part-time jobs to plump up the considerable amount of charity money from Father Xavier that must have come mainly from his own pocket. Luckily, Ethan knew an influential professor of Polish descent from the engineering department who helped them make travel arrangements and obtain passports and visas during a period of heightened Cold-War distrust. They researched at the Santa Margarita Library to find maps of the countryside surrounding Warsaw and its doomed ghetto.

Ariel was writing every day for hours, all the while wrapping one great arm around Svnoyi to nestle her tightly against his chest. Words gushed out, filling the pages in eruptions of verse like Hera's milk that had shot across the formless sky, creating the stars.

On the evening before their departure, Luz Luna made a surprise visit. She had brought a baby gift for Svnoyi, undoubtedly a telepathic purchase gleaned from Ariel's brain: Hans Christian Andersen's *Fairy Tales* with lurid but exquisitely refined illustrations. First, she hugged Ariel tightly to her, remarking on his *interesting protuberances*. Then she clapped him on the back with enough muscle to throw him off balance.

"Hey, Ari, congratulations. I hear you graduated with honors in English *and* a special commendation for the best creative writing *and* an award from the Cherokee Nation."

Then this woman with the stentorian voice that had terrified platoons of reluctant freshmen in ROTC proceeded in a husky whisper. "Ari, you don't have to go. Please, please reconsider."

"You know I have to, Luz."

She hugged him to her capacious khaki-covered bosom. "Yes, I do know. Don't forget we all love you."

***

The Owl Tree was not difficult to find. The little party trudged all the way from Warsaw following the paths and landmarks that matched Miriam's visual memories. She had described them in detail to Ariel on the only day during her long illness when he'd broken down and cried. Ariel was able to recognize every house, tree, field, and hillock, pointing them out one by one as they appeared on the horizon. He easily located the elder tree that had sheltered the last remnants of Danya's tiny bones for eighteen years. It stood only a few yards from the farmhouse and shed, now collapsed in ruins.

Ethan knelt beneath the tree's overhanging branches, weighed down by clusters of berries, and with his hands, he swept away last winter's debris to clear a circle of barren ground. If any owls peered down from above they gave no sign, although a flock of sparrows chirped in a raucous chorus, unseen among the sun-dappled leaves.

Ariel dropped to his knees, and with shaking fingers, opened the box containing Miriam's ashes. He distributed them evenly over the cleared space, then remained absolutely still with closed eyes to offer a silent farewell. A fragment of ash blew loose to land on his cheek. It burned him like a crumb of white phosphorus, but anguished as he was, he didn't notice. At last, he mixed the ashes into the soil.

Next Ethan said the *Kaddish*, which he had memorized with painstaking attention to every nuance. Later, his ego a bit puffed by his accomplishment, he would swear to Luz that even Nature listened—

that the sparrows grew silent and the elder tree's leaves drooped in sympathy.

Ariel had intended to read a sonnet he'd written as a last good-bye to the woman he loved, but he was in no condition to do so. He tried, but after a few broken starts, he crumpled up the paper and thrust it into his pocket. Weeping, he clutched Svnoyi to him, his face buried in her wispy baby-curls. He took a deep breath and pulled himself together.

"I will not be going back with you."

"Ari, that makes no sense. You can't just stay here all night by yourself."

"You're right. I can't stay at the Owl Tree because people will see me. I'll walk until I've reached the end of my Trail, somewhere in the Carpathian Mountains."

Ethan glanced at Svnoyi, who had scrunched herself against her father's chest. Two great tears, her first, gathered in the god-baby's saucer eyes. Ariel kissed her one last time, then placed her gently in Ethan's arms. Sparkling drops ran down her cheeks because she knew all. Eight months ago, the morning after Miriam died, Ariel had dragged his unwilling feet from La Iglesia de la Paz to Luna's Fork 'n Spoon. Somewhere during that one long block, he had made the irrevocable decision to end his life.

***

Before leaving for Poland, Ariel had emptied his closet and bookshelves, unbeknownst to Ethan, who had never been particularly observant. Then he had packed any useful belongings in cardboard boxes addressed to Father Xavier's church and had stacked them against the wall. On his desk, he had left the wedding rings and the illuminated page from an old bible for Svnoyi, a portfolio of strange bird paintings signed A. R. and his personal journal for Ethan, and his final manuscript simply titled *Poems for Miriam.*

Ethan could not bring himself to read past the first line. "Eurydice turned away, her cheeks washed in sorrow." If he knew anything, it was his Greek mythology; his mother had made sure of that. From then on, he could never shake the notion that Orpheus, the real living god, had briefly walked among them. Ethan had more publishing offers than he knew what to do with because all who read the poems were reduced to tears by their perfect beauty.

Chapter 8 Kidnapping of Svnoyi

After Ariel had hugged Ethan and kissed Svnoyi for the last time, he didn't look back at the Owl Tree. He walked in the opposite direction for days and days, sleeping by the side of the road whenever his limbs refused to take him further. The peace he'd hoped to find through the numbing repetition of putting one foot in front of the other didn't come. Sometimes he cried, but usually he fought the urge to return—to run his fingers through her ashes that called to him night and day.

Eventually, he reached the rugged High Tatras, the mightiest peaks in the Carpathian chain. He found them because their bulk beckoned, jutting out of the Polish flatlands and foothills. The High Tatras were like all giant mountains: indifferent to suffering, worse in the heat than in the cold, simply too big in scale for humans to comprehend.

Even before Ariel started climbing, he knew that he was dying. He hadn't touched food or water, and by now he could barely think straight or feel his own limbs. He labored higher and higher, often on his knees beneath the incandescent August sun. His shoes were long gone. His naked feet bled, the fine rivulets staining the moss that grew so bravely out of the crevices in the stone.

After all the years of yearning for one thing or another, Ariel had only one desire left—to find his and Miriam's vision of the lake beside the Trail of Tears. On the third day, he crawled to the top of a granite cliff and peered down at a snow-fed black pool nestled far below among jagged rocks. His search was over. Trembling in every joint, his wasted muscles sighed in distress as he struggled to reach his full height. Instinct alone made his toes grip the scree-covered lip of the precipice.

Now that Ariel had managed to stand upright, he recalled having to do something he could never undo, but he couldn't quite remember what it was. He only wanted to sleep, his eyes felt so heavy. He allowed them to close, but through the veins that laced his inner eyelids, he saw Svnoyi lying curled in her crib, her whole body heaving in paroxysms of baby-grief. He knew it was because of him.

Suddenly her saucer eyes sprang open. She let out a piercing scream directed into his brain—a rabbit's scream that went on and on. Ariel was torn out of his stupor. He grasped his head and started screaming over and over again, the horrendous racket bouncing off the mountain walls and echoing down the valley.

Then through his terror he saw Miriam drift toward him, her feet barely skimming a path of stars glittering like the Milky Way, and suddenly everything was all right. Her features were placid, her eyes gentle, her flesh rosy and warm. Her luxuriant black hair blew across her breasts as the billowing white dress sucked him close, wrapping him in its folds.

He let himself fall.

***

Ariel died, or thought he did. Why, then, was he still conscious, hovering over his own bloody and broken body that lay on the scree beside the water? He couldn't see it, exactly, because he had no eyes. His vision, hearing, touch, and the rest of his senses had vanished deep within that abandoned shell, although what was left of him continued to waft about like thistledown.

This new Ariel was devastated by his failure to die until it occurred to him that he might find Miriam if he could only learn to control his meanderings. Because Ariel had become *Thought*, the distillation of his being, he longed to sink to the bottom of the lake where he sensed Miriam waiting for him. He could almost see her looking radiantly lovely in her white gown, her long limbs stretched out on a spit of sparkling sand. He plunged into the still water.

Beneath the lake, Ariel found himself in an enclosed brick tunnel wading through a torrent that rushed furiously around his feet, its reflection making bright undulations against the ceiling. He didn't question why he had a body or at least the sensation of owning limbs, although he assumed that it was an illusion manufactured by his own thoughts. Some physical laws didn't seem to apply even though he was confined by the cylindrical walls; he could move fast or slow, up or down, walking or flying as he chose.

Ariel knew that Miriam was waiting for him in the blinding light at the tunnel's far-away mouth. So he flew, anxious for the moment when he would run his fingers through her black wavy hair once more, kiss her full lips, let himself grow huge and hot, love her through and through, and then lie contented in her arms. This would be only the beginning of their new existence together.

Ariel couldn't find Miriam anywhere, even though he searched the complete perimeter of the sandy shore that surrounded a lake red as blood. If his body were more than Thought, he would've wept, torn his hair, thrown himself beneath the choppy waves, but he knew it would be useless. Without flesh he couldn't die a second time.

At this moment, he cried out in a voice lacking sound or substance, although his utterance was entered in the journal on Ethan's desk. *If I had eyes, they would pour down tears. My Miriam is not here.*

Perhaps the power of his silent grief had moved some celestial beings. Without experiencing motion or the passage of time, he was snatched from that forsaken place. Now he found himself stretched out on a cold metallic surface inside a great yellow globe, his transparent self subjected to a flickering light.

***

Jaroslav was the head park ranger at the Mountain Service Rescue Headquarters in Stary Smokovec, the High Tatras' famous resort town. He knew every inch of the surrounding peaks, valleys, rivers and lakes. Although no one else was allowed such liberty, he and his wife Anichka lived in a cottage hugging the side of a mountain. Jaroslav had been taking a stroll, most people's version of an all-day hike, when he spotted Ariel's twisted body far below. Then he peered more carefully into the bottom of the ravine. He thought his eyes might be playing tricks on him; he had seen it twitch. He waited another minute, and no, he wasn't wrong. The person below was still alive.

Jaroslav had no trouble carrying Ariel up the steep, sliding stones and then on to his house. Jaroslav knew how. He had hauled up many foolish adventurers in his day, both dead and alive, and Ariel was so emaciated that the muscular ranger simply slung the comatose man over his shoulder.

Jaroslav laid Ariel carefully on soft bearskins in the corner of the one-room house, then made preparations to walk the long distance to the ranger station to get help. He had not anticipated his wife's reaction. The deeply religious Anichka would not let her husband go, but clung to his woolen coat, weeping. To show the depth of her conviction, she threw herself down before Ariel's bleeding feet and washed them with her long black hair. She was sure that Jaroslav had brought the true Christ to lie in their humble home during the days between His Death and Resurrection.

Jaroslav would have put up a fuss except he knew her too well. She was a proud Roma gifted in the medicinal arts, a better healer than the finest doctors at the hospital in distant Poprad. Besides, the move by helicopter and ambulance would probably finish him.

From then on, Anichka seldom left Ariel. She set his bones and healed his grievous wounds with fragrant salves made from the flora that Jaroslav gathered along the steep mountainsides. She breathed air into his lungs, all the while massaging his icy limbs. She fed him the nectar of the precious-juiced flowers from the meadows, being extra careful not to let him choke. And so Ariel continued to survive in a deep coma, his mind living a life of its own in far-away times and places.

***

It was September, and a new semester had started at Santa Margarita. Ethan began recovering from the dreadful loss of Ariel only two months earlier—simply by forcing himself not to think. This state of oblivion wouldn't last; he could feel Ariel's journal beckoning, crying out to be opened.

Svnoyi presented a different picture. She looked increasingly unhappy, even sick. Because of her peculiar god-baby anatomy, she didn't cry. At least she hadn't since the day she wept so bitterly at the Owl Tree. But she was losing weight, ounce by ounce, a bad sign for a child of ten months. Worse, her once shining saucer eyes looked opaque, and they drooped at the corners, just like her sad little bow-mouth.

Ethan was wise enough to steer clear of the pediatrician who scratched his head whenever he saw her and never had a thing to say. Instead, he called Luz, who hastened over as soon as she had finished terrorizing her ROTC class. Luz plopped onto Ethan's tired Victorian sofa with Svnoyi nestled on her lap. Then the two put their heads together for a silent chat. During the next half hour, Svnoyi's expressive eyes drooped further and Luz nodded gravely from time to time.

At last Luz looked up at Ethan as she cuddled Svnoyi in her hefty arms.

"Well, Ethan, it's been hard for her. She misses her father. She saw him do it."

"You mean …." Ethan felt a hot tear slide down his cheek before he could stop it. "Where? When?"

"She didn't say, exactly. She's too young to make whole sentences. She speaks in poetry."

Luz was affected, too. She wiped her eyes on a large handkerchief that she extracted from one of the many breast pockets on her uniform. Then she tucked it away and cleared her throat.

"About this fathering, Ethan. You'll have to pick up where Ariel left off. That's what he expected you to do."

Ethan responded defensively, "Jesus, I've been trying. I guess I'm just lousy at it."

Luz glared at him. "Don't pull that defeatist shit on me, Ethan. Ariel trusted you absolutely, so listen up. Svnoyi told me you don't hold her enough."

She softened her tone. "You know, Ethan, Ariel never put her down. Not for a minute, because somehow he knew that keeping her close helps a god-baby grow. That's why she's getting thinner now."

"But I have to go to class, Luz. Miss Montag babysits out of the goodness of her heart."

"Lord love a duck, Ethan, you are so dense. Get one of those snuggle things, those baby carriers like the native women wear. I bet they sell 'em in Berkeley, and take Svnoyi to class with you. Mark my words, she'll learn engineering long before *you* do. And one more thing. Get Moonshine out of here. Svnoyi is scared of her."

"You mean Miss Montag. She has a first name, you know. It's Bianca." He added with a smirk, "I think she has the hots for me."

"Don't flatter yourself, Ethan. You know perfectly well she was in love with Ariel. I hope that's why she's still hanging around his child and not for some other weird reason."

Then Luz smiled sadly and shook her head. "That Ari. I bet the whole female staff from two hospitals loved him. I adored him myself, and I happen to think most men are more ornamental than useful."

She paused to reflect. "Funny thing is, Ari never had a clue about any of 'em, he was so swept away by Miriam."

The very next day, Ethan took the Greyhound from Santa Cruz to San Jose and multiple additional buses to Berkeley to find a baby carrier for Svnoyi. On a street lined with import stores, he finally hit on The Sombrero. In a bin at the back, he located a *rebozo*. The Mexican saleslady taught him how to tie the large scarf, using her own child as a model to show off the design's simplicity and comfort.

***

On the long trip home, Ethan thought about Bianca Montag. He had been away from Aleta for so long that whenever he was with Bianca, he conveniently forgot that he was a man with a family, however estranged they now were. Bianca tended to linger way past her babysitting hours at his apartment in Little Mexico, and even asked him over to her house on Saturday afternoons. He tried not to notice that she always had a list of chores lined up for him such as mowing the lawn, changing the oil in her car, replacing the light bulbs she couldn't reach, or fixing her vacuum cleaner. Svnoyi, usually so cheerful at home, would twist away from them both, screwing her face into a scowl and slurping loudly on her thumb.

Ethan didn't get back from his Berkeley odyssey until nine. When he walked through the door, he dropped his package from The Sombrero in shock. Bianca was stretched out full-length on the sofa wearing a pink satin nightgown with a six-foot matching ostrich-feather boa draped around her neck and in dangling loops encircling her bare breasts. She had artfully arranged the lower part of the gown to show an expanse of leg and a tiny triangle of pink underpants. At first, Ethan wanted to laugh. How long had she been waiting for his return, frozen in place like a photo from a nudie calendar?

He supposed that his only choice was to react like a suave Casanova always ready for dalliance—partly as a kindness to save her from embarrassment. He stripped out of his clothes, then threw himself on top of her somewhat awkwardly, bruising his ankle on the wooden part of the sofa arm. He tried some deep kisses and lots of gyrating. Nothing.

At last Bianca asked in a small voice, "Don't you find me attractive?"

"You could get those feathers out of my face. I'm allergic to—" Ethan sneezed.

She simpered, "Ethan, I bought champagne to celebrate our new love. I'll get it from the kitchen. I bet you just need a tiny jump-start."

Ethan stared morosely at her receding backside bouncing above stubby legs, her feet encased in Lucite high heels with big pompoms on the toes. He thought, With those spooky panther eyes, she looks like a sphinx that fell into a pink cupcake. She's no match for Aleta.

Then he peered down at his limp penis. He had expected more from it after its long dormancy.

Bianca returned bearing the bubbly in juice glasses. He took a mighty gulp, then another, hoping for the elusive jump-start. What he got instead was a blurry view of the Victorian sofa's underside from a new vantage point on the rug.

***

The next thing he knew, Luz was towering above his supine body, one fist on her hip and the other grasping an empty water pitcher. He had been doused.

"Lord love a whole *flock* of ducks. Ethan, I told you there's only one man I ever wanted to see naked, and it isn't you. Someone slipped you a Mickey."

She glanced uneasily around the dawn-streaked apartment. "I had to break down your door. Svnoyi called to me in real terror during the night. Stupid me, I thought you were paying attention to her."

Luz stopped short as she had spied the pink boa on the sofa. She picked it up between her thumb and forefinger and dropped it on his face. "You fell for the oldest trick in the book, you dope. Don't be surprised if Svnoyi's crib is empty."

Luz was right about the crib. All Svnoyi's belongings had disappeared, too—her blankets, her clothes, even her toys. Ironically, as a follow-up to the parenting discussion, Ethan had moved Svnoyi into his room to keep her closer to him.

Luz steered him in the general direction of his battered dresser. "Hurry up, Ethan, put something on. We should go to the police."

Ethan mumbled in a choked voice, "Even the little dresses I picked out from the Sears Catalog are gone."

"Put a sock in it, Ethan. If I'd known I would be employed by the Blubber Family I might have refused the job, although come to think of it, feeling Ari's dorsals and other interesting protuberances at the front—Ethan, can't you even tie your shoes?"

Ethan wiped his eyes on his hand. "Would you just *shut up* for one minute, Luz? My baby … *my baby* is gone."

"Cool down, sweetheart. There has to be an explanation. Actually, let's think this through before we blast off to the police station."

Luz tied Ethan's shoes, then surrounded him briefly with her arms before sitting him down on his desk chair.

"Just how successful was your tryst with Miss Mooncalf? No shame, now. The boa alone would have turned *me* into an iceberg."

"We-ll—"

"Very expressive, Ethan. Her Plan A was to conceive her own god-baby, taking advantage of your proven abilities with Aleta."

"And Plan B?"

"To take the baby at hand."

"But why?" Ethan was bewildered.

"Well, I don't quite have an answer, except I bet she hopes she'll be allowed on the Moon People's trip with her own god-baby—"

Ethan interrupted, "What trip?"

Luz hesitated before coming up with an answer. "I don't actually know anything *about* the trip except you people with god-babies are going somewhere. Moonbeam and I don't have any so we weren't invited."

Ethan shook his head. "Why is having a god-baby so important? For some Superman repopulation scheme on Mars or something? Luz, admit it. For once, you're talking total bullshit."

He idly flipped through Ariel's journal that he'd started reading the day before. At the bottom of the last page, he found a new entry he'd never seen in Ariel's own handwriting, the ink fresh. *If I had eyes, they would pour down tears. My Miriam is not here.*

***

Miss Bianca Montag and Svnoyi were flying to Poland in the tattered, trembling cabin of a Soviet airliner. Bianca had plenty of time to muse. Too bad Svnoyi could read her every thought and make rude comments—and not in poetry. The little brat was sitting on her lap, keeping her elbows and heels in constant motion like a windmill. She also had sharp teeth and knew how to spit. At least she didn't talk out loud, scream or cry. Count your blessings where you can.

And thank goodness Svnoyi's passport and visa presented no problems at Airport Immigration. *Au contraire,* Miss Montag's Plan A, turning her panther eyes up to maximum stun to convince the agent that she was the Ethan Marcus pictured on her passport, was a miserable failure. She resorted to Plan B, this one requiring some hanky-panky in the men's room. She looked a fright too, only with time to throw Ethan's coat over her nightie and sweep Svnoyi's crap into a suitcase. The fat-slob agent was not really all that fun, especially with Svnoyi sitting on the grimy floor laughing at them.

Miss Montag tried sticking Svnoyi under Ethan's coat so she could think. *The $64,000 Question: How come I couldn't turn Ethan on? That racy calendar I found in his closet—I copied September right down to the panties.*

Plan A, which should have worked, goddammit, seemed watertight. She wanted a god-baby of her own so bad it hurt, and Ethan had a track-record making them. Not one, but two. With her own god-baby, she could get on that transport to wherever, thereby getting out of a lot of things she despised, including being a nurse, a nasty profession which meant being nice all the time and messing around with dead people.

Before Ethan came home from Berkeley—was it only yesterday?— Svnoyi had inadvertently handed her Plan B, made possible only because she had a kilo of chloral hydrate in her purse—lifted from the hospital to put her shitty old cat out of its misery.

The little brat thought her father hadn't died when he took a walk over a cliff in the Carpathians. Just that afternoon Svnoyi had received a poetic kick in the brain that anyone with half a gift could pick up from her: *If I had eyes, they would pour down tears. My Miriam is not here.*

She'd gotten a partial location and Svnoyi would help her pinpoint the right spot when they got there. With Ariel's Miriam-fixation it would be a lot harder getting him, much harder than Mr. Limp of Plan A. But screwing Sequoyah the Stud—now *that* would be *heaven!*

Svnoyi twisted free of her prison under the coat and smirked at her incensed captor.

Hey, Snot-nose, stick that laughter up your ass. You wanna know something? You have a dirty mind for a baby.

***

Jaroslav looked at the frozen female corpse with horror tinged with amusement. One of his trainees had carried the body to the ranger station where it lay in the back room, waiting to be ID'd. The head ranger had dealt with really stupid tourists over the years, but this one was the dumbest yet. Why would anybody in their right mind try walking a snow-covered trail in the High Tatras at midnight in a nightgown and high heels, especially with a baby?

And what a baby she was, poor mistreated darling. She wasn't even a year old, with huge round eyes and a little pouty mouth. But she was oh, so cold, maybe finished. At the very least, she would probably lose some of her pretty little fingers and toes. He wasn't putting up with any guff from his colleagues. He bundled Svnoyi tightly into his coat to take her home to Anichka. If anyone could do it, his wife would save the little one and fix her right up, nearly as good as new.

But this baby was tougher than she looked. As soon as Jaroslav laid her tenderly on the bearskin next to the comatose stranger, she clambered into his motionless arms, smiled blissfully, and fell into a heavy sleep.

***

Miss Montag's body was never identified. She had destroyed Ethan's passport sometime during the tortuous flight with Svnoyi. Not being apprised of certain vital facts about him such as his comatose condition, she had convinced herself that she would succeed in seducing Ariel with her nudie calendar charm. No more international travel for her! She could have a whole *slew* of his god-babies and get on that transport to god-knows-where. So she ripped the passport to shreds and flushed it down a toilet at the air terminal in Kraków. And even *she,* hypnotic eyes or not, had doubts of ever managing to board another flight as Ethan Marcus.

Miss Montag was sorely missed at San Jose Hospital. She had actually been a very good nurse, although a bit vicious when inserting IV's. Only one supervisor from Agnews made a negative comment about her otherwise exemplary record. He happened to mention in an aside to the Director of Mental Dysfunction that Miss Montag had spent entirely too much time during certain hours with one eye glued to an air duct in the hall outside Miriam's room.

The cat that was left inside her house had yowled so long and lustily that a neighbor called the SPCA. The fluffy white Persian was promptly adopted by an aged spinster who owned a palatial estate in Los Gatos. Sweetie Pie's only bad habit was upchucking hairballs on her velvet Louis Quatorze sofa.

And the doyenne of catdom wished she had an animal interpreter because he was a talker. *Meow, meow, meow. I could tell you a tale or two about Miss Bianca Montag. Whoohee! Will you scratch my gonads now?*

***

Jaroslav had never thought that the baby he had brought home was the daughter of the disgraceful Jezebel found frozen on the trail. But as the little darling continued to sleep in the stranger's arms almost as comatose as he, Jaroslav was pretty sure that the handsome giant was her father. Her delicate face kept its high color and her dainty toes and fingers grew rosy, recovering from the frostbite without Anichka's intervention. Indeed, it was irrefutable; the baby's presence had caused a miracle. The body of Anichka's patient filled out, slowly turning into the archetype for an Apollo, an Orpheus, a Baldr, a Prince Charming, or, in Anichka's eyes, a very attractive dark-skinned Jesus, preparing to rise on the third day.

Chapter 9 The Moon People

Ariel found himself plastered against a curved surface, bathed in an uncertain half-light pierced by fluctuating shadows. He combed his mind for any sentient thoughts. First, he remembered trying to die by falling a long, long way down. But what happened next? He must have floated free of his body that lay broken beside a lake, mangled by the sharp stones. Then he ran, maybe he flew, through a long tunnel that ended up at a horrible blood-red lake. Now it was coming back to him. He had been looking for Miriam, his beloved, all along its shores. But he couldn't find her anywhere. When he cried out, "My Miriam is not here," something or someone had brought him to this new place—the interior of a rivet-studded sphere.

He looked all around from his lofty perch on the ceiling, and below him was an apartment, the oddly angled rooms separated by flowered chintz curtains on brass rods. He felt like a squashed fly. Since his body had no weight of its own, he didn't know how to get down. Two ancient people, a man and a woman in threadbare bathrobes and tattered slippers, peered up at him from recliners that sprouted batting and springs through the leatherette upholstery.

They tried unsuccessfully to suppress laughter at his plight. Finally, the woman snorted through a guffaw, *Just think yourself down, my boy.* Then in an attempt at flirtatious charm, she crinkled up her faded blue eyes at the corners, looking more like the Wicked Witch of the West than a member of the neighborhood Meet and Greet Committee.

Ariel realized with a jolt that since he'd left his body behind in a broken heap, their communication with him would have to be entirely mind-to-mind.

The woman grinned, showing teeth that appeared as ancient as mammoth tusks. *Nice to make your acquaintance … at long last.* She swelled with pride. *We're your Moon People. I'm Nessie and he's Sasquatch.*

Ariel righted himself and fell onto a chair with a deteriorating plastic seat, very much like the ones he'd left behind in his and Ethan's Little Mexico apartment. Nessie stared rudely all up and down Ariel's non-existent self.

What the hell did you do to that stud body of yours, Sequoyah? You look like something the cat dragged in, ate, and digested.

Ariel glanced down in dismay at his unclothed, transparent legs that lacked flesh, muscle, and bone.

The resourceful woman had an answer for his plight. *Now think yourself some insides, son. That will have to do until you get your own body back. Don't forget your privates.*

Ariel's recreated body was crude at best.

Both Moon People roared with laughter until Nessie remarked, *I know someone who slept through Anatomy 101. Would you care to wrap yourself in a bedspread?*

Then she extended a gnarled hand, all skin-and-bone and age-spots. *Sequoyah Morgan Hummingbird, we brought you here. We've been protecting you since you were four years old.*

At last the old man managed to stick a word in, his voice quavering and cracked. *My wife Nessie means we've been controlling you by the short hairs since you were a tot, yanking your chain, jerking you around, making you kiss our butts—*

Nessie scowled at him. *Enough, you old coot.*

Her smile returned for Ariel's benefit. *Don't mind Sasquatch. My husband has indigestion which makes him disagreeable; Sugar Smacks will do it every time.*

She upped the volume to blast Sasquatch, *Besides, he's past his prime, long in the tooth, can't get it up, over the hill. In a word—senile.* She winked an eye to reassure Ariel that Sasquatch shouldn't be taken seriously, her creased eyelid lowering and raising like a stubborn window shade.

Ignoring the old couple's charmless antics, Ariel sprang up in alarm. He hadn't heard all three of his given names for years, and he hated them with a passion.

Oh please, please don't call me Sequoyah Morgan Hummingbird, call me Ariel. She gave me that name. Everyone calls me that now .... He ceased in confusion. *I mean called me that before I ... Ariel, or Ari for short.*

Having recovered from his wife's insults, Sasquatch spoke up. *Sure, Ari. Names don't matter a whole lot to my mind. We change ours now and then for entertainment. Breaks up the monotony, you know.*

Nessie was not as easily persuaded. *Don't listen to his nonsense, Ari. Of course names matter. What's on Svnoyi's birth certificate?*

In fact, Ariel had puzzled for a long time before choosing names for her and had finally settled on Svnoyi Marcowitz Sequoyah. At that moment he realized that if his eyes had been working properly they would have misted over.

You know, Nessie and Sasquatch, I really, really miss my little girl.

Sasquatch hefted himself out of the recliner and tottered with tiny shuffling steps as his frame was creaky and bent with arthritis. He wheezed, *If you want, Ari, we can fly on over and take a look at her. But time travel is not easy for us anymore. It's going to take a while to get there.*

Grasping the metal handrail and double-stepping on each tread, he carefully made his way down a spiral staircase to the engine room. His shoulder-length hair flew in all directions, and a long beard worthy of Confucius fell below his waist. Ariel guessed that some aspects of grooming might lose appeal after a certain age.

Sasquatch was frowning, concentrating on putting a sentence together. *We are old, Ari, our Moon is old. We used to blast all over the place, back and forth, but every move put years and years of wear-and-tear on her chassis.* He sighed. *Now we usually coast in orbit way, way ahead of your time because it saves energy, but we can burn rubber now and then.*

He twisted a few knobs on a control panel with the impressive word *TravLtron* emblazoned across it in faded gilt letters, although Ariel thought it looked like the dashboard of last year's Buick.

Just then Ariel observed the old man's glinting amber eyes beneath unusually thick white brows. One of them closed in a sly wink reminiscent of Groucho Marx in pursuit of some hot young starlet. Sasquatch was obviously dispensing with the endearing older-than-Methuselah act.

Not so long ago, the TravLtron was a powerhouse, and I was, too. Sasquatch leered and rolled his eyes, which even the accommodating Ariel considered a spectacularly hideous sight.

Yeah, I remember popping over to visit Aleta in a lightning bolt.

Ariel started with surprise. He asked suspiciously, *What did you have to do with her?*

Sasquatch chuckled. *Wouldn't you like to know!*

The old man had another memory to share. *You remember when you drove that crappy wreck, the Moon Bus? It started out fine and sleek, a real hot-rod of a Greyhound, but I just couldn't power her for all those round trips.*

Ariel remembered that day as the worst in his life, not that things were better now.

Sasquatch noticed right away. *Oh sorry, but I had nothing to do with it, honest. The wife, she has all the ideas. I'm just along for the ride.*

Ariel broke in, *Then you two knew about Miriam and me?*

Sasquatch's laugh sounded like a band saw. *Of course we knew, you big silly. We set you up, Sonny. She was some looker, that Miriam. What an ass she had on her, what an ass! I wanted her myself. Don't get me wrong, no offense. Just an old man dreaming.*

Ariel felt sick, even without a stomach. He left the engine room in dismay while Sasquatch fiddled some more with knobs and switches, peering with disgust from under his brows at the TravLtron's unresponsive dials.

***

Ariel rejoined Nessie, hoping to find a more pleasant companion.

Nessie poked him in the ribs, the eight or so he'd remembered to attach to his backbone and sternum. *Is my raunchy old Sasquatch too much for you? Where's your sense of humor, Sonny?*

Is it true what Sasquatch said about Miriam and me? That you and Sasquatch arranged it? Ariel tried to control his fury.

Nessie's smile vanished. *Listen, my boy. We happen to know a helluva lot better than you what's good for you. Sure, we set you up, but we never told you to fall in love. Never! Not Miriam, either. Your suicide is your own damn fault, and you almost destroyed our plans for you.*

Her voice grew sharper. *We warned you the first time around with Aleta. Hands off, she's not yours, no love allowed. But did you take our advice? Did you even listen?* Nessie scowled at him, her crimped visage resembling a week-old Halloween pumpkin.

At that moment, the still-grieving Ariel wished his emotions had been destroyed along with his body. Head bowed, he stumped over to the louvered window on his stiff legs and huge, flat feet. He turned his face toward the window to avoid having Nessie's angry glare drill into him, and he just happened to gaze down at the earth passing below.

Poor Ariel. He felt screams reverberate over and over inside his head because they couldn't come out of a throat with no vocal chords.

At last he managed to croak out, *My God, what happened to the earth? It looks horrible, all craters. There's ocean and sand, but no trees, no grass ... no nothing.*

Nessie poked a finger into his bedspread-covered arm even though he didn't notice her unkind stab. *Ah ha! You're seeing what your idiot children's children did. They finally blew themselves up. Call it what you want—the final war, World War III—oh let me think, when was it, anyway? Around the middle of the twenty-first century.*

Ariel found his inept body sliding to the floor of the globe, and it was trembling all by itself, so profound was his anguish. He remained there for a very long time, his back toward Nessie, clutching his head in jointless fingers.

Finally, Nessie shook his shoulder vehemently, which still failed to rouse him from his melancholy.

Sorry, you just got a shock seeing the earth, Sonny. And I'm happy to explain anything as long as it isn't about your idiotic love affairs.

Ariel didn't move.

She cajoled, *Don't you want to know how we got up here in orbit?* She showed her mammoth teeth in a grin.

Ariel was horrified by Nessie's lack of compassion for his feelings, but he had to find out from the only living witnesses of that final war what had happened to the rest of humanity. So he swallowed the pain and forced himself to listen.

Nessie pushed him down on a kitchen chair and she took the other, lowering herself with audible cricks and cracks from her aged joints.

Do you believe in parallel universes and multiple dimensions, Sonny? You know, sci-fi?

No, said Ariel.

Nessie frowned, lowering her skimpy eyebrows. She thundered, *I suggest you say yes.*

Ariel said, *Yes.*

Nessie reminisced, *Well, Ari, we lived a regular life in the U.S.A. until 1960, and then we took off in this Moon and started living up here in space.*

And that's how we happened to see civilization end in 2050, or thereabouts. We usually just jogged back and forth a bit in Time to meddle in your lives, but like idiots, one day we barged forward.

Jolted from his lethargy, Ariel turned toward her. *Why'd you meddle in our lives? You could have just left us alone.*

Nessie grew angry once more. *My goodness, Ariel, have some respect for your elders' needs. Haven't you ever been bored? It was fun. May I go on?*

But first, she poured herself a bowl of Rice Krispies minus milk. *Have some? Better not. You put on the body-part that matters, but I don't see a stomach under the bedspread.*

Ariel peeked beneath it. She was right. Nessie continued between crunchy mouthfuls, one hundred chews for every swallow.

Nessie poked Ariel's arm with her spoon. *Remember the private fallout shelters people with smarts were building in the fifties? Well, things were downright scary back then. First, the Cold War just wouldn't quit, and it kept getting hotter.*

Ariel nodded. On that at least, they agreed.

Well, we were all set to build a fallout shelter anyway, but we found a better solution. The company that makes the American Globe Trotter trailer, you know, those trailers all riveted and round at the back that look like armadillos. They started making these globes that they sold surreptitiously behind the showrooms for regular trailers.

She wiped out the bowl on the hem of her dressing gown. *Ari, we'd found our ideal retirement home—the orbiting fallout shelter! Because they'd stay way up high and not get touched by those nuclear mushrooms.*

She put back the Rice Krispies box next to the Sugar Smacks box on a shelf in the breakfast nook. Ariel noticed that besides a foldout table and two chairs, there was little else—no stove, refrigerator or sink. The area was made up entirely of shelves that presently held at least another hundred years' supply of cereal boxes.

Nessie observed the direction of his eyes. *You admiring our gourmet food cache? Don't bother. Anyway, we were shot into orbit from Area 51, you know, in Nevada, with help from the U.S. Government.* She added meditatively, *It was all rather experimental, post-Sputnik. Thing was, though, once you were up, you were up.*

Ariel was way out of his depth. He knew about the fallout shelter mania, but he had no idea any of *this* was going on.

He ventured, *What was it like up there, Nessie?*

Nessie sat back and closed her eyes, reminiscing. *Sonny, it was a sight to behold. Like Grand Central Station. For a year or two, there were so many Moons in orbit that we had to have traffic rules.*

Ariel nodded. *I can picture it. Orbiting trailer parks. What happened next?*

Nessie's toothy smile was cruel. *Well, heh, heh—people couldn't take it. They missed their golf, Ed Sullivan, hunting, taking a proper shower, you know, so they came down the hard way, every last one of 'em. The fools crashed their moons on purpose, or jumped, just like you.*

***

Just then Sasquatch started his labored, panting trip up the spiral stairs.

Hey, Ari, I finally got that fucking TravLtron to get its ass in gear. A few kicks, a few curses—works every time. Let's go downstairs to see the cabin in the High Tatras through the **Visionscope***.*

What? Ariel jumped up on his feeble excuses for legs.

Sasquatch nodded his head. *Yes. That's where Svnoyi is.*

Ariel peered through the engine room's Visionscope as the Moon passed over a little mountain house in the High Tatras. If he had been able to do it, he would have laughed and cried at the same time.

Is that Svnoyi, and is that me—or what's left of me? I don't look all that bad, and Svnoyi is … my baby is …, oh, God, she's gloriously beautiful. And she's grown bigger, too.

The moment had passed. Sasquatch was twisting and pulling the TravLtron's ancient knobs to take the globe home.

After completing his herculean labor, the three of them returned to the kitchen so Sasquatch could tuck into his Sugar Smacks. Nessie sat the astonished Ariel down near them on a filthy plaid couch, but he failed to notice its tatty condition. He was still enraptured from having seen his child.

The delighted father burst out, *How did Svnoyi get into my arms? Oh, if only her mama could see her now.*

Nessie reached out an ancient hand to touch his shoulder. *Ari, Svnoyi is actually healing your body, but it will take time.* She cleared her throat. *My dear, there is a lot you can do to help us while you wait for it to get fixed up.*

Her eyes crinkled endearingly. Sasquatch perked up, too, and stopped cleaning out his ears with his Sugar Smacks spoon.

Nessie grasped Ariel's stiff, doll-like hand. *Sasquatch and I had a really big idea once, and we put it into action. We can move people around with our minds, but you knew that already. We put people into places where terrible things happened a long time ago so that they can change the past, make the future better.*

Ariel squirmed; he knew what was coming.

Sasquatch and I are sending Aleta to a few hotspots where she can make a little dent in human suffering. Once we had a lot of people doing it; we called them our field agents. She's the last one, sad to say.

Ariel felt his non-existent blood start to boil. *What, exactly, have you done with my friend? And what makes you think she can change something that's already happened?*

Nessie swiveled her creaky neck to look Ariel directly in the eye. *Slow down, Sonny. She's fine. We sent her on a junior mission first to help the Japanese from California who got sent to internment camps in '42.*

Sasquatch took over where Nessie had left off. *Aleta is a sexy girl, Ari. Next, we sent her to Drancy in France in oh, let me think, 1943. It's a camp for Jews on their way to Auschwitz, and that's where she still is.*

Ariel couldn't believe what he was hearing. *But Sasquatch, she's in terrible danger. She's Jewish, for God's sake. She has her two children with her, and what the hell does sexy have to do with it?*

Sasquatch leered, smacking his lips. *Well, Ari, wouldn't you like to know. It sure is fun to watch her.*

Right now Ariel wanted to break the old man's wattled neck. *Sasquatch, you bastard. You shouldn't have done this to her. Bring her back.*

Tough luck, Ariel, we won't do that, Nessie chimed in. *But you can travel anywhere, now that you are outside of your body. Why not go to Drancy and give her a hand? And consider visiting the Trail of Tears while you're hopping about in your transparent angel suit. See it like it really was.*

One thing I do know. It wasn't like that stupid alpine lake stuffed with water lilies you and Miriam dreamed up.

By now Ariel felt cornered. *Why are you playing with people's lives? Where did this crazy idea come from?*

Nessie elbowed Sasquatch out of the way to stand two inches in front of Ariel's nose. *Simmer down, Sonny. You lose your dignity when you get mad. First of all, disregard the old coot and his crude remarks about Aleta.*

Indigestion, like I told you. Second of all, why keep asking questions? You think we don't know what we're doing?

Ariel tried to rise from the sofa, but Nessie held him down with her pincer-like fingers, making him furious. He yelled, *Okay then, tell me, what are you doing?*

Neither of the old people spoke at first. They were sharing a memory almost too painful to contemplate.

At last Nessie roused herself enough to speak. *Ari, everything we've done is because of World War III, everything. We saw it all through the window, and you can't ever forget seeing something so horrible.*

Nessie took her husband's hand, the first gesture of affection that she had displayed since Ariel's arrival. *There were mushroom clouds and explosions for days. Even the atmosphere caught on fire.*

Nessie threw her hands in the air. *And horror of horrors, Ari. After it was over, we looked at ourselves in the mirror inside the **Porto-Powder-My-Nose***. *Our hair had turned white and we were wrinkled all over, Ari. All over like we were 700 years old. Worse than elephants during a drought.*

Ariel was surprised to see tears in the eyes of the woman who had acted hard-as-nails until now.

We orbited the earth thousands of times — looking, and looking again. No one, not a single soul survived. And nothing else did either, as far as we could tell. There were no animals, no trees, only a few fires still burning a dull orange, the land scorched, and all the oceans black with ashes. We felt guilty for being alive.

She dried her eyes. *What you saw out the window just now, Ari, is actually an improvement. We've watched carefully, and 600 years forward, we can see tiny bits of green here and there. Even the **Aire-So-Kleen Meter** in the engine room checks in with a better atmosphere.*

Throughout Nessie's story, Sasquatch kept nodding his head like a dippy bird. But now he broke in with impatient excitement. *Then one morning we were sitting at breakfast eating our Sugar Smacks and Rice Krispies. It was like we got bonked on the head, an old-time religious conversion. We could bring people back, not right away, but after the earth got its shit together —*

Nessie punched him in the arm. *Shut up, I can tell it better. We'd contact a bunch of people from way before everybody had died. That is, all the people who could hear us because they had clairvoyant minds like ours. We could even try controlling their thoughts, make them do what we wanted.*

Ariel thought, My God. They've been in my head since I was four, I just didn't know why.

Nessie tapped her foot impatiently. *Sonny, you aren't listening. I'm getting to the good part. And when special people are carefully matched, their babies grow up even more advanced than the parents.*

And suddenly he knew. He and Miriam had made a god-baby at the Moon People's bidding.

Nessie glared at him. *Ari, what the hell's wrong with you? I'm talking to you.*

Ariel forced himself to look into the crinkled blue eyes he suddenly detested.

That's more like it, Sonny. Then we'd get the special people we picked to build a time machine with a helluva lot better TravLtron than our crappy old gizmo. They'd jump ahead millions of years to a time when the earth has recovered. They'd start the human race over. Her eyes were shining.

But then Nessie sighed theatrically. *The plan seemed perfect once; we found lots of people with special minds, but we just don't understand. Not everybody seemed to like us. They wouldn't play along, Ari.* She sniffed and wiped an eye with the corner of her sleeve. *It just broke our hearts.*

Her plea for sympathy did not touch Ariel. And he wasn't a bit surprised that the number of followers had dwindled.

Nessie cleared her throat, and Ariel felt a delicate request coming up, something the couple had planned carefully before they'd brought him so precipitously to their globe. *Sasquatch and I were thinking. We know how you felt about Miriam and even Aleta, but let's be practical. There have to be more kids. We think you should marry Luz before she passes childbearing age. Then she can be your new mate and be part of, well, destiny.*

Sasquatch interrupted enthusiastically, *Ooh, Luz, what a cushiony cuddle-bunny. What a helluva set of knockers, what a super-duper behind.*

Ariel refused to even acknowledge Sasquatch but spoke carefully to Nessie, who was obviously the lone brains of the outfit. *I respect your quest to bring people back. And you must believe me, I actually love Luz as a dear friend. But marrying her is impossible, unfair to her and to me —*

Suddenly he snarled at both of them, surprising himself. *I will never breed again for you, never, I won't do it with Luz or anyone else you throw at me. Now I can see that you stuck Miriam and me together for one reason only — to breed. Like hand-picked lab rats. Don't get me wrong, I'm glad you did. Oh, God, how we loved each other. But remember that you just saw me die by walking off a mountain, and I hurt so bad from missing her that I wish I'd been smashed to pieces. Did you think this would happen when you made your plans?*

Ariel took off the bedspread and dropped it on the threadbare sofa. He let the interior vanish from his ersatz body until it became transparent, leaving a mere vessel to contain his mind.

I'm not going to Drancy because you asked me to. I'm going because Aleta is my friend and I know she's in danger. I'll walk the real Trail of Tears to find out how my people suffered, not for you, but for me. About this journey to the

End of Time, or wherever it is. I'll think about it because maybe I can find Miriam there.

***

Nessie and Sasquatch watched him fade. They held hands and cried for a few minutes. How could Ariel, and such a sweet young man, have gotten so angry with them? He had said horrible things that weren't true because they were good people. Yes, they were even great, inspired people, god-like people, the last people in the world. And they had the power to change the future, to save the human race. *What was so bad about that?*

Chapter 10 Drancy

Ariel rather liked the freedom of traveling unfettered by his body. Before leaving for Drancy, he made two lightning-quick trips to visit the people he loved most. Svnoyi slept on and on deep in the High Tatras, lying snug within the arms of the chrysalis he'd become. Ariel extended a delicate finger of Thought, touching her forehead. She smiled but didn't stir.

Then he visited Ethan, who sat on the sagging Victorian sofa staring into space. Ariel was alarmed by his friend's increasing despair. He tried to extend a hopeful message about Aleta, although he did not believe it himself. Besides, Ethan lacked the capacity to receive it.

***

It was Saturday, and Ethan felt miserable. He heaved himself up from the sofa to watch the usual circus through his grimy window; two boys about six years old were punching each other viciously while their mothers pretended not to notice. Ethan sank back down on the sofa. Everyone was gone and he was so lonely. Aleta had never once touched the back of his brain, even though he tried touching hers from time to time. His children were as remote as strangers on another planet. Ari was dead, and he'd lost Svnoyi through his own folly. It was a dreadful betrayal, and besides, he had adored his precious little half-sister. He hadn't managed to forgive his dead mother for getting sick and deserting him. He'd never even known his father. He felt doubly sorry for himself at the moment because he'd finished his studying for the day and had nothing to do. He knew he should start reading Ariel's journal again after that first try he'd made in September, but the new entry still gave him the creeps.

***

Ethan had a sudden a brainstorm. Luz! He hadn't seen her for months. He'd call her up and ask her to dinner, or whatever you call Campbell's minestrone soup mixed with bean sprouts and ground beef.

Luz arrived, carrying a bouquet of wilted lilacs, which she thrust toward him. Ethan began reaching for them with the expected smile of thanks, but instead, he felt his jaw drop. Luz's abdomen protruded in an unmistakable direction.

Luz reddened, but only slightly. "Oh that. I was meaning to tell you." She gazed downward. "It's a gift from the gods when you're my age. I was fired from Santa Margarita, of course, but I'm so happy."

"So go on."

"Well, I never cared much for men because I couldn't get past their vanity ... except Ari, of course. But then this freshman came into my office. I'd given him an 'F' because he didn't know his right foot from his left, and that's a big liability when you have to march."

"And ...?"

"Well, he was an exchange student from the Congo, not so swift with English. I tried to show him which foot ... er, which *leg* was which, and we ended up on the floor."

Luz smiled sadly. "It was fun, but it had no future. He and his parents are like me. They read his mind and yanked him out of school." She murmured under her breath, "Not quite Ari in a Mr. America contest, but close."

Ethan felt a surprising stab of jealousy imagining a Mr. America contestant rolling on the floor with Luz, but he shrugged it off.

"Luz, Jumping Jesus, you'll have a god-baby."

Ethan visited Luz in the hospital a few days after the birth. Beaming with delight, she proudly cradled the male infant to her breast as she rocked him to and fro. He looked as creased and wrinkled as all newborns, although he already displayed the remarkable self-possession typical of god-babies. Luz called him her chocolate baby, a term Ethan detested immediately, although the official given name on the birth certificate, Lado Oscuro de la Luna, was not much better.

"Holy shit, Luz, how could you name your kid Dark Side of the Moon? He'll get destroyed in school."

"Watch your language, Ethan. You'll sully my son's childhood innocence." She kissed Lado Oscuro de la Luna's wizened face liberally, not forgetting his tiny ears and the tip of his nose.

In the end, she realized that Ethan had a point, and settled on Oscar as a nickname.

***

In addition to feeling depressed during the day, Ethan suffered from insomnia. As happened almost every night, he was still sitting on the Victorian sofa at 2:00 a.m. with his face buried in his hands. He knew he'd regret the lack of sleep in his morning classes and later at that awful job shelving books at the library. His mind was making its customary circular route from worry, to loneliness, to despair, and back to worry.

He jumped about a foot when someone pounded on the door. It was Luz, with little Oscar bundled up in the folds of her coat. She was not her usual collected self. In fact, she was weeping and out of breath from running across town.

"Ethan, someone just threw a brick through my window with a *death threat* attached to it."

He put what he hoped was a comforting arm around her and sat her on the sofa. He extracted Oscar from her coat because the saucer-eyed baby had begun screaming at the top of his lungs. With aching memories of Svnoyi, Ethan put him over one shoulder.

Ethan patted Luz's arm at the same time. "Calm down, Luz, sweetheart mine. What did it say?"

She pulled an enormous brick from Oscar's diaper bag with the note still tied on. "I-I have it here: 'If U R here 2morrow whore U die.'"

She went on through sobs, "That's what I get for living in a conservative Spanish neighborhood with my chocolate baby."

Ethan blurted out, "Luz, the solution is so simple. Stay tonight, I have a crib, and tomorrow, move in with me."

On the third night, Luz had seen enough. Some time after Ethan had settled into his insomniac misery, she whisked him off the sofa and took him into her bed. Wrapped within her warm, opulent flesh, his emptiness vanished. Luz became mother, father, Kuaray, Yacy, Svnoyi, Ari, Aleta. The sex was as simple as it was serene. He penetrated deep into her calmness while imagining flowery meadows, wide rivers, lofty treetops, the vaulted sky. At last Luz had found a lover who saw past the ROTC uniform. Once she had made up her mind on that third night, she loved Ethan fiercely with a pure, unquestioned devotion.

Luz was convinced that even Aleta's return couldn't break her new bond with Ethan, and Ethan remembered his vision of the moon-faced woman who had taken Aleta's place in Matka's white room. He realized that he was already joined with Luz, at least according to his own interpretation of his fever-induced dream. But Aleta's memory still plagued him.

***

Aleta stayed on in Puerto Seguro because she had nowhere else to go. The pink and yellow blossoms and emerald-green grass of spring gave way to the tall dry weeds of summer. Hostile winter, windy and wet, again surprised her with its bone-penetrating rawness. Two more years passed in Aleta's life—years with neither hope for her future nor desire for friendship and love. While the twins slept, she kept up her search for the Itos by writing interminable letters. She never saw

Scarlett's name on the movie posters at the Paramount, and she never went to Hollywood to find her.

She had her reasons. Moving about with two small children was difficult enough, even in the aisles of the grocery store and at the Five and Dime. Besides, she had to economize. Her income from violin teaching and the monthly stipend from the Ito's bank account paid for rent and food, but not much more.

One day she stopped lying to herself. Scarlett had never touched her own share of the Ito's money, so Aleta was sure that her dearest friend, along with little Tommy, had been swallowed up by California's least angelic city. And there was something else she was sure of, too. After her strange encounter with Ethan on the beach, she realized that he was not the one she missed. She missed Sequoyah with an ache that never ceased, day or night.

***

On a stiflingly hot summer evening a few days after the twins' third birthday, she and her peculiar offspring were swept away from Puerto Seguro. It happened the same day that Kuaray and Yacy's extremely patient, but God-fearing, nursery school teacher finally reached her limit, throwing them out of **Baby Buckle My Shoe.**

At cleanup time the good woman shielded her eyes from the sight of rag dolls, miniature cars and trucks, easels, paintbrushes, dripping poster-paint artworks, and Tinkertoys flying around in a maelstrom just below the ceiling. Never mind that the twins were doing what they had been asked to do since all the objects soon settled into the correct corners and drawers; it was the unholy method they had chosen. But it was their unnerving passivity that bothered her most. They sat through it all, prim in their little sailor suits, two pairs of flat amber eyes observing what was surely a compact with the Devil. Besides, Kuaray had resisted toilet training out of anger, stubbornness, or apathy.

Aleta had been expecting a blow-up like this ever since Nurse Isobel had warned her about the town's hostility toward her babies. She was glad to leave but was unprepared for the terrifying force of the tornado that ripped a great hole through the middle of the children's bedroom, sucking the three of them into blackness. After they had vanished along with the violin and a small suitcase she'd always kept packed in anticipation of this moment, the floor and walls of the apartment on Main and Orchard snapped back together, returning to normal.

***

Aleta landed, crashing into an unyielding wall. Drizzle fell in her face as she lay flat on her back in a muddy courtyard. She stared upward at a huge apartment building, and when she turned her head, she saw that there were more of them laid out in a U-shape. Barbed wire was everywhere.

A thought flashed through her mind as she stood up shakily, trying to orient up from down. *At last. I think those weird Moon People just sent me to the Itos' internment camp.*

The twins, usually so standoffish, clung to her skirt in fear. Aleta was frightened, too. Tough looking police in strange uniforms with guns at their waists were everywhere, marching about the huge complex with sullen faces. One of the men spotted the little trio and scuttled off.

Aleta's knees knocked together from the cold. As night fell, the drizzle rapidly turned into heavy rain. She fished her violin case out of the muck, along with the suitcase containing a change of clothing for each of them. Any gaunt and tattered inmate who happened to wander nearby turned away from them with unseeing eyes. And they didn't look at all Japanese like the Itos.

Aleta watched a tall uniformed man approach slowly with the carefully studied alignment of each boot, the toes turned out like the old paintings of Our Founding Fathers. She could tell by his bearing that he was some kind of mucky-muck born to intimidate the small and the weak. But he sidled up to her with caution, and in spite of his haughty good looks and a face masterfully controlled, he was unable to hide his bafflement, and even trepidation.

He commented under his breath, *"Maudit! Qu'est-ce que c'est ca ...?"*

Aleta tried to gather her muddled thoughts, further scattered by searing pain on one side of her head. "Can you speak English, please, sir? I-I don't know much French."

He collected himself as he peered at her down the length of his aristocratic nose. She seemed harmless enough, probably unarmed with no bombs hidden up her skirt.

"Of course I know English, mademoiselle. I am an educated man. Your accent, you are American? You should have been put in the American camp, not here." He whispered to himself, *"Maudit fonctionnaires!"*

"But tell me, please. How did you and these children happen to arrive inside the fence without going through the entrance? Your sudden appearance is unprecedented."

Aleta felt more confused than before. As he kept pressing her for answers she did not have, she gingerly explored her injured head with one finger. She started trembling, her eyes leaking tears.

"I don't know what to do, sir, I don't know where I am or even what year it is. I think I hit my head." In fact, her temple still streamed blood from her violent collision with the corner of the building. Just then she staggered and fell against a wall.

The man took her elbow to steady her, then answered her with a studied combination of pity and condescension. "Injured, are you? Or just a stupid American playing games in the wrong place? You are in Drancy near Paris, and it is January 1943. How do they say it in your country, 'Does that not ring a bell'?"

Just at that moment, his mind went somewhere else, straying from official business. Aleta knew the look—one of lascivious appraisal. She prepared herself for a crude comment that didn't arrive. Something entirely different came out of his mouth.

"Papers, please."

"I don't have any."

"Name?"

"Aleta Rosenthal Marcus and these are my twins Kuaray and—"

He didn't let her finish. "Ha, Jewish. I will get a room assignment for you." Then his lips curled up slightly at the corners. "On second thought, I am putting you in overnight police quarters. But note that you owe me, my beautiful little Jewess, and I hope you know the proper way to say *merci.*"

Aleta didn't know, but she had a pretty good idea. "Maybe I should live with the others."

"Oh, I do not think so. The rooms are meant to hold 700 and we have 7,000 in them right now. With your petite frame you would last about half a day."

He patted each of her children's heads, but only with his left hand. "To tell you the truth, *ma belle,* your little ones fascinate me more than you do. I do not want anything to happen to them. And, by the way, you are not a queen. You will work like everyone else."

It didn't take Aleta long to figure out that she was in a French concentration camp for Jews, run by the French. Word had traveled fast. She became an outcast on the very first day, mainly despised by the women for the special treatment she'd received from one of the highest ranking officials. As she stood in the long soup line, a few of them spat on her and backed away. Even without knowing any of the languages the inmates spoke at Drancy, she had no trouble understanding *putain* or *kurvah.*

The men's reactions were unsubtle as they looked her up and down while making crude comments that didn't need translating. Their hand gestures were quite specific. She was never befriended by anyone. Throughout the long days, she slunk about in the stinking mud of the courtyard, trying to look small by hunching her shoulders and drawing her neck into her collar.

As much as the women despised her, they hated her children even more. Their own young ones had been snatched away, so why had she been allowed to keep hers? They also sneered at Aleta's failure as a mother. It was obvious to anyone with a nose and eyes that Kuaray hadn't been toilet trained.

But what infuriated people most was the twins' newest obsession. They had taken up juggling with non-stop ferocity, using stones, broken pottery, or anything else that lay on the ground. At first, the men had stomped their feet and clapped, reacting to a theatrical novelty. It didn't last. The inmates knew demonic possession when they saw it, and the children were soon shunned by everyone. Aleta tried to protect her twins as she moved from one trash heap to another performing her assigned task to sort through the garbage looking for any useful objects that could carry water. On the first day, she made off with a little pail to wash Kuaray's clothes.

On the second day, the man who had rescued her from the mud entered her tiny room that abutted police headquarters. Aleta couldn't believe her own reaction. She was so relieved to have someone to talk to that she hugged him.

He brushed her off and removed a skin-tight leather jacket that he draped carefully over the single chair. Then he announced his name in an imperious tone to all three members of his new kingdom.

His arrogance came straight out of an earlier era. "I am Henri Rayon de Lune, from an ancient family of royal descent. I am a nobleman at heart, so do not ever cross me. With that one simple rule, you will find that we will get along splendidly."

He went straight for Aleta, forcing her into a corner in front of Kuaray and Yacy, who stared open-mouthed and unblinking. They were learning something new. He fondled Aleta's breasts, and then covered her mouth with his, inserting his tongue deep into her throat. But without warning, he yanked himself away from her and swung around in fury, pinching his nose.

"What is that horrible stink? One of your kids? I will fix that." The man did not touch Kuaray. But inexplicably, the screaming child dropped to the floor, writhing and grabbing the area between his legs, fore and aft.

"Disgusting, Aleta. How can you permit this? Well, your *cochon* is cured, and you should thank me for having a backbone. Now clean him up."

Aleta could hardly focus through her tears as she washed and changed her sobbing son into the fresh clothes that she'd scrubbed the day before in the little pail. The imprints of deep bruises in those tender areas took months to fade.

Then the twins picked up the spoons and soup bowls that Aleta had borrowed from the kitchen at police headquarters. As they started juggling, the objects flew aloft, perfectly synchronized. Faster and faster they whirled, with never a slip.

"Aleta, your twins are gifted, but you should not have stolen from the commissary. Tomorrow I will bring them rubber balls, and plates and spoons for you. Now come to me while they are busy."

"No, sir, I can't. My husband—"

"What a prude you are. You surprise me." Henri ran a hand around Aleta's little waist. "Mind you, I have a wife, but she is a perfect replica of the Venus of Willendorf. Besides, think about it. You do not have a choice."

The tall and sinewy Henri lay full length on top of Aleta, crushing her, his long legs and feet in fancy leather riding boots hanging over the end of the iron bedstead. With all her strength, she wriggled out from under him.

Suddenly the spoons and bowls crashed to the floor with a clatter of splintering glass as Yacy let out an earsplitting shriek.

"Well, my dear Aleta, as you must recognize from my little demonstration just now, I can penetrate your daughter just like I had intended doing to you. Do you prefer me to do it to her with my mind, or would you like me to do it the right way to you?"

Shaking all over, Aleta had to let him slide his hand up her skirt. Then she encountered a horrible and unexpected surprise; he was missing two fingers on his right hand. When she felt the one-inch stubs against her tender skin, she almost vomited.

The intercourse went on for a long, long time, pumping and pumping, an interminable bashing without variety or finesse. Perhaps Venus of Willendorf had never offered any helpful hints. After it was over, Aleta curled up into a ball, wounded deep inside her body and mind. She had no idea how much the children had seen, although she was almost sure that the whooshing and clinking of the flying spoons had ceased. Who could blame them? With the bowls broken, half the juggling stock had been destroyed.

Another shock was in store for Aleta. As Henri stood up and zipped his pants, he spotted her violin case sticking out from under the bed, the mud carefully wiped off.

He softened noticeably, changing into a different man. "Ah, *ma belle*, do you play? I was a good violinist before my injury. I graduated from the Paris Conservatoire."

118

He shook his fist at no one in particular. "Damn prisoner hacked my fingers right off two years ago; he paid a steep price of course. Can you play for me now?" He hid the offending hand behind his back and smiled at her expectantly.

"I-I can't. Two strings are broken and the back is open."

"Oh, do not worry. I will take your violin to a luthier this evening. Tomorrow night we will make love, and then you will play for me. Do you know *Après un rêve* arranged for violin? Fauré, of course. I weep whenever I hear it."

Aleta could hardly picture him weeping for any reason, and certainly not over a piece of music. Her heart fell precipitously. If she had ever assumed that Monsieur Henri Rayon de Lune would be satisfied with only one encounter, her hopes were dashed. And yet, it could not be denied. He had befriended her.

The next evening, Henri walked in, his arms full of packages. He carried not one, but three violins. Two were one-eighth size, made for young children. He had also brought colorful rubber balls for juggling, plates and silverware, Vichy water, fresh croissants, and soft cheese. Kuaray and Yacy gobbled almost every bite of food, but Aleta refused to nibble more than a few crumbs.

Henri took out the miniature violins. "You will see how easy it is to play, *mes enfants*, just like *Maman*. G Major, what a great scale. No sliding, no stretching between your tiny little fingers." Henri played two octaves, grasping the bow in his mangled right hand, and the children copied him, right down to the abominable tone.

Then he lay on top of Aleta, pumping and pumping, G Major driving on and on, up and down, over and over, whining and wheezing, like two great augers drilling, drilling into Aleta's head. She could not abide this man's touch, but she craved his attention. And she had to admit that he was handsome in an aloof sort of way.

Afterward, Henri asked Aleta to play for him. She remembered his request from the night before—to hear *Après un rêve.*

Henri wept from ecstasy, rolling his eyes and clasping his hands. "Ah, my sweet. So, so beautiful. I am dying from pleasure hearing your music."

Aleta's knees turned to putty. For the first time in years, someone had expressed appreciation for her accomplishment.

The grotesque routine continued for another month. All day Kuaray and Yacy juggled with delighted, sparkling amber eyes, antagonizing, and even terrifying the other inmates. They advanced on their violins to A and D Major, even combining the juggling and playing skills. As they did their scales in canon—up and down, up and down—they bounced the balls back and forth to each other, using their tiny feet.

At night, Henri arrived with food and little surprise gifts for the twins. They grew chubby, but Aleta would only eat a mouthful or two. The relentless pumping went on every night as he pressed his wiry, muscular body against hers.

Soon Aleta began to anticipate the sex, no matter how awful it always was, because she loved the violin recital that would follow. How Monsieur Henri Rayon de Lune adored her playing! He tilted his head back, swayed and wept, often singing the melody with an excess of vibrato and florid ornaments. Unable to contain his ecstasy, he proclaimed, "Berlioz, Fauré, Debussy, Ravel, Satie, ah, glorious, glorious."

No one had ever responded to her music quite like this. Sometimes she wished she could melt into his arms and declare undying love as this was the effect the unaccustomed admiration had on her.

***

One day Henri arrived with sharp little scissors. He cut the threads holding the Stars of David on their coats. Then he told them that a deportation train would be leaving for wretched places to the east of Paris that very afternoon and they didn't want to be on it.

He added, "You should thank me for looking after you."

He turned to Aleta without warmth, and she felt inexplicably wounded by his indifference. "I am a nobleman and you have received that legacy. I am sorry that my Venus of Willendorf never let me make babies with her."

She expected at least a kiss but did not receive one.

He escorted the little family to the gate and gave each of them excruciating jabs in their calves to make them run. "Make haste. Do not stop until you see open fields."

Aleta and the children ran as fast as they could, the little ones' legs making circular blurs. Then they slowed to a walk that went on for two days. At last Aleta fell down in a green meadow, thick with daisies and cornflowers. She retched into the coarse grass, but with a stomach so empty, nothing came up. She knew then this was morning sickness, and she was carrying Henri's child.

The earth below Aleta and the twins collapsed under them. A sucking whirlwind pulled them and the violins down and down, up, and sideways. The direction did not matter. The green meadow above, thick with daisies and cornflowers, showed no remaining traces of a sick mother and her two robust children.

***

Ariel feared for Aleta's sanity in the hellhole of Drancy but hadn't managed to get her out, or even to talk to her. In final desperation, he decided to visit the Moon People to beg for their help. He expected to be thrown out but received an unexpectedly warm welcome considering his last visit. When he popped in, they were sitting at the foldout table in the breakfast nook eating Rice Krispies and Cheerios.

Nessie spoke first, mind-to-mind, offering Ariel a hint of a smile that exposed her yellowed canines. *If it isn't Sonny. Would you like some Rice Krispies? Oh, I guess not. You are a transparent Ken doll today. Would you care to flesh up so I can lend you a bedspread?*

No thanks, Nessie. I'm actually in fancy dress. Usually, I just float.

Sasquatch chewed his last Cheerio before he spoke. *So, how's my buddy Ari? You said some real shitty things last time you were here. We hope you're in a better mood.*

He extended a hand in Ariel's direction. *How can we help you?*

Ariel knew he was groveling, but he couldn't help himself. *I've been to Drancy, and it's horrible—a concentration camp. Can you send Aleta somewhere else, or please, please bring her home to Ethan? During the day, she works in filthy garbage dumps, and at night—I can't tell you how bad it is.*

Nessie's smile disappeared. *Is that why you're here? How many times do I have to tell you we're running this show?*

Ariel felt a stab of the old hostility, which she noticed immediately.

She sighed. *You are one tough customer, Sonny. We'll explain everything you need to know. Let's move to the parlor.*

Sasquatch barked unpleasantly, *She means the place with those rotten recliners.*

Nessie settled herself on one of the La-Z-Boys with a crunch of unhappy springs, pulling a ratty afghan over her legs, and Sasquatch took the other. Ariel floated here and there, finally settling on the roof of the Porto-Powder-My-Nose. The ancient couple resumed a half-finished game of Scrabble, the letters barely visible on the worn tiles.

Nessie held the board perched on her bony knees as she waved a tile aloft. *So Ariel, did you talk to Aleta?* She smiled gleefully, anticipating the answer.

Ariel sighed. *I tried, I really did, but I couldn't get through to her. She just didn't read my thoughts. And she couldn't see me, so she had no idea I was there.*

Nessie murmured, *Surprise, surprise.*

She frowned at the Scrabble board. *That word's not in the dictionary, Sasquatch. Who's ever heard of "sexsome"?*

He glared at his wife as he removed the last four letters. She placed her letters, spelling a word that used the "x" and hit a triple-word red square.

Ariel continued, *I don't get it. A long time ago Aleta sent me a message in words that I delivered to Ethan.*

Nessie grew impatient. *Ari, don't be an idiot. I sent that to you, she didn't. She and Ethan have the puniest abilities of any of our recruits. They could barely understand each other's thoughts even after they took all their clothes off.*

Ariel cringed at the crudeness of Nessie's remark as Sasquatch scowled at his wife from under his great thatch of eyebrows. *I told you I didn't want a couple of halfwits on the team, but you're always so damn bossy—you insisted.*

She threw Sasquatch a warning glance. *I had my reasons. I knew Aleta would be dumb enough to ferry the kids around in the worst … hells you human maniacs have created. And we need Ethan to design the transport.*

Sasquatch grumbled under his breath, *Aleta has one redeeming feature: her cute ass.*

Not acknowledging the despicable Sasquatch, Ariel turned to Nessie to make a last plea. *Please, Nessie. Please help Aleta. She's no use to anyone at Drancy. The other prisoners hate her. She's being raped every night by the chief of police in front of her children.*

Sasquatch leered, grinning from ear to ear until Nessie slapped him.

Ari, disregard my husband's rude behavior toward Aleta. We ran out of Sugar Smacks, and Cheerios don't agree with him.

She twisted around abruptly to look at the game. *Sasquatch, as an ex-speechwriter for Nixon, your spelling stinks. "Saten"?*

She turned back to Ariel. *You are so dim, Sonny. Those trips aren't for her, they're for her kids! We want the little tykes to see what went wrong the first time around so they don't repeat the same errors in the New World.*

Her tone turned to acid. *Smart-ass that you are, Ari, you figured out our itty-bitty untruth last time you were here, and I quote, "And what makes you think she can change anything that's already happened?"*

Sasquatch laid out his replacement word on the Scrabble board: "salteen."

Nessie blew up. *Sasquatch, you damned fool. It's "s-a-l-t-i-n-e."*

The board crashed to the floor as she rose, hands on hips, her face red.

Listen up, Sequoyah. We're talking old-fashioned decency now. Luz whores around without our permission, and she's dropping litters like a rabbit in perpetual heat!

Please, Nessie, Ariel begged, *she's my friend.*

Oh shut up, Sonny, I'm talking. She and that awful woman now deceased, Miss Bianca Montag—or maybe you aren't fully acquainted with that sordid story? Both very gifted minds, but with the morals of alley cats.

She sniffed with self-righteous indignation. *Don't think we can't finish Luz off for misbehaving. We had to kill Miriam for a much lesser offense.*

Ariel cried out, *Oh God, why? How could you? We loved each other so much.*

His agonized outburst did not arouse Nessie's sympathy. *Cut the emotional crap, Ari. Toughen up. We made a one-child-per-couple rule because we need all the genetic variety we can get. And we got tired of watching you two spontaneously combust every damn day about five times. Too perfect a match, all that intensity. You and Miriam would have self-destructed anyway sooner rather than later.*

Sasquatch smirked knowingly. *And with your big endowment, if you know what I mean, we need you to spread the love.*

Nessie continued with pride, *The brain tumor was a cinch. She never got over killing her first baby. Her crime stayed inside her like a tiny grain of sand. I just added layers, like making a perfect pearl. I made it grow and grow, harden, invade.*

She moved her hands in widening arcs to illustrate. *The Power of Thought. It is a wonderful tool, my boy. Don't ever consider misusing it.*

Ariel was falling apart inside, his mind reeling from the horror of Miriam's murder, but he tried not to let them see it.

He stammered, *Y-you let Aleta and Ethan have t-two babies.*

Nessie laughed bitterly. *The old coot I'm married to says he's the father. I thought it sounded a bit theatrical myself, like Zeus zipped up in a swan suit or God hiding inside the Holy Ghost, but Sasquatch says he impregnated her in that lightning bolt.* With contempt, she observed her groaning husband as he crept around on painful knees, gathering up the Scrabble tiles.

Men. Such morons. At the same time, she kept tabs on Ariel's slipping self-control to gauge the precise moment.

Nessie jutted her chin forward and hissed at Ariel, *We trust you'll keep your mouth shut. Tell any one of your friends about Miriam, and you'll be mourning over Svnoyi's corpse.*

Ariel burst out, *Oh please, Nessie, just kill me now. I tried to die.*

Nessie interrupted, *You think we weren't watching? We slowed your fall.*

Suddenly she grew charming, crinkling her blue eyes once more. *We had to save you, silly boy. Of the whole bunch, Sequoyah Morgan Hummingbird, you are the only one fit to rule at the End of Time—until Kuaray comes of age. Don't you fancy being an emperor? And I recommend that you don't forget what I said about little Svnoyi.*

Ariel left them, falling straight down.

At last, he let out his invisible tears accompanied by a silent cry, *My Miriam murdered, Aleta violated.*

With barely a second to spare, he summoned the minimal presence of mind needed to establish a new landing point before crashing into the devastated earth below the Yellow Moon. His trajectory altered, he descended lightly onto the curb of the Santa's Village parking lot next to the reindeer pen—the very spot where he and Ethan had shoved and punched each other on his longest day three years before. His despair mingled not inharmoniously with chipmunk voices singing *Deck the Halls* through hidden loudspeakers and the odor of the captive Lapland beasts panting in the California sun.

But who was this? A little boy wearing short pants, a hand-knit argyle sweater, and scuffed saddle shoes stared directly at him, attempting to soothe his anguish with thought. He had rich brown skin, and eyes like Svnoyi's.

He was also deft at communicating mind to mind. *Mister, don't cry. It can't be that bad.*

Ariel replied, *It is that bad, and worse. But how can you see me?*

The little boy gave Ariel a sly wink. *I see lots of things, and my Mama and Papa don't know it, at least not yet.*

He squatted to pick up a cigarette butt. *Interesting, these delivery systems for carcinogens. I'm Oscar, but my real name is Lado Oscuro de la Luna.*

Mine is Sequoyah Morgan Hummingbird, but call me Ari.

A big woman swept the child into her arms. "Oscar, my sweetie, drop that filthy thing. Don't you want to see Santa?"

Ariel felt like crying again, but from joy. *It really is Luz, and she's with Ethan. She's pregnant. No one's pairing up right. No wonder the Moon People are so angry with her.*

***

The very next day, Luz thrust Ariel's journal into Ethan's hands. "Ethan, you must read this. Don't freak out, but I think Ari is alive and he was much closer to Aleta than you realize. You should know about it."

"Ari alive? *What?*"

"I can't explain it, except Oscar sees things, like spirits and even ghosts. It's his god-baby gift. He saw Ari's spirit yesterday at Santa's Village. So Ari is alive, maybe in a coma."

Luz paused, wondering if she was dropping too many bombs at the same time. "Oh, a letter arrived. You should know that Svnoyi's passport has been found. It was at a ranger station in some mountains between Poland and Czechoslovakia."

Ethan would have been upset with Luz for reading the journal, except he had left it lying around for anyone to see. He smoothed his hand over the maroon cloth cover and opened it to the second page. He had read the first page already, a brief note explaining that it had been written in great haste expressly for him. The script was small and surprisingly elegant with only a few crossed-out words. Ethan caressed the rich matte paper and sat at his desk to read.

***

June 1963

As soon as I met you and Aleta in September at Santa Margarita, I knew that you were the ones the Moon People wanted me to protect. The difference between the two of you was how you saw me. You saw a big, nice guy who was stupid and wouldn't mind being called Fuck. Aleta saw an unhappy person paralyzed by self-doubt, a little like herself. In early October we hiked to the end of the Cove Crest Trail into the valley below where there is a redwood grove. The attraction we felt for each other was always intense. We lay close all afternoon under the trees. I told her about the Moon People, and I said I was frightened for her. We promised to love each other always as the closest of friends.

I have never understood why the Moon People chose me, but they have been a part of my life for as long as I can remember. I knew Aleta would be taken somewhere soon, but I didn't know why. I was with her when it happened on that day in November. I held her hand as long as I could, but then she was gone. She tried to write notes to you and to her parents. She didn't have time to finish them. I forged them which I did not like doing. The Moon People would not let me tell you anything.

Your suffering was almost more than I could bear. I tried to watch over you without being noticed. I followed you up the Cove Crest Trail twice because I thought you might try to kill yourself. I worried about your health; I brought you home from your vigils at the Bell Tower. To close the police investigation, I testified that Aleta had jumped off the Golden Gate Bridge. This lie tormented me, but after that, you were no longer a murder suspect.

I know I will cause you pain at my death. And I can no longer protect you; I don't know the consequences of that. I am leaving the world too soon. May we meet in the next world, if there is one.

You will find more on the following pages about Miriam and me. I suggest that you hold off reading it until you are less angry. I grieve that I damaged our friendship by loving her. Just know that she alone opened my heart and freed my mind. When she died, my life was finished. The last page is about my daughter. I adore my little one and wrong her terribly by leaving her.

Aleta gave me paintings of birds that she did in high school. They are yours now. Hold them dear; her heart lies deep in the birds' eyes.

***

Ethan sniffled all the way through the pages with a Kleenex box on hand. If Ari had intended to protect Ethan's feelings by writing in an unadorned and factual style, its terse revelations only hurt him more.

And a certain sentence was already beginning to nag at him. *We lay close all afternoon under the trees. What the fuck?* Ethan took a deep breath. *Grow up, dumb-ass. Be thankful that maybe he's alive.*

Something compelled him to look at the entry on the blank page at the back. There was a new one below *My Miriam is not here,* the ink barely dry: *My Miriam murdered, Aleta violated.*

Chapter 11 The Trail of Tears

When the sun rose, Unalii woke beside an unconscious newcomer lying in the covered wagon, who had somehow become tightly wedged between her dying mother and herself. Unalii was sick, too, but not as seriously afflicted. Measles was the culprit, and she thanked her lucky stars that it wasn't the flux. The stranger was a white woman, barely more than a girl. This wagon was reserved for the sick, and in Unalii's opinion, the wispy creature certainly fit the bill. She was obviously pregnant but looked hardly robust enough to carry the burden, with the delicate blue veins of her thin limbs pulsing beneath the surface of her skin. Her skirt was too short to be practical, and odder still, she was clutching a fiddle.

Unalii nudged her gently. *"Osiyo. Gado detsadoa?"*

Aleta opened her eyes, which bulged with fright. As she sat up, she managed to whisper, "I don't understand you and I don't know where I am." Then tears filled her huge brown eyes.

Unalii answered in English, trying to sound soothing. "I said 'hello' in Cherokee and asked who you might be, miss. Did the soldiers put you in the wagon last night when we slept?"

Aleta shook her head; she was trembling.

"Are you sick, maybe have a high fever?"

Aleta almost gagged then, right in front of her new acquaintance. "Oh, no, it's my stomach."

Then Aleta peered above her head at the dusty canvas on wooden hoops. She exclaimed, "This is a covered wagon. Are you pioneers, going west like we studied in fifth grade? Why isn't it moving?"

Unalii gave Aleta an odd look. "Oh, it will when the oxen are hitched. And an awful ride it is. But how do you not know where we go, miss? Did the soldiers hurt your head?"

Aleta nodded, the brimming tears flowing down her cheeks. "Oh, yes, yes, one of them did hurt me. But that was somewhere else, far away."

Unalii patted her hand. "Someone hurt you very painfully, poor little miss. We go to Oklahoma. We had to leave our homes; the Government forced—"

Aleta interrupted, "My husband, Sequoyah Morgan Hummingbird, he's from Okla ...." Aleta trailed off. Her *husband?* Why had she said that? Suddenly she wanted Ariel so much that she sobbed out loud, hunching over her violin case.

Unalii put an arm around her shoulder. "Oh, miss, now you make sense. Your husband is Cherokee and you do not know where he can be. Maybe he is with the forward party. The soldiers take us too fast, we lose children, husbands, our old parents."

Just then, the wagon started to move, straining in every timber. Unalii had to yell over the rumbling, "We ask everyone, we find him."

***

But Ariel was already on the Trail of Tears—as Thought. His mind resisted understanding a sight so abysmal. When he finally took it in, he mourned. *My God, these are my people, hundreds of them, marching with bowed heads, some even weeping! It's the real Trail of Tears. I know so much about it, but I could never have pictured this, never. No history books and no stories could show the degradation, the misery. Oh, it's awful.*

Ariel knew the terrain of most of Oklahoma, so this desolate land must be further to the southeast, perhaps in Arkansas. The heat was brutal. He saw his people filling the rutted road and overflowing onto the once undulating grass on either side, the sword-like blades now crushed to a slimy mass under hundreds of slogging feet, animal and human. On the road itself, oxen and horses pulled lurching carriages, carts, and covered wagons. Livestock, driven alongside, further pulverized the rank greenery under their stomping hooves. The people flowed forward like a great river, sliding on the slick pulp. An eerie silence prevailed. Ariel guessed that the sheer effort of putting one leg in front of the other killed the desire for human contact. And the sulfurous trail dust that rose in spreading clouds suffocated the entire party.

When he drew closer, Ariel saw whole families shouldering heavy loads of household goods—pots and pans, bedding, even a cradle— sometimes their backs bent double from the weight. Here were mothers and fathers holding little children by their sweaty hands, dragging them, forcing them, to match the adult pace.

An old man tottered past carrying a motherless infant in his arms, her stick-thin legs and filthy bare feet protruding below his torn cloak. In the midst of this misery, a magnificent horse-drawn carriage pulled up by the side of the road. Ariel assumed that it must belong to a wealthy Indian landowner because no one was exempt from the relocation. First, two black slaves climbed down from the perch to open the carriage doors. A fashionably dressed young man and woman stepped out, but they were weeping, caressing a limp bundle. It was their first-born who must have perished just moments ago.

Then Ariel saw the soldiers, and he remembered his history. Most of the later parties had been conducted by Indian leaders and their hired trail masters, so this must be an 1838 summer group. It was certainly hot enough.

These were the most disastrous trips of them all. Disease, deaths by the hundreds, half the trip in steamboats that ran aground. And Aleta, my beloved friend, she's on this hellish march? Oklahoma, not much of a prize, so bleak when I was growing up. How long does it take for a people to overcome something as devastating as the spectacle that stretches before me now?

Ariel made a vow. *If I live through this, the whole world will read about the Trail of Tears in poetry. I promise from my heart, I promise.*

Ariel found the twins first, and they weren't with their mother. Not by a long shot. They had become favorites of the militia, a motley bunch selected to manage the horrors of mass deportation, some sympathetic, some vicious, most just doing a job. All of them were exhausted by heat, disease, long hours, and the unvaried diet of salt pork—except the human dynamos Kuaray and Yacy. The twins had picked up a few new skills, which they dispensed liberally. In addition to the juggling, their violin repertory had moved past G, A, and D Major scales. They could play all manner of rapid dance tunes—jigs, reels, and hornpipes—even as they danced the steps in perfect synchronicity. In exchange for their non-stop entertainment, the army put them up and also taught them how to shoot game as well as the occasional deserter who had lost the will to continue along the disease-ridden trail.

***

Unalii's mother succumbed to measles the day after Aleta's sudden appearance in the wagon, and her first Indian friend and confidante perished two days later from the same disease. Since the dangerously hot weather encouraged pestilence, Unalii's two younger sisters and a brother buried first their mother, and then Unalii as soon as possible in shallow graves by the trail.

Aleta was devastated. In the midst of her tears, she remembered her own mild case of measles at age six when her usually unsympathetic mother hovered over her solicitously as she lay itchy and feverish in her frilly pink bed.

Aleta's next friend was Magnolia who took the vacated place next to her in the wagon. Weak from coughing, she had fainted on the trail that she walked as long as possible to avoid the sick wagons' death knell. Magnolia had pneumonia that she'd caught in Camp Cherokee, the detention camp at Ross's Landing.

Aleta, thinking about Drancy, asked Magnolia about the camp, but she received only a cursory description. "Lord, it was a stink-hole of rapine and starvation, like you never seen. The march startin' up were a blessing, even on them Devil steamboat rides."

The motherly woman was a freed slave with a bit more to say about her past. "But I's happy now, belongin' to nobody. My Indian family was good Christian souls, stood by me workin' in the fields, then they give me my liberty. And now the Lord makes us all equal in His eyes. Bless Jesus, but we suffer, every one, like the Israelites in Egypt."

Four days later Magnolia died in her sleep. The pneumonia that she had fought for so long carried her off before she could say goodbye to her grown sons who had gone ahead to scout out new trails.

Several weeks later a pimple-faced soldier still in his teens asked Aleta to give up her violin for bartering. Kuaray and Yacy had outgrown their clothes and shoes. Although they were perfectly happy to run around with nothing on, the Captain himself had asked them to "appear decently attired, or immediately depart the regiment." Aleta detected a note of hostility in the soldier's voice. Were the non-stop dance routines growing tiresome? Confined to the wagon, she could barely care for herself, let alone her manic offspring. Weeping, she handed over her most precious possession and the last remaining connection to her past.

***

Ariel found Aleta at last, after weeks of searching for her. The time for her delivery was close, and in her weakened condition, she was afflicted by a new, unnamed disease, not yet endemic. She had a high fever and a rash, unlike the telltale blisters of measles, and she coughed, gasping for breath. Ariel hovered ineffectually over her head. There was nothing he could do.

He tried to understand his feelings for Aleta—aching love and gloomy foreboding that swept over him. For Miriam's grip had begun to loosen, imperceptibly at first. But now it fell away, leaving him unmoored and drowning in self-doubt. He had certainly tried his best to join his beloved in death, but he had failed. And since Drancy, why had he continued to search for Aleta all along the Trail of Tears, peering into hundreds of miserable faces day after day, both along the road and inside the sick wagons? But he couldn't help thinking, *If this is a release from old sorrow, why isn't it happier?*

***

Luckily Aleta had not been deserted after Magnolia died. Unalii's sisters walked behind the wagon in the acrid dust, laying cool leaves dipped in their own scarce drinking water on Aleta's burning forehead. Her last night in the wagon's confines had been a torture of bruising bumps as she wheezed, hacked, and flailed about, burning up with fever. The next morning the sun heated the enclosed space, stifling the sick and dying inside. Aleta begged the sisters to leave her in a little copse away from the trail.

"I will die soon in the wagon anyway. I would rather lie in the shade of these trees." They offered to stay with her, but two soldiers displaying bayonets on their rifles would not let them straggle behind the rest, so her new friends left reluctantly.

Aleta was alone. She tried to resign herself to death by closing her aching eyes and folding her hands her high round belly. She could hear insects buzzing in the tall grass and the rustling of the cottonwoods' leaves. The air smelled of summer's rotting vegetation, still an improvement over the stench of human misery in the wagon.

***

A huge bird, a golden eagle, plummeted from the sky, crashing by Aleta's side. Aleta could see blood streaming from the bird's breast staining her feathers; she had been shot. Still alive, the eagle turned her majestic head to show one eye, just as the backyard birds used to do so long ago when she had painted them. Aleta looked deep, deep, into the eye's core.

And she was not surprised when the eagle spoke directly into her brain. *Your husband Sequoyah Morgan Hummingbird has been near you all along the Trail of Tears. You will see him soon.*

Aleta wished she could staunch the flow from the eagle's two gunshot wounds, one through her wing and the other directly into her heart. But she was almost as close to death as the bird—she could barely wiggle her fingers.

She could still weep, and at the same time, she directed a question with her mind. *Who did this, my poor dear Eagle?*

Kuaray and Yacy. The light faded from the eagle's eye.

As she died, Ariel appeared to Aleta, seemingly in the flesh, his beautiful athletic limbs burnished by the sun. At the same time, she saw the eagle's mate in a halo of radiant light, circling above. When the bereaved bird landed, he flapped about in terrible distress emitting raucous cries, even as he tried to rouse his beloved from the dead.

Ariel knelt at Aleta's side.

She couldn't move, but she sighed with happiness and closed her heavy eyes, murmuring, "I knew you'd find me. At last, my Sequoyah."

Ariel lay beside her just as he had years before beneath the redwoods at the end of the Cove Crest Trail. He kissed her burning cheeks, her cracked lips, her throat, her red-gold hair, dusty from the pitted road.

He took both her hands in his. "You must not leave me, Aleta. I love you so much, and I will be back."

He turned to the eagle. "Stay with her, my Eagle Friend, keep her on this earth."

Ariel, in reality only a wisp of Thought, left Aleta to find the Moon People. *They must help me, or my last spark of life will wink out with hers.*

The eagle's head sank to his breast in grief. But he stayed by Aleta, fanning her hot face with a mighty outstretched wing.

***

Petitioning the Moon People again was not something Ariel wanted to do. He arrived at the decrepit globe, covered with dings and scratches, while it was orbiting the night side of the ruined earth. He knew that barging in on Sasquatch and Nessie when they were sleeping would seriously damage his cause. But he was too desperate to wait until morning. Aleta was so close to death that she had envisioned him within his physical body—a sure sign that she had begun her symbolic passage to the world beyond.

The interior of the Moon was pitch-black, but Ariel could see the ancient pair kneeling on the cracked and curled linoleum squares that constituted the floor. As they bent their foreheads toward their respective sagging, smelly recliners, they held trembling hands palm to palm. Ariel had caught Sasquatch and Nessie saying their bedtime prayers.

Dear God, bless Richard Nixon, Herbert Hoover, Otto von Bismarck, Napoleon, Machiavelli .... They worked backward, and by the time they had reached Nero and Caligula, Ariel felt it was time to intervene.

Ahem.

The effect was startling. Sasquatch and Nessie sprang from the floor with agility borne of terror, collided, and fell into a tangled mass of bony limbs.

Sasquatch squeaked, *Goddammit, we should have brought the .45.*

It was then that Ariel realized something. The Yellow Moon's light bulbs must have burnt out some time ago. Although he could see the quaking couple, they could only hear his disembodied voice and were apparently too frightened to figure out who he was.

Who … who … who's there? Nessie whispered as they righted themselves.

Sasquatch echoed, *Ho! Who's there?*

Urgency gave Ariel strength—and inspiration. *It is I, the Ghost of Christmas Past, come to take my revenge on you two sinners!*

Wh-wh-what have we d-d-done? Sasquatch barely managed.

Ariel thundered from a different location on the ceiling, *You don't know? You have injured the good Christian, Lady Aleta.*

Nessie took over. *I thought she was Jewish, you know, ultra-smart but expendable.*

Ariel moved to his old spot above the Porto-Powder-My-Nose. *Wrong. You have offended me. Prepare to die.*

The pair whined in unison, *Just like that, with our life's work unfinished?*

Ariel roared inches above their heads, *Just like that. Snicker-snack.*

Oh-h-h, groaned Sasquatch. *Sounds horrible.*

Nessie, who was more in tune with the criminal element, piped up, *Mr. Christmas, how about a little deal, you know, we could grease a few palms.*

Ariel bellowed, *You provoke God Himself with such a depraved suggestion, but … but, I do spy a kind of hope. Send the Lady Aleta, without those odious twins, to the High Tatras. You know the place, the house of Jaroslav and Anichka. And mind you, I expect a gentle landing—or snicker-snack!*

Chapter 12 The Wolves

Ariel made a rapid about-face in order to spirit himself to the High Tatras. He fervently hoped that the Moon People had been convinced by his improvisation and would act before thinking too analytically about just who would do that. When he arrived inside the little log house, Aleta lay unconscious next to Svnoyi and his own body. No doubt about it, the bearskins looked overpopulated.

Svnoyi woke up, rubbing her eyes. My God, thought Ariel. She's four years old and pretty as a picture.

Svnoyi sat cross-legged and began to caress the comatose man's face with her stubby little fingers even as she shed her precious crystal tears over him. Ariel felt himself whooshing into that long-abandoned flesh, his very own being giving it a tingling new life. As he sat up with a creaking of hip and knee joints, he thought of the surprise that Frankenstein must have felt watching his manufactured creature attain an animate state.

Jaroslav and Anichka stood by gawking as they observed two unexpected miracles in close succession. Anichka would have fallen on her knees to give thanks for the Resurrection of Jesus if Aleta's meteoric arrival hadn't added yet another deviation from the Word.

Aleta gave a faint groan and her eyelids fluttered. Anichka's mouth snapped shut. Her raven-black eyes sparkled and flashed as she took in the condition of the sick newcomer, burning with a high fever. Then the Roma healer bent over Aleta to make a number of knowledgeable probes all over her protruding belly. She straightened up, putting her hands on her hips authoritatively because she had a lot to say.

Svnoyi translated, speaking aloud in English for the first time in her life. "Anichka wants you, Jesus Daddy, and me to get out of the room, or we sit in the corner and not look. Jaroslav, you boil water and get clean towels."

Svnoyi began to prance about, clapping her hands. "The lady, the lady, the lady is having a *baby!*"

Before the long night was over, Anichka put everyone to work. Svnoyi ground willow bark and herbs to make a fever-reducing tea and held cooling cloths to Aleta's forehead. She also sang songs to promote healing that she made up on the spur of the moment, her sweet child's soprano bouncing off the rafters.

Ariel wandered outside for a half hour to get used to his legs. Svnoyi and Anichka had taken good care of him; he was in remarkable shape, considering, and he had not aged. He returned to hold Aleta's hands as she dug her nails deep into his flesh to counteract the agony of her contractions. He loved her so much at these moments that he became faint from the racing of his heart.

Jaroslav, with his mountain-rescue medical training, helped Anichka bring Aleta through a life-threatening breech birth. She predicted that Aleta's convalescence after both scarlet fever and the delivery would be a long one, which proved to be true.

But when the baby, a handsome boy with turquoise eyes shaped like Svnoyi's, finally entered the world, Aleta refused to look at him. Instead, she turned her face to the wall and wept. Aleta faced the wall for an entire day while the others agonized about the newborn's chances, caring for him as best they could.

Eventually, Anichka had had enough. She thrust the baby into Aleta's arms, resurrecting the English she'd learned working as a maid at the ritziest hotel in the High Tatras' Stary Smokovek. "You give milk, we give love."

And so a bargain of sorts was struck; Ariel, Jaroslav, and Anichka, with Svnoyi's help, became 'round-the-clock nannies.

It was Jaroslav who gave the baby a temporary name, Sine Nomine. He had been born into a huge and devout Czech-Catholic family. Like his older brothers, his parents made him sing in Prague's St. Vitus Cathedral boys' choir, where his soaring soprano won him undesired fame. He was mercilessly teased in school but was adored by the church elders and pious women, especially overdressed and over-perfumed dowagers. He recalled singing a *Missa sine nomine* by some long-gone composer. Calling the baby Sine Nomine or "without a name" seemed appropriate until Aleta warmed up enough to choose a lasting one for him.

Jaroslav took Ariel aside. "Aleta sick for long time. We have big family now. We build new log bedroom by house."

Ariel was deeply touched by his hosts' generosity. He, too, saw no other option except a long stay. How Jaroslav and Anichka could shelter strangers, comatose or sentient, for years on end was a mystery to him.

Jaroslav suggested an immediate hike into the valley for a shopping trip in Stary Smokovec. Building supplies for the annex had to be purchased and a blueprint drawn up. In addition to obtaining baby items for Sine Nomine, the three newcomers needed almost complete wardrobes. As it was, barefoot Svnoyi presently wore an ancient red silk blouse of Anichka's pinned small at the shoulders that billowed past her knees. The torn and bloody clothes that Ariel had on during his rescue had long since been tossed out, and Aleta's only skirt had not survived the fourth cataclysmic journey through space and time.

***

The family fell into an easy rhythm caring for Sine Nomine, leaving the nighttime shifts to Ariel, who wanted to be alone with Aleta. Unfortunately, he was a true glutton for punishment, for even after several weeks, she had remained silent and aloof. After feeding Sine Nomine, Aleta handed him to Ariel with distaste, not bothering to support his tender neck. Ariel held Sine Nomine close, tucking the infant against his chest the way he used to hold Svnoyi.

Aleta whispered, "I wish that kid had never been born. You should've let me die."

Ariel was overjoyed that she had finally spoken to him, even in bitterness. "Aleta, I know how you feel about the baby, but what happened wasn't your fault." He tried to touch her shoulder, but she shrugged off his hand.

"How do you know what happened? You weren't there. Maybe I wanted that man, did you ever think of that?" Aleta began crying from anger and humiliation.

"Aleta, I was there, my mind was anyway, when I was in the coma. I saw you, I tried to help you, but you couldn't hear me or see me."

Aleta sat very still, staring straight ahead. Then she jerked around to face him. "You *watched* me?" With the speed of a boxer, she punched Ariel full in the chest with a closed fist—just missing Sine Nomine's head.

Ariel curled himself over the infant in case more blows came as Sine Nomine began howling, his turquoise eyes wide with fear. Ariel crossed the room, rocking him until he had quieted down, then laid him in his basket. The punch had hurt only a little, but Ariel felt his own eyes fill. He knelt by Aleta but didn't dare to touch her. Even though he was bewildered that she could endanger her own child and not even notice, he still wanted to apologize, to say something affectionate.

Before he opened his mouth, she hissed with venom, "By the way, that Trail of Tears. I hate you. *I hate you* because I saw *your* people die."

Ariel didn't know exactly what she meant, but he was stunned by her vehemence, by her choice of ugly words, by her vindictiveness. He felt a great ache grab his heart and stomach. He couldn't stay inside any longer. On his way out the door, he picked up a lantern and walked around the house to the construction site where the log walls for the new room were almost waist-height. He began to work hard and fast, partly to fight off the cold. Whenever the tears started, he angrily wiped them away, causing the wet sawdust to streak on his cheeks.

The dawn broke, staining the highest peaks a new pink. Jaroslav came out back and led Ariel inside. A cup of hot broth was waiting for him on the kitchen table.

"I rock baby this time, you sleep." Then he added sadly, "I hear what Aleta say. She hurt very much. You hurt very much, you do not help. Anichka talk to Aleta."

Ariel couldn't bring himself to taste the broth. He murmured a thank you through trembling lips. He unlaced and kicked off his cold-stiffened boots, but didn't bother to undress. He lay down on his bed of quilts and pulled one of them over his head, bringing his knees up to his chest. *If I just make myself small enough, maybe she won't see me.* He gripped his face in his hands. Something had broken inside him, and he had no idea how to fix it.

Then Svnoyi was kneeling beside him, searching for his hand beneath the quilt. She spoke into his head. *Daddy, don't do this again. It's like Jaroslav said. You are still too hurt to help Aleta. She is too hurt. Sleep now. It's the only thing you can do.*

***

Out of gratitude to his hosts, Ariel threw himself into the construction of the annex, really a simple log box with windows, a door, and a sloped roof to keep snow from collecting. He also had to distance himself from Aleta, who had perfected the use of sexual temptation to torture a most vulnerable subject. Whenever Ariel was in the main house, he noticed that she watched him constantly from beneath her long lashes, inflaming him with occasional provocative stares.

Worse, her oversized nightgown borrowed from Anichka often slid well off her shoulders, and whenever Ariel was nearby, she was not inclined to adjust it. And then there was the potently erotic breastfeeding during which she would peek at him out of the corner of her eye to gauge his reaction.

The magnetism was not one-sided. Ariel was unaware of it, but every chop of the ax, heft of a log, or hammer-strike against a nail had increased the appeal of his long muscular limbs, trunk, and shoulders. And so Aleta was also on fire, although Ariel remained oblivious of his power over her. The other members of the household, including Svnoyi, observed the tableau with fascination and growing alarm. The distraught pair had managed to construct a particularly volatile trap for themselves.

***

Now that the annex's exterior was finished, Ariel laid the hand-smoothed pine floor and installed shelves for Svnoyi's clothes, toy collection and books, and a tall closet with a burlap curtain. As the last steps, a glazier from Stary Smokovec was summoned to fit the windowpanes. A pot-bellied iron woodstove with a curving chimney pipe was hooked up for winter heating. The new bedroom lacked nothing except occupants.

The sleeping arrangements were never discussed but always assumed; the annex would be for Ariel and Svnoyi, and everyone else would remain in the house—the couple's end of the long room separated by a cheerful red curtain.

But when Aleta noticed Ariel's preparations to move his bedding and few possessions, she begged him not to leave her, although nothing else in her behavior towards him had changed. Heartened by her request, he knelt beside her and reached to stroke her arm. At first, she gave him a come-hither look, then smacked his hand, thus spurning him once again without a hint of pity.

Svnoyi had already arranged her blankets in the annex's clothes closet. She refused to move, announcing that she was snug as a bug in a rug, especially with the curtain drawn. She carefully hung her only dress, pink and ruffled, that Ariel had bought for her in town, on a handy peg. Her "boy's clothes," as she called them, were neatly folded on a shelf.

She laid out with precision her baby toys that the unfortunate Bianca Montag had carried off inside the battered suitcase from Ethan's apartment. Her nature collection—pretty pebbles and tiny crystals, autumn leaves, ferns, pinecones and blue jay feathers—sat on the top shelf next to her dog-eared books, mainly travelogues in English and Czech that Jaroslav had brought home from the ranger station, and *Mother Goose and other Poems for Children* that Ariel had bought in town. Her dearest treasure from the suitcase was Hans Christian Andersen's *Fairy Tales*, which she had read and reread. It took the place of honor at the center of her belongings.

In the end, to accommodate Aleta's wishes, Jaroslav and Anichka moved into the annex with Svnoyi, saying politely that they liked the change of scenery.

***

A few days later, after Ariel had rocked Sine Nomine to sleep and laid the infant in the rush basket, Aleta begged him to sit by her. His heart leaped. Maybe she would show a little warmth.

Aleta began with an accusation. "Svnoyi told me that you jumped off a mountain right around here and almost died, which is why you were in a coma. Is that true?"

Ariel was immediately disappointed. Warmth was not evident, and he hadn't wanted to tell her about his past so early in her recovery. "Svnoyi talks too much, but yes, it's true." He looked down at his own tensely clutched fingers.

Even though Aleta talked about suicide all the time, she skewered him, "That's horrific and disgusting, you know that, don't you?" The ferocity of her tone increased. "And Jesus, Sequoyah. What about Svnoyi? Didn't you think of her, your own kid?"

He struggled on lamely, "I did think of her, and yes, it was a very desperate, terrible thing to do. Do we have to talk about this now?"

"So why'd you do it, then? Actually, Svnoyi told me you did it for love, but I can't believe you'd be so nuts." She looked triumphant as if she had scored a point.

"My wife died. I didn't want to live after that." Even four years after Miriam's death, Ariel felt his throat tighten.

Aleta stiffened. "What do you mean, your *wife?* I thought you and me, we had something special. And you turn around and get married to someone else in six months?"

"But Aleta, you were Ethan's girl, and besides, you were *gone.*"

Aleta hung her head. "Do you still love her, then?"

Ariel knew that his answer would be too honest to please her, and he was right. "Of course I do, but now my feelings are buried deep inside like she's a part of me."

Aleta's shoulders drooped. After a pause, she asked wistfully, "Do you still miss her?"

"Yes, all the time."

Aleta sounded jealous and angry now. "So obviously since she wasn't me, she must have been some other lucky lady. Who *was* she?"

Ariel twisted his hands. "Aleta, this is not easy to talk about. She was ... she was Miriam, Ethan's mother."

Aleta was momentarily silent, but then she threw her head back and laughed in his face. "Good gravy, Sequoyah, not that Crazy at Agnews. You and she were ... she's Svnoyi's *mother?"* Suddenly tears hung on her lashes. "You bold, bad man. I'm sure Ethan's reaction was priceless."

"Yes. He was pretty upset."

Aleta went on bitterly, "Ethan's living with some fat ROTC dyke and you're in love with a dead woman. And not just *any* dead woman, Ethan's mother."

"Aleta, that's not fair. I know she's dead and I've gotten over it … mostly. You are living, you are here, and I've always loved you in a different way."

Aleta was not interested in his attempted declaration of affection. She changed the subject, facing him angrily. "You know Luz and Ethan had a baby girl."

"Is this more information from Svnoyi?" As much as he didn't want to, he would have to confront his gossipy daughter.

After her show of indignation, Aleta looked deflated. "Yes. She does that mind-talk with Oscar all the time and then tells me what he said. It seems Ethan has forgotten me." Tears filled her eyes once more.

Even before the words left his mouth Ariel realized that his timing was bad. "I haven't forgotten you. Don't you want to know how *I* feel?"

She turned her back on him and covered her face with her hands. "No, I don't. You men are pathetic. I hate you both, especially you, Sequoyah Morgan Hummingbird, and that includes your stupid childhood in the orphanage—"

"You *hate* me? My childhood, too? Aleta, I can't talk to you when you get like this." Ariel stood up to leave. As usual, after any conversation with her, he felt crushed, but this time was worse.

"Fine. Then leave. You make me sick." She added one more jab. "Would you die for *me?* I don't think so." Aleta burst into tears.

Ariel felt like crying, too, right in front of her, but he wouldn't give her the satisfaction.

***

The sun had set behind the peaks across the valley as Ariel started to run up the narrow trail, now barely visible. He knew he was being foolish, but he was in dreadful turmoil, even shedding tears from time to time so that he found himself tripping and sliding on the jagged stones.

Then he heard Svnoyi's little flying feet pattering behind him as she raced to catch up. "Daddy, come back, *come back*. You're scaring me."

Ariel turned on his daughter in fury, partly because she always knew when he was suffering and came to the rescue, never allowing him any time alone.

Spoken directly into her mind, his words were cutting. *Svnoyi Marcowitz Sequoyah, you made big trouble blabbing all that private stuff about me to Aleta. You gotta learn when to shut your trap.* Ariel watched Svnoyi shrink and back away, but he didn't stop himself. *And … and you are smothering me, killing me! Just leave me alone, get out of my head.*

Even as he did it, he knew that he had stooped low, even below Aleta's level, and had hurt Svnoyi terribly. Her mouth crumpled and two of the rare crystal tears filled her drooping eyes, sparkling in the moonlight as they slid down her cheeks. Before Ariel could stop her, she turned and flew up the dark trail into the night.

A tall figure rushed past, feet thumping. It was Jaroslav in pursuit of Svnoyi. Five minutes later he returned, carrying the little girl home to safety in his strong arms. Svnoyi's head was buried into his chest; she would not look up. As Jaroslav passed Ariel, he growled, "I talk to you later."

Ariel could hardly have injured himself any worse if he had chopped his foot off with an ax. He veered off the trail, crouching down under the low-slung branches of a pine tree. His whole body shook with sobs as he bit his clenched fist hard to keep from wailing out loud.

Jaroslav found him in this sorry state when he returned with a lantern. He put a big hand on Ariel's shoulder. "We talk out here. Maybe Svnoyi not hear so good."

Ariel couldn't reply.

Jaroslav sighed and patted his arm. "Is time you learn about mountains. You work with me at ranger station. You learn job fast." He winked, smiling at last, "Then you bring Svnoyi. She learn to read topographic maps."

Ariel managed to nod. Jaroslav went on. "My sister lives in town, luckily she has spare room. You and Svnoyi move in few days. She like children. Better for you there."

Ariel regained his voice. "But I can't leave Aleta, she's still sick. She needs me. And what about Sine Nomine?"

Jaroslav stood up to go home. "No, we manage. You visit weekends." Ariel got up, too, even though he dreaded seeing Svnoyi.

Jaroslav turned towards him, his face illuminated by the eerie half-light of the lantern. He chuckled. "I hear what you think, what Aleta think. You not know that." He added slowly, "Maybe she love again after hurt." Then he went on with relief, "Good thing I hear Svnoyi. Is how I save her."

***

Ariel and Jaroslav left early the next morning for the ranger station. Anichka and Svnoyi kept Aleta company as they took turns caring for the cast-off Sine Nomine. That afternoon when Sine Nomine slept and Svnoyi was busy in the annex talking mind-to-mind with her faraway friend Oscar, Anichka saw her chance to be alone with Aleta. The Gypsy sat beside her, looking very serious, her eyes lowered. She cleared her throat to attract her difficult guest's attention.

"My English not good. I tell my story. You hear it, you like Sine Nomine and Ariel better. Is like your story, also from war, maybe is sadder, more awful."

Aleta had been dozing in the square of warm afternoon sunshine that stretched across the floor and over the bed of bearskins. But when Anichka's comments registered, she sat up abruptly with her forehead wrinkled in a frown.

"That's impossible, and I don't believe you. Mine is much more awful, worse than anybody's."

Anichka looked annoyed. "Okay, my story I not tell."

Even Aleta realized that she had overstepped the bounds of politeness. She pulled up her knees and clasped them, looking like a child about to hear *Goldilocks and the Three Bears*.

She pasted on a superficial smile. "Oh, sorry. I want to hear it, really. It's just that you woke me up."

Anichka glared in Aleta's direction before taking a deep breath to begin.

"I am in Auschwitz Camp, many die. I am Roma, I am a young girl, sixteen. And you in French camp, different time."

Aleta's whole body twitched as if she had accidentally stuck her finger in a light socket. "H-how did you *know* that, Anichka?"

The mysterious dark-skinned Roma with the sparkling black eyes smiled with amusement at her own shock tactic. "You not know? Even from far away I see what you think. I hear what you talk."

Her triumph over, she lowered her voice to a husky whisper. "I see you hurt in camp. I see you and bad man, he make baby. Now I tell story about me—"

Aleta interrupted, snapping at her, "You're worse than that Ariel creeping around outside his body. You *spied* on me … with your mind. And I know you're just going to steal *my* story."

"You rude and selfish girl, Aleta. I go now." Anichka stood up in disgust.

Then Aleta's curiosity took over, "Please don't go. I want to know. Did it happen in the camp, like it did to me?"

Anichka sat back down, surly with annoyance. "No. Auschwitz commander send me to work in German auto factory. Boss's son make baby with me. End of story."

Aleta begged, "Don't be angry, Anichka. Oh, *please* tell me. Did it happen the same way? Did the boss's son make threats, then force you … you know … into his bed?"

Unexpectedly Anichka's pique vanished and her eyes glistened with tears. She shook her head vigorously, reaching for Aleta's hand. "No, no. Not same way, very, very different."

Then she burst out, "Boss's son, his name is Werther. The father, he wish for a great warrior, a Siegfried. But this he not get. His Werther is born with thin legs that not hold him up. He walks with the braces, but he is eighteen, he is beautiful. His eyes are huge and blue, they look only at me, all day. By evening I speak to him with my eyes.

"In the night he tells to me German poems from a long time ago, he sings to me sad songs. Then Werther and me, we are like Adam and Eve on God's new earth. We lie together in love behind the big auto presses."

Watching the wistful yearning in Anichka's eyes as she recalled her Werther, Aleta let out a little gasp as suddenly she saw herself deep in a redwood forest grasping Sequoyah's muscular hand. Then she felt the flame of his fingers running along her spine. Gulls circled in the fog overhead crying, "Awk, aawk, aaawk, aaaawk, aaaaawk."

Anichka broke through Aleta's reverie. "But you know what is next. We love many nights, and a baby grow inside me. One day the father of Werther take a long look. My belly is round and hard under my blue striped smock. He ... how you say it? He 'put two and two together.' His face turn purple.

"He make a lion's roar, 'Werther Tristan Wolfenbüttel, I not even *guess* you have balls between your ragdoll legs, but is obvious I misjudge.'

"He point his pistol at my head. 'I shoot you, *Zigeunermädchen*, I shoot you dead.' But his hand, it is trembling. 'How, *how* I kill my own grandchild?'

"He make another roar. 'You leave auto factory, you leave my idiot son, you go far away before sunrise tomorrow.'

"Then he turn around. He shoot about one hundred bullets into shiny new Daimler we just finish for *Generalfeldmarschall* Wilhelm Keitel."

***

Anichka stared out the window at the tall peaks, already outlined in silhouette by the last glow of late afternoon. When she continued her story she seemed distracted, her eyes gazing inward at a rutted road filled with gray-faced refugees.

"I start to go home. For Roma is dangerous to walk on road, and I am big, many months big. And I cry all the days I walk. I know Werther is crying back in factory, I can hear him in my head."

Aleta could barely see Anichka in the growing darkness of the room. She pictured her friend alone and helpless under a brazen sun, weeping without pause for her Werther as she stumbled beneath the weight of her belly.

"My time come. I meet two good Russian soldiers. They take me to nursing station — lucky for me is close by. I have baby, then I walk and walk home. My baby is boy, very beautiful boy."

Anichka got up to light the evening lamp before going on. But she wheeled about suddenly, clenching and shaking her fists, her brows knit together above smoldering eyes.

"I remember this, always I get angry. The war, it end. I stay home and my baby grows, I watch his hair get more blond, his eyes get more bright blue. My mother, my sister, my people send me away. They say I am Nazi slut with enemy blond baby that bring curse of white skin."

Anichka struggled on, but now tears streamed down her cheeks. "My baby, I call him Little Werther from day he is born. I walk and walk nowhere, I get lost in mountains. I get very sick. Little Werther, soon he is dying." She stopped talking for a moment to wipe her eyes on an embroidered handkerchief that she took from her skirt pocket.

"Baby is very heavy, I fall down, sleep in snow, here in high mountain."

Aleta asked gently, hoping to hear a happy ending, "Did Jaroslav find you and save you and Little Werther ... well, kind of like Ariel found me?"

"Yes. Jaroslav save me. He wake me from snow, I go to hospital. But my baby, my Little Werther, is gone."

"Where *was* the baby?" Aleta asked in alarm.

Anichka's eyes were dry again as she answered with an unnatural calm, "No one find. Maybe wolves take him. Very deep snow, wolves very hungry in 1947 winter."

Still reeling from this revelation, Aleta asked hesitantly, "Did you ever see Werther again?"

Silence hung heavy in the air.

Finally, Anichka found her voice. "No. My Werther die at same time as Little Werther. I sleep in snow. I have horrible dream that I know is true. Men in khaki, they hang him in woods behind auto factory. So gentle Werther, my first love, they take from him all he has left — his precious life."

Then Anichka spoke so quietly that Aleta had to strain her ears to hear. "For a long time I cry. I cannot stop. But Jaroslav is patient and kind. He waits. After one year we marry. In our big soft bed we make love every night under icon of Pregnant Mary with baby Jesus painted on front of her blue dress. We cannot make baby.

"One day I see vision. God say, 'You not have baby again, Anichka. You go different path; you help people with Roma medicine. You love Me, I am God.'"

***

Anichka left Aleta's side to set cups on the table and bring the teapot and a plate of cookies that she and Svnoyi had made the night before. As self-absorbed as Aleta was, she had no trouble anticipating what Anichka was thinking, or what she would say next.

"Sine Nomine born two months now, Aleta. You get more strong. Sit in your chair, I not bring tea to you. And I tell you, baby too old for No Name. You choose name!"

She helped Aleta to her feet. "Another thing. I not tell you your heart with Ariel. But I ask you this because I lose Werther, my first love. Your first love you have; *why you throw him away?*"

Aleta began walking to the table but then turned abruptly. Agape and trembling, she stared hard at Anichka as tears welled up in her eyes.

"Anichka, suddenly I saw the strangest picture in my mind. I know why Little Werther disappeared when he did. The wolves didn't hurt him. They lifted him gently with their mouths, and then they ran so fast they looked like silver streaks. The wolves brought Little Werther to his daddy so they could comfort each other when they died."

Anichka sobbed into her hands, "Oh my darling ones ...." But soon she straightened up. "Aleta. This not sound like you."

Aleta quickly dried her eyes, nodding her head solemnly. "No, I suppose it doesn't."

***

After considering Jaroslav's advice for the lovelorn, Ariel saw the wisdom of moving into town. He packed his and Svnoyi's few belongings, planning an early start the next morning as soon as the sunlight reached the hazardous trail. He waited until the household was asleep to tell Aleta, assuming that she would still be tossing and turning, stewing in her own personal hell.

When he sat beside her on her bearskins and blankets, he had no clue how she would react. He placed his arms around her cautiously, expecting some sort of rebuff. Instead, Aleta drew herself deep into his embrace with a subdued whimper, curling up almost like the infants he had nurtured.

She whispered into his neck, "What took you so long? I've been waiting and waiting."

Ariel had nothing to say. And right now, he didn't trust her. But she closed her eyes as she ran her hands up and down his back, caressing the smoothly knit muscles, grown powerful from building the annex. In response, his hands reached down the length of her spine, his fingers splaying over her hips and buttocks. The two savored these first moments of arousal, feeling suspended as if the world had ceased rotating. Delicate kisses, the gentlest of touches, their flesh prickled and pulsed, crying out for more.

Aleta lifted the borrowed muslin nightgown off over her head revealing her lovely breasts—round and full with new milk. As Ariel molded them tenderly in his hands, she reached beneath his nightshirt to touch his penis. Both of them gasped as she ran her fingers up its full distended length.

Every nerve in Ariel's body screamed out to finish what he had craved for so long. *Aleta, so sweet, the consummation achingly close. But wait, Aleta isn't sweet. She was viciously cruel only yesterday. God, all this is so confusing.*

Her fingers began an extensive exploration under his shirt.

"Aleta, we have to talk about this first. That isn't helping." He sighed with regret as he pulled her hand away. "You and me, we've been through a lot, I know that. But ever since we got here, you've hurt me, over and over. It's gotten so awful to be around you that I plan to leave tomorrow."

There was a silence between them.

Then Aleta laid her head against his chest and threw her arms around his neck. "Sequoyah, to keep going on the Trail of Tears, I imagined you were my husband. I knew you were close by. That's what the poor eagle said before she died. If you leave now, the both of us, how will we stand it?"

She weighed her next words before going on. "I have been so unhappy. I-I was often cruel to you on purpose to watch you suffer." She kissed him through her tears. "But ever since the Moon People took me away, you've always been my beacon, my only reason for staying alive."

Ariel kissed her with physical longing and at least some of the love he'd felt before she had inflicted so much pain.

He helped her back into her nightgown. "I would like to sleep beside you. I won't touch you, and tomorrow we'll talk, try to make things right."

Nature thwarted Ariel's chivalrous intentions long before the night was over. They succumbed to the pull of desire that had obsessed them long before that autumn afternoon under the coastal redwoods at Santa Margarita. Ariel was a gentle, considerate lover who understood the dreadful punishments that Aleta's body and mind had endured. He penetrated slowly, kissing her all the while. Aleta put up no resistance, and soon melted with tiny cries.

At dawn, the irrepressible Svnoyi jumped onto their bearskin bed since no secrets could be kept from her. *Daddy, I see you finally got the point.* She giggled and bounced about on his chest.

Ariel opened one eye and mumbled, *Has anyone ever told you that you have a dirty mind for a little kid?*

Svnoyi had a ready answer. *In fact, yes, Daddy, but that was a long time ago. Just try to keep the Gingham Dog wagging his tail and the Calico Cat purring.* She winked one of her saucer eyes and left to get dressed in her boy's clothes—jeans and a flannel shirt.

Ariel hurried to pull on his pants so his hosts wouldn't find him naked in Aleta's bed. Needless to say, his gesture meant nothing; in a houseful of clairvoyants they already knew. Even Sine Nomine was fully aware of a change. Aleta, who held her baby willingly for the first time, noticed that he had just learned to laugh while flailing his tiny arms and legs, his sparkling turquoise eyes crimped in a paroxysm of infant delight.

Everyone except Sine Nomine decided to celebrate by having a party that evening. In a flash, Ariel recognized the import of the moment. For the first time, he was a vital part of an *almost* conventional family that spanned three generations.

During dinner, a delicious venison stew prepared by Anichka and Svnoyi, Aleta unveiled the names she had selected for Sine Nomine, who lay contentedly in her arms, soaking up knowledge through his turquoise saucer eyes.

"I'm calling him Phoenix Sequoyah Werther Rosenthal. I chose Phoenix because I want him to have a name from Greek mythology like mine. And today he's like the sun rising again to give me a second chance." She added offhandedly, "Besides, I like birds. An eagle talked to me once."

She went on softly, "The Sequoyah is easy to explain. Besides, you all know anyway. And Werther, that's my secret and Anichka's."

Anichka had tears in her eyes. "I love you like my children. Will not always be so easy. I know."

"Right," chirped Svnoyi as she fluffed up the pink ruffles along the hem of her only dress. "I listen in on the Moon People all the time. They want to kill us as soon as we leave the magic circle of the mountains."

Her comment electrified the group, and Ariel glared at his wayward child. "Svnoyi, what did I say about not telling everything you know?"

Jaroslav interrupted, "Svnoyi speak true. We have serious talk tomorrow or next day. Now is for love."

Svnoyi grabbed at all the hands she could reach as she jumped up and down. "'Now is for love,' even for children? Aleta, now can I call you *Etsi*? It means 'Mama' in Cherokee. I read it in Daddy's brain."

Ariel wanted to frown at his daughter, but his forehead wouldn't cooperate. "Really, Svnoyi, I don't remember that word."

Aleta hugged the bouncing girl. "Of course, Svnoyi. How I love the sound of it. Etsi, Etsi. And I love what it means."

***

That night, Ariel and Aleta chose to deny the ominous threats of the unforeseeable future by losing themselves in the present. Lying in each other's arms within the protection of the High Tatras' peaks, they felt safe for the first time.

During lovemaking, beginning on this night and continuing for a thousand more, Ariel would always feel the ghostly presence of Miriam. But he knew that at last, she would bless him. For Aleta, it was not so simple. True, Ethan's feelings had not touched hers since she had left Santa Margarita, but she could tell that he was keeping track of her. She sensed anger and self-pity festering just beneath the surface of his conscious mind.

Chapter 13 Aleta's Violin

Head over heels in love, Ariel and Aleta were soon married by a magistrate in Stary Smokovec. Only the immediate family attended the exchange of vows, but thanks to Jaroslav's popularity and prestige as head forester, almost the entire town turned up for the bacchanalian reception at the local tavern. The mountain folk had no problem accepting the blushing bride with the red-gold hair. But they shied away from the reticent groom with his all-knowing black eyes, dark skin, and intimidating physique.

As time passed Ariel acquired impressive mountaineering skills and the respect he deserved at the ranger station. Unfortunately, his success did not alter public opinion. He could never entirely block out the distrustful glances of his neighbors, who drilled nasty holes through his back from behind twitching lace curtains and half-closed shutters. And he had not managed to start the epic poem he'd so solemnly promised to write after experiencing the visceral horror of the Trail of Tears. Something else was nagging at him, too. Sooner or later he'd have to tell Ethan about the ruined earth that he'd witnessed from the window of the Yellow Moon.

***

As sometimes happened when he was faced with troubles that overwhelmed him, he experienced a shattering vision.

At the start of this one, he was assailed by memories from his youthful years that he desperately wanted to forget. "Please," he whispered, "Don't stick me here. I hate Tahlequah." But here he was anyway, and it was midday and hot. A boisterous crowd milled about him, moving too close as if determined to drown him in sweat. Just then, the tempting aroma of fresh fry bread laid out for sale on long tables, extended tendrils of pleasure that wooed and soothed him.

A parade, of course. That's why we're on Muskogee Avenue. He figured the red banner stretched high above his head would tell the story. He backed away to read the giant block letters: THE CHEROKEE NATION PROUDLY SALUTES THE 134TH ANNIVERSARY OF THE TRAIL OF TEARS. *His insides churned a little: it seemed odd that the Removal could ever be the cause for a celebration, but then, none of them had seen the real thing. At that moment, a smartly attired high-school marching band began a cacophonous salute accompanied by precision military high-stepping.*

The music stopped. Ariel and everyone else—the marching band, Cherokees he thought he recognized, and a few whites weighed down by Kodak cameras—turned eastward just in time for a resounding crunch that generated shockwaves beneath their feet. A plane, gaudily striped pink and orange with green wings and shaped like a fat sausage, had split apart in the forested foothills of the nearby Ozarks, its jaunty blue tail sticking absurdly into the air. Ariel wanted to cry out, "Hey, everybody, don't panic. It's a hoax, a toy." But his voice caught in his throat.

He stood amazed and paralyzed: the impact was all too real. White-hot flames roared through the wreckage, the scorched wind propelling fiery cinders into the crowd. A costumed Cherokee wearing a feather bonnet fell writhing, devoured by fire, as his two daughters threw themselves onto his charred remains. Parents with clothes aflame trampled their children underfoot as they fled to the cover of nearby buildings—their open mouths shaped in screaming O's.

Ariel wanted to help, to reach protective arms around the children. But with shaking knees and watering eyes he stared stupidly upward as blowing smoke and ash fell on his head in a fine white powder. Surprising himself, he doubled over from the pain in his stomach, gripping his hair and yelling, "How I hate myself. It's all my fault that this is happening. I never talked to Ethan about what I saw from the Yellow Moon, the End of the World. And now I will die before I write my poem, The Trail of Tears." He added in utter despair, "Aleta, you deserved better."

In the midst of his anguished soliloquy, two misshapen cinder-blackened imps with batwings and forked tails slithered out of the smoke, peering about to find him, their amber eyes rotating 360 degrees on protruding stalks.

"My God, it's Kuaray and Yacy."

He tried to fend them off, but they sidled up close, cackling and grimacing. Wiggling bony webbed fingers in front of his face, they smirked and stuttered, "We-we-we love-love-love a good plane crash, don't you-you-you?"

Ariel didn't know whether to laugh or run as fast as he could in any direction. With perfectly synchronized voices, hands, and feet, the antic pair sang and danced to the Hokey Pokey:

Put your right hand near, put your left hand far,
Shame on you for leaving us, poor bastards that we are!
Put your right foot far, put your left foot near,
Come get Mom's violin before it bites your ear.

***

Sweating and trembling violently, Ariel tore himself out of the vision by abruptly sitting up. Aleta was jarred awake. She sat up, too, reaching out her arms to him.

With great gulping sobs that made him almost unintelligible, Ariel revealed a few of his bottled-up secrets. "I just had a vision about the end of the world and some other stuff, and-and I'm just so *useless.*"

Aleta pulled him into her lap, where in spite of his size, he curled up like a baby.

Ariel mumbled into her leg, "I never told you this before, but when I was in a coma, *I really did see the end of the world* from the window of the Yellow Moon. The ground was all torn up and everyone and everything—they were dead."

Aleta didn't sound convinced. "Darling, I don't know what you're talking about."

"Oh God, Aleta, l tell you it's true. It happens about 100 years from now, and it's only us, you and me, our kids and Ethan's family who can try to fix things." Still shaking, Ariel sat up and dried off his sweaty tear-streaked face with the bed sheet. "If *you* don't believe me, who will?"

Aleta straightened her mussed nightgown and when she finally spoke, she wasn't sympathetic. "Pull yourself together, Ariel. You plan to tell Ethan that tall tale? If he believes it even half way, don't expect much help; he hates you, you know. You had a nasty habit of stealing his women."

Ariel sighed. "I have to talk to him. Maybe I won't get anywhere, but he's the only one who can build the ship."

Aleta interrupted angrily, "Oh don't tell me. You mean the transport those nasty Moon People want? That will travel through Time to land millenniums beyond the catastrophe with us in it?"

Ariel jerked away from her, "Who told you?"

"Your little girl gossip, Svnoyi, who else? Although at the time I didn't know what the hell she was talking about." Aleta's voice rose in fury. "It's not enough that they threw me all over creation like a rag doll. Now my whole family has to suffer?"

Ariel pulled Aleta towards him in an attempt to soothe her. He murmured, "I'm going to find your violin first because I think it's in my hometown. I know how much you miss making music; you always look so sad when the birds sing."

She wriggled out of his embrace. "Oh, don't consider *me* or *my* feelings." She turned her back, to Ariel it seemed like forever, only to whip around and throw her arms around his neck. She burst into a storm of tears, even more abandoned than his had been. "Oh, do, *do be careful.* The Moon People have it in for you, and I'll miss you so."

They held each other in silence, trying to heal the damage done. Then they made love as if it would be for the last time.

The following day Ariel sought new travel documents to the United States and Canada, where Ethan was finishing his graduate work at McGill University.

On the morning of Ariel's departure, Aleta, who had been acting overly emotional lately, cried bitterly. She clung to his neck, caressing his hands and face. Two crystal tears fell from Svnoyi's droopy eyes onto his hands as he reached to embrace her. She told him that the tears would protect him—up to a point. Phoenix wrapped his chubby arms around Ariel's knees, sobbing without tears as was his nature because he adored the warm-hearted giant, his *Táta*. Jaroslav and Anichka, who loved Ariel like a son, hugged him almost to the point of suffocation. Then Anichka handed him a tiny vial of healing herbs and a package of fresh-baked cookies. Jaroslav, while denying its efficacy, slipped a St. Christopher medal over his head.

With unshed tears constricting his throat, Ariel walked out the door, wondering if he would ever return. To comfort himself as he descended the stone-strewn trail lined with gently swaying pines, he reviewed in his mind the story of Aleta's violin. In fact, he owed that violin a huge debt. In a roundabout way, it had brought the two of them together.

***

Ariel had first met the violin back in Slime's rooming house at Santa Margarita where he got to know it almost as well as Aleta. He was so captivated by her that his outsize passion almost destroyed what little motivation he still possessed to pass his English and history courses. To satisfy an aggressive need to outshine everyone else in his classes, Ethan had simply ejected Aleta from his room in the evenings in order to study. This left a convenient opening for Ariel. Aleta often asked him if she could practice her violin in his room to avoid disturbing the scholar.

Ariel should've been studying, too. But he couldn't resist Aleta's request because she would end up standing so very close to him in his tiny studio apartment. She unfolded her metal stand first and then placed the music books with care, arranging them in the order that she would use them. Before delving into Bach, Vivaldi, or Beethoven, she'd always begin the same way, playing scales and etudes, her turned-out feet poised in the center of his circular hooked rug. Ariel watched her bow fly across the strings, the tips of her fingers piercing the fingerboard like arrows. The way she arched her back, raising her already high breasts, drove him half mad.

Occasionally Aleta would look inward, her brow furrowed in concentration, or she'd do the opposite, soaring above the phrases with far-away eyes. At these times, he could feel her pulling him into the center of the music. It was a place where he was afraid to go, a place too intimate, too close to his own center, his racing heart.

To keep from losing himself in her, he concentrated on the characteristics of the violin. He memorized every line and knot in the wood, lustrous with red-gold varnish that swept over the hills of the front and back and the female waist and hips of the sides. He sealed into his brain the smiling f-holes and the spiral of the scroll that unfurled like a new frond.

Aleta told him that the violin had been made by a man who had lived in Turin, Italy, during the nineteenth century. One evening, they put their heads together and peered through an f-hole to read the label inside. As her long hair that matched the violin's gleaming coat brushed his cheek and neck, she said out loud, "Joannes Franciscus Pressenda q. raphael fecit Taurini anno Domini 1838." He never forgot the maker's name, which reverberated in his head like the thumping hooves of a stallion.

A few days later his ardor was reciprocated. After several such practicing sessions, they walked the length of the Cove Crest Trail to lie together for an entire afternoon beneath the redwoods.

***

Tahlequah was the Cherokee town at the end of the Trail of Tears, home of the Cherokee Nation. It was the town he'd hoped never to see again because it was so near the orphanage where he'd grown up—where he'd so carefully hidden his misery behind a wall of silence.

The town hadn't changed much since he'd left. It had more than its share of flophouse neighborhoods, but it was still pretty, with the puffy moss-green forests of the Ozarks rising in the haze behind it. But when the Greyhound bus rolled through the town's outskirts, the debilitating poverty of his people, some living in corrugated iron shacks, smacked him in the face, leaving him vulnerable.

Oh, help me to know what to do. How can I honor my promise to write my epic poem if I can't even accept where I come from or who I am?

Ariel went to the old town first. At a guitar store on Choctaw Street and then a pawnshop on Chickasaw Street, he asked after the red-gold violin sold or deserted on the Trail of Tears. Both proprietors looked uncomfortable and shook their heads.

At the antique shop **CHEROKEE TREASURES** around the corner, the owner also refused to answer his query directly. But she elaborated nonetheless. She said that everyone knew the story of the violin, but that she, personally, didn't like to talk about it. When Ariel asked for specifics, she clammed up and shook her head vehemently, her mouth pinched tight. With both hands firmly planted on the gathers of her long dirndl skirt, she nodded emphatically in the direction of the door.

But after Ariel purchased one of her handmade patchwork quilts, she spoke in an undertone, "Don't ever, ever tell *who* you hear this from, they won't buy from me no more. No one likes haunted things." She lowered her voice to a whisper. "It belongs to the old Cherokee who boozes at *The Red Tavern* on South Street."

***

The Red Tavern had seen better days. The neon sign that hung precariously on the bulging brick storefront blinked the inconsistent rhythm of imminent mechanical failure. But the tidy interior felt surprisingly intimate, with the rosy light of late afternoon filtering through high windows. The bartender and his two young daughters, or so Ariel assumed from their sullen expressions, were wiping down everything in sight, from the glass tabletops to the ancient hardwood floor, bleached almost white by the daily scrubbings. There was only one customer; it was still too early for the boisterous after-work crowd.

On a hunch, Ariel decided that the tall, craggy-faced Cherokee who sat at the furthest table was his "boozer." When Ariel asked if he might join him, the man coldly scrutinized him through bloodshot eyes.

He mumbled without inflection, "Hey, big feller, if you is some stuck-up university antripologist t' ask about the fiddle story, forget it, an' fuck off." He added as an afterthought, "Because it ain't no story, it's all true. It go down my family from geneeration to geneeration."

Then he peered at Ariel more closely, focusing his bleary gaze to take in the athlete's unforgettable musculature and good looks. He sprang up a little unsteadily, craning his neck to focus.

"What the devil? Ain't you Sequoyah, the high school football hero from '59? From the orphanage? Same goddam school as mine twenty-five years before. An' all them girls couldn't help droolin' over you after every win. I *never* miss a home game back then."

Ariel was embarrassed. He didn't remember the girls. When it came to his female admirers during high school, he'd been almost clueless.

The man obviously had a good memory. "An' after that you left for some highbrow college in California with a big scholarship. You was the town celebrity."

He extended a hand towards Ariel. "Name's Mohe, but everyone in town call me Fiddle Mo—an' worse for my inebriatin' ways. Waddya up to now?"

After a firm handshake, they both sat down. The last thing Ariel had wanted was to be recognized, although it had helped break the ice.

Ariel tried a synopsis. "Well, I-I live in Europe. I'm a forest ranger, and a writer, a poet. The book of poetry I wrote ... about someone ... sold really well."

Ariel stopped and looked away until the tightness left his throat. "Life's been tough, but I'm married now with two kids and I'm really happy."

He wasn't sure how the next sentence would go over, and so he spoke with a hint of diffidence. "It's my wife's family that owned the violin on the Trail of Tears."

Frowning, Mohe mulled the line over long enough to make Ariel feel uncomfortable.

He went on suspiciously, "No one say nothin' like this to me before. I thought *my* family owned the fiddle. How come you have a claim on it?"

Ariel had lied often enough to aid the ones he loved, and he hated doing it. But there was a lot of truth to the tale he'd concocted during the long bus ride to Tahlequah. He wasn't sure quite how to begin, and he needed to soothe Mohe's ruffled feathers at the same time. He figured alcohol would do the trick, but when he asked the Cherokee if he'd like a fresh beer, Mohe shook his head. His curiosity had overcome his momentary anger.

Ariel hoped he could improvise until he discovered a bit more about how Mohe had come by the violin, so he started in. "My wife's great-great grandmother was on the Trail. Her name was Aleta and she was carrying the violin. She was white, married to a Cherokee. She rode in the sick wagon with a woman named Unalii who had the measles—"

An agitated Mohe interrupted. "Oh, Unalii! She's an ancestor of mine. Everyone remember her. She help all the lost 'n miserable souls on the Trail before she sicken."

He lowered his voice, "'Cause she love the girl with the fiddle, her sisters take care of the girl after Unalii die. And one of those sisters, Tsula, she's my great-great grandmother."

Then Mohe leaped up in excitement because he felt history was about to unfold. "That white girl, what's her name again? Aleta? Everyone remember her, too. She was thin as a stick with her belly poppin' with child." To demonstrate, he moved his hands in a great arc over his red flannel shirt.

"She cry all the time for her husband, Sequoyah. Hey, same name as you! He was lost somewhere up front on the Trail."

Ariel couldn't help smiling. *What a coup.*

Mohe sat back down and leaned forward for emphasis, gripping his beer glass with both hands, his voice husky. "But soon she was dyin'.

The sisters left her in the woods so she can breathe her last in a nice place. Then they feel very bad an' sneak back to bury her."

Mohe paused, and Ariel could see his hands trembling, sloshing the beer about in the glass.

He went on in a whisper, astonished by what he was about to say. "But what do they find? No human corpse, the girl was gone. But instead there's two golden eagles, and they ain't soarin' on the breeze. The violin girl, somehow—*somehow* she turn into the woman eagle, an' she's lyin' dead, bleedin' all over the place. Her husband that was named Sequoyah must have found her at last, 'cause this eagle is cryin' an' flappin' his wings, makin' a terrible racket over his dead wife."

Mohe turned contemplative, his voice dropping to a whisper. "You gotta wonder what kinda Power turn people into birds."

It was obvious to Ariel that Mohe had wanted to tell someone the entire story for a long time. He went on eagerly, after downing the beer in one gulp. "But that ain't all. The sisters brung the fiddle-girl's two kids to say goodbye to their mother. These kids was boy and girl twins. They hung out with the army, and they was weird ones. They had her fiddle, an' they was jiggin' an' laughin', fightin' over which one would play it.

He stumbled over his words in agitation, "Be-before they decide who gets it, that fiddle start up all by itself, *all by itself,* right inside the case, howlin' an weepin' like the eagle done!

"So everyone run away they're so scairt, even the kids, except my great-great grandmother, Tsula. She was pure piss an' vinegar. She tie a rope around the neck of the fiddle case and drug it, that thing howlin' up a storm inside, all the way to Oklahoma like a pup on a leash."

Ariel wondered if the violin had survived the trip, and soon he would know. "Can you still hear it, making that noise?"

Mohe answered uneasily, "Sure, I hear it, but only after I had a few, if you know what I mean. And I keep it in the cellar so's most of the time I'm too far away to hear that god-awful moanin'. Makes you wanna bawl for no reason!"

Ariel was curious, "Did you ever dare open the case?"

Mohe recalled what must have been a frightening experience with the pride of a conqueror. "I sure did. One day I get brave an' wonder what's inside. I lift the beat-up old lid and look through them fancy holes with a flashlight right into the fiddle's guts. An' wadya think I find? A little sign pasted in there with some Dago name that don't mean nothin' to me, and a date, 1838."

The full import of the date affected them both, and Mohe had a hard time going on.

"It is the year the dead fiddle-girl and her mournin' husband turn into birds *because* it's the year of the Trail of Tears. No wonder the fiddle cries. Everyone and everything did back then—birds, people, rocks, trees. It just tear a Cherokee's heart right out ...."

Mohe stopped mid-sentence, and neither the man who had jumped off a mountain nor the man drinking himself to death spoke for a full minute, joined as they were by the ruinous aftershocks of that appalling journey.

Then Mohe clapped a leathery hand on Ariel's shoulder as they stood up to leave. "There's too many spooky things goin' on with that fiddle. If you can tell me the name inside, I'll give it to you for nothing and maybe then I can get a good night's sleep and reform my ways."

Hearing the galloping stallion in his head, Ariel murmured, "Joannes Franciscus Pressenda."

Mohe gave a short nod. "You got it. But my friend, don't let that fiddle bite your ear."

***

Ariel stayed the night at Mohe's house, a modest foursquare sorely in need of paint, where the violin was indeed kept in the cellar.

"This is the family mansion," Mohe explained with a touch of pride. "I inherited it from my sister when she die too young of the TB." The old Cherokee attempted a carefree laugh. "I expect I'll die here soon since my time is coming."

Ariel was moved almost to tears by the peculiar offer that came next.

"The place ain't worth kindling, but if I can talk you into being my son, it'll go to you. It kinda belong with the fiddle, if you know what I mean."

Trying to gather his thoughts, Ariel stared hard at the cracked linoleum squares of the kitchen floor. *Me Mohe's son. Just maybe. Oh, please, please let it be true.*

***

The next morning Ariel boarded the first of four connecting Greyhound buses bound northeast for Montreal. As it rolled out, he waved from the window, awkwardly embracing the fragments of the violin case wrapped in the bulky quilt from Cherokee Treasures.

He thought he heard Mohe call over the grinding gears, "*Donadagohvi!* See you again, and travel safe, son."

Chapter 14 Montreal

Ariel couldn't sleep on the three-day bus trip because he was bursting with excitement over the remote possibility that he had found his father. Keeping a protective arm around the swaddled violin, Ariel sat hour after hour debating whether he might simply look into Mohe's thoughts because if he *were* his son, this fact would surely be uppermost in the old man's mind. The truth was that Ariel had his own peculiar code of ethics. He refused to pry out of curiosity, although he couldn't control the mental invasion that went along with extreme emotional stress or passionate love-making. By contrast, Svnoyi had never hesitated to poke her enquiring mind into anything and everything.

In a perverse one-time experiment, Ariel tried his skill on the bus driver, a handsome young black man with a perfectly spherical afro. He regretted his intrusion immediately because his probe exposed a deeply personal secret. The man much preferred fly-fishing with a homosexual buddy to sleeping with his curvaceous young bride.

***

By the time Ariel reached Montreal and the second-floor flat over a Greek restaurant on Avenue Desrochers, he was close to collapse. The sweltering bus station had been so confusing with the rush of foreign voices, sharp elbows, and pointed umbrellas that he never located an empty taxi. He walked in a light drizzle for what seemed like miles, clutching the quilt-covered violin case to his chest.

Moonfaced Luz threw open the front door to greet him, exclaiming, "You're a sight for sore eyes, handsome. How have I survived without you?" She drew him into one of her full-length embraces, violin and all.

To his relief, she refrained from making a remark about interesting protuberances, as she always had in the past, because he saw a number of children hiding behind her African-patterned skirt. But Ariel was worried. Although she looked enticingly thinner, her greeting lacked the warm spontaneity of the old days, as if her lively spirit had shrunk along with her robust frame.

Luz urged Ariel to look around, but as he stumbled about the narrow flat trying to appreciate its stained wallpaper and buckling floors, his eyes drooped from exhaustion. Luz noticed right away. She escorted him to the musty-smelling guest room at the very back where he'd be sleeping during his stay.

Except for an overfed gray and white cat stretched full length on a sofa, he was alone and delighted to lie down in total quiet. He dropped beside the cat, who obligingly moved over a few inches. The sofa was already made up for him, covered with freshly ironed sheets and four puffy quilts.

Ariel instantly fell asleep. But his slumber was disrupted by a short, disturbing vision in startling Technicolor.

Mohe, his creased cheeks damp, slid a cardboard box containing Ariel himself as baby-boy Sequoyah into the whitewater of the spring-swollen Illinois River. With choking sobs, he yelled over the roar of the cascades, "Goodbye, little Moses, and don't forget to lay my bleached bones in the Promised Land."

Ariel woke with a start. Was the vision a prophecy somehow involving the biblical Moses, or was it about Mohe being his real father? Or was it merely a distorted reflection of his orphaned past? The strangest thing about it was that Mohe was speaking *Tsalagi*, the Cherokee language that Ariel had been forced to suppress and forget by age five.

And what did he know about Moses? Precious little, since he had sat through obligatory Sunday services throughout his years at the residential school, refusing to listen to or accept the anecdotes that he remembered his aunties calling "that devil white man's crap-trap." However, he did recall that during a particularly boring sermon he'd come up with the following epic gem:

Old man Moses ate the roses.
Meanie Matron broke his noses.

He liked it even if it didn't make sense.

***

From the length of the hall, Ariel heard Luz bellow in the stentorian voice of her ROTC days, "Chow time, troops. *Now or never.*" Ariel was famished. His diet of the last three days had consisted of rest-stop BLTs and Milky Ways washed down with watery black coffee.

Ethan emerged from his study and they walked down the hall together. His old friend looked the same, although worried and drawn like Luz. And wasn't his curly brown hair thinning at the crown? Ariel noticed wire-rimmed glasses, a new addition since their college days, peeking out of his breast pocket.

Sadly, Ariel's warm greeting was met with a chilly nod. His heart sank. Perhaps Ethan hadn't appreciated Luz's welcoming embrace, or else Aleta was right. Resentment still lingered over Ariel's choices of women at Santa Margarita.

Oscar and Lucy left a toy-stuffed bedroom to join them for the last few feet before they entered the front room's double doors. Ariel had never seen a more elegant child than eight-year-old Oscar, who bowed from the hips like a Little Lord Fauntleroy.

Taking the tips of Ariel's fingers, he purred, "I'm so happy to meet you, sir … for the second time. Your lovely daughter might just be my best friend. I live for our daily conversations."

But Ariel wasn't fooled. Deep within the boy's sincere black eyes lurked terrifying pits of loneliness. He wondered, *Is this what seeing ghosts does to a person?*

Tiny fair-haired Lucy was already whining about the food even before they'd sat down. "I won't eat any dinner, *I won't*. And Mama can't make me. Mr. Ariel, before the butcher cut off Mrs. Chicken's head, she said, 'cluck-cluck.' Maybe she said really, 'I love laying pretty brown eggs.'

"What happened next, Mr. Ariel?" Lucy grasped her straining neck in both hands, lolling out her tongue and rolling her eyes into her head to simulate the beheading. Then she sank to the floor in slow motion, rippling her arms as gracefully as a Dying Swan before twitching in death's throes for at least a minute.

At first, Ariel thought she might be a six-year-old clowning around, but then he noticed that she was serious enough to hide her face in her hands after her theatrical reenactment.

Kuaray and Yacy arrived late after the others had already sat down at the scratched oak table, its oval top centered over four curvy legs with lion's ball-and-claw feet. Neither had washed their filthy faces and hands. Kuaray appeared as swarthy as a pirate and tall and broad in the shoulders for his ten years. He whistled as he looked Ariel up and down with rude directness, taking in the former football player's height and muscular frame.

"So *you're* the one the Moon People picked for my advisor 'til I come of age. It's okay with me, but you just might end up dead day after tomorrow." He grinned, drawing a finger across his neck.

Yacy, delicate and fair, punched Kuaray hard on the arm. "Just shut your trap, you mean shit-face! Or I won't speak to you again … ever."

Only Ariel noticed that her pale lips trembled after her outburst.

Luz appeared rosy from the hot kitchen, carrying a platter of roast chicken. She was not fazed by the twins' forthright and original entrance.

She exclaimed heartily, "Meet Yacy and Kuaray, Ariel. One morning last year they showed up on our doorstep—whoosh. Just like that. Said the Moon People yanked them off the Trail of Tears ... whatever that is."

Then she glared at the smirking pair through the rising aromatic steam. "I'm warning you two goons. We have a guest, so behave yourselves and don't mess with Mama. Just in case you forget, I fought Chinks in Korea!"

***

After a relatively uneventful meal, Ariel retired early. But he should've known better than to expect privacy. Yacy materialized in the doorway of his room so silently that he hadn't heard the latch click. She stretched herself up the frame, then sidled over to the sofa.

My God, thought Ariel. She's as slinky as a Siamese cat and only a few months older than Svnoyi.

Yacy swept sticky hair out of her amber eyes with the flick of a liquid wrist. "Can I sleep in your bed?"

Ariel recoiled. "No, Yacy, no. Go back to your own room."

Yacy slipped one grimy foot under Ariel's covers. "I can't go back. Kuaray keeps touching me."

Ariel was immune to shock. There had been enough of that, and much, much more at the residential school in spite of Matron's watchful eye. But Yacy and Kuaray?

Ariel removed her foot. "Okay, we'll line up the sofa pillows on the floor and I'll give you a few of my quilts." He had plenty. Although it was mid-summer, Luz had supplied bedding for subzero temperatures at the North Pole.

"And tomorrow we'll talk to Stepmama Luz and your daddy about this ... this *touching*. It can't go on."

Yacy remarked, "They don't listen to me anyways, and besides, you can't talk to my dad. He lives in the Moon."

Ariel's heart sank. *So the Moon People have fed the twins that story, too.*

Then he grabbed her skinny shoulders and twirled her in the direction of the door. "Go take a bath before bed. And scrub out the tub afterward. You share it with a lot of people."

He couldn't refrain from asking, "How'd you get so filthy?"

She mumbled her next words, perhaps trying to disguise their content. "Kuaray and me, we was makin' bombs. An' like I always do, I helped 'cause he says to."

"Kuaray and I *were* making, Yacy."

She bellowed from down the hall, "Yeah, Stepdaddy Sequoyah, I know how to talk. I'm just lazy."

Next morning, Ariel's spirits soared as sunbeams illuminated the dust motes floating in front of the uncurtained window. Little blond Yacy looked unbearably innocent curled in sleep on the sofa pillows that lay by a monstrous oak armoire carved all over with fruits and griffins.

Perhaps the strange child would survive her past and unlikely present after all.

But then he recalled the conversation of the previous evening. Were she and Kuaray, barely ten years of age, really experimenting with bomb-making? Did Luz and Ethan know, or did they have too much on their minds to care? Ariel wondered if he should bring it up, sooner rather than later.

***

Ariel's mission that morning was to prepare the violin for Aleta, and he couldn't wait for the moment when he would present it to her. He dressed, then wrapped the serendipitous Cherokee quilt around the battered and broken case. His destination was **Varkonyi Violons** on Ontario Street where he planned to buy a new case and plenty of extra strings, get an appraisal, and have it adjusted. Then he had an idea. Perhaps he should bring Yacy along to test the violin after it was shipshape.

The two started out with Yacy doubling the distance by zigzagging back and forth while simultaneously explaining the sights.

"Here's the mountain—it's so huge it's fit for a king. Mont-réal, get it?" She reached her arms wide and high above her head as a visual demonstration. "And here's the bus stop to Ethan's college. And look. You can see the World's Fair from here. Will you take me?"

Ariel was about to say that he wouldn't be staying long enough when Yacy nearly tripped him. Standing on the toes of his hiking boots, she pointed her finger at the city below.

"Do you like the skyscrapers? I don't, they're ugly and square and they don't really scrape the sky. Can we walk across the Jacques Cartier Bridge someday? Can you speak French?"

After about twenty minutes Ariel was thankful for his mountaineering skills. Yacy kept the pace of a cross-country competitor even while using up half her breath in non-stop chatter.

He thought to himself, Has anyone ever taken the time to listen to this poor child?

Just before they reached downtown, Yacy sank dramatically to the sidewalk, clutching her stomach. "I'm starving, Stepdaddy Sequoyah. Buy me an ice cream?"

Once they entered the violin shop, Yacy hid behind Ariel as if she were three years old. And when the adjustments were completed, she refused to play.

She stared down at her feet, whispering, "Kuaray won't let me touch our violin, Stepdaddy Sequoyah, he says it's only for him. He says it's 'cause I sound like fingernails on a blackboard and I can't jig very good at the same time."

She wrinkled up her nose. "It sounds kinda rotten anyway. Stepmama Luz bought it at the flea market."

Ariel noticed that the ends of Yarcy's dress sash had been dragging on the parquet floor. Kneeling down to match Yacy's height, he tied it into a big loopy bow before laying his hands gently on her shoulders.

"Yacy, there's a song I simply adore, and I heard you play it once on the Trail … well, somewhere. It's called *Fare Thee Well*, you know, *Ah Perdona* by Mozart. Can you play it now, not for them, just for me?"

Suddenly Yacy gave him a melting smile that lit up the entire room and began to play with sure fingers and a sweeping bow. The Hungarian shop owner Mr. Varkonyi and his three apprenticed sons gathered one-by-one in the showroom. The octogenarian in the long royal-blue work apron showed his approval by kissing Yacy on the top of her head.

He murmured, *"Te úgy játszol, mint egy angyal!* You play like an angel!"

Yacy turned a vivid red as tears of both delight and embarrassment glittered in her eyes. The moment was magical, and Ariel promised himself that one day he would purchase a good violin just for her.

***

In the afternoon Ethan invited Ariel into his study, a narrow room near the back of the flat that barely fit his cluttered desk and overflowing floor-to-ceiling bookcase. A few other odd furnishings were incongruously scattered here and there, but the comfortable old Victorian sofa and the Turkish rug had apparently not made the move. Ariel felt a momentary stab of homesickness for the derelict Little Mexico apartment where he'd held Svnoyi tight to his chest for her first eight months.

Ethan moved a stack of hefty library books from a green painted chair to an end table before thrusting it in front of his scarred oak desk. The chair had a rush seat that spewed broken cane and even though Ariel sat down gingerly, the aged frame groaned. Ethan took a seat behind his desk, relieved that it created a broad barrier between the two of them. Without Luz and the children serving as buffers, the very air hung thick with mistrust.

It was caused by the entry Ariel had written in his diary about the illicit afternoon he'd spent with Aleta. The lines were stamped in Ethan's memory; he had reread them often enough. *In early October we hiked to the end of the Cove Crest Trail where there is a redwood grove. The attraction we felt for each other was always intense. We lay close all afternoon under the trees.*

Ethan frowned and sighed before looking Ariel in the eye. "Well, Ari …." His voice died out, and there was another uncomfortable pause.

Finally, Ariel hazarded, "If you're worried about what I wrote in the diary—"

Ethan interrupted, "Damned right. Genius deduction."

Ariel wondered to himself if his real motive for bringing it up hadn't been to wound Ethan for not taking him seriously, but he tried to put the best face on it.

"I probably shouldn't have written it. But I wanted you to know what happened and how I cared for both of you. I was trying to look after her and I—"

Ethan turned beet-red. He banged a fist on the desk, causing the reams of paper that made up his dissertation to cascade into Ariel's lap.

"Don't even try to finish that sentence 'cause you know it'll end up sounding like a pile of steaming horseshit. What you wrote was a smart way of letting your buddy Ethan know that you fucked—"

Ariel leaped to his feet, the precious dissertation scattering. He stabbed his forefinger at Ethan, "You want the truth? Here it is. I figured, who gives a shit, I sure don't. I'll be dead when he reads it!"

Ethan sprang up from his desk chair, shaking. "You are one insensitive prick, you know that? You think I didn't know something was going on? You forget that I shared feelings with her back then. Even now I sometimes get a jolt when you two do it."

He ran his fingers through his hair, grimacing. "So here I am, taking this chemistry test, and *wham* goes an explosion in the back of my brain. I know she's with *someone*. And it isn't me."

He rushed Ariel, fists at the ready, but collided with the coffee table that cast off its piles of books in a massive avalanche. He knelt to rub his injured shins muttering curses, his fury mushrooming.

"Goddammit, Fuck, how many fathers do those nutty brats have? You, me? *They* say the Man in the Moon." Ariel extended a hand to help Ethan to his feet, but he batted it away in disgust and staggered upright, glaring.

"First she doesn't tell me she's pregnant. Then comes the morning sickness. Poor little Aleta, *so misunderstood*. And I have to just swallow what I know and forgive and forget."

He added coldly, "I should kill you."

Even Ariel knew his response sounded pathetic. "If you hadn't thrown her out of your room every night, Mr. Grade-grubber, we wouldn't have gotten to know each other. Besides, I always knew she was your girlfriend—"

Ethan interrupted, flailing his arms. "Who are you calling Grade-grubber, you jerk? It's not like you gave a flying fuck about school."

His legs stamped inexorably in Ariel's direction as every twinge in his hurt shins made him angrier. Luckily, he barged into an art deco floor lamp, which distracted him from the intended physical attack that he would surely have regretted.

He extricated himself from the shade, his voice taunting. "Let me think. How many times did you have to repeat English 101? Or Early Modern European History? If it weren't for that Minority Assistance Scholarship which some do-gooder so graciously paid over and over, you'd have been out on your ass."

He was shouting now, "Until my mother, *my mother, punched* some kind of inspiration button located in your—" He completed his discourse by shaking his middle finger directly into Ariel's face.

Adrenaline flooded Ariel's stomach. Flexing his muscular arms and tightening his fists, he backed Ethan into the bookcase with a resounding thump, which let loose a hailstorm of green *Physical Review* magazines. During the commotion, the rush-bottomed chair lost the battle with gravity, smacking the hardwood floor. But Ariel knew just how much damage he could inflict and stopped short of slamming a fist into his cowering opponent.

Instead, he bellowed, tears lurking behind his rage. "You should hear yourself, you racist. Do you want to know how you treated me? Like this. 'Nice big, ugly Fuck, with the funny brown skin. Borrow his stuff and never return it. Even his money. Insult him behind his back. Call him slow, even stupid. He can take it, he'll bounce back, in—*in humble adoration.*'"

Ariel turned abruptly toward the window clenching and unclenching his fists as he pretended to admire the backyard's crabgrass and struggling hydrangeas.

He mumbled through a choked throat more to himself than to Ethan, "'He's just a *dumb Indian*, so he's not sensitive like you and me. God forbid he should be attracted to our women, or touch them, or worse, *fall in love.*'"

The door flew open, the oval brass knob ramming the wall. A great hunk of loose plaster fell to the floor, bringing down strips of tattered wallpaper with it. Luz entered with arms outspread like an avenging angel, her voice chilly and tight with indignation.

"Holy Mother of God, am I the only adult left?" She surveyed the scattered papers, fallen books, and downed lamp and chair. At the same time, she took in her husband making himself small against the towering shelves and her friend staring resolutely out the window to keep from breaking down.

"Why do I bother reading minds when I can hear you yelling and throwing furniture all the way from the kitchen?"

She turned on Ethan first, both hands on her hips. "How does *that woman* still manage to create so much drama?" Tears flooded her eyes, which she brushed away angrily. "I thought you resolved the Aleta question about the time you said 'I do' to me, Ethan — *to me.*"

She moved on to Ariel and asked him directly into his brain without a hint of pity, *What's with the "dumb Indian" stuff? When do you start liking yourself?*

Then she spoke to both of them. "Instead of fighting over who's Daddy, why not put your heads together and ponder how to keep those hell-raisers out of the slammer?"

Luz's homily proved effective. A heavy silence overtook the room as neither man dared speak.

***

It was broken by the sudden crack of an explosion. Seconds later, a bushy gray and white cat's tail, freed forever from its owner's fluffy backside, sailed past the window and landed on a hydrangea bush. Nor was there much left of the backside, or any other part belonging to a cat.

Chapter 15 The Loon Dynasty

Dinner that night was a somber affair, indeed funereal. If Lucy's saucer eyes had been made like Svnoyi's, she would have wept torrents of crystalline tears. Instead, she sat in Ethan's lap with her face buried in his chest, her fair ringlets bouncing as she sighed into his pectorals.

Both Ariel and Luz understood perfectly that Lucy had lost her closest companion and confidante from whom she had learned an intimate cat-language—Maltese. In fact, Tybalt and Lucy had argued only once during their friendship, over the cat's wanton, and apparently uncontrollable, slaughter of songbirds.

Oscar's comprehension of Lucy's grief went a step further. He had seen Tybalt's soul leave his dispersed body to navigate the stygian depths.

Yacy arrived late after everyone but Lucy had started eating spaghetti bolognese in subdued silence. The look on Yacy's face easily revealed what she was thinking, and her torment went straight to Ariel's heart. For starters, she wanted to be held like Lucy. And according to her own estimation of the family, that would never happen in a million years.

I can see inside people as easy as Luz can, and I know she doesn't like me 'cause I'm not hers but Ethan and Aleta's kid, and Ethan doesn't like me 'cause he's not sure I'm his kid at all.

Ariel surprised the others by pulling the little girl onto his lap where she created a fair imitation of Lucy's grieving, right down to the head in the pectorals. For the rest of his visit, Ariel and Yacy remained close, which both baffled Ethan and made him jealous.

Shit, even if she is my kid, I don't feel a thing for her. And I sure wish those two Looney-Tune twins weren't peas in a pod, close as thieves. The family pet just blew sky-high for Jesus' sake, and Ari feels sorry for her?

Kuaray had the good grace not to show up for dinner. In fact, he was no longer in the flat, but downtown at the trendy Place Jacques-Cartier earning fast money by sweetening the air with tunes played on the priceless Pressenda violin—the new case open to receive coins and bills.

***

After all the children, except the absent Kuaray, had been put to bed, Ethan and Ariel holed up in the study, joined by a watchful Luz. The afternoon's vicious fight was essentially over but far from forgotten. As long as Luz placed herself between the two men, they earnestly tried to repair the damage done. To Yacy's credit, the place was spotless. In an effort to make amends for Tybalt's demise, she had slipped in just before bed and cleaned it up by object rotation, nursery-school style.

Ethan started off with an attempt at humor. "Ari, unless you'd like the doubtful honor, let's hold the Man in the Moon responsible for the twins' conception."

Ariel replied by changing the subject. "Which would you rather discuss first, keeping them out of the slammer as Luz suggested, or what I really came here to talk about in the first place?"

Luz had a ready answer. "You can kill two birds with one stone, and I sure hope Lucy didn't hear me say that. If you want to keep Kuaray out of trouble, and he's the leader of the pack, I'm afraid, divert him. Put him to work on the time machine, Ethan."

She sent her husband a winning smile that would melt the hardest heart. "I've been listening in on Oscar and Svnoyi for years now, and I know we all have to make the trip even if the Moon People haven't agreed on the passenger list. It's the only answer." She winked at him as she turned to leave. "Oh, I'll leave you two now to work out the details. Don't disappoint me, Ethan, or I won't keep you warm tonight."

Ethan looked lost. "I don't know what the hell she's talking about. What trip, what time machine? So far it sounds downright dubious scientifically."

Ariel laughed gently at his confusion. "Dubious? Without a doubt, but that's where you come in. I'll explain everything."

Ethan replied with forced joviality, "Shit, Ari, if I'd known you had a mysterious scientific project up your sleeve, we could have avoided that fight. It upsets me every time I think how ugly it got."

Ariel thrust his palms upward and shrugged. "No, it had to happen. Aleta is just so beautiful. Men lose their minds over her. You did. I did, and I still do every time I look at her." He sighed. "She's a bit of a mess, though. She was sent by the Moon People to the worst pits of hell, she had to raise Yacy and Kuaray alone, and she almost died twice. I could go on and on."

With the words barely out of his mouth, Ariel wished he could take them back; the very mention of Aleta had destroyed the new mood so carefully established by Luz. Oppressed by the sudden silence, he shifted his weight on the abominably uncomfortable green rush chair. Ethan squirmed behind his ugly oak desk, his forehead drawn into a frown.

Ethan couldn't help what issued next from his mouth. "I have to ask. I keep thinking about you and Aleta under those redwood trees. Did you really do it … I mean, did you two *go all the way?*"

Ariel stared at Ethan, his jaw hanging. "Jesus, Ethan, you sound like you're still in high school. No answer will make you happy one way or the other, *and you happen to be talking about me and my wife.* So could you just drop it?"

He paused, his face darkening like a thundercloud. "On second thought, fuck this. I'm leaving."

He pushed the chair backward, the spindly legs scraping against the hardwood floor. Once again, it teetered and fell.

Something about the crash made Ariel lose the control that usually kept him out of other people's minds. Seething with anger, he leaned across the desk, thrusting his face aggressively close to Ethan's. He no longer cared if he invaded the head of his rival from long ago and what he found in there explained a lot, unfortunately.

The inner Ethan gripped his skull as burning white-hot spikes jack-hammered oozing holes right through his brain. And even now after years and years, Fuck's dark skin, coupled with his massive mental and physical maleness penetrated all the way through Aleta's body from her vagina into her brain. She lay in spread-eagled abandon with convulsing limbs as she gibbered and moaned. In this state, she could hardly distinguish between pleasure and pain.

So was this the tortuous jealousy that had plagued Ethan ever since he'd read the diary? No, even before that, ever since they'd met at Slime's? Was this the Fuck that Ethan saw, huge, virile, and different?

Ariel was horrified but not surprised. He put his hands over his eyes while sucking in great gulps of the poisoned air.

He blurted, "Ethan, *Ethan!* This is how you see me? This is what jealousy has done to you, how you think I have sex? How you see my people just because we're not white like you?"

His voice grew strident. "God, it hurts, because I know you're reacting like almost everyone else, *but you have to make yourself stop.*"

Ethan started trembling. He closed his eyes tight as tears leaked out, rolling down his cheeks. He laid his head on the desk sobbing, "I can't, I can't, because I really, *really* want to kill you."

Ariel moved around the desk to Ethan's side, his voice gentle. "Ethan, you know killing me won't solve anything. Besides, from what I can see, the person you're killing is yourself. Instead, why not say, 'I want to get over this.'"

Ethan snuffled for a while before whispering almost inaudibly, "Okey-dokey, I'm trying." He raised his head high enough to stare down at his slide rule and compass. "All right, I want to."

Ariel replied sternly, "Not good enough."

Ethan spoke louder through tense lips, "Yes. I want to get over this, I really want to."

Ariel relaxed. "Okay, good enough for now. It won't happen in a day. But please, please, try to see my people differently, even if not me."

He moved back to his side of the desk and sat down gingerly on the uprighted chair. "How do you think hateful eyes and sneers feel drilling right into your back? Or insults thrown at your face? In Poland, your mother knew. Anywhere, in small towns and even in big cities, I get it every day."

He went on, softly. "We've all been jealous, especially when it comes to … to sex. But keep race out of it."

Ethan wiped his nose on his sleeve. Then he raked his fingers through his rumpled hair to flatten it. At the same time, he fervently hoped that his churning stomach would shut up and settle down.

Ariel watched Ethan. In the center of his friend's head, he thought he could see those white-hot spikes lift half way up, which was, at least, a start, and he certainly could hear Luz in the back bedroom sigh with tearful relief. Ariel felt himself reaching out to her in sympathy. How dreadful the past eight years must have been watching Ethan's jealous hatred and not being able to do a thing about it.

Ariel clapped Ethan on the shoulder. "Okay, man, get two beers, and we'll start in on the dubious scientific mystery."

As Ethan headed for the kitchen, Ariel stopped him. "Or better yet, is there a park close by where we can talk, preferably with a comfortable bench?"

***

As twilight fell, Ethan and Ariel walked along Avenue Desrochers searching for a neighborhood park. They found one, a tiny sliver of green sandwiched between a garage and a bakery. No comfortable bench beckoned, but it had possibilities; a refreshing breeze carried the combined scent of rain, mock orange, and baking bread as it rustled the surrounding elms' sodden leaves. A flat boulder at the back of the park's sparse lawn offered them a place to sit. Ethan and Ariel found two reasonable spots on its gritty surface and settled down under the overhanging juniper bushes. Irritating spiny branches fell in their faces, but just in time, the thatched canopy above partially protected them from a sudden, thumping downpour.

Neither man spoke. Ethan still felt deeply humiliated, and Ariel knew that he had unfairly probed Ethan's inner thoughts.

He mused, *Sometimes I hate this power. If I can't control where my mind goes, how can I use it wisely?*

He remarked carefully, "You must know something about the Moon People, at least you know that they took Aleta away when we were at Santa Margarita, and of course you've overheard what the twins think."

To lighten their spirits, Ethan replied overeagerly, waving his hands. "My Lord, yes. I know way too much about the Moon People, and I ask you, Ari, do you think being a father is always fun?"

Ariel frowned. He hadn't a clue just where the conversation was going.

"Your Svnoyi and Oscar are like two old biddies in housecoats and curlers gossiping over the back fence. In case you didn't know, your little girl first picks your brain, then broadcasts the more interesting bits to my stepson."

Ariel did know that, and it had never made him happy.

Ethan continued, "We get a complete synopsis at the dinner table every evening. Of course, Oscar's in competition with Lucy, our animal lover, complaining about the food. Listening to Kuaray hurl death threats at Yacy and everyone else is almost preferable."

Ariel was relieved not to start from scratch, although he was uncomfortable that his daughter dispensed his private thoughts so freely. "Well, I guess I don't have to deliver a lecture, then. What kind of things do you know?"

Ethan laughed. "I know they named themselves after the Loch Ness monster and Big Foot from the wild forests. I know everything about the inside of that tacky Moon, also known as an orbiting fallout shelter. I know about the portable toilet and the smelly beds, about Sasquatch's crappy spelling, Nessie's horrible teeth, the Sugar Smacks—"

Ariel broke in, "Those are details. Do you know what they're up to?"

Ethan nodded. "I have a pretty good idea how they operate, and it stinks. Sad to say, the main gist is, these old folks, and I mean *old*, are so damned pissy that they want to kill just about everybody. That is, everybody except their pet, Kuaray.

"And through some kind of mental coercion, they recruited us for a weird, uh, *breeding experiment* that is actually working."

He forced a laugh. "It produced our misfit kids. I love Oscar and Lucy with all my heart, but can you picture them in grade school? Oscar would tell little Janey with the pigtails that he talks to her dead grandmother, and Lucy would link minds with the pet hamster. Kuaray and Yacy … better not to think about it."

Both of them sat silently as a siren pierced the stillness of the humid evening air. When the wailing finally stopped, Ariel asked cautiously, "Ethan, you do know that I was inside their Moon, don't you?"

Ethan nodded. As hard as it was for him to picture Ariel's mind separated from his body, he'd gotten a pretty clear idea from Svnoyi's conversations with Oscar.

"Well then, I have to tell you what I saw from their window." But going on was harder than Ariel had anticipated, and he shivered in spite of the stifling heat that hadn't abated with the downpour.

He thought, God, how can I tell this? He took a deep breath.

"In the twenty-first century, the Moon People saw humanity destroy itself in the final world war. When I saw what was left of the earth—"

He stopped abruptly, for it was his turn to cry and he surprised himself because he hadn't felt it coming.

He struggled to go on. "You ... you have to believe me. These huge craters—"

Ethan put an arm around Ariel's shoulders, his voice suddenly compassionate. "Okay, you don't have to explain. Listen, I do believe you, and I think I know how you feel. It's not something you see every day."

Ariel stood up and slogged to the opposite end of the park and back again to regain his control as the mud between the clumps of grass slurped beneath his boots.

Wringing his hands, he began a halting explanation, "That's why ... that's why the Moon People recruited us because we're one of the last generations before *it* happened. And here's the part that concerns our families ...." He hastily wiped the sweat and tears off his face with his sleeve. "They have a plan to restore the human population in the far, far future after the earth's atmosphere and surviving plant and animal species have made some kind of recovery. They want us to go there by moving far enough ahead in time to start over in a pristine world. Maybe it won't work."

Ethan leaped up. "*Maybe it won't work*? How about maybe we'll all end up dead. Besides, why us? There are millions of people they could have picked."

Ariel shook his head. "Unfortunately, that's not true. The Moon People found us because we are highly telepathic, just like they are. Besides, there aren't that many of us."

Ethan replied grumpily, "Hasn't it occurred to you that their plan isn't just about saving mankind? They're setting up the Loon Dynasty run by Little Lord Kuaray. They're preparing him right now because they can't rule themselves. They have to stay behind because their feeble little Moon can't go the distance—"

Ariel interrupted, sensing Ethan's resentment over being less gifted than the others. "Don't be bitter, Ethan. What we can do is pretty useless, actually. They chose you for a very specific reason—your scientific genius. They know you're the best … no, the *only* person to design our ship."

After a long pause Ethan crowed, "At last it all comes together. I've been waiting for this moment of revelation to sum up my worth: *the trip and the ship.* Invent the damn thing. Travel in time millions of years into the future and establish the Loon Dynasty. Is that all? I guess I better buckle down and apply for a post-doc in physics and engineering."

Then, even though he had sounded cynical at first, his tone suddenly changed to rapture. "You know what, Ari, there won't be a Nobel Prize committee to greet us where we're going. But *just imagine* science like that actually working."

As they walked home through a new cloudburst, Ariel cleared his throat. "I'm flying out before dawn tomorrow, so this is it, for now. You … you mean a lot to me, you know." He shook Ethan's hand too formally, then gave him a quick hug. "For Luz and the kids."

He added sadly, "I know we have to make the trip like Luz said. And *if* you can get Kuaray to help with the drive for the time machine, whatever that's going to be like, he might feel like he's part of the family."

Ethan nodded. "It won't be easy. I'm no mind reader like you, but I think Kuaray, with lots of help from Yacy, blew up the cat. They put the explosive together and then one of them fed it to the poor dumb beast, and *whamo.* Kuaray detonated it with his thoughts."

Ariel bowed his head in tribute to the unfortunate victim. "Poor Tybalt. We took a snooze together only the day before."

***

The Polish airliner out of Moscow rose trembling and groaning in a clumsy takeoff. Ariel slumped down into his seat's seedy upholstery, welcoming the flight to Kraków, the last leg of his long journey home. He smiled, stretching his tired limbs as far as they would go beneath the seat in front of him.

His easeful pleasure was short-lived. He jerked one leg back again, grimacing with painful surprise. The imp straight out of his vision grasped his shin with wiry fingers, its razor-sharp nails digging into his flesh. The creature emerged from under the seat, snake-like and soot-blackened, to plop down beside him.

"Yacy, you scared me half to death."

The merciless child clamped a grimy hand over his mouth. "Shut up and give me the violin. Now."

"Mumpf, mumpf." Ariel emitted smothered laughter through her fingers before gasping, "Is this a Wild West stick-up?"

At that moment he heard a rabbit scream in his brain for the second time in his life. It was Svnoyi's most desperate warning cry. *Give it to her, Daddy.*

Ariel hastily thrust the instrument, lucky survivor of extensive probes during customs, into Yacy's outstretched arms.

With the delicacy of an expert surgeon, Yacy wormed her slim fingers into an f-hole. Letting loose a soft whoop of victory, she extracted a miniature explosive that had been glued just within reach. Then, with her sharp young teeth, she severed the red hot-wire. She completed the operation by swallowing the evidence.

Yacy grinned like a Cheshire Cat. "Daddy Sequoyah, you could be my daddy. I'm not deaf, you know, I heard Ethan an' you duking it out in the study. Kuaray woulda crashed the plane ten minutes from now."

She stuck out her tongue. "The farty old Moon People wanted you dead for playing Christmas Ghost that time in their Moon, an' Nessie told Kuaray to explode the bomb with his mind."

Such relief surged through Ariel that he remained silent. He thought, A plane crash killing maybe 100 people. 'Don't let that fiddle bite your ear' was some namby-pamby euphemism.

Then he sat up straight. *Hearing it in my own vision is one thing. But how the hell did Mohe know?*

At last, he accepted with reluctance a most unwelcome thought. *I'm no sleuth, but most likely Yacy glued the explosive inside the front of the violin. And she helped to blow up Tybalt. Was that experiment a practice run for the big one?*

The sooty imp grew impatient. "You ain't gonna ask me *nothing?* I rode in a wheel well all the way from Montreal. An' I have a passport."

She pulled a crumpled rectangle from the elastic band of her underwear. Ariel smiled at the crude forgery, but when he imagined Yacy hunched over her artwork preparing her secret means of escape, he grew serious.

"Yacy, first of all, you should say, *'Aren't* you going to ask me *anything.'* And I *am* going to ask you something. Why did you help Kuaray do such horrible things? Because I know you helped him. You said so the night you hid out in my room."

The little girl seemed to deflate like a punctured balloon. "Daddy Sequoyah, maybe you won't believe me, but Kuaray made me. He said if I stopped helping, he'd do much worser things than touching. He said he'd make me *marry* him."

An inebriated stewardess weaved her way down the aisle, grasping at the rows of empty seat backs and the occasional passenger's arm.

Ariel panicked. "Hurry, dear. Go wash up and turn your dress wrong-side-out to the clean side. And don't leave mud all over the sink."

Yacy registered both amazement and delight. "You called me *dear*?"

Ariel sighed, but not from distress. *Won't the others be surprised? I seem to have gained a daughter.*

Chapter 16 Yacy

The sun had long since disappeared from all but the highest mountain peaks. But Yacy made little forward progress, stalling more and more frequently during the last half mile of the mountain trail between Stary Smokovec and Jaroslav's cabin. Ariel continued to urge her on with fatherly patience, even turning her gently by the shoulders to show her the valley below, now obscured by forbidding purple shadows.

Just then Yacy made a grab for her hair as a chill evening breeze whipped it around her head in a swirl of tangles. She was not deterred; indeed, her artful delays increased in frequency and variety. First, she lingered for a good five minutes, enraptured by a perfectly conical pine tree. Then she picked up a stone to explore every millimeter of its lichen-encrusted surface. Finally, she stooped to sniff an entire row of unassuming mountain daisies that had already closed their narrow petals for the night.

Ariel stared anxiously at the sun's departing rays that had left a mere afterglow along the rim of the mountain crests. He surmised rightly that there was much more on Yacy's mind than simple appreciation for the High Tatras' natural wonders.

"Yacy, are you tired?"

She shook her head with conviction, but then changed her mind, exclaiming, "Yes, yes, Daddy Sequoyah, I'm just so, so tired. Can we stop for a little while?"

Ariel knelt on one knee to look her straight in the eye. "Something's up, Yacy. You're worried about meeting the new people, aren't you?" He rested his hands on her shoulders. "Jaroslav's big and nice like a teddy-bear, and Anichka is a real gypsy. Svnoyi is just your age, and Phoenix can make anything grow, even delicious strawberries—"

Yacy interrupted him in a pet. "I'm *never* gonna tell you what's wrong, so don't bother to ask."

She whirled around and started running down the trail as Ariel sprang up, mumbling imprecations under his breath about temperamental little girls.

Suddenly he had an inspiration. He bellowed at the top of his lungs after her receding figure, "I know your mother will be so surprised and happy to see her pretty little Yacy all grown up."

Yacy stopped in her tracks and turned in a fury, stomping her foot. "Daddy Sequoyah, don't *ever* talk about my mother 'cause I wish she was dead. You wanna know why? *She left me on the Trail of Tears.*" As an afterthought, she made a last jab. "An' I don't care if she's your wife. I *hate* her."

She zoomed down the trail at breakneck speed, sliding precariously on the loose stones as Ariel rushed after her. The violin and suitcase flapped behind him as he clutched them in sweaty hands.

He called out as he went, "No, dear, it was me—*me!* Aleta was too sick to know what was happening."

Yacy turned once more, this time in shock. "But Daddy Sequoyah, you wasn't even there."

Ariel came to a halt in front of her, panting from the exertion. "Believe me, Yacy, I was, even if you couldn't see me. And I left you and Kuaray behind. I kind of had to."

The blunt horror of that truth swept over Yacy as her mouth fell into an "O." Then, rubbing her eyes with her grubby fists, she sank down in the middle of the trail weeping for the first time since Ariel had known her. His heart melted, for he had no idea that she *could* cry, since the other children, with the exception of Svnoyi, seemed incapable of shedding tears from their saucer eyes.

She mumbled, "Sometimes people do terrible mean things. Me an' Kuaray almost blew you up on the airplane, so I guess you and me are about even doing what's awfullest. Daddy Sequoyah, can we jus' hold hands now 'n say we're so, so sorry about everything?"

Ariel knelt down on the sharp stones to take her in his arms. No words were exchanged, for sometimes words simply aren't necessary.

At that moment Jaroslav rounded the bend, his lantern illuminating the blackness around him. To Ariel, the scene seemed eerily familiar, an unwanted reminder of his shameful treatment of little Svnoyi that had required Jaroslav's lightning-quick rescue.

The seasoned ranger put down the lantern before clasping his dear friend in a breath-stopping bear hug. But his voice was stern.

"My best forester still not know first rule of mountain so I make rescue *again?* Not ever walk trail in the night."

Then Jaroslav swept Yacy into his capable arms as he began the ascent towards home, each measured step making a gritty crunch against the stones. He whispered in her ear, "We see you on airplane, so all persons wait for our big girl, Yacy. Anichka, Svnoyi, and Phoenix bake *huge* cake, and Mama Aleta cry all day long she is so happy."

***

The first chance he got, Ariel whisked Aleta off to the annex, the only truly private place in the whole house. When he slipped the violin into her waiting arms, she clasped it to her heart both laughing and crying.

The pair could not refrain from giving each other deep kisses and impassioned touches all over their eager bodies, although the timing couldn't have been worse. Yacy's party was about to start in the next room, and their absence had already been noticed by everyone. Even Svnoyi, who always looked out for her father's happiness, couldn't think up a single excuse to cover for them. They tried to ignore the rising din, but the crescendo punctuated by whoops of laughter ended their tryst. Ariel sighed in defeat.

But then he noticed that Aleta's dress was not hanging quite right in the front and he remembered feeling something oddly rounded where he'd expected to find her slender waist.

Aleta rubbed her belly, blushing. "It's true, my love, and miracle of miracles. Anichka's pregnant, too." Her eyes crinkled with laughter. "You'll be happy to know even *she* doesn't think God is totally responsible."

The flushed lovers emerged from the annex demurely holding hands and stepped into a virtual fairyland. The kitchen table had been pulled into the main room and covered with Anichka's best starched linen cloth. Someone had hung coiled paper streamers across the ceiling and run aromatic pine boughs along the mantel of the big fireplace and over the frame of the front door. Candles twinkled everywhere, illuminating the faces of the excited children and adults encircling Yacy.

But she huddled against the wall, utterly petrified. So Svnoyi and Phoenix took her hands, leading her ceremoniously to Jaroslav's big armchair at the head of the table as the *pater familias* accompanied the procession by whistling a few bars of Verdi's *Triumphal March* from *Aida.* Suddenly the focal point of an appreciative throng, the beaming child looked both painfully shy and absolutely radiant as unexpected tears gathered in her eyes.

Apparently, Yacy had been given a scrub-down with homemade soap followed by a bubble bath in the big kitchen tub because her translucent skin shone. This bracing treatment had been followed by a manicure and a thorough dousing with Anichka's favorite perfume. Svnoyi had loaned her new friend her very best dress for this most special occasion—a sparkling neon-pink confection covered with tulle netting and an abundance of sequins. To complete the perfect princess look, Yacy's team of dressers had precariously stacked her squeaky-clean hair high on her head and secured it with flowing silvery ribbons and a sparkling rhinestone tiara. The cake had her name written on it in pink icing, and, to top off the evening, she and Svnoyi were allowed two sips of champagne each.

Aleta spent the entire party clutching Ariel's hand and staring in wonder at her willowy daughter in her unaccustomed finery. To the astounded and trembling mother, she looked like a newly opened flower covered with fresh dew. The last time Aleta had received any knowledge of Yacy's whereabouts, an army private had visited her in the sick wagon on the Trail of Tears. Then he'd taken her violin away to pay for the twins' upkeep since the plump little monsters who jigged manically to entertain the troops had outgrown their clothes. No doubt they had stolen the instrument back from the private before it was sold, or she wouldn't have it now.

The suddenly penitent mother had never meant to abandon her children. In fact, she had loved and cared for them in terrible circumstances for as long as she was physically able. But she had to admit the truth, however reluctantly. Ever since life with her Sequoyah had begun in the High Tatras, she had not missed them at all, except momentarily when Svnoyi had mentioned their sudden ejection from the Trail of Tears.

Looking at Yacy now, she was overcome with the fragile hope that she could nurture once again the lone twin so providentially returned to her. During the stolen time alone with Ariel before the party, he'd said enough about his Montreal visit and the plane trip home to reveal that her daughter was not growing up in a promising direction. She wondered if it was too late to change that.

The first opportunity to be alone with Yacy came when Svnoyi and Phoenix were busy dismantling the party's flammable pine boughs and streamers. Yacy was by herself in the annex, and Aleta overheard a varied repertory of sophisticated curses coming through the door. She pushed it open timidly to find the poor girl ensnared in the complicated neon-pink dress with her hair caught in the zipper. Aleta extricated her daughter from the trap while murmuring with unusual inner courage how much she loved her. Yacy eyed Aleta suspiciously but did not refuse the lacy pink nightgown scented with lavender that Aleta had brought from her own dresser.

***

After the children had been put to bed, the adults returned to the main room to make convivial small talk that filled in the gaps for Ariel after his long absence. Any serious discussion of his trips to Tahlequah and Montreal would come at a later date. Then, at precisely 9:00 p.m. on this particular Tuesday evening, they sat cross-legged on bearskins in a semi-circle in front of a newly kindled fire. Anichka passed around cups of rich hot chocolate, mainly to serve as hand-warmers for warding off the high-altitude chill. The friendly gathering had just turned into a formal weekly meeting, and as always, Jaroslav served as chair, the others deferring to his position as head-of-household. This traditional hierarchy had always worked in the past and was not about to change. Also from long habit, the speakers lowered their voices, even though they knew that unless the little clairvoyants in the annex were sleeping soundly, they would catch every word.

First Jaroslav turned to Ariel. "Yacy look sweet, but she dangerous girl. You swear she okay?"

Ariel considered before replying. "Yes, I'm sure of it. We have an understanding."

Jaroslav frowned. "All that work fine if you love her like daughter. She think you are father."

"Jaroslav, I'll be honest. Of course I love her, but I just don't know about this paternity thing." He shifted his gaze uneasily, wringing his nervous hands. An unnatural silence lasted seemingly for hours as everyone noticed that Aleta's eyes were glued to the utterly fascinating bubbles on the surface of her hot chocolate.

Ariel struggled on with his long withheld confession. "Aleta and me, it was just once."

Anichka tried to keep a straight face as Jaroslav cleared his throat. He spoke with absolute authority. "Well, my son, here in mountain, you are father. This keep us safe."

Then with Jaroslav's permission, Anichka spoke. "I bring Aleta's new baby into world, but how I bring my baby?"

At that moment Svnoyi appeared, her bare feet squeaking on the waxed floor. She sat down uninvited in the very center of the group as if the adults had been expecting her all along. Seemingly oblivious to the four frowns that greeted her, she placed a monstrous medical book from the Stary Smokovec Public Library on her nightgown-clad knees, the explicitly illustrated volume already opened to the chapter on childbirth.

She smiled beseechingly. "I can help you, Jaroslav. I bet I already know more than almost anyone about obstetrics, and Petr the veterinarian said I could help deliver Farmer Michal's foals. I've always wanted to be a doctor, and—"

Jaroslav peered at her under his bushy eyebrows. "Okay, Svnoyi, but until baby, you help at Stary Smokovec clinic. That mean you clean up anything and everything."

Svnoyi leaped up to embrace and kiss Jaroslav before sitting down again in the same centrally located spot. She obviously had no intention of leaving. Jaroslav sighed. He was quite familiar with this pattern because it had happened at almost every meeting for as long as he could remember. He nodded to Anichka who bustled into the kitchen, returning with a cup of steaming hot chocolate for the inquisitive and thoroughly practical child.

Openmouthed, Ariel stared at Anichka's distinctive waddle of pregnancy, noticing for the first time that she was already popping out of her skirt and blouse in several strategic directions.

Jaroslav called the meeting to order once more. "Now we talk about building new annex for big new family."

Yacy and Phoenix made a furtive entrance, creeping on tiptoe to the back of the semi-circle.

Svnoyi bounced up to whisper in her father's ear, "Don't worry, Daddy, they didn't hear *you-know-what*. I woke them up just now because they want to help with the new bedrooms."

She turned to Jaroslav and the others. "I already drew real plans on graph paper following *all* the building codes, and I know about how to construct Cherokee log houses. Yacy can float the logs just above the ground with her mind, and Phoenix can help, too. Remember the nice big doghouse he built? Too bad Barkus died before he finished it."

Jaroslav tried to smother a laugh as the newcomers looked at Anichka expectantly. She smiled indulgently as she brought two fresh cups of hot chocolate from the kitchen.

But at the end of the meeting, Jaroslav glanced around the assembly, his face drawn with worry. "I not expect all big and little people, but good thing everyone here."

He turned to Anichka. "Maybe you tell, you hear bad things on radio every day."

Anichka turned pink with pleasure because she was not often consulted about serious matters at the meetings. She stood up and moved to the front of the gathering, her swelling body outlined by the crackling fire behind her. But a sudden stab of fear crossed her face that said as much as her words.

"Politics not good now, the *Komunistická* not good. People disappear. It make me remember old days and I cry."

She stopped, weighing her next thoughts before going on. "I think maybe police come soon. They ask many questions, so you make good answers, have right papers."

***

Just before midnight, Ariel disobeyed Jaroslav's first rule of mountaineering for the second time in one day. But it didn't matter since the moon shone so brightly that the trail stood out like a snaking band of silver. Ariel and Aleta followed it until he found the very same pine where he'd wept in disgrace after hurting four-year-old Svnoyi. The hungry pair crawled beneath the needled boughs, free at last to make love without being overheard.

Aleta chided him for embarrassing her publicly over their secret consummation in the Santa Margarita redwood grove. Ariel whispered, "We can talk about that later." He sealed her lips with a sumptuous and prolonged kiss.

Then he simply bubbled over. "Aleta, we're having a baby. I'm so excited. If it's a girl, let's name her Agali, which means 'sunny' in Cherokee. And I think I found my real father. I don't know for sure. If I did, he'd love a Cherokee name for our daughter."

It was Aleta's turn to silence him, covering his face, neck, and torso with at least thirty little nipping kisses.

They lost all restraint. His buoyant fingers circled over her swelling breasts and rounded belly, reaching down below. For the lovers, the rest of that moonlit night beneath the silver-tipped pine branches flew by in a mere moment.

***

In the next few weeks, Aleta made progress breaking the ice with Yacy. She often found her daughter hanging by the door while she practiced. One day, she handed the violin to Yacy, but the little girl backed away.

Aleta pleaded, "Don't you want to play it?"

Yacy shook her head. "No, Mama. You sound too good, and Kuaray said—"

Aleta, who had heard all about the trip to Mr. Varkonyi's shop, interrupted, "Never mind what Kuaray said. I heard something entirely different about your playing from your Daddy Sequoyah."

Yacy blushed at the compliment. "Okay, Mama, but I don't like your violin. It's haunted 'cause I heard it scream once. So I need my own violin an' I don't care if it don't sound good like yours." She added under her breath, "An' I need lessons 'cause I never had any."

Aleta asked shyly, "If we can get a violin for you, would you be willing to study with me?"

***

Just days later, a violin fell into Ariel's hands. The circumstances were unusual, although all in a day's work. He rescued Jörg Anton Schmidt-Eulenspiegel, a first-time hiker who left the trail to make an unwise scramble up an exposed rock face, and then couldn't get down.

Luckily for the young man, Ariel was close by delivering a propane cylinder to a high-altitude hostel when he overheard whimpering cries for help.

Jörg's mother was the wealthy widow of an industrial magnate who had amassed a fortune during the war. To indulge her son, Frau Ephigenia Schmidt-Eulenspiegel was spending the summer at a swank hotel in Stary Smokovec where she'd taken a suite with him and her lapdogs. The day after Ariel's providential rescue, she invited the shy ranger to tea in order to offer her heartfelt thanks.

From the hotel's impressive mirrored hallway, Ariel was surprised to hear the familiar sound of violin scales issuing from behind the closed door, mingled with the dogs' lilliputian yips and scuffling toenails on the hardwood floor. As it turned out, Jörg's mother was an avid amateur violinist from West Berlin who kept up her passion "in the wilderness," bringing what she called her "second-rate practice fiddle."

When Ariel told her he was looking for an inexpensive violin for his daughter, she sized him up, from his worn hiking boots to his frayed collar. Guessing at a forest ranger's yearly salary, the good woman simply handed the instrument to him.

"It is the least I can do for the handsome hero who saved my only son from the Jaws of Death." Her heavy German accent reminded him of the Moravian missionaries, intent on converting the heathen of Oklahoma.

A sloppy and far too arduous kiss accompanied the gift, obliging Ariel to make appreciative pecks on both of her fuchsia-colored cheeks. Even the dogs slobbered affectionately on his boots as he bowed himself out, making an obsequious, if somewhat hasty, retreat.

The *second-rate* violin turned out to be very nice—a German nineteenth-century anonymous instrument with warm dark-brown varnish, a high arched belly, and a silken sound.

***

Once Yacy had a violin of her own, the lessons with Aleta began daily at ten sharp. Yacy had grown fonder of her mother, especially since she did little things that no one else had thought of such as gently combing out her daughter's snarled blond hair in the morning while slipping her handfuls of forbidden sweets. But Aleta knew in advance that the lessons wouldn't be easy for the headstrong Yacy to take. Although a mother first, Aleta was a purposeful, no-nonsense teacher— the strict-but-fair type who offered praise only when it was earned. This was the way she herself had been taught, which was one reason she was such a good violinist. Aleta turned out to be right.

Any family member who happened to be home cringed during Yacy's blow-ups, which brought almost every lesson to an abrupt end. First, the little vixen would levitate her instrument back into the case and slam the lid down. Then she would stomp out, screaming, "I *hate* you, Mama. You are *so mean.*"

After a dozen such lessons, Aleta considered giving up until Yacy was older. On a particularly bad day, she made the mistake of gently criticizing Yacy's bowing during the very first etude.

"You play like a Paganini when you do the *spiccato* in measure eight, but for the rest of it, please give me a simple, singing tone using your whole arm."

Yacy flung her violin into the case nursery-school style, closing the lid with a resounding smack. Then, once again, she lost all the newly gained control she'd been working on during the past month. But this time, she screeched something far worse than usual into her mother's face.

"Say that one more time, an' *I'll break your fingers.*"

A trembling Phoenix, the designated family peacemaker, barged into the room.

Yacy didn't give him a chance to open his mouth but turned on him, yelling directly into his sensitive ears, "What do *you* want, *Drancy fuck-face?*" Her last words hung in the empty air, dripping with venom.

Then Aleta's powerful bow-arm rose up in slow motion to strike the girl who crumpled, cringing at her mother's feet. She patiently awaited the blow, knowing she deserved it. Aleta stopped short, wondering how many times Kuaray, or maybe the soldiers on the Trail of Tears, had hit her daughter. Her open hand did not land.

Instead, she stooped, gathering her little girl onto the lap that had almost vanished under the bulge filled with new life. Aleta hugged Yacy close, stroking her hair as she rocked her. "Baby, I almost did it, but I love you too much. I promise I'll never, never hurt you."

At last, Yacy answered in a strangled whisper, tears flowing. "I love you, too, Mama an' I like the lessons, kind of. I jus' show it funny."

***

Svnoyi began snooping in her father's head more often than usual after his return because he had changed in ways she didn't understand. She had always taken care of her daddy from the moment of her birth and now she thought he might be getting into something bigger than he could handle. Whatever it was, it seemed to lighten his spirit and fill him with hope.

But at the same time, he yearned for something he'd never had and he seemed torn. She knew exactly why, too. He wanted to find out what that something was, but couldn't make himself practice her brand of intrusive snooping. In minutes, the clever and loving Svnoyi figured everything out. Ariel had located his father, or hoped he had, but he simply wasn't sure he was right. And if he weren't, just how would he bear it?

Svnoyi easily located the man, for he was none other than Mohe, who had kept Aleta's violin in his cellar. She knew because Mohe dominated her father's thoughts, just as Ariel dominated Mohe's. She began talking almost daily to the garrulous Cherokee since he turned out to be as clairvoyant as she was. He told her immediately that he was indeed Ariel's father and her grandfather, too. Although he claimed to understand Ariel's reluctance to communicate, it pained him that his very own son was too afraid to speak to him. Svnoyi was faced with a dilemma—whether to tell her father what she had discovered, or for once, to let him overcome his debilitating doubts by himself. She decided on the latter.

What stunned her even more were her father's dreams, which even she was usually not crass enough to invade except when she was overcome with insatiable curiosity, as she now was. Something else was stirring within Ariel's heart. He wanted to find out, even if not consciously, who he was. Ever since he had returned to the High Tatras, he often dreamt in *Tsalagi*, but in sentences and images of a four-year-old, the age he had been when his first language was snatched from him at the residential school. She had picked up isolated words before, but never whole dreams.

And so Svnoyi listened and learned to speak in her father's childish tongue because she acknowledged with secret pride that this was her language, too. She shared her newly acquired knowledge with Yacy, her best friend and possible half-sister, whenever they worked on the second annex together. The language lessons were accompanied by whispering, laughter, and dress-up in their own invented costumes. They had founded an exclusive club of their own—no boys or grownups allowed.

***

The same day the new annex was completed, with much additional help from the muscular men of the house on weekends and after-hours, the glazier and building inspector from Stary Smokovec showed up. Both were thoroughly unnerved by the design. It was huge and shaped like a true star divided into five adjoining arrow-shaped rooms with outside doors and windows at the star's points. A central stove heated all five chambers, and the spiked roof had ten sloping surfaces, each containing a skylight. The inspector kicked the structure to test its durability, and he also searched for chinks or other flaws. He found none. The annex was as strong as a battleship. He also noted with approval the tiny gesture toward Communist symbolism inherent in the star design.

The adults admitted privately that it had been much more expensive than they'd hoped and excruciatingly difficult to build out of logs. It was also a bit of an eyesore, looking like a spiky roundhouse for locomotives. Only sleeping bags, quilts, and bearskins would fit inside the narrow, pie-shaped rooms. No matter, the children were ecstatic with pleasure beholding their one-of-a-kind masterpiece, called the Star Annex by everyone.

During the week following the completion of the new annex, both babies were born. Svnoyi made quite a remarkable assistant to Jaroslav at both births because Anichka was in no condition to take charge at Aleta's delivery since her own had occurred only the day before. Svnoyi admitted later that neither her reading of the mighty medical tomes nor her helping out at the delivery of Farmer Michal's foals had prepared her for a human birth.

Phoenix was delighted to no longer be the baby of the family and to finally have a boy-child to befriend. Jaroslav and Anichka's child was that boy—a handsome ten-pounder they named Alexej. He had huge black saucer eyes and glossy ringlets that curled all over his head. Both parents wept for joy when Svnoyi severed and tied the umbilical cord.

Aleta and Ariel named their newborn Agali as Ariel had suggested six months earlier during the night they'd spent in a thrall under the pine branches tipped with moonbeams. The delicate infant girl was olive-skinned like Ariel but with blond hair and saucer eyes the color of oxidized silver. Her coloring suggested early-morning shadows streaked by light that lined the mountain peaks at sunrise.

Only Yacy turned her back at both births, sobbing uncontrollably amidst the rejoicing. The idea of carrying a child inside her own belly terrified her. She had gathered up the courage to ask Daddy Sequoyah how they got in there, but he said that topic was best discussed with her mother. Yacy never dared to ask such a personal question because her beautiful mama just kept smiling like she was having the time of her life, getting fatter and fatter like Holy Mary in the picture over Jaroslav and Anichka's bed.

Unbeknownst to all but the protective Svnoyi, Kuaray had threatened Yacy with marriage every single day since she'd arrived in the High Tatras. After reading in secret the chapter on male sexuality in

Svnoyi's medical book, Yacy was sure Kuaray's threat meant a lot more than wearing a pretty white dress and saying, "I do" in front of the preacher. Besides, Svnoyi had told her over and over that brothers and sisters couldn't get married because it was breaking the law and they might have ugly babies born without enough fingers and toes.

Svnoyi led Yacy away from the rejoicing families to the privacy of the Star Annex where the weeping girl climbed under her bed-quilts beneath the peaked ceiling decorated gaily with the streamers from her party. It took courage, but finally, she uncovered her head to whisper to her best friend how Henri Rayon de Lune had injured her most secret place with his mind a long time ago and how Kuaray had penetrated her with his dirty fingers only last year.

For hours, Svnoyi couldn't console her.

Chapter 17 Interrogation

Now and then, the adults wondered why the police were taking their own sweet time to show up at Jaroslav's cabin. It had been almost two years since the first rumors of secret nighttime disappearances had become public. When Jaroslav was in one of his darkest moods, he imagined roomfuls of bureaucrats with green eyeshades on their foreheads assembling piles of damning documents.

With all the mental build-up, the first visit came almost as a relief. The two rangers were just stepping out the front door on their way to work when Jaroslav cocked his head to one side.

"Ariel, listen. Ravens make a fuss, cry warnings like watchdogs. Strangers come up trail."

Sure enough, three men in unfamiliar dress rounded the final stretch leading to the cabin. Jaroslav and Ariel hoped they hadn't been spotted as they rushed inside the house to send the rest of the family into the Star Annex.

Ariel hissed at the whole lot, "It's the police. Don't show yourselves unless we call you." Everyone fled the breakfast table, although Yacy managed to grab a full plate of fresh-baked kolacky for nourishment during their enforced confinement away from the kitchen.

Then Ariel and Jaroslav hastily threw off their coats as they balled up the tablecloth with the extra dishes and thrust it in a cupboard. Although they weren't particularly adept actors, they sprawled at the newly vacated table, legs akimbo, hoping to look like they'd just wound up a leisurely bachelor breakfast.

Two of the men peered in through the window, just as Jaroslav hoped they would, enabling him to see whom they would be dealing with. The third one was the local constable who arrived late, gasping for air. He wiped sweat off his fat cheeks with a huge blue and white handkerchief, trying not to mess up his luxuriant handlebar mustache. The man was a longtime friend who had once raised a glorious tenor voice to honor Jaroslav and Anichka at their wedding party. His bulk was barely contained within his straining black uniform with three popped buttons on the front.

Jaroslav couldn't believe the constable posed a threat, although he was undoubtedly under the thumbs of the other two who looked particularly intimidating in the sweeping long leather coats that investigators for the Party wore. One was fat and frowning, and the other was narrow and featureless behind giant dark glasses. Soon the fat one pounded rudely on the door with both his fists.

The three men glanced around the cabin that smelled enticingly of sweet pastry and freshly brewed coffee.

The fat one bellowed, jabbing a finger into Ariel's chest, "I spik the English for American spy to knowing we mean the business."

He made the same jab into Jaroslav's chest. "Family where is, and dumb gypsy wife we eat for refreshment?"

Ariel bridled instinctively, and Jaroslav threw him a warning glance. Then he murmured with studied humility, "Children sleep. I call Anichka."

She appeared, producing a fresh batch of fruit-filled rolls hot from the oven and a pot of steaming coffee. She set down three plates and cups, meanwhile smiling broadly at Ariel. At the same time, she sent him a message so piercing that it hurt his brain.

Be proud. You are Cherokee.

Jaroslav threw her an inquiring glance, but she refused to look his way. Ariel reeled as sudden inspiration struck.

The constable sat down and began gobbling rolls as he winked at Anichka. The fat inspector rapped his fingers with a pencil, although he, too, surreptitiously crammed four of the delicacies into his squirrel-like cheeks. The thin one resisted the second breakfast as he glared at the other two over his dark glasses. He raised his voice in annoyance and speaking in Slovak, sent them back to headquarters, slamming the front door behind them.

Now Jaroslav knew who the boss was. The leader-apparent took off his dark glasses and slid them into his coat pocket, revealing watery blue eyes embedded deep within worried creases. Clearing his throat, he quickly slid thick horn-rims up his nose to peer at Ariel with intense curiosity.

"I introduce myself. I am Dr. Benjamin Tulak. But you, you are American, but not white, not Negro? I never see odd name like Sequoyah Morgan Hummingbird."

Emboldened by Anichka, Ariel took a chance. He puffed out his chest and flexed his arms, hoping to intimidate his interrogator with his spectacular sets of muscles. "I am no one to fool around with, Tulak. I am Sequoyah, proud Cherokee of the Cherokee Nation."

Dr. Tulak was immediately impressed. "Ah. You are Indian. You ride Plains on a wild pinto horse, your noble brow in high white feathers down to feet. You wear little loincloth. You kill white man with bow and—"

Ariel raised a mighty fist. "I am *not* that Indian. I am Cherokee who speaks own language in Oklahoma, home of Cherokee Nation."

Dr. Tulak quailed. "Own language in middle of United States?" Recovering, he countered, "Speak it, then."

Later Ariel marveled that his little girls had managed to save his credibility before the powerful Tulak, perhaps saving the lives of them all. For on cue, Svnoyi and Yacy swept into the room wrapped in bedspreads with a few owl feathers protruding from their hair. They carried overgrown pumpkins and zucchini squash in their arms, purloined from Phoenix's pride and joy, his very own vegetable garden, lovingly planted behind the Star Annex. The girls bowed low, depositing the giant squashes at Dr. Tulak's feet. The interpretive dance that followed would have made Isadora Duncan proud if they hadn't kept tripping on the bedspreads.

At last, with a whole series of knee-dipping curtsies, Svnoyi and Yacy intoned sentences in Cherokee that sounded impressive: *"Osiyo, gago nihi? Hatlvtegvi? Utohitsvkayisi gohi iga!"* In fact, they were simple greetings gleaned from Ariel's immature vocabulary: 'Hello, who are you? Where are you from? It is a nice day!' Then the Indian beauties exited, their feet stomping and their immature hips twitching to a silent drumbeat.

Perhaps Tulak was fond of little girls. Or men in loincloths. Or the fantastic notion that Indians had once roamed freely all over the Western Hemisphere. Most likely, he simply loved the idea of a powerful nation challenging the United States from within its borders.

He asked Ariel one more question just to make sure he'd got it right. "Then the Cherokee are independent people with their own nation right in the middle of the United States?"

Ariel nodded. Tulak's grin signaled his enthusiasm, but it looked unnatural, even scary — all teeth and no lips.

Dr. Tulak returned several times after that, but always in the middle of the night, scrambling up the treacherous trail by flashlight to talk to Ariel alone after the others were asleep. The Communist agent told his wary superiors that he was checking facts and ever more facts. In truth, he was mulling over ways to help the endangered families escape.

Unfortunately, Ariel was new to international intrigue. He never guessed that Tulak's clandestine arrangements might come with a hefty price tag.

***

Just as outside pressure threatened their little world, the family suddenly found itself torn apart from the inside. In the middle of the night, an unearthly screech tore through the tranquil cabin, breaching even the sturdy hand-hewn logs. The blue pines that stretched protective branches over the peaked roof dropped half their needles in agitation as the two families, snug beneath layers of homemade quilts, sat bolt upright. The babies howled and everyone else quaked in terror. Even sensible Svnoyi, who had finished reading *Dracula* the night before, yanked her quilt over her head. *Didn't I just hear ivory-fanged vampires rip out the throats of wailing virgins, and a thousand ghosts keen in ear-splitting unison?*

There were patters of bare feet as the household gathered by the great stone hearth. They stared into the soot-blackened depths of the fireplace beneath its broad mantel for five agonizing minutes while the babies, taking cues from their elders, grew uncharacteristically silent. The assembly shivered in thin nightclothes, wriggling their ice-cold toes on the stone flags. They remained helpless, watching Jaroslav's fruitless attempt to kindle a fire. As match after match slipped through the ranger's twitching fingers and went out, Ariel took charge, or tried to.

Bouncing little Agali and Alexej in his sturdy arms, he ventured, "Don't worry, everyone, and remain calm. It can't be all that bad. Wasn't that horrible noise just a howling wolf pack?"

Only Svnoyi came up with an answer. "Daddy, wolves don't sound like that, even in a huge pack. Besides, the noise came from inside our house. It can be only one thing—the violin!"

She stopped to consider how her next words might affect the nervous gathering before whispering, "Prepare yourselves. Something is terribly, terribly wrong, or the violin would still be sleeping."

Everybody craned their necks toward the dark corner where Aleta kept the instrument when she wasn't practicing. The moonlight danced on the shiny surface of the new case, and Jaroslav swore later that at that moment the violin moaned from deep within its green velvet cocoon.

Aleta suddenly came to life and she sounded thoroughly irritated by the slight to her most beloved possession. "You think I don't know my own violin? What's your plan, you psychics? Are you going to ask it to give you an explanation?"

As if to dilute the hostile remark, Anichka emerged from the kitchen with a wicker tray in one hand and a kerosene lantern in the other. She offered everyone in the circle big brown mugs filled with steaming herb tea. Two were left over.

She exclaimed in alarm, "Holy Lord Jesus, some of our darlings are missing. Find them before you drink one sip of my good tea!"

It was true. Both Yacy and Phoenix had left the circle on the hearth.

Ariel found Yacy huddled under her bed quilts, shaking. He held the little girl close, stroking her night-tangled hair. When she finally managed to get the words out, she reverted to the strange colloquial speech that Svnoyi had taken such pains to erase.

"Oh, Daddy Sequoyah, that sad, sad Trail of Tears with people cryin' an' dyin' all over the place, 'n Kuaray, he made me shoot the eagle! The fiddle don't shut up 'cause its heart is broke like all the Indians' hearts, an' I know it screamed 'n screamed 'cause it jus' hate me.

"Then the Moon People make a tornado that suck us under the dirt 'n rocks, it swallow us whole 'n I don't see no light for days 'n days. It throw us on Ethan's front porch all dirty 'n broken."

The second missing child, the intuitive Phoenix who wore his heart on his sleeve, had not gone far away. He sat in the corner, cradling his mother's violin case in his arms. He opened it with a reverence reserved for jewel-encrusted reliquaries housing sacred bones.

"Watch this, everybody, 'cause the beautiful violin is alive."

He whispered inside an f-hole to get its attention. Then he traced a finger along the shell-like scroll while stroking the striated neck with his other hand.

"I'm jus' gonna put my fingers on its front now, but real carefully 'cause Mama doesn't like prints all over the shiny varnish. He palpated the violin's belly with delicate swirls as his face paled.

Ariel returned, carrying Yacy against his shoulder as if she were a baby, the same age as Agali and Alexej. He had missed Phoenix's conversation with the violin, but once he'd put Yacy down on the bearskins, Phoenix slipped a tiny hand into one of his great paws. Afraid to hurt Ariel, the tender-hearted child stared at his feet for a long time before raising his drooping turquoise saucer-eyes.

"Oh, Táta, the violin says Mohe is really, really sick."

With the sentence barely out of his mouth, Svnoyi gazed inward. Without saying a word out loud, she spoke directly into her father's mind. *Daddy, Phoenix is right, and there's no time to lose. Just get on a plane. Go to Oklahoma right now.*

After the household had settled down for the night a second time, Aleta and Ariel made love, trying to commit to memory every nerve beneath the surfaces of their mutually aroused flesh. When they finally drew apart, they comforted each other during the remaining hours as both feared separation during such uncertain times.

At last Aleta voiced what weighed most heavily on her mind. "Sequoyah, the sacred ring of our beloved High Tatras protects us from the Moon People, but not from our very own neighbors. Soon the mountains will be filled with evil, I'm sure of it." She leaned on one elbow, staring at his unseen face in the dark. "Those horrible places I went to in the past … I thought none of it could ever happen again. I thought people had learned."

Ariel squeezed her hand, offering a platitude meant to soothe her. "Don't fret, darling. Meanwhile, we can love each other, and our families."

Aleta shivered in the chilly predawn, replying bitterly, "How's that supposed to help? I know thousands will die just because some people think they're right and everyone else is wrong. And not just this time. It's going to happen over and over."

***

Ariel's departure the next morning was even more somber than the last one had been. The whole family gathered outside the front door, hovering around the man they all loved.

Ariel tried to steady his voice. "Dear ones, I don't know how much longer we can live here safely, or even if I'll be able to return. After Oklahoma, I might have to head directly for Frobisher Bay where Ethan and his family are. That's where you'll all join me—"

Yacy interrupted, "But Daddy Sequoyah, I don't want to go there, 'cause Kuaray—"

"Of course, Yacy. We'll do our best to watch out for you." He rubbed the crown of her head affectionately.

Svnoyi hurried across the circle to gather Yacy into her arms. In a rare flash of anger, she spoke directly into her father's head. *Daddy, sometimes you're a big disappointment. You could at least try to understand that she's scared of him for a good reason.*

Aleta called to Yacy gently. "We'll take care of each other, shall we?"

Ariel felt a tug on his jacket sleeve. Phoenix stared up at him, his saucer eyes wide open with fear. "What about the rest of us? You're going, but how will we get there?"

Ariel tried to sound reassuring, "Don't worry, dears. I think I worked that part out. Most of it, anyway."

Then the child asked plaintively, "Why do they hate us, Táta?"

Ariel faced the whole group. "By now, you've seen enough inside my mind to know why we're going to Frobisher Bay where Ethan is doing post-doc work at a place called … The Geophysical Arctic Studies Project."

It might have been Ariel's imagination, but just then he thought Aleta gave a startled gasp of recognition. He looked at her quizzically before going on.

"I've hidden nothing from you about the journey to a distant place that we're all going to make. It's just that there's so much I don't know about it myself. I guess we'll find out when we get there."

Last of all, he threw his arms around Aleta and ran his fingers through Agali's bouncing silver curls as she perched in his wife's arms. The child had been born with sunshine in her heart; she smiled while the others mourned, blessed with an uncanny optimism in the midst of any turmoil. Not caring about the others looking on, Ariel bent to fervently bestow a long, long kiss on his darling wife's lips knowing it would have to last a long time before they would see each other again.

Then he was gone.

Chapter 18 Mohe

Ariel arrived in Tahlequah by bus much as he had before, except this time Mohe's illness weighed down his heart. Ever since he'd found Aleta in a sick wagon on the Trail of Tears after searching inside what seemed like hundreds of them—he'd turned squeamish around sick people. The acrid stench of ox manure rising from the clouds of choking trail dust, the sight of the patients' flapping feet hanging over the wagon gates, the pressingly hot, humid air. This was illness. That his destination was none other than the end of the Trail of Tears made him positively gloomy.

***

Ariel was relieved to find Mohe's big, boxy house, so different in appearance from the low-slung log cabin in the High Tatras, looking cheery with a coat of fresh, yellow paint. Someone had planted chrysanthemums in newly dug flowerbeds running the length of the house below the pillared porch. They were blooming now in great splashes of reds and yellows. But then he noticed that all the curtains were drawn. Ariel froze; was he too late?

He was not. His knock brought to the door a comely young woman with waist-length black hair pulled back into a practical ponytail. With a broad smile of undisguised delight, she grasped both his hands in hers.

"Sequoyah, may I call you that? I'm so glad you're here." She introduced herself as Tsaquolade, one of Mohe's nieces. She explained that her name meant "bluebird" in Cherokee, but all her friends called her Birdie.

"I hope you'll call me Birdie, too. And you have *no idea* how excited Mohe is to see you."

Following this outburst, she started up the stairs to put his suitcase in a bedroom, showing strong, capable legs and feet clad in white oxfords. Halfway, she turned her head, "Mohe can't stop talking about you. You wouldn't believe, he's a different man because of you, less of a loner and no longer a drinker."

When she returned, she explained that both she and her sister Atsina had degrees in nursing. They traded off caring for Mohe when they weren't working at the Indian Hospital or staying home with their husbands and growing families.

With tears in her eyes, Birdie whispered that her uncle continued to refuse all medical care. Both she and her sister expected him to slip into a coma and expire within a few days—the cause of death from both cirrhosis and kidney failure.

She warned Ariel, "His body is swollen from the toxins. He's never been a vain man, but try not to notice, for his sake."

Then she dried her eyes and took Ariel's arm to walk him into Mohe's bedroom, made up downstairs in the dining room, conveniently close to the kitchen and bathroom.

Brightening visibly, she announced too loudly, "Uncle Mohe, Sequoyah's here."

She turned to Ariel, patting his arm. "You know, back in high school all of us girls were *so in love* with you, Sequoyah. The football hero from the famous Vocational School team. I bet you didn't even know it."

Near tears himself, Ariel took Birdie's cue, rearranging his long face into one that he hoped held a smile. Birdie gathered up Mohe's untouched lunch tray and blew her patient a kiss as she relinquished the room to the two men.

Thanks to the hard work of Mohe's nieces, the indifferent room was bright with several vases of the garden flowers. They must have scrubbed every inch in anticipation of his visit because there was no telltale odor of illness.

Mohe lay propped on several pillows in freshly ironed striped cotton pajamas, his hands clasped above his hugely distended belly. Its size shocked Ariel, reminding him that during the telling of the violin story, Mohe had described the pregnant Aleta by drawing his arms in a flamboyant arc over his abdomen, then quite concave beneath his red flannel shirt.

Bursting with excitement, Mohe unlinked his fingers and extended his arms as far as they would go in a wide welcome. Ariel's sickroom qualms vanished. Mohe was the same expressive, craggy-faced man Ariel remembered. Only now he was painfully gaunt everywhere, except that belly.

And just then, great tears started rolling down his jaundiced cheeks. Ariel figured that now a few of his own wouldn't matter as he threw his arms somewhat awkwardly around Mohe in a spontaneous gesture that pleased them both.

He couldn't help thinking, *Like father, like son. Both way too emotional.*

After a good while, as each man tried to comfort the other, Ariel broke loose to pull up a battered kitchen chair. He sat as close to Mohe as he could without climbing on the bed. He knew the moment had come. But how would he ask the question that had driven him half crazy for two years? He twisted his hands, tongue-tied and overcome with confusion. His heart pounded in his throat.

What if Mohe says no? Will I be able to stand it?

"I know what you been thinkin', Son, *for you is my son.*"

Ariel expelled a great sigh of relief. His wait was over.

"But get ready for a real sad love story ... way, way sadder than Hollywood can do. An' it's like you and Miriam done near the same one. I know 'cause I been talkin' all the time to Svnoyi, your little girl an' *my granddaughter.*"

He shook his head sadly. "I coulda been chattin' regular with you for two years now exceptin' your high moral principles don't allow it."

Ariel's jaw dropped once he had processed the last bit of information; he'd inherited the unnatural clairvoyance from his father. Then he wondered if part of his principles weren't based on cowardice—on not wanting to know.

Ariel tried to assemble his thoughts, blurting out the first thing that entered his head. "Then ... then Birdie must be my cousin."

Mohe nodded. "She's the nicest girl, that Birdie, an' Atsina, too. An' they was born lucky. My sister have the mind-readin', too, but these girls don't get it to make 'em miserable."

Then Ariel asked shyly, "Mohe, can I call you Dad?"

Mohe smiled, but his eyes filled. "How about you call me what I call my father? That's Edoda, to us Cherokees. I don't have him for long, jus' 'til I was four an' then he die." Mohe added in a whisper, "An' you won't have me too long neither. My nieces don't say much, but I'm thinkin' only a few more days."

Ariel didn't know what to say, so he took his father's hand in both of his.

Mohe brightened. "Well, son, you would be Uwetsi. But you got a good name already, an' that's Sequoyah."

Ariel had been too young to learn much about his dead mother from his aunts. But the malicious gossip that he overheard at the residential school, especially from teachers and staff, gave him enough information to form a dreary picture. On some points, everyone agreed. Her name was Sunali. She was a Cherokee beauty who had worked in a fancy bordello near the center of town, and since she had a home of sorts, she gave most of her earnings to her family. Cook and Matron even said that her two sisters, his aunties, had four huge pots of Sunali's hard-earned money buried in their back yards.

They never tired of talking about the heroin overdose that killed her, leaving him behind, orphaned at three days of age. Long ago he had accepted the gossip about her profession and death as the dismal truth.

It hadn't occurred to him that she might have had more than a passing acquaintance with the man who fathered him.

To comfort himself after lights-out in the little boys' dormitory, Ariel sometimes imagined a lady both gentle and fierce, named Sunali. Her eyes shone like twin stars, but her midnight-black hair swirled about her head like a storm cloud. Then he imagined a rocking chair for her with magic runners that threw sparks across the pine boards of her cottage floor. Sunali held him in her arms as she rocked and rocked, which made the winds roar about the house. But when she smiled, no one could hurt him in the calm center of the maelstrom, and when she kissed him, the whole world fell away. He was asleep.

"Sequoyah. Your mind keeps driftin' off, but I can hear the Grim Reaper sharpenin' that harvest knife of his. So I best tell you 'bout Sunali—means 'mornin' to you. She's the only woman I ever love."

Ariel gave Mohe a sip of water from the mug on the night table. Then the old man joined his long fingers in a bridge and cleared his throat.

"Maybe I'm wrong about you bein' my own son, but I don't think so, an' she was sure about you, too. An' I see you thinkin', 'how can old Mohe know that?' Well, 'cause she was real careful with the clients an' not ever with me."

Mohe smiled sadly and took his time with the next sentences. "We love each other like there was no tomorrow, Sequoyah. We talk about gettin' married all the time, an' here's why we love like we do. Both of us know what we is thinkin' without sayin' a word out loud."

Ariel gasped, "So you both gave me the gift."

Then Mohe's eloquent face drooped. "But she die just after you is born. I curse the white man's heroin that kill her but it's not really their fault. It's just like my booze. She can't never kick it.

"After Sunali die, I try tellin' your aunties I'm Sunali's husband-to-be an' your father. An' that she give you some names: Sequoyah for the Cherokee hero of writin', an' Morgan for the name teachers make me take at the damn orphanage, same's yours. An' a new last name we don't either of us have, Hummin'bird. That word sound better in Cherokee. But they ain't listenin'. We is at the funeral, an' they is cryin' an' swayin' about like trees in a hurricane, but I notice they hear enough to use the names."

Ariel felt like both laughing and crying. "So *she* named me. And all these years I've hated the names because I didn't know where they came from. In California at college they sounded stupid and embarrassing, so when Miriam called me Ariel, I took to it and kept it. And I only put Hummingbird on official documents."

Mohe nodded. "It's strange. We have trouble givin' up bein' our Cherokee selves an' then 'round other people we have trouble bein' ourselves."

Mohe paused for so long that Ariel grew concerned. When he went on, his voice shook, maybe from exhaustion, but most likely from recalling the worst days of his life.

"I jus' come apart after that. I cry an' cry an' drink meself half to death.

"Then one day your aunties start a big embarrassin' paternity suit. They finger a client of Sunali's who meet her all the time at the *Royal Flush*, an' he's the richest big-name Cherokee in the whole county, an' a family man."

Ariel registered shock. "That's horrible. My aunts were trying to make money off me?"

Suddenly Mohe's old eyes sparkled. He was getting to the entertaining part of the story.

"The way your aunties done the lawsuit make chickens look smart. They hire a white Tahlequah lawyer with dollar signs for eyes. An' Mr. Big-Name, he hire a better lawyer that make the case go on for three years 'til Dollar-Signs piss away all Sunali's money makin' himself rich."

Mohe went on with a frown. "Believe me, your aunties know exactly who I is, an' sure as hell don't want me hangin' around my baby boy ruinin' their chances of collectin'. In that one way, they ain't dumb clucks, but cleverer 'n weasels. After I lose four construction jobs in a row 'cause of their insinuatin' to the foreman, what with that an' a little drinkin', I know I'm done for around there."

A look of anger long unforgiven flicked across Mohe's face, turning it red.

"I give names to them sisters, your aunties, an' they ain't real ugly but not near so pretty as your mama. But they is as smelly an' mean as the animals I pick. One I name Dili, which mean 'skunk,' 'cause she have an interestin' white streak in her long black hair. T'other is Inada, or 'snake,' 'cause she have a way of swirlin' around her tongue that give a man excitin' thoughts."

Mohe's face darkened some more to a shade of vermillion. "An' their no-good husbands is Dili-Pee an' Inada-Piss for reasons that's obvious. Not neither of 'em work a lick since they is waitin' for the lawsuit to hit the jackpot, just sittin' around on their propity wi' shotguns on their knees.

"So when I come to see my baby, one say, 'I'll blow your head off,' an' t'other say, 'I'll blow off your balls.' Given a choice, I prefer the balls, but I jus' slink home instead."

Ariel tried to calm his father by offering him more water. "It's amazing what children don't see. I didn't think my aunts loved me particularly, or that my uncles could care less about me, but not this. Besides, they were my only family."

Mohe interrupted, "It get worse, Sequoyah. When the lawsuit finally fizzle out, them sisters put their heads together an' rise above the level of chicken-brains. The money in Mr. Big-Name's family is his wife's. She is Osage from Fairfax, an' it turn out, her dirt-poor family is sittin' on an oil well. All of a sudden, this Indian maiden is Miss Most Eligible Debutante. Never mind that she look like a dyin' houseplant."

Mohe suddenly chuckled to himself. "So the extortin' an' blackmailin' begin. Dili an' Inada threaten to trot you right out front 'n center 'cause resemblance 'tween you an' Houseplant's old man is clear as day. I don't see it, natur'ly, but folks'll believe anythin'. She's afraid her white Baptist lady-friends'll stop askin' her to luncheons, so she pay up, big bucks ev'ry month.

"An' then the gun-totin' Dili-Pee 'n Inada-Piss show up on my doorstep wavin' their pieces in my face. For the time bein' anyways, I know I lost you."

From the way Mohe hesitated, shrugging his shoulders and opening his hands, Ariel knew the plan must have developed critical flaws.

"By the time you reach four, the plot begin unravelin'. Mr. Big-Name find out what his wife's been up to protectin' his good name, an' don't appreciate the family fortune bein' frittered away. He send a threatnin' letter to Dili an' Inada sayin', 'One more month of blackmailin', an' I will personally kill the little bastard.'"

"My God!" Ariel broke in. "Do you think he was serious?"

Mohe nodded. "You bet your moccasins, Sequoyah. Your aunties been pesterin' Big-Name's family for four long years, an' everyone, almost, own a gun back then an' still do."

He continued apologetically, "I is too scairt to let you stay another minute in that vipers' nest of a county. An' that's when I enroll you in the Orphan Training School, secret-like so's Big-Name don't know where you disappear to. Your aunties don't put up a fuss, an' a gov'ment agent from the Bureau of Indian Affairs come to fetch you."

Wringing his hands involuntarily, Ariel abruptly turned his head to hide from his father the look of desolation that must have crossed his face. Even now, he remembered vividly the days that ended his childhood.

First, both his aunties fiercely scrubbed him down in the galvanized metal kitchen tub and dressed him in assorted clothes belonging to their own children. When they yanked a comb through the impossible tangles in his long hair, he wondered if he'd been bad. Then a man dressed in a suit arrived in a big black car to take him away. He tried not to cry because his aunties, uncles, and eight cousins were watching from the road.

A full week of humiliation passed in the terrifying new place. They shaved his head and fed him strange food that made him sick. Everything in the big rooms scared him—the line of steaming silver pots in the kitchen, the rows of identical beds in the little boys' dormitory, and most of all, the white porcelain toilets in the bathroom.

The worst thing was, no one seemed to understand what he was saying. But he still hoped that this confusing nightmare would end when his aunties took him home. He climbed out a window every night after lights-out to wait for them at the front driveway, which always made fat Matron so angry that she hit his hands with a ruler, and sometimes she had a big boy hit his back with a leather belt.

His aunties didn't come.

On the seventh night of his persistent vigil, he saw a beautiful princess. She was pale, with red-gold hair, and she held his hands tenderly in hers before vanishing in a burst of multi-colored light. He ran after her down the road, the first of many nighttime breakouts. The princess had been his final hope. After that, whenever he walked outside by the fishpond, he considered throwing himself in.

Mohe hadn't missed the look on Ariel's face, and once he saw that, he scrutinized the unhealed wounds in his son's thoughts. The passage of more than twenty-five years had done little to assuage them. Seeing how stricken his Uwetsi was, he hastened to wrap up the story that he had yearned to tell for two long years, his voice hoarse and sagging at the conclusion of each new revelation.

"Your aunties has let you run around half neked an' taught you no manners an' no English, so you take to school real hard.

"After about a week I see the problem of you breakin' out ain't goin' away by itself, so I watch for you ev'ry night to cut short them witless escapes you keep doin', an' bring you back. You don't know who I is, just some man finds you dropped down in the road all wrecked from them punishments, beatin's, castor oil 'n such."

The sick man winced as he twisted his rusty vertebrae to look Ariel in the eye. "Do you remember, son, just where you was tryin' to git to?"

Ariel took a long time answering. "The Moon People started talking to me all the time after I saw, don't laugh, a princess. They lured me into running away. They promised to take me to the magical place where she lived—"

Mohe interrupted, "Believe me, son, I ain't laughin'. I *am* sorry you have to truck with them. They try to recruit me an' Sunali before you is born."

Ariel felt choked. He wasn't sure he could bear having much more of his soul stripped off the way kids pull loose bark from a tree. "Edoda, let's stop for now. I'll call Birdie to make you comfortable."

"Uwetsi, I'm about done."

Mohe closed his eyes in hapless resignation. "An' so we make it through one year, you an' me. By then you start learnin' English an' catch on to the rules. I know you is safe now an' gettin' no more punishments. I got no choice. I start lettin' you alone an' don't see you no more."

***

Ariel took off his hiking boots, the only footwear he'd worn since starting work at the High Tatras' ranger station. Then he stretched out exhausted on his bed. He didn't turn a light on, but stared at the ceiling, watching the dusk-filled bedroom go dark. More chrysanthemums, in many European countries the overly showy flowers at funerals, stood in a Mason jar on the night table. They emitted their bitter perfume, somehow giving him permission to let the long withheld tears leak out the sides of his eyes onto the pillow.

Edoda made me suffer because he loved me, but God, it hurts. Being reminded makes those old scars on my back itch. I know he did it to save my life, so why, oh why can't I forgive him?

Just then an unwelcome thought crept in, erasing the comfort of self-flagellation. *I gave my baby daughter away before walking off a mountain, and not once has she thrown it in my face. She always loves me and helps me every time I need her—*

As if on cue, Svnoyi's pert voice invaded his thoughts.

Daddy, yes, I love you, too—but listen. Things are just awful here since you left. That Dr. Tulak couldn't reach the Cherokee Nation on the phone to check out what you said about Independent People. He can't protect us from the police much longer.

Ariel could feel his daughter's anxiety, so he put on his best fatherly tone, even if unspoken. *Svnoyi, darling, go slow. Do you know what they're planning? Maybe it's a false alarm.*

But she insisted, *No, Daddy, it's not. I'm pretty sure they want to take Anichka to a prison camp for being a Gypsy, and another thing you won't believe.*

She giggled, which felt like frothy bubbles in Ariel's head. *They think Yacy rubbed dirt all over that ugly passport she made herself to hide something.*

Ariel started to whisper his thoughts to Svnoyi, even though their conversation would never be intercepted.

Svnoyi, Dr. Tulak just loves Indians. I didn't mean that, as a people, you know.

He felt Svnoyi laughing at his inept clarification, so he hurried on. *I already made arrangements with him, and he'll help all of you except Jaroslav, Anichka, and the baby get to Denmark and then Frobisher Bay. Just say "Hiawatha" to him three times; that's the code we arranged.* Ariel pictured Svnoyi rolling her eyes.

That Hiawatha stuff is simply hilarious, Daddy. But what about Jaroslav, Anichka, and Alexej?

Ariel knew this moment would come, sooner or later. *Svnoyi, give me a few days. I'm figuring out what to do—*

Someone knocked on the door. Before Ariel could reach it, Birdie cracked it open and whispered, "You'd better come downstairs. Uncle Mohe has something to say. Just leave your boots off, but be careful not to slip on the stairs."

Ariel's heart jumped, but a gentle probe aimed his father's way showed no reason for concern. Nonetheless, he rushed into the dining room. He found Mohe sitting up in bed looking far more rested than he should considering his condition and also immodestly pleased with himself.

"Don't forget, now, Sequoyah, 'til I bite the dust in a day or two, I'm the eldest an' smartest."

He grinned and then whistled a tuneless ditty. "I got a lifesavin' notion for them friends of yours livin' on that two-bit Communist mountain. An' Birdie, here, says she can make it work. Tell 'im, Birdie."

Ariel threw back his head and laughed aloud for the first time in weeks. "Edoda, you eavesdropper. So much for private conversations in this house."

Birdie suddenly looked embarrassed, so Mohe cheered her on. "C'mon, Birdie. Sequoyah don't bite."

"Well," she began slowly, "Indian Hospital and Northeastern State College," but then the words tumbled out because the idea was actually quite brilliant, if far-fetched, "they collaborate on a course in native healing. It's sad, but mostly anthropologists and hippies take it, not medical staff. It's a great course, mainly about our medicine, old-time Cherokee. Anyway, I loved it."

She literally danced a few steps. "Just think, Sequoyah. You combine that with gypsy medicine, and you have something tremendous. If your friend Anichka's anything like you, she'd make a great guest professor."

Beaming, Mohe patted her hand. He burst out, "Anyways, first Anichka get a personal invite from the Principal Chief of the Cherokee Nation to teach gypsy-healin'. Then Svnoyi 'n Yacy put on Indian get-ups with them knockout bird feathers *an'* bat four pretty eyes at Dr. Tulip the Red, who's so nuts over us Cherokee. I bet he jus' 'bout break his butt talkin' up our Nation to them stuffed-shirt buracrat commissars."

His eyes sparkled, and he thrust a finger into the air. "Now see if old Mohe don't know his current e-vents from the TV from them blabbin' anchors like Walter Cronkite sayin', 'And that's the way it is.' 'Cause I'm *uppin' the ante.* The Anichka family come to the great U.S. of A. an' be counter-counter Commie-American-Cherokee Nation spies."

After Ariel had picked himself off the floor from laughing, he decided not to reject the idea outright. Leaving off Mohe's "upping the ante," it had a great deal of promise.

First he hugged Birdie, whispering, "Thanks, Cuz."

She turned a vivid red and began plumping up Mohe's pillows.

Then he hugged his father tightly for a long time, eventually holding the old man at arms' length to look into his eyes. "You mean the world to me, Edoda, and you *are* the smartest. And, there's nothing to forgive."

***

Ariel slept late. By the time he looked in on Mohe the next morning, it was already 10:00 o'clock. His father was sleeping, his cheeks visibly sunken since the night before. Birdie's sister Atsina looked up from her flower arranging. It seemed that the fresh chrysanthemums sat on the night table tossing snakey red-orange heads in a sinister greeting. Stunned by Mohe's decline, Ariel looked helplessly at the new cousin.

Atsina, just as handsome as her younger sister Birdie but a head shorter, put a finger to her lips and motioned him into the hall. She stood on tiptoe to peck him on the cheek, and as Birdie had done, took his hands.

"Cousin Sequoyah, I'm Atsina, and Birdie sure didn't lie. You look like you walked straight off the football field, almost, that is."

Ariel noticed fresh tears on her cheeks. "Is it that bad, Atsina?"

She thought before answering. "Yes and no. He's lasted much, much longer than anyone thought he would, probably because of you coming. He's stopped eating now that you're here; he wants it to end." She whispered, head bowed, "It's just a matter of time."

Ariel couldn't help comparing the two sisters. True, they looked much alike, with the same opulent hair, athletic limbs, and friendly faces. But in spite of Atsina's cheery greeting, Ariel suspected that she was tougher and not as optimistic as the sunshiny Birdie.

Then he detected something else in Atsina: an inner core of righteous indignation. And it was she who brought up the subject of his faraway friends' need for asylum.

"Listen, Sequoyah. Birdie filled me in about the people in the Czech mountains—how the amazing gypsy healer and her family have to escape."

Ariel felt his heart beat faster. "So do you and Birdie think Mohe's plan has a chance? It's a wild idea, but what a great way for Mohe to leave us, knowing he did something this fine."

The two of them sat at the kitchen table, leaning their elbows on the slick red-and-white checkered oilcloth.

Putting their heads together like conspirators, Atsina whispered, "There may be a problem. I hope Mohe's *buracrats* don't find out that the Cherokee Nation isn't very powerful right now, although it sure used to be."

Ariel did know because he'd lived through its forced decline. And he'd read his history. Furthermore, his subscription to the *Cherokee Nation News* had brought the paper, a bit dog-eared, to the ranger station until the Party cracked down on "foreign propaganda."

Atsina's voice rose, filled with pride. "Then you must know we're getting stronger. Not so long ago we elected our own Principal Chief for the first time in years and years, and I helped with the election."

Atsina grabbed a chewed pencil from a jar and started taking notes on a paper napkin, starting with THINGS TO DO in block letters at the top. She wrote, *1. Meet w. Chief.*

She looked up. "I think Chief Keeler will invite your friends here if we both talk to him this afternoon."

Ariel broke in. "You know him? I'm getting nervous already."

"What, you? Ex-football player, published poet, maybe the only Cherokee living in Czechoslovakia? And yes, I know him. I helped get him elected, remember?" Atsina's brisk retort silenced Ariel, so she went on.

"Good. That's settled."

She wrote down, *2. Hospital,* and *3. College.*

"Indian Hospital is easy. I think they will love the course idea. Birdie's working on them this morning. Northeastern should be easy, too. Both of us got our undergrad degrees there."

By now Ariel was thoroughly dumbstruck. His lovely cousin Atsina was an activist and a superb organizer.

Atsina stood up, knees bent, to look at her reflection in the shiny chromed toaster on the kitchen counter. She brushed an errant strand of black hair behind her ear before going on.

"So we can handle this end. I hope what's-his-name, Tulip the Red, gets the family's passports in order. And transportation."

She turned to Ariel, her face serious. "Won't this guy have to go underground to escape deportation to the Siberian salt mines?"

Ariel grinned. "What's-his-name is actually Tulak, and you can drop 'the Red.' Cuz, do you read spy novels on top of everything else?"

Atsina bristled, then smiled winningly. "Yes, Cuz. I happen to live in the Cherokee Nation and the real world, too."

***

In the sickroom, Ariel sat in the kitchen chair watching his father sleep while Atsina swatted a feather duster at offending grime that seemed invisible to him. He made a quick calculation in his head; his father couldn't be much older than fifty-five. Mohe's chest rose and fell evenly, and just then, a smile turned up the corner of his dry lips.

He whispered hoarsely, "Sequoyah, I know you is sittin' here by your old man. An' it warms my heart, but I'm too tired to open my eyes."

Ariel squeezed Mohe's cool, bony hand with relief. "Edoda, I'm so glad you're awake. I have to tell you where I'm going. I don't quite know myself where we'll end up, but it's far away. Maybe some background—"

Mohe interrupted in his raspy voice, "You don't give your old man enough credit for bein' a snoop just like Svnoyi. I been checkin' in on you regular for two years, so I already been let in on the surprise."

Ariel shifted uneasily. He should've known.

With Atsina's practiced assistance, Mohe sat up. Groaning, he leaned his weight back against four fluffed pillows and Ariel's extended arm. Then Mohe nodded to his niece, who dutifully slipped out of the room.

"Uwetsi, I got one a them real serious stories to tell." In preparation, Mohe took a sip of water from the mug that Ariel offered him.

"I use' to sit through them monster-long sermons in the school church ev'ry Sunday, same as you, listenin' to the honeybees buzzin' outside. But when I hit ten, along come the bible tale of Moses, an' my eyes spring open like I been bit by a stingin' wasp. I'm thinkin' … finally. This *is* a story worth hearin' 'cause old man Moses do the Trail of Tears backward, takin' his people where *they* want to go. To the Promised Land."

Ariel asked guardedly, "Is this leading up to my vision in Montreal?"

Mohe tried to look embarrassed. "Right. I sneak into your head an' see that pow'rful sight when you was sleepin' by the kitty that blow up nex' day. An' it bother me, a cardboard box ain't a floatable choice for raftin'. One of them mind-shrinks would say it's 'bout me givin' you up too young."

Ariel tightened his hand and arm on Mohe's shoulder in a forgiving gesture as his father went on. "What I take most serious is the part about my old bones. About you totin' 'em to the Promised Land. So ever since I sicken, I been thinkin' on it, an' what I choose is cremation. Then my bones is almost feather-light, an' fit in a box. Please, Uwetsi, take 'em to your new land, an' put 'em someplace beautiful. What I see in my mind is a spot under a big, green shade tree."

Neither man spoke after that. Then Ariel walked around the room several times, his head bowed in thought.

Finally, he returned to sit on the narrow bed close to Mohe, his arm draped over the old man's shoulders, and one foot dangling on the floor.

He spoke gently, "Of course I'll take them, Edoda, if that's your wish. But so many things could go wrong. We don't even have the ship yet."

Mohe sounded impatient. "I see your worries all the time in my own head, Uwetsi, an' I know you can fix 'em."

When he went on, he sounded exactly like his niece, Atsina. "Good. That's settled. 'Bout my bones, anyway.

"Movin' on, let's talk 'bout you bein' leader in the new land." He added as an afterthought, "An' don't act all shy like you don't know."

Ariel replied cautiously. "I never thought I'd be taking charge, but since half the people making the trip seem to be my family—"

Mohe interrupted, "It's way more 'n that, Uwetsi, an' you know it. But there's two things you gotta learn. First is, how to train that mind of yours to see better what people is thinkin'."

Even though Ariel resisted this frank criticism, he knew his father was right.

"An' second, don't trust everyone all the time like you done usually, 'cause they ain't all good people, or normal in the head. That Kuaray with his two fathers, maybe you is the one, is plannin' to kill you."

On that forbidding note, Atsina poked her head around the doorjamb. "Birdie's coming soon, Uncle Mohe, and I'm taking Sequoyah to see Chief Keeler so we can discuss your plan. Besides, you've been talking a blue streak; it's time to rest."

Birdie, her ponytail flying, burst into the sickroom like a ray of sunlight. She was holding yet another bouquet of ruby-red chrysanthemums, which she had harvested on her way in.

"Listen to this great news, everyone. I talked to a whole tableful of people at Indian Hospital this morning, and they all think Anichka's course is a great idea."

She laughed, dancing a jig step. "Someone's already named it 'Comparative Native Medicinal Practices from Two Diverse Cultures.'"

***

Later that afternoon, Atsina dropped Ariel off at the corner. She was in a hurry; she had barely enough time to keep her appointment with the dean at Northeastern before her evening shift at the hospital.

Flushed with success from the meeting with the Principal Chief, Ariel flung open the front door to make a grand entrance as Birdie had done earlier. But Birdie intercepted him in the hall with tragedy written all over her face.

"Sequoyah, Uncle Mohe's slipped into a coma. I couldn't reach you, I've tried everything, but this is what we knew would happen."

Ariel felt tears flood his eyes, but he didn't care if Birdie saw.

Then, as he sat close to Mohe grasping the cold, blue hands, Ariel tried reaching directly into his father's mind. And Mohe spoke into his.

Uwetsi, I'm deep inside a laid-stone well an' everything's cool an' dark. I don't see no way out.

Ariel cradled the old man's head and smoothed his cheek, searching for a remnant of sentience on the glassy black surface of his father's consciousness. When Ariel found a tiny light-filled crevice, he touched it delicately.

Edoda, I have a question. When I write my poem about the Trail of Tears, can I use your story about the violin?

Mohe had a ready answer, *Sure, son, but don't forget, it ain't no story.*

Ariel smiled through his grief. *I know it's no story because Aleta plays the violin every day and it's still magic. Did you know it brought Aleta and me together at college and brought me to you—twice?*

Mohe remained silent, his mind empty, as Ariel massaged his forehead.

He rallied once more. *The house, Uwetsi. It's yours, like I said before. First invite your friends from the mountain to stay here for the healin' class.*

Ariel nodded. *Of course. I will.*

Minutes ticked by before Mohe broke in with another thought. *After that, why don't we all four give it to the Cherokee Nation—you, me, Atsina an' Birdie?*

Ariel squeezed his father's hand in approval as another silence, much longer than the others, sent him into a panic. There was so little time to make up for the lost years—to express his immense love.

The dying man had a last thought. *Uwetsi, when I go, take me inside of you, next to your heart. Sunali is already restin' in mine, but she won't bother you none.*

***

Ariel walked steadily, eyes downcast, until he reached the corner. He held his suitcase in his left hand and the pine box carrying Mohe's ashes slung awkwardly under his right arm. Birdie and Atsina had wrapped and taped it carefully in newspaper to protect it from accidental bumps during his five-day journey to Frobisher Bay by bus, plane, and barge. As the powdery bits of bone jostled with each footstep, Ariel felt an eerie sensation that his father was searching for a more comfortable position to lie beside his son's own radiantly beating heart.

Uwetsi glanced back at the boxy house for the last time where, if all went well, Anichka, Jaroslav, and Alexej would be staying. Silhouetted against the cheerful yellow paint only a few flowers remained, their drooping heads blackened by an early frost.

Chapter 19 Frobisher Bay

Compared to the robust towns nestled in the High Tatras, tiny Frobisher Bay was an anemic pinprick perched on Baffin Island's frigid alien expanse. Ariel's hopes shriveled. At first sight, he despised the ominous cliffs that rose from the ocean to sweep into the vast grayness of an endless plain. Where were summer's placid bays with the bobbing fishing boats painted in bold primary colors that he'd seen in *National Geographic?* The boats were long gone, frozen into the ice, or stored in dry-dock. Ariel had missed the few short months that made the town bearable; the first big storms of the Arctic winter had obliterated any color from the uniformly featureless landscape.

The town lay among lumpy hills covered in filthy, wind-sculpted snow. Overflowing garbage picked apart by scavenging ravens, thawing mud, bubbling puddles, and mounds of ice encrusted with dirt melted into the gravel roads. In his whole life, even in the poorest neighborhoods of Indian Country, he had never seen such desolate houses—a sorry jumble of prefabs and tumbledown shacks. To make things worse, Ariel found himself shivering in his light denim jacket. In his preoccupied state back in the heat and humidity of Oklahoma, he had forgotten to pack a coat, hat, or gloves.

Ariel took a taxi to the Geophysical Arctic Studies Project, which was about ten miles out of town. The road had been plowed in the morning but had iced over as the temperature fell. The Eskimo driver, who never revealed more than a slit of his brown face and lined eyes beneath the wolf-trimmed hood of an oversized parka, seemed to take pleasure in skidding sideways, which he did with the mastery of a movie stuntman.

From the mud-spattered window, Ariel noticed occasional clumps of laboratory buildings set at apparently random angles behind chain link fences. Ethan's workplace was no different. The monotonous group of almost windowless stucco boxes and a dotting of corrugated metal shacks stood behind a ten-foot fence topped with razor wire. As the taxi pulled up, Ariel noticed that the whole place buzzed with life. He could make out stick figures silhouetted against the low sun, darting about with purposeful strides.

He wondered, Why do scientists always walk so fast?

The driver dropped Ariel at the guard station, then whirled the taxi around with a gratuitous grinding of gears. He headed back the way he had come, making artful esses and looping circles all along the empty road.

Ariel's arrival had been on the books for a long time, and the guard should have admitted him into the complex right away. Instead, the wary Eskimo concealed his agitation behind an inscrutable mask as he asked in a gruff staccato just what the devil the newcomer kept hidden inside the newspaper-covered box.

Ariel patted the reliquary with reverence, murmuring truthfully, "These are the last remains of my father."

He had not anticipated the effect of the simple words. The Eskimo turned abruptly, jerking his whole body toward the tiny window to gaze across the furrowed snow on the other side of the road, all the while twisting his wool watch cap in nervous fingers. Then with an effort, he recovered his original impassive stare to nod Ariel through the gate. But he closed his eyes tight as Ariel carried the modest box with its rattling contents past him.

Ariel stood on the inner side of the fence. Shaking all over from the bitter cold that accompanied early dusk, he turned away from the wind that tore relentlessly over the barren waste. He put down the suitcase and the little casket, silently entreating his father's pardon for laying the bones on the frozen ground. Then he stomped his feet while walking in hurried circles, rapidly rubbing and clapping his folded arms with cupped hands to warm them. Nothing helped.

Ariel tried to ignore his misery by concentrating on the people he was about to see. If he could only recall at least a few pleasant details about his visit in Montreal. He finally settled on the trip to the violin shop with Yacy, and the belated understanding he and Ethan had reached. Everything in between had been pretty awful. He hoped his old college friend had gotten over a ruinous obsession for Aleta at seventeen and had rekindled his passion for Luz. And for the future happiness of everyone going on the trip, he hoped that Ethan somehow had managed to welcome the unlovable Kuaray into the bosom of the Marcus family.

At first, Ariel was delighted to see Ethan and Kuaray emerge together from a nearby building. Ethan was muffled from head to toe in a woolen great-coat, while the swaggering Kuaray kept his arms conspicuously bare. The pair held their heads together, engaged in an overly loud discussion concerning gravity's effect on a sphere's interior.

Then, seeing Ariel, Ethan stopped in his tracks, beaming. He appeared to have spread outward around the middle, which was evident even beneath the heavy folds of his coat. Ariel guessed that his workload didn't leave much time for exercise, and he recalled that not so long ago in Montreal, Ethan had possessed an almost full head of hair.

Kuaray had changed even more. He was at least a head taller, sporting a thick, wavy mane that flowed down to his shoulders, and his pudgy adolescent cheeks displayed endearing dimples. Perhaps Ariel had worried unnecessarily about them both. But just then a warning bell clanged deep within his brain, for he sensed something not quite right behind the surface of Kuaray's flat amber eyes.

Ethan met Ariel with an open smile, a powerful handshake, and a resounding slap on the back. "So good to see you, Old Man. You're in great shape. I'd be jealous if I didn't feel real bad for you, losing your father like that! I'm so sorry, that's terrible."

Ariel turned away as his eyes watered involuntarily, the wound still raw apparently. With his head bowed he hurried along the lone road, his suitcase flapping in the wind and the bones bouncing with his every stride. He headed in the only direction possible, toward the low-slung prefab housing laid out in orderly rows beside the perimeter's chain link fence. Once Ethan caught up, gasping for breath in the cold air, he pretended not to notice Ariel's tears that froze as they fell.

To cover for him, Ethan explained Kuaray's presence too loudly. "Ariel, you wouldn't believe it. After you left, Kuaray took to physics like a fish to water. I was shocked by his talent and persistence. Anyway, the lab lets him work as my unpaid assistant."

Ariel's throat seized up with fear, for his premonition about Kuaray seemed right on the mark. The grinning youth had missed nothing. He looked Ariel up and down, contempt lurking just beneath his studied veneer. He knew his rival was weak, physically depleted by the cold and emotionally drained by his father's death. He grasped Ariel's hand, shaking it vigorously with a showy enthusiasm designed to impress Ethan. But at the same time, he maliciously dug his untrimmed nails deep into the tender flesh of Ariel's palm, piercing the icy skin.

Responding to the hurt, Ariel writhed, hoping that Kuaray hadn't noticed. Oh, God! he thought. How can I lose this meaningless battle even before it starts?

Just then, Ariel felt something warm stirring close to his heart, and he heard Edoda's voice inside his head, *There's two things you gotta learn. First is, how to train that mind of yours to see better what people is thinkin'. An' second, don't trust everyone all the time like you done usually, 'cause they ain't all good people, or normal in the head.*

So there it was. Even as Kuaray blasted his hatred, the newly empowered man willed himself to stay calm enough to intercept and analyze the barrage.

Kuaray let loose. *Well, Stepdaddy Sequoyah, you senile piece of shit, it's too bad I'm still shorter than you, but I'm at least ten times stronger.*

His jagged nails dug deeper. *Good grief, you're such a crybaby. I only want my friendly handshake to show you who's boss, but you're almost bawling. Oh, by the way. Thanks a million for stealing my sister.*

Ariel answered coolly, *If you really want to pick a fight, be my guest, but it's no contest. I could flatten you in five seconds.* He paused to stare Kuaray down and didn't back off until the boy's nails loosened.

Even then, Ariel refused to let up. *About your sister. She belongs to herself, not to me or you, and I'll knock your head off if you ever need a reminder.*

Kuaray stepped backward, but just for a moment. Then he tried a different tack to unnerve Ariel. *Did you forget your old acquaintances, the Moon People? Boy, are they pissed at you and Sis for ruining their little bomb plot. Believe me, those Moonies don't fool around when they get riled up. So, Stepdaddy Sequoyah, I hope you don't mind dying, but first, you just might find your little pet Yacy swinging from the rafters.* He yawned to broadcast his indifference, displaying a perfect set of sparkling white teeth.

Ariel winced deep inside but smiled suavely. *Mark my words, Kuaray. Since you seem to have a direct pipeline to the old buggers, please let them know that killing off their hand-picked breeding stock won't leave anyone to repopulate the earth.*

To Ariel's amazement, Kuaray's twisted mind and reddened face relaxed as his lips bent upward at the corners. Ariel had inadvertently stimulated the youth's prurient, and pitifully immature, thoughts by using the word "breed."

Kuaray leered suggestively before letting out a guffaw of amusement. *That's so funny. Killing off the breeding stock. What it means is, if everybody's dead, I'll get no "you know what."*

Ariel refrained from laughing aloud, trying to remember if he'd ever been so clueless himself. He rubbed his hands. Through blind luck, he had stumbled upon Kuaray's weak spot. The randy youth was sexually backward and totally inexperienced, which made him less of a monster on one level, at least. Was it possible that Kuaray's threat to marry Yacy was not a nasty sexual proposition but an expression of brotherly affection? Ariel rather doubted that Kuaray's intent was totally innocent, and to be honest, he didn't know quite *what* to think. He made a mental note to bring the uncomfortable subject up with Kuaray someday, or to ask Ethan to do it.

During this exchange, Ethan had been prattling on non-stop, totally unaware that Kuaray had usurped Ariel's attention. Gesturing toward the housing, he remarked cheerfully, "All of us who work at the lab live in prefabs that are exactly alike with three bedrooms lined up in a row like a railroad car. There's no preferential treatment here. But lucky for you and me, someone went on vacation this fall and I got an extra one right next to mine. Now your family and what's-their-names have a great apartment."

In order to answer Ethan, Ariel wrenched himself back into the here-and-now, smiling graciously. "My goodness, Ethan, how thoughtful of you. With all my worries, I completely forgot to find a place to live. All of us, including Jaroslav, Anichka and their baby boy Alexej will be overjoyed. I can't thank you enough, buddy."

***

Ariel sank down on the Victorian sofa in his empty prefab apartment, a stone's throw from Ethan's family-filled one. He rubbed his hand along its familiar arm, recalling how the sofa had once filled most of Ethan's living room at Slime's. But by now the tattered green velvet upholstery had faded to a gray as bleak as the horizon outside the window. It was the same sofa that had survived the clumsy two-man move to the Little Mexico apartment where he had sat for hours nestling with the infant Svnoyi, imagining just how soothing death would feel. It was the same sofa where Ethan had spent many insomniac nights until Luz had swept him into her warm bed. Although Ariel had looked for the ancient piece of furniture in their Montreal apartment, he hadn't found it; perhaps it had been buried beneath piles of children's books, toys, clothing, and Luz's seemingly endless supply of quilts.

Ethan had kindly loaned the sofa to Ariel until he came up with something better. And so he let the broken springs hold him as he gripped his face in both hands, giving way to the misery that seemed to be getting worse by the minute. He missed his family and had no clue where they were other than somewhere between Czechoslovakia and Denmark. He missed his other family, the gentle Jaroslav and Anichka. He missed his father who just then no longer seemed to be nestled by his heart. He missed the High Tatras and even Oklahoma; he despised the frigid wasteland that surrounded the lab on every side. He couldn't make himself write his poetry.

Staring at his feet, Ariel scraped his fingers through his hair, digging his nails into his scalp. Why had he let the Moon People ruin his life starting back when he was four at the orphanage and culminating with the murder of Miriam? And why, oh why had he ever consented to a terrifying journey to nowhere? Ariel contemplated shedding a few tears but realized that indulging in further self-pity would not change how he felt.

***

Without knocking, Luz burst into the room accompanied by Lucy, who carried an orange tomcat slung over her shoulder. Purring and twitching the end of his tail, the cat was clearly docile enough to put up with a capacious bandana tied around his neck. In her free hand, Lucy held a dubious looking sandwich that she extended towards him with a sweet smile. It was a vegetarian offering sprouting uncooked broccoli from all four sides, liberally spread with peanut butter and jam. Ariel noticed a few tufts of stray orange hair stuck in the mix. He had too much respect for his stomach and intestines to attempt eating it, but he thanked the little girl nonetheless. After Lucy had set it down on the sofa arm, she introduced him to Marmalade before retiring to a corner to converse with the genial creature.

Luz stood over Ariel with her hands on her hips. At first, he thought she would scold him for acting spineless, but then she plopped down beside him, causing the tired sofa springs to emit squawks of protest. She took his hand.

"Ariel, my dear, excuse me for barging in, but you are blasting your distress for miles, at least to those of us who can hear it inside our heads. That includes vindictive little Kuaray, so I thought I should trot on over."

Then she lowered her voice, even though she knew Lucy wasn't the eavesdropping type.

"And this is a great opportunity. There are a few more things you should know about the Moon People, and I guess that means I'll have to tell you a little about my past." She gave him a wink. "Don't get your hopes up for anything too racy."

Ariel was intrigued. He knew very little about Luz's life before he'd met her in Luna's Fork 'n Spoon on that awful day after Miriam died. He remembered what she had said after she dropped the quaint Mexican accent that had fooled him completely. *There, there, I truly am your mamacita for today.* He could still remember how it felt when she wrapped her big warm arms around him as he cried.

Luz squeezed his hand. "Jesu Maria, Ariel, weren't you ever curious why I became an Air Force ROTC instructor, not so coincidently at *your* college?" Ariel was embarrassed. He guessed that he had always been too self-absorbed to think about it.

He jumped up, waving his arms. "Luz, I do want to know. It's just that—"

She pulled him back down. "For Christ's sake, why *all* the drama *all* the time? Just let me tell you why.

"I grew up in an Air Force family. We lived on bases all over the place in houses more-or-less like this one, a new base every two years or so. There were ten of us kids. My parents were Catholics. It was no surprise when all those babies arrived.

"My mother died in childbirth with the last one, not with me I'm glad to say. I couldn't have taken the guilt." Luz crossed herself, more from childhood habit than from any lingering religious feeling.

Ariel asked in a hushed voice, "Were you the oldest? Did you have to take care of about nine little ones?"

Luz shrugged. "Yeah, I did. I was twelve when she died, and my father drank too much which is why I got the hell out of there as fast as I could. Career track in the Air Force, Ari. I was big, tough, and pushy, too. I made it to Project Blue Book—"

"You mean tracking UFOs? That's how you discovered the Moon People? In orbit?" His eyes bugged out and his jaw dropped with awe.

Luz chuckled. She felt gratified that Ariel seemed impressed by her high-ranking position, but her eyes were sad. "No Ariel, I had this telepathy for as long as I can remember. I didn't want it, you can be sure of that. I was born with it, like the rest of us. The Moon People have been after me since I was four years old."

"Just like me," Ariel gasped. Then he stopped short, finding it hard to admit even to Luz how utterly miserable he'd been when they found him. Did she know that he'd spent whole nights crying under the covers with his fist in his mouth so no one could hear him?

He asked hesitantly, "Luz, were you lonely, too, you know, so that you kind of started loving them?" Then he shrugged, trying to make light of the question. "I knew it was a bit sick to feel that way, but I couldn't help it. I guess they did fill a hole in my heart."

Luz put her arm on his shoulder and her voice grew gentle. "Yes Ariel, it was like that, I loved them, too. But your childhood was far worse than mine. It was criminal what that school did to you. At least I could jabber in Spanish anytime I wanted and I had my own family, even if it wasn't a happy one."

Ariel wanted Luz to stop rubbing in those awful years, but she didn't let up. "You realize that the Moon People exploited your terrible sadness by promising to take you away from it all. By disappointing you, they made you feel more unhappy than you already did and more in need of the love you weren't getting from other people."

She sighed. "What's worse, they didn't quit after you left the residential school. They took everyone you loved. First Aleta … you think I didn't know about you two? Then Miriam. I was the only one who saw your suicide coming years before you tried it. I even expected it."

Ariel cleared his throat. "God, Luz, can't we talk about something else?"

Then he turned bitter. "Your Air Force Brass must have seen 'em. Why didn't they just shoot the damn globe down?"

"Good question, Ari. But believe it or not, the brass adored those old crazies, and even now they get special protection whenever they show up in our time. You gotta admit, they're unique. They use an amazing technology that the U.S. invented a long time ago, but still can't replicate."

"So the military is clueless about how the Moon People operate? What they're up to? But they must scare *you*, Luz."

"Sure they do. They scare the hell out of me, the cattle-breeding, the coercion—I don't have to tell *you* about that. But something makes me do what they want."

Luz began pacing around the uncarpeted floor, her heels pinging, which he had never seen her do before.

"I got furious once and pleaded with those old farts to shoot the Moonies down. I'll tell you exactly when that happened. It was when they first started pushing Aleta around in Time, the poor little thing. How could she understand? She's never been a particularly good telepath, and she was only fifteen."

Luz sat down again, her voice catching in sympathy for Aleta and for him. "You actually know exactly what they did because it changed your whole life, but you haven't faced it head-on yet. That's all I can say until you figure it out for yourself. And it changed Ethan's life, too." She looked grim. "He'll find out soon enough."

Ariel wrung his hands, overcome with uncertainty. *What's Luz getting at, anyway? She's acting so enigmatic.*

Then Luz shrugged. "Long story short, I was demoted real fast. That's why I ended up teaching ROTC at Santa Margarita. The job was open and it was in sunny California, so I took it." She smiled. "It was actually a lucky break because I could be closer to you, Ethan and Aleta, to either protect you like the Moonies wanted or save you from them. I wasn't sure which. Sometimes I wonder if they set it up."

Ariel nudged Luz's arm. "Now I think I can understand exactly why the Moon People have it in for you."

Luz laughed aloud for the first time. "Because I wanted them shot out of the sky? That is only *one* of the reasons and hardly the clincher. It's probably the one that occurs to Sasquatch occasionally when he isn't swooning over my Rubenesque proportions. But Nessie, that old Baba Yaga. *She's* the lady with the vendetta. And you heard her say it yourself. Something about a 'gifted mind, but the morals of an alley cat.'

"First she had a fit over the ROTC student, but then, so did the Santa Margarita administration. But when Ethan and I, the man who wasn't mine to take—well, the crazy old bitch's puritanical notions about family values kicked in. It raised her hackles, you know, the fur along a dog's back when it gets ready to leap at your jugular vein."

Blushing, Luz hesitated, something Ariel had never seen her do before. "The truth is, before I fell for Ethan my love life was pretty short on action. I always said men were complete dolts, utterly beneath my contempt, but I didn't totally believe it. It was just that most men wouldn't have me. But I wasn't immune. The first time I fell madly in love, head over heels, in fact, was with *you*, Ari."

Ariel was deeply touched by her admission. *She fell head over heels in love with me? Ah, dear Luz. She never let on how she felt because she knew I was mourning for Miriam.*

Ariel had figured her all wrong on a number of points, but he had another surprise coming. "So Luz, after all this, even with the Moon People still kicking up a fuss about you, how can you possibly be the most enthusiastic supporter of our journey?"

"Ariel, darling, you don't know the inner me. You *could* get over yourself long enough to take a look inside to see how I tick. Of course I supported the journey as soon as I understood just what the Moonies had been up to all those years with their plotting and planning." She smiled in such a winsome way that for a moment Ariel understood exactly why Ethan had fallen for her.

"How do you think I found out, Ariel? I know I should be embarrassed to tell you this, but I peeked. I took the liberty of reading your anguished mind up there in that Moon when you saw the earth in ruins. That did it for *me*. Don't forget I'm an Air Force brat and a true patriot. I'll do anything to preserve the good old U.S. of A." She added with a theatrical sigh, "Even if it means starting over from scratch."

Luz stood up to leave, kissing him warmly on the cheek before taking her daughter's diminutive hand in her big one. The cat led the way out, turning its head from side to side sniffing the air, bidding goodbye to the uneaten sandwich.

Luz turned back. "And incidentally, I like you a lot better now, inside your own flesh. Your disembodied mind never did much for me except to make me terribly, terribly sad."

Ariel felt better. He hadn't realized that Luz had been watching over him even after Santa Margarita, and although she didn't intervene in his life, she would always be there like a guardian angel. *Dear, dear Luz. Ethan is a lucky man.*

He rose to make coffee on the oil stove and to dispose of the sandwich that had fallen behind one of the sofa's bowlegs.

***

From the kitchen, a staccato pounding on the front door made Ariel jump. Was that Ethan's voice? He was yelling in terror through the flimsy wood muffled by the long hallway leading to the living room.

"Oh, please, *please* let me in, Ari. *Help me.*"

When Ariel opened the door, Ethan fell onto the floor, his face ashen and his chest incongruously bare beneath an unzipped parka. Ariel lugged him the length of the hall to the sofa.

"Good God, Ethan, what's happened? I'll get Luz."

Once Ariel plunked him down, the overwrought man managed through chattering teeth, "No, no, only you can help me with this."

As soon as Ethan could sit upright, Ariel took off the parka and helped him into one of his own sweaters. Then he put a cup of fresh hot coffee into his friend's trembling hands. At last Ethan began his story, stuttering at first.

"I-I was at the airport to pick up a package for the lab, and I was standing on the tarmac waiting for the plane. I started hopping up and down; it was as cold as it ever gets with a mean wind blowing. And the Northern Lights, they were on full, looking like big green wheels. And then this girl *crash-lands* at my feet. God knows where she came from. I swear I only looked away for a second up at the sky. Those damned cargo planes are always late."

He stopped to drink some coffee and organize his thoughts. "Ari, she was only a kid, maybe fourteen or fifteen years old. I think she must've bumped her head hard because I had to help her stand up."

Ethan stared into space for a minute. "If you think that was weird, I'm just getting started. Here it is a freezing night in the middle of winter with the Northern Lights putting on a great show and she's wearing only this short nightgown with no coat. And Jesus, she's barefoot! She's shaking and looking at the Lights, freaking out, and I swear, turning blue."

Ethan stopped, the muscles in his jaw twitching uncontrollably.

Ariel prodded him on, gently. "So what did you do?"

Ethan drained his coffee cup and put it on the floor. "Well, I wanted to warm her up, but at the same time I figured I should get the police to help her." Then Ethan hesitated, almost as if asking Ariel if he had behaved badly.

"I didn't want her to take it wrong, Ari. I mean, she was a teenager. I-I took off my sweatshirt and gave it to her, and I helped her put it on. It was that one I bought a few days ago from the clearance bin at The Trading Post. It was like a million others; you saw it. It was red with a big cartoon polar bear and a 1974 on it."

Ariel thought that Ethan should have found the police before touching the girl, but he refrained from saying so. Instead, he made a facetious remark. "Losing that ugly shirt wasn't so bad then, and I'm glad to know why you showed up here half naked."

Ethan looked so distressed by the comment that Ariel hurried to take it back. "Uh, listen, Ethan, I guess you did the right thing. After all, she *was* freezing."

Ethan didn't take comfort from Ariel's hasty revision, and if possible, his face grew more contorted beneath his wrinkled brow.

"Now comes the part that's really confusing. Terrifying, too." He sounded increasingly ill-at-ease as his story progressed. "I-I tried to warm her up inside my parka by putting my arms around her."

Ariel thought to himself, Against his bare chest? If the gift of the sweatshirt hadn't shook up the girl enough, surely she must have taken his embrace inside the parka all wrong. Wait 'til Lucy gets older. He'll figure it out.

Ethan dropped his head into his hands for a moment, and after that could barely get out the next part.

"Ari, it was then that I recognized her. She was Aleta, no doubt about it. I couldn't tell so much from her looks, it's been so long, except for that red-gold hair no one could ever forget. It was that *feeling* we used to have deep inside our heads. Well, still do sometimes. And please don't make me explain it again because I told you about it when I saw you in Montreal."

Suddenly Ariel's heart jumped. Something about the red-gold hair jogged a deeply buried memory. It crept upward with an insistence he couldn't control. *Did I see Aleta, too, before Santa Margarita?*

Ethan went on in a whisper, "I called out her name. I sure didn't mean to, it just popped out. When I said it, she started struggling, really scared. I held her tighter, I guess to reassure her, and she was gone. Just like that, gone."

He was shaking again and stuttering. "Well, th-that was all I could take. I-I said fuck the damn package and grabbed a taxi for home—you know, the one driven by that crazy Eskimo we all call The Skidder. We were doing this ice dance all over the road when it hit me. I suddenly remembered the sweatshirt. That I'd seen it a long time ago. Long before last week when I bought it."

Then Ethan looked away from Ariel, his silence acknowledging a sensitive subject coming up. "Aleta gave it to me the first time we … we made love at Santa Margarita. Although we'd sworn eternal 'death do us part' and all that, I thought the sweatshirt looked stupid with that ugly polar bear on it, and the numbers didn't make sense." He shook his head. "I didn't even think they might be a year because back then it was only 1961. I never wore it after that night. I kind of remember throwing it away."

Ariel was at a loss how to explain things to Ethan. He had a very good idea what had happened to Ethan from what Luz had just told him, how she had begged the Brass to shoot down the Moon People after they started pushing fifteen-year-old Aleta around in Time. To add to his discomfort, the vision of the fairy princess from his most vulnerable days at the horrible residential school began to resurface.

Luz's prophetic sentences made more sense now as his own memories seeped back into his conscious mind. *You actually know exactly what they did because it changed your whole life, but you haven't faced it head-on yet. And it changed Ethan's life, too. He'll find out soon enough.*

Ariel put a hand on Ethan's shoulder, his voice surprisingly steady considering how he felt inside.

"Listen, Old Man. I think I've figured out what happened to you at the airport, but there's one person who knows much more than I do and that's Luz. We talked earlier this afternoon, and she told me a lot." He pleaded, "Ethan, she loves you so much. Please just hug her and tell her what you saw. She'll explain everything."

He went on hesitantly, "I hope Aleta isn't still a problem for you and Luz. I'm sure *we* don't have anything to worry about. At least I don't think we do." He stood up, opening his hands for emphasis. "You have to be sure, Ethan, you *have* to and so does Luz. All of us will be living together peacefully for a long, long time — with any luck, that is."

Ethan replied in measured tones with an unnatural calm, "Then, Ari, if you *really* want peace so much, you owe me the truth, better late than never. I'll see if I can take it. Did you sleep with Aleta at Santa Margarita?"

For once, Ariel's answer was a simple, unadorned yes.

Ethan sighed, then rose to put on his parka and left without a word.

With trepidation, Ariel looked into Ethan's thoughts. There was no anger, only a bone-deep weariness, tempered by relief, and an overwhelming desire to hold Luz in his arms.

***

Even though the room had been thoroughly heated by the oil stove, Ariel shook with chills in his temporary bed made up of Luz's thick quilts. Of course deep down, the first moment he saw Aleta at Santa Margarita he'd recognized that she was the fairy princess. That was why he'd been so drawn to her — so much so that he could hardly concentrate on his studies or on anything else. By age nineteen, Ariel had hidden the brilliant vision of a maiden surrounded by light deep beneath many protective layers, along with the rest of his Cherokee self.

But at this moment Aleta's halo of red-gold hair and her tender hands caressing his stubby child's fingers came flooding back with enough force to make him cry out. How the Moon People had tortured the young Sequoyah, constantly dangling her image before his dazzled eyes, promising that she would come for him any day if he would but love them.

Ariel tossed and turned, throwing off the quilts. Had the Moon People sent poor teenage Aleta both backward and forward in Time in some warped trial to test her preference for either Ethan or himself? Or, as Nessie had suggested, because she and Sasquatch were bored? It occurred to him that in her confusion Aleta had slept with them both, one right after the other. But in the depths of her heart, she had been torn between the passion she felt for him and the duty she felt towards Ethan, the Moon People's choice for her. Then the Moon People had ripped her away from the world she knew to thrust her alone and pregnant into an alien past.

Next, he thought of Miriam stuck in the middle. Without remorse they had killed the woman he loved after using her compliant womb, undoubtedly so that he would move on to others. They had said as much.

Suddenly he sat up, burning with hatred, a fire smoldering with such intensity that he doubled over, groaning aloud and beating his fists against his temples. *If those monsters fell from the sky this moment, I wouldn't care. I'd celebrate, I'd die of happiness, I'd crunch their bones beneath my boots, I'd even bathe my hands in their ancient blackened blood.*

Chapter 20 The Cabbages

During the next few weeks, Ariel turned the prefab into a home for the arriving families. He bought used furniture and household goods advertised on lab bulletin boards since even the hardiest souls often left the relentless gray of Baffin Island's arctic winter once they lost the courage to tough it out. His prized find was an antique brass bed purchased for his lovely wife, who had often mentioned how much she wanted one. Unfortunately, the spools and knobs that he burnished until they shone did not totally make up for the broken-down mattress and springs. And Ariel never found a sofa as satisfactory as the Victorian, which remained in the center of the living room, a faded belle from yesteryear's cotillion.

Arranging the apartment kept Ariel occupied for a while, but once it was finished, he found that waiting for Aleta and the children became almost unbearable. He learned from Svnoyi that they were on their way. All of them had been laid low for weeks in Denmark by the Hong Kong flu, with Aleta and Phoenix hardest hit. Anichka let him know that her course on gypsy medicine at Indian Hospital in Tahlequah was going well, but that Jaroslav had fallen into a crippling depression after leaving his alpine home. Only strenuous day hikes through the foothills of the Ozarks with little Alexej riding on his broad back seemed to soothe him.

Ariel was hardly better off. He sat on the old sofa for hours, contemplating the arctic silence. Whenever he looked out the living room window at the blowing snow that met the horizon in a wash of absent color, he felt as if he might lose his mind. Then, to break the winter spell cast by Frobisher Bay, he would pace the length of the prefab listening to the thudding of his own heart.

One sunny morning he decided to save his sanity by hiking along the road to the slipshod town of Frobisher Bay. He walked slowly, his head bent in thought as he methodically kicked his worn boots into the plowed snow bank along its edge. But without warning a sudden storm swept in, leaving him blind and fearful, hunkering down where he stood.

Just then a taxi spewing snow from its tires screeched to a halt at his side. At the wheel was the Eskimo whom he and everyone else called The Skidder. Without ado, The Skidder threw Ariel into the back seat, leaving him lying prone and breathless, near tears from awed relief. In the first place, what sixth sense had guided this man to find him, and second, how could he then navigate back to the Project in whiteout conditions that obliterated the road? At the end of the journey, the Eskimo refused to accept a fare, remaining impassive behind his wolf-trimmed parka. But for the briefest of seconds, Ariel thought he felt a flash of kinship.

Ariel had long since given up any attempt to start his epic poem about the Trail of Tears. Of course, Luz knew how unhappy he was, and invited him over almost every evening for dinner. He often stayed late into the night to discuss plans for the trip, even talking to Kuaray, whose eyes glinted at the prospect of leaving behind the world that had always been hostile towards him. Both Oscar and Lucy contributed their ideas as they slipped slender hands into Ariel's great ones, hoping to comfort their stricken Uncle Sequoyah.

On one particularly fruitful night of brainstorming, everyone agreed that the physical design of the vehicle didn't matter much since time travel wouldn't require it to rise above the earth. Unlike the Moon People's little globe condemned to circle forever, their vehicle would never need to reach an orbit. Ethan and Kuaray's main challenge would be to start it going and then stop its forward advance through Time after it had passed well beyond the ravages of the world's final war. Everyone also agreed that the earth's magnetic field, particularly strong this far north, would somehow power the vehicle in conjunction with the unified force of fourteen interconnected minds.

The younger children knew exactly where the perfect vehicle lay hidden—in plain sight. In the shadow of the towering back fence, a circa 1950s Greyhound bus stood unnoticed behind the huge rectangular trash bins, empty wire spools, rotting fiberboard, and old oil stoves with their splitting seams. The sturdy bus was sound of body, the sleek canine still running tirelessly on both of its metallic sides, although it had been stripped of its seats and wheels. Perhaps the bus had once housed an impoverished Eskimo family before the lab's new fence had shut them out, or perhaps it had been hauled there by some long-departed public transportation buff intent on restoring it to its former glory.

Both Ariel and Ethan recalled the Moon People's Greyhound of the Future that lost its ability to rise off the ground the day after Miriam died, its tailpipe spewing clouds of black exhaust all along Highway 17. Sometimes Ariel wondered what had happened to its rusting carcass, flattened into a pancake at the Santa Clara junkyard. Oh, how fervently they hoped that this Greyhound would fulfill its unprecedented mission—a clandestine departure from behind the trash bins and a propitious arrival in the renewed world.

***

Several months later, the day Ariel had been longing for finally arrived. With butterflies in his stomach, he walked the ten miles to the airport at Frobisher Bay to meet his beloved family—Aleta, Svnoyi, Yacy, Phoenix, and Agali—for they were finally flying in from Greenland. He had bought warm presents for all of them to wear home in the taxi: sealskin mitts with pretty fox trim for Aleta and the girls, and caribou mitts for Phoenix. He had also remembered cozy hats with ear flaps that could be worn under the parkas that they would surely purchase soon. At home, he had hidden something additional for Aleta in the night-table drawer—a newly scripted love poem that had taken him two weeks to perfect.

As the plane taxied to a stop, Ariel's heart rose into his throat with excitement. Svnoyi and Yacy bounded down the stairs first, looking radiantly lovely. They threw their arms around him while jumping up and down. The little blond and the brunette, identical in height, exclaimed in perfect unison, "We love you, we love you, Daddy!"

Yacy had called him Daddy along with Svnoyi? At first, she had called him Stepdaddy Sequoyah, and later Daddy Sequoyah. He almost wept when he heard a simple Daddy. Phoenix and Agali ran to him, their unbuttoned woolen coats flying behind them.

Only Aleta brushed past Ariel without a glance, her eyes squinting in the snow's glare above the thin, angry line of her mouth. She waved at the lone cab, then hustled the children into the back seat, shoving both violins onto their laps. Tossing her head to show her disdain for him, she slammed the door ferociously before taking her own place in the front.

Ariel stood on the tarmac, too stunned to react as the cab drove off, allowing the warm gifts that he'd intended for their trip home to slip from his lax fingers.

Just then, as if summoned, The Skidder pulled up. As was his wont, he didn't say a word but got out of his cab to retrieve the package that lay forgotten on the ground. Ariel slid into the back seat, averting his wet face. The Skidder restrained his usual acrobatics, driving relatively straight as if commiserating with Ariel. For the second time, he refused to accept a fare.

***

Ariel tiptoed into his apartment not knowing what to expect. Phoenix and Agali had apparently gone next door to meet Luz, Oscar, and Lucy. He could picture the lunch treat in store for them — peanut butter and broccoli sandwiches with cat-hair garnish.

Behind one of the bedroom doors Ariel heard Yacy crying and Svnoyi murmuring words of comfort. He knew that he had wronged his new daughter by bringing her back to face Kuaray, but at the moment, his wife's behavior worried him even more.

Aleta had vanished into their bedroom, leaving all of her belongings in the hall. The violins straddled the width of it, providing the kind of barrier that would not survive an inadvertent kick. So Ariel moved them into the cramped living room, carefully stacking the almost identical cases beside one of the Victorian sofa's arms. Then he stood in front of the bedroom door, puzzling out his next move. Since none of the doors had locks, he could simply walk in on Aleta, although he hesitated to do so.

A quick peek at her thoughts revealed a mind in conflict; she wanted to be left in peace just as fervently as she wanted to yell at him. But there was something else. A tiny part of her desired to lie beside him.

Ariel took a gamble. He walked in without knocking and sat on the bed as close as possible to Aleta's aggressively displayed C-shaped back with its prominent vertebrae. She had curled herself into a tight ball so theatrically posed that it sent an unexpected message: she wanted him to challenge her misery and anger. Ariel knew then that if he pulled her close, she would acquiesce rather than fight. So he did.

But then she lay still, too mentally and physically exhausted to respond to his gentle advances. They remained in silence for the rest of the afternoon, at least lying on the same bed a few feet from each other, sometimes dozing, sometimes thinking of nothing in particular. He had fantasized for months about their impassioned reunion. But considering the scene at the airport, he was relieved that they were in the same room together. He marveled at the intensity of his feelings in spite of her rebuff. He was more in love with her than ever.

As the days passed, their relationship didn't improve. Although Aleta occasionally let Ariel put his arms around her, she wouldn't permit his hands to stray over her breasts or reach below her waist. He was also denied any kissing more passionate than a peck on the cheek. Every night Ariel begged his wife to give him an explanation for her coldness, but she cut off his entreaties with a decisive shake of her head followed by a haughty sniff.

Ariel couldn't help remembering how after Phoenix's birth she had driven him nearly mad by purposely revealing an expanse of tender flesh above the neckline of Anichka's nightgown, but there was none of that now. Instead, she buttoned a nun-like robe up to her neck, and with a wide yawn that signaled her bedtime, she turned toward the wall with a monumental heaving of the worn mattress and springs. Often, he considered plowing through her thoughts to uncover the reason for her apparent dislike of him, but couldn't bring himself to do it.

When Ariel's breaking point came, he was almost as amazed as she was.

He burst out, "I can't stand this. Obviously, you hate me." He hastily gathered up his clothing and boots, dropping them again as he tripped on the corner of an imitation Turkish rug. Then he turned toward her, stabbing a finger in her direction even though her back was turned. He announced in a fury, "Oh, don't worry about *me*, sweetheart. There are plenty of women out there who would have me in a second."

Aleta remained curled in her habitual ball, but whispered just loudly enough for him to hear her, "Ariel, where are you going?"

"Oh," he replied airily, "To Frobisher Bay. There are bars all over the damn town, and Ethan says the one called the **Lazy Daisy** has a girl perched on every barstool, just dying to get picked up by someone good-looking like me."

Ariel certainly didn't expect the rush of words that followed. Aleta begged in a voice just short of whining, "Ariel, don't go there, please. Find someplace else. That's where Kuaray plays violin every night in his top hat and tails, and he dances and does magic tricks. Svnoyi says it's because he wants the money for something. Please."

She raised her voice anxiously. "If he sees you, well then, everyone will know."

Ariel couldn't believe his ears. Aleta was perfectly willing to let him seduce strange women but was bothered by appearances. How baffling she had become.

Aleta sat up suddenly, tucking her nightgown demurely over her knees and down under her toes. Then she patted the bed, mutely begging him to sit down.

When she finally spoke, he had to strain his ears to hear her. "It's not true that I want you to find someone else. It's just that I can't do *it* anymore. You know, have sex."

She paused for a long time, raking her fingers through her long red-gold hair, which he noticed had a few prematurely gray streaks in it.

She went on with obvious reluctance, "I want to tell you a story about something that happened, and I don't know what it means. But it bothers me all the time because it's connected to how I feel." She covered her face with trembling fingers. "Please pardon me, I don't tell stories well."

Ariel sat beside her. He didn't dare take her into his arms, although he pressed her hand encouragingly.

"It-it was after you left for Tahlequah, and Tulak was helping us get our papers. Anichka sent me outside behind the Star Annex to get two cabbages from Phoenix's vegetable garden for the borscht she was making." Aleta stopped to wipe tears off her face with a handkerchief that she kept tightly clutched in her fingers.

"Then like always, Anichka asked me to chop them up, but when I cut them in half, each one had a big red worm in it as thick as your finger. The leaves around the worm were eaten away leaving a black cave, and all the other leaves on the inside had turned a slimy brown."

Ariel put a hand on her shoulder, but she refused any comfort, brushing it off with her free hand. She could sit by him no longer, so she rose abruptly from the squeaky bed. Sliding on her mules, she shuffled the few feet to the back of the room, the soles slapping against her heels. Only then was she able to finish her story, her eyes staring at the shuttered window.

"Anichka took one look at the cabbages and told me to throw them out. And-and I'd never seen her do what happened next. She started crying so hard she had to put her apron over her head."

***

Ariel couldn't fathom Aleta's excruciating story of the two rotten cabbages. So when Svnoyi set up a secret meeting in the Greyhound bus, he hoped she'd be willing to enlighten him. He also wanted to know why on earth Kuaray had reverted to his habit from the old Montreal days of playing the buffoon for money.

Clearly, Svnoyi had another subject in mind. She slipped her mitts into Ariel's big paws and turned toward him, her face solemn.

"You may not want to hear this, Daddy, but you have to go back to Oklahoma before we leave. There's a good reason."

Ariel stopped her by grabbing her arm. "That's crazy, I can't go all that way. And what about Aleta? I can't just take off."

Svnoyi went on as if oblivious to his objections. "Right now Etsi would be happier without you. Oh, Daddy, I know that hurts, but listen. Anichka and Alexej are arriving here any day now because her course is finished, but Jaroslav didn't come with her. He stayed behind in Mohe's house and you have to go get him."

"But why isn't he with them? What's going on?"

There was a lengthy silence as the cloud from his warm breath dissipated in the frosty air. In early May it was still winter-cold in this perpetually overcast land.

Svnoyi's sudden frown changed to a scowl as she pulled her hands from his, thrusting her fists against her hips through the bulk of her parka.

"Daddy, how are you *ever* going to lead us if you don't use your abilities? You have to keep track of everybody's feelings, you just have to."

Then she spoke louder and more angrily. "When will you get it through your thick head that it's not spying to look at people's thoughts, Daddy? Jaroslav and Anichka are having their troubles, and you should have seen that a long time ago. Obviously, it's too late now to talk to him, so you have to go to Oklahoma and try to fix things."

Svnoyi kept at him, tossing her head for emphasis. Ariel couldn't help noticing the similarity to Aleta's gesture from the infamous scene at the airport.

"Why do I have to be your teacher, Daddy? Why?"

Svnoyi's voice softened, but only a bit. "You can do it. I've seen you. You got it right once or twice, like with Kuaray on your first day here, but most of the time you just think about yourself, and about not hurting anyone's feelings. You use your emotions all the time, not your head.

"Just try to remember what Mohe said before he died, that you have to see better what people are thinking. Have you forgotten your Edoda? He's lying right next to your heart, Daddy."

Svnoyi began pulling her earflaps down to prepare for the cold wind outside. But as she rose, Ariel looked at her with such pleading in his eyes that she sat down again.

"Svnoyi, please don't go." He stopped. "Th-there's just something … something I want to tell you before I leave for Oklahoma. It's a story that might explain why I don't look into other people's minds very easily and I *know* it doesn't let me off the hook." He wrung his hands.

"My first year at the residential school, I ran away almost every night. Maybe it was because the Moon People were in my head all the time promising me something better, or maybe it was less complicated than that. I was just plain miserable, you know."

Svnoyi did know, even though he seldom talked about his past.

"When I broke out, I would climb out of a window in the little boys' dormitory and then run straight down the road until I fell down. Suddenly, a tall man would appear from nowhere and carry me back to the school. He never spoke, but he was kind, and I usually fell asleep in his arms." Ariel was shivering now, but not from the cold.

"Even at four I already knew I was different, and something told me that if I looked inside him, I could find out who he was. But I also knew that *if* I looked, he would leave and never come back. I never looked, but one day he vanished anyway.

"Now I know who he was because he's the one lying right next to my heart. And I also know why he stopped coming because he told me, and it was simple really; I didn't need him anymore. But I missed him so much, I always thought he disappeared because I *almost* pried."

There were tears on his cheeks. "Svnoyi, please don't laugh. I know I am just a coward making excuses."

Chapter 21 Departure

Even in springtime, unpredictable Oklahoma greeted Ariel with ninety-degree heat and a ferocious wind. It may have ripped loose a banging shutter that hung by one remaining hinge from his yellow foursquare, but he doubted that the damage was recent.

The moment Ariel reluctantly entered the front door, the smell of garbage making the transition from overripe to rotten hit him square in the face. His feet followed his nose into the kitchen as dust wafted in front of him in little puffs. The kitchen was a mess. Crusted dishes threatened to topple out of the sink onto the grease-slicked linoleum, joining others that had already made the trip. Dozens of discarded wine bottles lay everywhere, the dregs filling the air with a lugubrious stench.

Ariel thought back to his first view of the house when he'd entered at Mohe's invitation. As the alcoholic led him through the streets laughing at nothing and swaying from side to side, Ariel had anticipated the worst. But the tired old place had looked surprisingly clean and orderly. Mohe couldn't wait to show Ariel around. Never one for house tours, he had followed dutifully, perversely hoping that the violin would let off an ear-splitting wail from the cellar.

The old man was proud of his belongings. He lovingly had run work-roughened hands over the pillows of a threadbare sofa upholstered in blue plaid, and across the kitchen table with its top scoured down to the bare wood. Then he had offered Ariel a chair and uttered the sentence that had changed everything: "If I can talk you into being my son …."

Ariel's thoughts jumped ahead to Birdie and Atsina who had worked so hard to spruce up their uncle's last refuge, painting the house inside and out, sewing bright red curtains, and planting a flower garden out front. He bent to pick up the cracked mug with the elk on it that had been sitting on the night table by Mohe's bed. Cradling it in his big hands, he turned it over and over, thinking bitterly, *Just stay cool. There's nothing here that can't be fixed, except perhaps Jaroslav's mind.*

Ariel found Jaroslav in the same second-floor bedroom where he himself had slept not so long ago. Even though it was midday, Jaroslav was still buried under the covers, most certainly wide awake but pretending to sleep, hoping Ariel would leave. The rank odor of old sweat and the fake snoring disgusted Ariel, but one mud-caked hiking boot protruding from the swirled mass of blankets and sheets was the last straw. Ariel stripped off the bedding with a whoosh, quaking with a white-hot fury that bubbled up from nowhere.

Suddenly he stopped short. In the middle of yanking Jaroslav's supine frame feet-first onto the floor with a bone-rattling thump, he happened to glimpse the once-proud ranger's harrowed thoughts coiling behind his clenched eyes. Filled with pity, Ariel bent down, thrusting his hands beneath Jaroslav's elbows to help him stand, but the drunken man's rubbery knees wouldn't cooperate. At last, Ariel knelt down, gathering him as close as the other would allow in his humiliated state.

Before Ariel could speak, Jaroslav whimpered, then roared angrily, "It not my fault. I tell you what happen, Ariel, I tell you. But not today, *not today.*" Then he peered at Ariel from beneath puffy eyelids, asking in a trembling voice, "Aleta not say *anything?*"

Nervous words tumbled out of Ariel's mouth. "Okay, okay, calm down. She didn't say anything, but whatever it is, tell me later, it can wait. Everything's gonna be fine, I'm here, I'm here ...." His voice trailed off as he groaned from the effort of hoisting Jaroslav back onto the bed. "Listen, friend, get up now, and take a bath. Meanwhile, I'll wash the dishes and make us some really, really strong coffee."

An hour later the two sat at the scrubbed breakfast table in silence. Eventually, Ariel cleared his throat and spoke offhandedly, "Hey, Jaroslav, I'm thinking of hiking every single day that the weather's good. I've been snowbound for too long, and could sure use your company if you'll join me."

Jaroslav turned away, frowning. When he finally answered, he shrugged as if making a concession. "Okay, maybe ... maybe I go, too."

His pose was short-lived. Hanging his head with embarrassment, he tried to hide his shaking hands by gripping his coffee mug.

He mumbled, "Ariel, I know what you really ask, and I-I try. In mountain, I not drink. At home, I not drink so much."

So in the following weeks that stretched to months, Ariel and Jaroslav fell into a daily routine. They hiked at top speed in the foothills of the Ozarks until the hot afternoon sun drove them to find a shady grove by the trail, usually one bordered by a spring-swollen brook. Gasping for breath, Ariel would flop down on his back to gaze upward at the tree branches, the clusters of leaves trembling and sighing high above his head. At the same time, he slapped at the tiny biting flies that circled in aimless black clouds.

But once he drew his notebook and pen from his knapsack, the rest of the afternoon would vanish as the words for his epic poem *Trail of Tears* filled page after page.

Ariel's proximity to those dolorous sites where the Cherokee had dragged unwilling feet spirited him into the past. Did Aleta ride this trail in the sick wagon with Unalii and Magnolia in the cruel summer heat of 1838? Was it here, or somewhere else, that he found her lying beside the corpse of a golden eagle with wing and heart shot through? Or over here where Mohe's great-great grandmother Tsula had roped the screaming violin to drag it to Tahlequah, or here, a mile or two down the trail, where a roaring vortex had sucked Kuaray and Yacy into the center of the earth?

Ariel lay back, dizzy with happiness, as a silky soft Cherokee word from his childhood took shape in the back of his brain, rolled along his tongue and slipped out of his mouth. It was a question, actually. *Diquenvsvis?*

God, he thought. I just asked myself if this is my home.

Jaroslav sat up with a jerk. "What? You say something?" As usual, the man who yearned for his alpine past had been sleeping the afternoon away even though he wasn't tired.

"It's nothing," Ariel whispered. "Just a word I remembered." But tears stood in his eyes.

***

Once summer ended and the rainy season had taken the pleasure out of hiking, Jaroslav's addiction to drink worsened. The frustrated head ranger, who had famously traversed every inch of the rugged High Tatras, spent whole days plunked in an old pink armchair glowering at the streaming windowpane—bottle in hand.

Hoping to impress the locals with the seriousness of his request, Ariel tried out his emerging child's Cherokee at every native-owned liquor store in Tahlequah. He begged the shopkeepers not to sell to Jaroslav, even though he knew that they started snickering the minute he turned his back. No doubt they found his labored attempt at speaking the mother tongue hilarious. But mainly they couldn't resist accepting the morose foreigner's money, and they also took a contrary delight in witnessing a white customer's fall into degradation.

As autumn turned to winter, Ariel's despair grew. He had to acknowledge that it was almost time to return to Frobisher Bay with Jaroslav in tow, uncured, dangerously volatile, more miserable than before. During the long hours when Ariel was shut up in the house doing mundane chores, he felt the pull of his father's bones beckoning from the little pine box on Baffin Island, where they had lain for more than a year.

This morbid fancy was compelling enough, but a more essential fact finally jerked him out of his indolence. He counted up the weeks. Early in December Ethan had submitted his resignation to the lab, requiring the little band to leave the world they knew by the end of January at the latest.

Without warning, Ariel felt a stab of homesickness for his family almost as intense as the inexplicable ache for his aunties from the old days at the residential school. Jaroslav's illness be damned; they could delay no longer.

Once Ariel was certain that Jaroslav was dead out for the night, he tried to reach his daughter. After his third attempt, Svnoyi answered with an impulsive laugh that rushed through his head like a snow-fed mountain rivulet.

Daddy, I'm in the back of the Greyhound with Oscar. She felt her father recoil and laughed again. *No, it's not like that, but I am getting older, you know. We're trying to make the hoes and rakes fit. And the tools for building houses. And the —*

Ariel broke in, *How's the ship's drive? Is it ready?*

Svnoyi had reason to celebrate, and Ariel could sense Oscar cheering along with her.

Ethan and Kuaray got it, Daddy, just today. It has to do with the Northern Lights and using the sun somehow, and the earth like a big magnet, but mostly it's us.

A thrill shot through Ariel. He knew what was coming.

Ethan and Kuaray, they looked so funny prancing around, all puffed up. Ethan's glasses kept sliding off his nose. They explained how they can harness our minds to move the ship.

All the bits and pieces were falling into place.

Svnoyi, darling, we're coming home, Jaroslav and me. How's Etsi, and how's Yacy?

Svnoyi didn't answer. She had abruptly cut off the conversation. The sudden ending unnerved Ariel, and he struggled against his impulse to bother Svnoyi again. He sighed. Svnoyi always had a reason for the things she did, so if she was covering something up, it was better if he didn't know about it, at least not yet. But he took it as a warning, nonetheless, and paced around his bedroom for hours deciding just how to clear up his affairs in Tahlequah by the end of the week.

He ticked the jobs off on his fingers. Luckily his poem was already at the publishers in New York, and he'd almost gotten over the new title they'd forced on him: *Sing From Thy Broken Heart, O Fiddle!* First thing tomorrow he'd arrange turning over his house to the new Principal Chief Swimmer and the Cherokee Nation. Some of the furniture could stay, the rest would be given away. But first, he'd invite his cousins Birdie and Atsina with their husbands and children to a nostalgic dinner with toasts and speeches, a farewell feast like none other to celebrate the renewal of his roots. He fell asleep, at peace with himself for the first time in weeks.

Ariel wasn't alone in wanting to make the dinner party a memorable occasion. His cousins decided to present him with parting gifts so thoughtful, *so meaningful* that he would feel homesick enough to return. The sisters simply couldn't fathom why Ariel preferred an ugly two-bit town at the Arctic Circle over gracious Tahlequah, especially now that he'd found *them*.

After spending two hours at the Northeastern State bookstore, they settled on a Cherokee dictionary to help him plump up his vocabulary, and a handsome two-volume set containing the legends of his ancestors, the Eastern Cherokee. Of course, Ariel knew the legends already from doing research for his poem at the library, but they were sure he'd shed a tear or two when he received his very own copy.

Privately, each hoped he'd write now and then, winding up his letters with romantic postscripts, in Cherokee, that the husbands couldn't read. Ariel didn't realize it, but his undeniably attractive person sometimes made Birdie and Atsina wish they weren't related to him.

***

By afternoon, Ariel had a hearty beef stew, the party's main dish, simmering on the stove, the recipe adapted from one of Anichka's most savory High Tatras' specialties. To be fair, Jaroslav had tried to help out by slicing the carrots and potatoes, but a few hopelessly random slashes with the gleaming knife disqualified him instantly. Ariel threw Jaroslav out of the kitchen but could hear him upstairs drunkenly bellowing the hymns of his choirboy days.

As the enticing aroma of the meat and vegetables permeated the whole house, Ariel sat at the kitchen table to write farewell poems on textured linen paper for each of his beloved cousins. Then he set the dining table with any plates and glassware that had survived Jaroslav's drunken rages. He prayed that Jaroslav's good mood would last. What Ariel wouldn't give to have the man act half decently in front of the two people in Tahlequah he cherished most.

Everything had been going so well. Ariel took no chances with alcoholic beverages at the table; the company raised glasses of bubbly ginger ale for the informal toasts that made everyone laugh and cheer and tear up sometimes. With sparkling eyes, Birdie rose and rapped on her glass with a spoon. Dancing a little jig in place, she toasted Mohe's ingenious plan to spirit Anichka out of Czechoslovakia, letting slip the name Tulip the Red.

Not even an ex-football player of Ariel's caliber could have caught a flying tureen of leftover stew. The contents, mainly hot root vegetables and thick broth, hit the wall above Birdie's head and ricocheted across the table, splatting her two perfectly behaved young sons and Atsina's sweet toddler twin girls squarely in their terrified faces. The husbands, who had so far sat gamely at the sidelines, sprang into action, wrestling the intoxicated Jaroslav to the floor. Knocked flat on his back, he bayed like a wolf at the overhead light fixture before passing out.

Ariel found himself weeping, and he was not the only one. His cousins, tears streaming down their wholesome cheeks, herded the bawling children out the door without a goodbye. The husbands followed directly, after giving the unconscious Jaroslav a few parting kicks aimed at his kidneys.

First Ariel poured a glass of ginger ale onto Jaroslav's face. He came round and stood up shakily, his back hunched over as he massaged his bruised abdomen. Ariel drove him back to the floor with expert punches designed to hurt.

He snarled, "You bastard! I should kill you." Then he sat on Jaroslav so he couldn't get up.

"No, Jaroslav! Make that I *will* kill you if you don't cut out the crap and talk."

The older man twisted and kicked ineffectually as Ariel hissed, his face beet-red, "If you don't, I'll tear your skull apart and *pry* out your fucking secrets." He added under his breath with bitterness, "Like Svnoyi wanted in the first place."

Jaroslav found his tongue. "Okay, I talk, I talk. But get off me."

Ariel wasn't taking any chances. He let Jaroslav stand but then thrust him down by the shoulders into the pink armchair, whose pillow let out a rude squawk.

Jaroslav tried to form a sentence. But all he could manage was, "Ruski bad, *bad!*"

Ariel shook him. "*What* Ruski, you jerk? Tulak? He's Czech."

Suddenly Jaroslav spat on the floor, his face contorted into a purple knot. "Same goddam difference, *same goddam difference.*"

Ariel sat on the adjacent sofa but looked away to give Jaroslav a bit of privacy to compose himself. The defeated man sniffled back tears, mumbling in Czech. Then he stretched out a long arm to grab a used napkin from off the table. He took at least five minutes to mop the sticky ginger ale from his face and neck. He then wiped his eyes and blew his nose before diving in.

"Is simple story. Old, old, like War, Trail of Tears, all that."

Ariel felt his mouth drop in surprise. Even though Jaroslav had been drunk half the time, during the past year he'd apparently caught on to his surroundings. Could it be possible that hiking all those trails had made him feel even worse?

Jaroslav hesitated, struggling with what came next. "Y-you not think Tulak satisfy by Svnoyi and Yacy make harvest dance with squashes."

"What?"

Jaroslav glared at his dim friend. "Shut up. Is as I say. Every day he bring one new paper for travel. He give it only after he take Anichka to bed. Every day."

Jaroslav bowed his head, gripping his hair with white knuckles. "I stand outside, I do nothing, every day. After, my Anichka, she pick up Alexej, go to America, go teach healing course. Why she is tough like plow horse, like strong lady in circus."

Then Jaroslav paused, inviting Ariel to glimpse his next thought within his head; he simply couldn't bring himself to say it aloud.

Ariel felt his face grow hotter and hotter watching Jaroslav's vision of Aleta's pretty lips being crushed by Tulak's teeth. He covered his eyes.

"Oh, God, Aleta, too? It was all my fault, I set it up. The worms in the cabbages …."

He took off running as if he could escape from himself.

***

A big scaly fish kept smacking Ariel hard in the face with its tail. Plap, plap, plap, plap, plap, plap, plap. No, it was someone pumping giant hands up and down on his naked chest, forcing him to cough out his insides and vomit about a gallon of water. His eyes flew open. Why were sinister oaks writhing above his head, menacing him with the moonbeams grasped in their fingers? When he twisted his neck, he saw a blur of hunters in red jackets with rifles over their shoulders. He had sandy mud in his eyes, his mouth, down the front of his pants. Ariel sat up, shaking his hair like a wet dog.

Addressing his question to no one, he asked, "Where the hell am I?"

Jaroslav was right there, holding him up, rubbing his back and arms with a wool sweater.

"A goddam lake. You run, run all the way, yelling like crazy man. I teach you about mountain but not how to swim? Ptah."

"I can swim. Every Indian kid—"

Jaroslav sounded annoyed. "You not kid, you big man act stupid." Then he waved his arms at the rubbernecking hunters. "Show all gone now. You go home."

Ariel couldn't believe what he'd done. Why would any sane person run for an hour, then wade into a lake way over his head just to get caught in the reeds? He had a long time to think about it. He and Jaroslav slogged the many miles home with frequent stops because he kept bending double, clutching his chest and coughing. He noticed with humility that the man he'd wanted to kill not so long ago had given him half his clothing, the sopping-wet layers better than nothing.

Jaroslav had something important to say, but his approach vacillated between pity and anger. "Now you know Tulak hurt Aleta every day, you try the suicide again?" He added decisively, "Ariel, that why I not tell you."

Ariel tried to concentrate; he was quite sure something else had happened. "No, Jaroslav, I-I think it was a vision. They happen every once in a while when things in my life get really rough, more than I can handle." Using a long-forgotten college expression, he added, "Holy shit, I guess my timing could have been better."

***

The sun rose behind the house just as they walked through the front door. Ariel was exhausted. Shaking from the cold and still coughing, he sank down on the sofa and stretched out. He must have dozed off, for when he woke up, he was swaddled up to his neck in itchy gray army blankets. Once he'd kicked them off, he found himself staring for a long, long time at a pair of muscular limbs protruding from his own flannel nightshirt. Then Jaroslav bent over him with a mug of steaming coffee, whistling a cheerful folk-tune.

Ariel shook his head, trying to gather his scattered thoughts. There was no doubt about it. Sometime during the night, their roles had been reversed.

Clutching the hot mug tightly in both hands, Ariel coughed and cleared his aching throat. He asked, "Do you want to hear it?"

"What, your vision? I not miss for whole world." Jaroslav laughed wickedly.

Ariel paused again, concentrating on the curling threads of steam rising from his coffee. When he went on, he measured his words. "I've been thinking about it, though, and the funny thing is, maybe I got trapped inside someone else's story."

He coughed yet again before continuing in a raspy voice, "Somehow I got sucked into a terrifying whirlpool in the middle of Lake Tenkiller. You know, the lake where I almost drowned last night.

"God, it was scary. Right at the bottom of the whirlpool, these cold, slimy fingers reached up and grabbed my ankles. I looked down and saw Yacy. Dead. She was a white corpse crying huge red tears like blood."

Ariel exhaled a shaky breath. "There was someone else with her. I waited for the current to turn him over, and it was *me*, with a great slash across my—"

"I know that story," Jaroslav interrupted. "Is Czech from dark forest."

Ariel sprang up, holding a fist over his head in triumph, his mug shattering on the floor. "I get it now. It's a Cherokee legend from Tennessee. *The Haunted Whirlpool.* I read it at the library."

He sank back down slowly, surveying the mess around him. "Jaroslav, let's clean this place up and get the hell out of here." He added, "It won't be easy. Going home, I mean."

Jaroslav nodded gravely with his mouth drawn down at the corners, but his eyes were shining.

***

The first thing Ariel did after walking through the prefab's front door and down the long hallway was to gather Aleta into his arms, right in front of his open-mouthed family. Without a word, he carried her into their bedroom. Before she could protest, he covered her lips with kisses.

Then he nuzzled her neck, murmuring, "My darling, I know about everything that's happened to you. Jaroslav told me. Please forgive me."

Aleta didn't answer immediately. When she did, tears stood in her eyes. "I forgave you, but only a long time after you left for Oklahoma because you didn't do anything, really, at least not intentionally."

"That's the point. I didn't do anything. I made a lousy decision by trusting the wrong person to help you escape and I deserted you in the High Tatras."

Aleta looked deep into his eyes. "I'll admit it, I hated you at first. More than that, because of what *he* did, I couldn't stand you for being, well, for being a *man*. And you didn't even *try* to understand the story about the cabbages. Instead, you left right away to take care of Jaroslav."

Then she looked down, whispering, "But listen to me, Sequoyah. You made a bad mistake letting that Tulak fool you. He never cared all that much about Indians. Sometimes you aren't a very good judge of character; you let all sorts of emotional things cloud your thinking."

As soon as the couple had shut their bedroom door for the evening, Ariel rummaged in his suitcase. He withdrew an oblong package covered with tissue paper that Aleta unwrapped slowly, blushing with pleasure. Beneath the crinkly layers lay a pair of hand-beaded deerskin moccasins that he'd bought at Cherokee Treasures. When he slid them on her feet with a reverence bordering on the abject, he uttered a little speech. Obviously, he had prepared it in advance.

"Every step you take in these slippers is one step I should have taken for you. Every brightly hued bead is one of my repentant tears."

Aleta put a hand over her mouth; she wanted to laugh. She thought better of it, and instead, kissed his eyes and lips, and any other place not covered by clothing. She moved on, undoing every button on his shirt, kissing him all the way down his abdomen. Then she slid off his pants. How many kisses can a woman bestow on the flesh of the man she loves? Surely not an infinite number, but something close to it.

***

The very next day, Ariel invited both families to a feast that he planned in every detail. Although canned vegetables and tinned beef would have to substitute for fresh ingredients, he hoped to recreate the stew he'd made in Tahlequah. Aleta bowed out early on, claiming she had a headache, although Ariel suspected that she couldn't face the long estranged Kuaray. As his preparations commenced, he collected chairs from both apartments, cramming them around the oilcloth-topped kitchen table. Soon the families gathered in the hot kitchen. Even Marmalade was there, hidden not too successfully beneath Lucy's sweater.

Ariel couldn't help noticing that Anichka and Jaroslav had their hands all over each other. He had no idea where his friends could have spent the night in the overcrowded apartments. Jaroslav pulled him aside and with a lot of winking and other unsubtle gestures, he proudly described a romantic tryst spent at the finest hotel in Frobisher Bay, the only one that featured an igloo-shaped bar and invitingly lush polar bear skins draped across the bed.

Once the hungry guests had scrambled to fill the available places, two chairs still stood empty, sticking out like toothless gaps in a six-year-old's mouth. But who was missing? Everyone looked around; apparently, Kuaray and Yacy hadn't bothered to show up. Ariel sprang up from his place at the head of the table, glaring and muttering under his breath. Surely the errant pair had received his hand-written invitation with the artfully worded poem extolling the reunion of a clan long separated. They must have realized how much the occasion meant to all of them. Everyone started babbling at once, although no one seemed to be saying anything informative. At last Svnoyi's voice overpowered the general din.

"Daddy, Kuaray, and Yacy have moved out of the prefabs. They're living inside the bus in a little hideaway behind the tarps and stuff, but you don't want to go there, not right now, anyway."

***

The next day Yacy shambled into the prefab on her own accord, looking pale and unkempt. Her hair hung in strings, she kept wiping her runny nose on a filthy bandana pilfered from the supplies, and she had forgotten to put on a winter coat. Ariel thought he should embrace her, but he turned away instead. Where was the charmingly eccentric child he'd known in the High Tatras? Or the exquisite blond-haired girl who had greeted him at the airport calling him Daddy?

Ariel offered her a chair which she accepted, dropping into it without a word of thanks. Then he fetched coffee from the stove, but she shoved it away impatiently. Once Yacy started in, except for a few euphemisms, she didn't mince her words.

"I'm living with Kuaray now. The first time he did 'you know what' to me, I bled all over the place, and that's what you saw in your scary vision at the lake ... if you want to know."

Ariel wasn't sure why, but the ghastliness of that experience, which oddly, he'd witnessed himself, made him reach out for her hands.

With a violent jerk of her elbows, she yanked both hands away, sitting on them for emphasis.

Ariel pretended not to be hurt by her rebuff.

"But Yacy, why did you go to him in the first place? We were so happy doing things together, we went on hikes in the mountains, we picked mushrooms—"

Yacy interrupted, "That was a long time ago before any of us moved here. Once that happened you never talked to me, *not ever.* And why did you take off for Oklahoma without even saying goodbye?

"And after that, Mama just got weirder and weirder. She shut herself in her room all day and yelled curse words at me through the door when I wanted to take my violin lessons. *Did you even know that?*"

Yacy let out a rattling cough and spat into the bandana before going on. "I know Svnoyi tried to be friends with me. But hey, I can see inside minds like everybody else. Ever since we got here, she's put up with me because she thought she was supposed to. But all she *really* wanted was to be someplace else, making out with Oscar."

Then Yacy looked down her nose to preface a smug remark. "Who cares if everybody else loves her more 'n me? In the end, she's gonna marry a pathetic loser. Because guess who bought me a fox fur muff and matching gloves with little pompoms on the cuffs *and* a real silver ID bracelet that says, 'I love you'?"

She thrust her wrist into Ariel's face. The bracelet sparkled in the sunlight, the engraved sentiment glinting on the polished surface.

Ariel tried the moral approach. "But Yacy, listen to me. You can't keep doing this, it's just plain wrong. Both of you are too young, and … and he's your *brother*. You'll get pregnant. Then the Moon People will kill you."

Yacy stared at him bug-eyed, her mouth twisting with contempt. "The Moon People would kill their own grandmothers!

"And what makes *you* so damned superior that you can tell *me* what to do? You fucked a crazy woman, who just happened to be Ethan's mother, inside the nuthouse. Did *you* care about making a baby?"

Then she stood up, shaking with rage, her fists clenching and unclenching at her sides. "You're a goddam cheat, too. You fucked my mother right under Ethan's nose and afterward, you lied about it for the longest time. You think I didn't hear you admit it to Jaroslav at the grown-ups' meeting in front of the fireplace, *finally*, in a teeny-tiny coward's voice?"

Ariel reached out a hand to soothe her, but she slapped it down, ratcheting up the volume to an ear-splitting high. "Sometimes Kuaray thinks you're his father and other times he thinks Ethan is. But I made up my mind a long time ago that *you* were my father, *up to now, that is*. Because if you aren't his father, too, it can't go both ways, can it?"

She turned to leave. "Think about it, *whoever you are*. At least *my* kids will know who their daddy is."

Ariel could hardly breathe; her last remarks had wounded him so. No, he thought, it can't go both ways. Worse, he had to acknowledge that after this, even if he and Yacy *were* father and daughter, the relationship was all but dead. Furthermore, now that she had fallen into Kuaray's clutches, she would most likely spend her remaining years in unspeakable misery.

But his guilt went much deeper. He had abandoned Yacy long before leaving for Oklahoma. He had never taken seriously her fears over the marriage threats, and the first day he arrived at Frobisher Bay, he had failed to see Kuaray for what he was: a merciless sexual predator.

***

The chaotic night of January 7, 1976, would never be forgotten by anyone who worked at the Geophysical Arctic Studies Project, although only the Eskimo guard realized the date's true significance. By then the Greyhound bus was ready to leave, stuffed with the bare necessities required to settle a new land. All that remained to be done was to sell the families' accumulated household goods via the bulletin boards. Preparations had been furtive, for everyone agreed that the departure should go unnoticed, leaving no physical trace.

Even without Kuaray and Yacy, dinner that night at both households seemed like any other. Plates were passed, children kicked each other under the table, and the events of the day related by the adults bored them all. Marmalade rubbed against Lucy's legs, receiving the vegetarian handouts that he barely sniffed anymore.

But what came next was a detonation so huge that the earth shook and the back walls of both prefabs blew in. Was it an earthquake? There had been a really big one back in 1933. Probably not, for the noise at impact shattered half the windows and temporarily paralyzed everyone's eardrums. At first, the littlest ones howled and the rest sat in rigid silence. Then they ran outside.

The Yellow Moon had come down. It lay in a deep crater of its own making, about ten yards from the Greyhound bus. Its metal skin had cracked open like an eggshell as raging flames shot twenty feet into the air, eating away the interior: the rotten La-Z-Boys, the breakfast nook, the Rice Krispies and Cheerios, the Scrabble set, the Porto-Powder-My-Nose, the TravLtron and the Visionscope. Somewhere within its smoldering depths, the broken carcasses of the Moon People lay intertwined, fused by the heat.

Everyone was there, even Kuaray and Yacy who shakily exited the Greyhound bus, still deafened by the explosion. All their faces, from the very youngest to the middle-aged, registered horror, followed by ugly suspicion as they peered furtively from squinted eyes around the impromptu circle.

At last Luz burst out, her stentorian ROTC voice aimed directly at Kuaray. "Holy Mother of God, they were monsters, but *why* did you do it? *How* did you do it? With your mind?"

Kuaray lashed back, *"I didn't.* I didn't do it."

Turning to no one in particular, he screeched, his voice cracking, "Listen, everybody, I know you all hate me, but it wasn't me. It was Luz. Or Sequoyah. Just look at him covering his eyes. He's ashamed to show his face."

Just then the Pressenda violin, already packed inside the bus, began to howl louder than Luz and Kuaray put together, louder than the screeching children, the sparing adults, louder than the approaching sirens.

In seconds, Kuaray had the instrument on the ground in the midst of the gathering. After catching his mother's eye, he flung back his head in spiteful ecstasy. Then he stomped and stomped on it until nothing remained but a pile of red-gold splinters that still whimpered beneath the demolished bridge, the ebony pegs, the skewed strings, the cracked scroll.

Aleta fell to her knees, sifting the remains between her fingers. She rocked back and forth keening with even more pathos than the mythical Niobe lamenting over the corpses of her children.

At first, no one noticed The Skidder who stood outside the circle, his flat features beneath the wolf-trimmed hood illuminated by the conflagration. Then with urgency, he pushed his way into the center of the group, surprising everyone. They stood silently as he scanned their faces, one after the other, and although they knew quite well who he was, not one of them had ever heard him speak … until that moment.

"Crash make big, big noise. My brother at gate hold off police for now, but you leave quick. You all packed, you *go.*"

He expanded, "You go to new world. I know. I see you think big, big thoughts all the time."

Then he singled out Ariel. "My brother say, 'Mr. Ariel, bury father's bones under green shade tree like he ask.'" He paused, smiling to himself, perhaps pondering the almost total lack of any kind of tree on Baffin Island.

The Skidder then wagged his finger, frowning from seriousness. "Mr. Ariel, do not, *do not* forget. Only spirit of father help calm anger."

He turned to Lucy. "Cat stay here. Mr. Marmalade go inside my warm coat. He ride in taxi, he have fun every day."

As the tearful and guilty-faced Lucy extracted the stowaway from her jacket, everyone scrambled aboard. The police cars' lights were already flashing a mere fifteen yards away.

***

The Skidder saw the Greyhound bus wink out, leaving a black rectangle of bare gravel where it had once rested behind the trash bins. He inched his way back to the front gate in the shadow of the fence, tightly hugging the unprotesting Marmalade inside his parka.

He whispered over and over into the animal's ear, "May the Spirits protect them. May the Spirits protect them."

Chapter 22 The Last Shade Tree

The bus skittered and torqued, ending up more-or-less horizontal as stomach-churning lurches sent everyone rolling into a heap at the front. The forward end sank into some kind of slurpy goo. At the same time, a fearful scraping against a gritty surface raised its back end into the air. The entire group held its collective breath as the staunch vehicle settled, trembling, the volleys of metallic squeaks and groans resembling the conclusion of a particularly long-winded symphony.

In the new silence, everyone sighed with relief. Yet not one of them made a motion to stand up even though the aisle's slant was hardly more than a gentle incline. And for a good reason: the ice-rimed windows revealed not a comforting sky blue, but an unnerving iridescent green the color of unripe grapes. They turned away from that alien outdoors, preferring to take in the towering piles of equipment secured inelegantly by the still vibrating ropes.

For the first time since their frenetic departure, Captain Ethan Marcus left his position at the very front of the bus to look about him. He winced. The bags, boxes, and camping supplies reminded him of a certain Cub Scout summer trip his mother insisted that he go on to make him, as she put it, "more tough, like real American boys."

Twenty of them, screaming at the top of their lungs, had careened along rutted red dirt roads in just such an overladen vehicle, their destination the unbearably hot, dusty foothills of the Sierra Nevadas, dotted with sparse digger pines and little else. Here he had come down with trench mouth. He lay sweaty in a flannel-lined sleeping bag for the trip's duration, barely able to sip water through his swollen gums.

The prolonged silence was broken by Agali's high treble voice as she reached for her father's comforting hand.

"Daddy, I don't *want* to live in Oz. The flying monkeys scare me."

Ariel stood up, pulling her along with him. He tousled her hair.

"If we're in Oz, it's Oz a million years from now, I mean a million years from *then*. I don't know what I mean."

Everyone laughed uneasily as they glanced at the watery ice sheets oozing down the green glass.

Then Ariel cleared his throat to make a noble and encouraging speech. "We are about to embark on an adventure no less important than the renewal of history itself! With humility, we bring the best we have to offer, salvaged from a world doomed to die through a combination of human arrogance and hatred. Can we do any better? It is devoutly to be hoped. But before we leave our little nest, let's all give a round of applause to Ethan and Kuaray for bringing us this far—"

Kuaray interrupted Ariel's diplomatic endeavor by leaping up, bowing repeatedly from his hips like an obsequious footman.

He announced, "Ah, my dear friends, I gladly accept your applause, but to reduce the unmistakable tension brought on by our, um, *hasty* departure, let me explain about the busted violin and a few other things."

Ethan whispered over a fresh outburst of tears from Aleta, "Kuaray, please not now. Save it for later."

But he could not be dissuaded. "It's important, everybody. You all think just because I'm not *fuzzy-wuzzy* like the rest of you I don't need love? Well, I do. And those ... those fucking ice-cold Moon People could never fill this lonely aching heart. Believe me, they tried." He gripped his chest, making smacking clown's kisses before going on.

"And by the way, I didn't kill them." He burst into manic stage laughter, shaking all over for dramatic effect.

"They wanted to crash the Moon on top of the Greyhound to ruin our trip. They preferred death. *Yes, death over life*, just to put a stop to their failed experiment. And why?"

Leering, he yanked Yacy off the floor where she lay crumpled in a miserable heap, her unusually pale features suddenly turning scarlet with shame.

"'Cause Yacy and me, I went a little bit too far with her, even for Sasquatch."

He dropped Yacy before summing up. "Ha ha. Crappy eyesight 'n shit-for-brains, I guess. The old farts just plain missed the bus. Get it? *They missed the bus.*"

No one laughed, and Luz sprang up, quaking with fury. "You egomaniac, you have *some nerve* taking all the credit for their geriatric Moon crash. They hated me, too, they hated Ari, they hated all of us for not listening to them anymore, for choosing the wrong people to love. But *you* ... you monster. Even *they* finally figured out you belong in the rubber room, that you'd make a perfectly crappy king."

She lunged for Kuaray's neck. "And I swear I'll kill you if you don't leave your sister alone. Your *sister*, Kuaray."

Kuaray stepped aside so that Luz fell, colliding with a box of canned goods. As she sank to the rubber runner on the bus's floor, he shook a finger at her in a stagy scolding.

"Tsk, tsk, little *mamacita*, over-exerting yourself like that. And you in a *family way*—just like my sweet Yacy."

In the midst of a stunned silence, Ethan leaped up from the circle of spectators to kneel at Luz's side, gathering her into his arms. He refused to acknowledge Kuaray's nasty theatrics.

He whispered ecstatically into Luz's ear that peeked out from beneath her silver-streaked hair, "Really, my love? *A new baby?* You didn't tell me."

Just then Kuaray dropped to his knees and burst into tears, either the real thing or a convincing stage imitation. He choked out a few almost incoherent sentences to no one in particular.

"Ethan and Luz so in love. *Look at 'em.* My mama, she didn't love me ever, not since I was four years old; she didn't say one word to me since she got to Frobisher Bay. She left me crying on the Trail of Tears. Me and Yacy, *crying.* On the Trail of Tears! And just who is my daddy? I ask you, everyone, 'cause your guess is as good as mine."

Then he wiped his eyes on his shirt, looking repentant as he murmured, "At least I got Mama's attention when I broke her violin."

He lurched to a standing position and began his stage-grimacing again, crossing his arms and bowing his head piously. "Ladies and Gents, how I loved that fiddle. How I loved it. It was my best friend, my other half in times both thick and thin."

But soon his eulogy fell apart. He covered his face with his hands. He barely managed, "Oh, Jesus, Mama, I'm so sorry. *Poor, poor* wooden devil, *requiescat in pace, Franciscus Pressenda, anno Domini 1838,* rest in peace."

Almost everyone turned away. They shuffled to the door at the front of the bus, finally ready to face an unknown world hardly more threatening than Kuaray's distracted ramblings.

As Ariel put an arm around sobbing Aleta's waist to steady her, he thought to himself, We'll have to treat that one with kid gloves.

Both Ethan and Anichka helped Luz to her feet. She had become a fragile vessel—a bearer of new life. Only Svnoyi saw to Yacy, who was clutching her stomach, doubled over with a bout of morning sickness.

Jaroslav lifted Alexej and Agali high on each shoulder as Lucy and Phoenix clung to his jacket.

He announced encouragingly, "You will see, little ones. We stay together, we love our oceans and mountains, all will be good."

Lucy chimed in, "And the animals, Jaroslav. We will love them, too."

Phoenix murmured in a small voice as they walked down the aisle to the Greyhound's door, "And the plants."

Only Oscar stayed behind with Kuaray, who sat cross-legged next to the farm equipment, gripping his head and rocking back and forth.

"Kuaray…."

Oscar hesitated because he hated being called Little Black Sambo, the older boy's customary name for him as long as no adults were present.

But Kuaray said nothing.

Oscar went on in what he hoped was a soothing voice. "Kuaray, the Moon People didn't exactly go away, did they? Just because their bodies died doesn't mean—"

Kuaray pleaded, "Oh, help me, Oscar. They're hanging out in my head all the time. Nessie keeps saying, 'You can be *king*, Kuaray.' That moron Sasquatch keeps echoing her, 'Ahem, yes, right, ho, ho, you can be king.'"

Kuaray turned to him imploringly. "Are they real? Tell me, please, please, that it's just from getting really fucked up about it 'cause let's face it, I disappointed them so much that in a way I killed them."

Oscar's reply was not what Kuaray wanted to hear.

"When they died, Kuaray, you let them get inside you. They are as real as you think they are."

***

The bus door opened with a hiss like an angry snake. Everyone but Kuaray and Oscar stepped out gingerly, reaching for each other's hands. First, they tested the ground, taking tiny steps in place. Then they inhaled three or four breaths of air, pungent with the scent of pine. They looked up and all around, taking in a seemingly endless forest that formed a thick canopy over their heads.

Suddenly Ariel shocked himself and caught everyone else off guard by falling to the ground. First, he kissed the layer of aromatic needles that cushioned his outstretched limbs. Then he gathered a handful of sandy soil in his cupped hands.

With his head bent and eyes full of tears he whispered, "I am touching you at last, Mother Earth, but I shall never own you, and I shall never knowingly hurt you."

Only Svnoyi, the half-Cherokee child who understood her father best, knew exactly what he meant. She sank down beside him.

Then Alexej and Agali fell flat, kissing the pine carpet. With bursts of bubbly laughter they cried out, "Mother Earth, Mother Earth, we love you, too."

Lucy and Phoenix dropped down next, followed by Jaroslav and Anichka.

Luz, in her fourth month of pregnancy, was already too portly around the middle for such athleticism. Ethan stood at her side looking adoringly into her eyes, perhaps unconsciously linking the life within her to the earth beneath their feet and the green boughs arching high above their heads.

Yacy was not doing as well as the others. She lay curled up in the nearby juniper bushes, prostrated by morning sickness as Aleta, putting aside her own troubles, hovered over her. The two had hardly said a word since the termination of the violin lessons at Frobisher Bay, but presently Yacy was too sick to refuse her mother's gentle offer of comfort.

Phoenix spoke up first. "No wonder the bus windows looked green. They were covered with ice so we couldn't see anything outside. But the green came shining through because we're in a forest. And look! The air is full of yellow pollen from the pines and cedars, so it must be late spring."

He added sagely, "It's almost past planting time for us; we better hurry."

Svnoyi remarked soberly, "Good thing there was a little opening for the bus to stand in." Then she threw her arms wide in ecstasy.

"Look at the sky, everybody. It's so clear, it's almost navy blue."

Alexej and Agali jumped up linking arms, joyously skipping the length of the bus and back again to check out its condition after the wild finish. When they returned, the crowd still lay on the ground mesmerized, staring skyward.

Agali reported in her piping treble, "The bus is crooked. The front is stuck in a huge puddle—"

Alexej finished for her, "And the back is stuck on some rocks."

Soon Jaroslav took charge. "Ariel, my friend, now is time for real mountain rangers. You and me, we go away from trees, we make survey." All the children sighed in unison from disappointment.

Catching Jaroslav's eye, Ariel added hastily, "Of course we'll all go, children, too."

He called toward the bushes, "Aleta and Yacy, I hope you'll come along if you're feeling better. We'll walk slowly."

He issued instructions, "Stay in single file, and watch every step you take. And no one get in front of Jaroslav. I'll bring up the rear."

By the time the sun was overhead, the little party had left the forest and reached a ring of cliffs towering above an endless watery expanse. From there, they could see a curving beach below, slapped rhythmically by azure waves. When they turned around, they could just make out far away mountains, covered with snow.

Then they sat down to rest. Anichka had planned ahead. Before leaving the bus, she'd hastily thrust crackers, cheese, oranges, and chocolate into a paper sack, which she now distributed equally among everyone. They all glanced hopefully at a sparkling rivulet that ran over the cliff, tumbling down to the ocean below. Ariel was appointed the taster, so he took the first sip from a flat tin cup he'd unhooked from his belt. He found the water pure and sweet, tinged with a faint bouquet of pine resin.

Following the rush of excitement, the crowd turned morose.

Ariel spoke first, doing his best not to sound disappointed. "I don't think we've moved to a new place at all because I recognize the landscape. We're still on Baffin Island right where Frobisher Bay used to be, even though we've jumped ahead millions and millions of years."

Phoenix added, "The pine forests will mean infertile soil for crops. It'll be tough to get anything to grow."

Everyone fell silent.

Then Lucy murmured, "I didn't see a single animal—not even a chipmunk or a bird. Or an earthworm."

The adults said nothing, although all of them were thinking the same thing, even if their worries were more practical than Lucy's. Game was essential to their existence.

Only Svnoyi spoke up heartily. "All of you should be happy. We arrived safely, most of us feel pretty good, and hey, Luz and Yacy are expecting babies. And you'll see. There are trees, so there have to be animals and insects and even nematodes and micro-organisms."

She swatted a mosquito that settled on her arm. Then she laughed. "See? Some things never change."

Just as the sun was setting, the adults discovered three caves in the cliffs above the beach. Everyone seemed relieved; if they had found adequate shelter for at least a few nights, the families wouldn't have to sleep in the airless Greyhound bus, especially with Kuaray in it.

Each pair selected a cave at random. When Ariel and Aleta entered theirs they hesitated, not knowing what to expect. They almost fled. Their flickering candles projected massive shadows everywhere, rippling up and down the walls. But as they tiptoed further in and grew accustomed to the light, they suddenly sank to the gritty floor clasping each other. High above their heads and cascading to their feet, sculptures of plants and animals bulged from every inch of the stone. They were speechless. How and when had mere humans made anything so life-like? Such perfection terrified them.

Soon the desire to see more overcame their fear. Vines heavy with raindrops sheltered toucans and mynahs; lemurs crouched, popping open their perfectly round eyes. And a little way above their heads brown bats settled in orchard trees folding their membranous wings as tamarin monkeys reached tiny hands toward branches laden with fruit. Did the rock forests and their fauna emit an irresistible perfume, a faint odor of incense? Perhaps, because Ariel and Aleta found themselves locked together twisting and thrashing, their ecstasy observed by a thousand pairs of stone eyes. Later, Ariel would murmur shyly that the night creatures told him to do it, but Aleta had heard them, too: the peeps, chirps, and screeches sounding in canon along with two humans in spontaneous song.

Aleta woke the next morning feeling dwarfed by the forest frieze that wiggled and winked above her head in the gray-pink dawn. Suddenly she was swept up by renewed passion stirring deep inside her, urging her to unite with Ariel again. He knew what she was thinking. He smiled, barely opening his heavy lids as he pulled her close. Aleta had never believed in prayer, but she sent a tiny one into the morning light, thanking the unknown strangers for giving them such a beautiful cave.

***

At dusk, after a long day spent prudently exploring the area closest to the caves, most members of the three families ate together on the beach. The menu was hardly a culinary inspiration—canned baked beans heated over a campfire with tender ostrich-fern fiddleheads gathered by Phoenix. He was thrilled to discover them in the forest and assured the doubtful crowd that the unfamiliar greens were not poisonous if consumed in small quantities.

Ethan and Luz, followed by Jaroslav and Anichka, made a hasty exit as soon as they could gracefully leave. Everyone understood why. The caves still lacked partitions. Since the sleeping arrangements hadn't been sorted out yet, no one could blame them for wanting to spend some time by themselves.

Oscar showed up briefly to eat but left quickly for the Greyhound carrying a plate of beans and fiddleheads for Kuaray, hoping that the curly vegetables wouldn't remind him of the Pressenda's scroll. They had slept in the bus the night before and had also spent the whole day huddled behind its closed door. By now, the adults had begun to worry. Ethan, especially, was concerned about his buddy Kuaray, the only other stalwart man of science besides himself. Luz figured that Oscar was the best person around to cope with Kuaray's ghosts as long as her visionary son's captivity in the bus ended soon.

***

Beneath a sky illumined with stars, the campfire burned low. Ariel stood up to ask a question that he knew would stimulate the imaginations of the children gathered around him. He crouched down to place his hands on his knees, looking at each of them individually.

"How do you think the cave sculptures got there? All three caves have them."

Lucy crowed instantly, "That's so easy. I have the answer because I thought about it all day long."

She dropped down to a mysterious whisper to capture everyone's attention. "The Skidder knew where we were going. He even kind of said so just before we left. So *this* is what he told his family that night at dinnertime—in the Eskimo language, of course."

Deepening her voice to imitate The Skidder, she intoned, "'The world is coming to an end in less than one-hundred years from now! All the people and all the animals will die except maybe a few tough ones—'"

Phoenix interrupted, "And all the plants will die, except the coniferous ones that hold their seeds tight in pinecones, and some other hardy plants like bamboo and ferns, and—"

Agali and Alexej broke in, piping in unison, "Go on, Lucy. What happened next?"

"Well!" Lucy caught everyone's eye; she loved an audience.

"The Skidder family knew how to make really fine carvings of polar bears and things out of soapstone. They'd done it for years and years, father to son. So the littlest girl in the family whose name was Minnie said, 'Daddy Skidder, there are caves right here on the shore where Ariel and his family are going to live—way, way later from now. Let's carve animals and plants from all over the whole world on the walls inside the caves.'"

Still playing Minnie, Lucy went on with enthusiasm, "'Here's why, Daddy Skidder. Because when Lucy and everybody else see the animals for the first time, right by their beds, they get together to decide the best way to bring them back to life.'"

Then Lucy's voice faltered. Unable to hide her sorrow, she could no longer sustain Minnie's cheerful character. "But what can we do? It's too late now. All those wonderful animals are gone, forever ...." Her voice trailed away to nothing.

Soon she sobbed, "When I was a really little girl, I had a favorite poem. It was *The Gingham Dog and the Calico Cat*, and in it, they got so mad that they ate each other up so there was nothing left of them. Not a single scrap of cloth or a piece of stuffing or a button eye. I always thought, *That's impossible.* But now I see it's not. The animals have disappeared without a trace and all we have left are cave pictures."

Svnoyi hurried to Lucy's side and threw comforting arms around her.

"I loved that poem, too, but it never made sense how the cat and dog could simply digest each other, even though I knew they were only pretend.

"Lucy, I see what you're trying to say, though, but I don't agree. We *will* find animals in this new land. They may not look the same anymore, but they're around here somewhere. And I'll bet they'll come to you, just like the old earth animals used to."

She directed her next remark to the whole circle. "Look, everybody." Pointing to the swollen red lump on her arm she announced brightly, "*Cherchez la mosquito,* and you'll find the animals. And not just any animals. Warm-blooded ones like us."

Yacy absorbed the story about The Skidder's daughter Minnie from her spot by the fire. She looked a sickly green, her face cadaverous in the flickering light. But even in her weakened condition, she obviously had an important contribution to make.

"Last night Svnoyi and me stayed in Jaroslav 'n Anichka's cave. Maybe you think Lucy's story is just made-up, but it isn't. 'Cause listen to this. Where I slept, there are all kinds of cats, big and small, carved in the stone. Roaring lions and tigers with their mouths full of sharp teeth are hiding in the grass, and a leopard is stretched out high up on a branch. And right beside my head I saw *Marmalade*, real as life, with that stupid bandana around his neck."

Then Yacy whispered in awe, "That's not all. I think Marmalade has something to tell us. Because there he is, sitting under *a big shade tree*, just the kind where Grandpa Mohe asked for his ashes to go. So today I looked around everywhere, and I think maybe the real shade trees are gone, every one of them. *Gone from all over the whole world.*"

Ariel felt tears well up in his eyes. First, he embraced Lucy and kissed her forehead to show how much he loved her story and also to acknowledge her grief for the missing animals. How he wished he could hug Yacy, but he knew it wasn't possible so soon after their bitter argument.

He addressed them all. "Girls, you have no idea how meaningful this is. Lucy has just created *our* story, the first story of our new life." He lost himself in the enthusiasm of the moment. "Write down what everybody said, word for word. I have paper and pencils. I know the pencils will eventually wear down to nothing and the paper will run out, but I brought them for occasions like this."

Ariel thought of the disorganized boxes spread all over the beach where everyone's personal treasures lay. "Once I find my books of Cherokee legends, we'll put the story right inside the front cover of Volume I."

Svnoyi knew exactly how the story should start—with her father's own words, "I am touching you at last, Mother Earth, but I shall never own you, and I shall never knowingly hurt you."

Lastly, Ariel considered Mohe's ashes, which were never far from his thoughts. They were still packed safely inside the bus, waiting for him to locate their final resting place. And he knew Yacy had found just the right spot. He'd put them below the shade tree in a little niche in the cave wall, and although he realized that a flat stone replica was not precisely what Mohe had asked for, the ashes would still lie next to the flora and fauna of his father's own time. Ariel felt deep down in his heart that Edoda would be satisfied.

He didn't say it aloud, but he hoped Yacy would hear him anyway. *Thank you, thank you, dear Yacy, for finding the last shade tree in the whole world.*

***

Svnoyi, Lucy, and Yacy sat by the embers until the last of them had flickered out. After dousing the pit as a precaution against the flames restarting, the three made up their minds to bed down in Aleta and Ariel's cave because they hadn't seen that one yet. The rest of the evening was better than any slumber party. By candlelight, the friends looked at every one of the exquisite sculptures. Each chose a favorite animal, and Svnoyi suggested a project to record the complete cave walls in line drawings for Ariel's proposed history. Giggling, they wrapped themselves up like mummies, snuggling in the quilts chosen from Luz's generous supply. Lucy fell asleep instantly to dream of animals long gone, and in particular, of her Marmalade who had been so very obliging to wear that stupid bandana.

Yacy wasn't tired, and Svnoyi was just as wide awake as she was. Yacy reached for her friend's hand in the dark.

She spoke hesitantly, "Svnoyi, I have a question, but it's so hard to ask." She paused then, carefully planning out her next words.

"I know I'm supposed to love Kuaray because we made a baby, but lots of times I don't like him at all. It's partly because I love the other people he says he really hates, like Mama and you."

Then she whispered, "And Daddy Sequoyah. I love him too, so much ... but do you think he *really is my daddy?*"

Svnoyi had been both expecting and dreading that question for years. She gripped Yacy's hand tighter. "I think ... I think maybe he is your father because of the way he loves you. But I don't know for sure. No one knows."

Yacy had pinned all her hopes on an irrefutable yes. Perhaps Svnoyi was hiding something from her. But when Yacy slid beneath the surface of Svnoyi's mind to make sure, all she saw was the gelatinous gray of ambiguity.

Svnoyi could hear Yacy sniffling, and sensed through the blackness that copious tears were running down the poor girl's cheeks.

In truth, as soon as the words had left her mouth, Svnoyi wished she could take them back. But what reply would have been better? She blurted out an addition that was no help at all.

"Yacy, when Sequoyah tries to talk to you, you won't even answer him. You could at least fix that."

Yacy wailed, "I can't! I was so mean to him I can never be his friend again. Oh, Svnoyi, I have no one to call Daddy anymore inside my heart. Sometimes I wish I'd never been born."

***

With their quilts tucked under their arms, Aleta and Ariel sought a comfortable spot to sleep outside—once again disobeying Jaroslav's hard-and-fast rule not to wander about after dark. Like young lovers, they walked hand in hand, gazing at the heavens arching overhead, the starlight painting their upturned faces a molten silver. Soon they discovered a nearly flat rock not far from the caves. It was ideal, almost totally concealed by an overhanging juniper, gnarled by winds that blew in from the cove. Inevitably they embraced with a passion as undiminished as the first time they'd touched under the redwoods at Santa Margarita.

But then Ariel sat up. "Aleta, let's discuss something important first before we … it's about Kuaray."

He felt Aleta stiffen and pull away.

"Listen, I-I find this hard to say, but now that we're in the new land, I do want to unite the whole family."

He hesitated before adding, "For something as special as Mohe's memorial service, if you could just ask Kuaray to be there—"

Aleta felt her face grow hot. Then she jumped up in a fury. "Thanks so very much for turning me into your errand boy. Can you seriously think I'll talk to that-that *monster* after what he did to Yacy? And my violin? My God, you saw him carrying on in the bus. He's *crazy.*"

Ariel sprang up, too, just as angry as she was.

With his hands on his hips and his head thrust forward aggressively, he stared her down, hissing, "And just how do you expect to spend the rest of your days living right next to him without saying a word to him *ever again? He's your son* if that means anything to you.

"And something else. We'll never pull this family together because you won't let it happen. You, Aleta, *you.*"

Aleta was boiling mad. She rolled up her quilt in fumbling haste and headed for Jaroslav and Anichka's cave.

She yelled over her shoulder, "You talk to him then. Why is it all my responsibility? *How do you know he isn't your son, too?*"

***

The next day brought rain and plenty of it. With Agali acting as supervisor, Alexej carried all the boxes still lying on the beach into the caves. At the age of four, he was already putty in Agali's hands. He never tired of showing off his strength that rivaled that of the fabled child Hercules.

Once the chore was completed, the children had nothing to do. They slumped down on the spiny tufts of grass that speckled the shore and pined for their mothers, but after a while, they grew bored with such a useless pursuit. Hand in hand, they began walking in an ever-expanding spiral, scuffing the rain-pocked sand with their bare feet.

Agali brightened suddenly. "Alexej, I know what we can do. *Let's run away.*"

***

Lucy and Luz bustled about, preparing johnnycake and strong coffee under a huge tarpaulin hastily stretched and tied to four pine trees by Jaroslav and Ethan. Jaroslav glared at everyone from beneath his lowering brows.

"Girls go to bed last night and forget to cover woodpile. How lucky here is Jaroslav to light good fire."

Luz swatted him with her spatula. "Just shove it, big boy. You could've come home to teach us about survival instead of moping in Tahlequah for months and months."

Just then Phoenix stomped in from the rain fretting loudly, "We should have planted by now, and we haven't cleared a single inch of ground. All that rain is going to waste."

When he noticed that no one was paying attention, he grumbled, "So what do I care if we all starve? Come winter, it'll be like the Donner Party all over again."

Svnoyi and Oscar belatedly appeared to pick up breakfast for themselves and their patients. Svnoyi had her hands full taking care of Yacy and her morning sickness, and Oscar looked drawn after two days and nights sitting through Kuaray's unhinged monologs. Oscar and

Svnoyi kissed each other sweetly on the lips, seemingly unaware of the moody audience surrounding them. Then they clasped each other, eyes closed.

They broke apart when Anichka shambled in, her eyes bleary and her hair uncombed. She mumbled that she was looking after Aleta who had a cold, but everyone had already heard the real truth from Jaroslav. Aleta had spent the whole night in Anichka's arms, crying bitterly.

Ariel was unaccounted for.

Luz had reached the end of her rope. She climbed on an upside-down galvanized bucket. Then in her trademark ROTC bellow, she addressed the damp and shivering crowd. "Listen up, people. In the unexplained absence of our fearless leader, I appoint myself second-in-command. Sit down, all of you. I have *a lot* to say."

She paused as Agali and Alexej wandered in, wet to the skin.

Alexej whimpered, "We run away."

Agali concluded, wiping her streaming face on her sleeve, "But we got hungry."

"For heaven's sake," Luz blustered. "Please tell me *why* our precious youngest children were left outside all by themselves? Get off your duff, someone, fetch them dry clothes and give them some johnnycake."

She rolled her eyes. "Lord love a duck. Don't we *care* anymore?"

She began her lecture anew. "Ever since we got here, we seem to be practicing what some of you might call *communal living*, but what I call anarchy. Where, in God's name, are the *parents?*"

With withering condemnation, her eyes swept over the entire crowd, sparing no one. "The sickest kid in camp is Kuaray. He has *three parents*, well, more-or-less. All cowards! So meanwhile, my own darling son has been stuck with him for two days in a disgusting Greyhound bus while his very own mother spends the night sniveling in Anichka's cave."

Then she summed up. "If Aleta can't deal with him, and the two fathers can't come up with some kind of solution, like putting him to work, I say *drop him off a cliff* as the first human sacrifice to the inclement weather gods.

"You think I'm joking?"

Luz wasn't finished. "Now on to our fearless leader. No, he's not tending to Kuaray like he should be. Last night he acted like a complete idiot, running off in a snit after arguing with his wife about that very subject. If you want to know exactly where he's gotten to, try using your gifted minds." At this point, she glared at Svnoyi in particular.

"Ah, Bingo. Svnoyi has found him, four miles due west with both his arms and legs tied up by the world's toughest vines. But come now folks. Just *how* did that happen, d'you think?"

She peered around the group. "Ah, let me see, who should I appoint as the rescue party? I have it. Jaroslav, you go so no one careens off a cliff, and Anichka, you go in case Ariel has sustained a few injuries. And Lucy Dolittle, you go as dogcatcher, or whatever. I expect it'll be right up your alley."

Luz stepped off the bucket as everyone stood up to leave, much subdued by the scolding. But she was not quite finished.

"Anichka, before you go, tell Aleta I want a word with her about her son Kuaray, and that I don't intend to coddle her." She muttered under her breath, "That one's been spoiled rotten by Ariel. Rotten!"

She turned to Svnoyi. "I can cure Yacy of that morning sickness in two shakes of a lamb's tail. Feed her a couple of crackers and then send her here to help me wash the dishes and start lunch."

She smiled for the first time that morning. "Okay, Svnoyi, I know how you feel. Bring Yacy here, and then why not take the day off, you want to be with your father so bad. Run along and join the rescue party."

***

Aleta rapped timidly on the door of the Greyhound bus. Her heart was in her throat, she felt like vomiting, and for a moment she contemplated running away. But how could she? What Ariel had said about her breaking up the family was bad enough, but what Luz said was devastating. Her ears grew red as she recalled the exact words, *No one seems to want him. Even Oscar couldn't take it anymore. But the one who wants him least of all is his very own mother. Let's just drop him over a cliff, shall we?*

It was too late anyway; she heard Kuaray's footsteps scraping inside along the rubber runner of the aisle. He flung open the door, extending his arms. They embraced awkwardly for a second or two.

"Mother, how enchanting to see you, and you looking so lovely. I haven't had the pleasure of such a *close* encounter since I was four." Aleta was put off by his sarcasm but could hardly blame him for trying to cover up a hideously uncomfortable moment.

Close up, she was bowled over by his virility—at fourteen, yet. Although she'd never get used to her daughter's behavior, she was not entirely surprised that Yacy had fallen for him out of loneliness, at least long enough to climb into his bed once or twice. For a fleeting moment, she thought she saw a bit of Ariel in him, perhaps around his high cheekbones.

But he was looking at her expectantly, so she answered, "Kuaray, I feel the same, of course. It's ever so nice to see you, too."

Aleta glanced around wishing she could spot an emergency exit, although she knew full well that even if the bus had one, it would be blocked by towers of boxes.

She asked timidly, "Can we sit down?"

They walked to the middle of the Greyhound where some of the camping supplies had been moved out, leaving an enclosed space, not unlike an improvised clubhouse. She lowered herself gingerly onto a stack of wobbly cardboard cartons full of canned goods. But Kuaray preferred to stand, intimidating her with his compactly muscled adolescent frame.

He announced heartily, his hands placed nonchalantly on his hips, "I happen to have the same remarkable abilities to eavesdrop as everyone else around here, except maybe you, Mother, and Ethan, of course. A little bird told me you wanted to ask me to go to a memorial service, although I did sense that some coercion may have brought you to my door."

He bowed like a courtier. "Oh well, not to worry. *Here you are,* and who could ask for more?"

Her heart pounding, Aleta stuttered, "Y-yes, the memorial service. For your grandfather Mohe, or maybe not your actual grandfather, but …."

Kuaray smiled at her tongue-tied confusion. "Ah, Mother, just the topic I wished to pursue, and you brought it up. How curious that my parentage remains a mystery."

Suddenly, Kuaray's demeanor changed from friendly to imperious. He spit out the next sentence, "So, Mother, if you don't know whose kid I am, at least tell me which of my two fathers you loved more."

Aleta's blanched complexion grew red in blotches as she shrank away from him. "How can I answer a question like that, Kuaray? I was seventeen, and-and it's none of your business."

Kuaray snickered. "Don't forget that memorial service. I know for a fact that if I refuse to go, a certain person out there will be mighty pissed off with you."

Aleta stood up, but he pushed her down by the shoulders, adding, "Besides, you'll be refusing your very own son who you've managed to avoid for *ten years.*"

Aleta was overwhelmed by self-doubt and shame. Although she didn't know it, she was hardly the first person to fall victim to Kuaray's tactics. Considering how he'd treated Ariel, the practiced tormentor had barely shown her his claws.

Then Kuaray barked unpleasantly, shaking a fist. "Get on with it, Mother. Which one?"

"Well," Aleta began. "I think the Moon People had a lot to do with it."

Kuaray sniggered, "That goes without saying. Don't they always?"

He rudely poked her in the back to get her started. "Mother, so what about the first one—Ethan?" He tapped his foot impatiently.

Aleta should have pulled away, angry and hurt, but she didn't. Suddenly she sat absolutely still, her mind elsewhere. She had wandered back to a perfumed morning at Santa Margarita in the early fall. She was in her bedroom practicing Bach—the impossibly difficult *Ciaconna* from the *Partita in D Minor* that she had foolishly agreed to play in a concert that evening. She remembered peeking out from behind her window curtain and there was Ethan, glued to a lamppost with his knees shaking. She had loved him madly for a whole day until their first date at the Momus Cafe. After that, she still loved him, but not nearly so much, although the affair had been set in motion, like a runaway train.

Kuaray poked Aleta again, making her jump.

"Okay, Kuaray."

She went on in a trembling voice, "I'll tell you, but *only* if you go to Mohe's memorial at Anichka and Jaroslav's cave and act like a gentleman."

He smiled ingratiatingly, taking a seat near her on a wooden crate full of oranges. "I promise I'll go if I can stay by the entrance. Dark places freak me out ever since that vortex swallowed me up on the Trail of Tears."

Then his voice turned nasty. "Now, Mother, get on with it. You should know that I can see your thoughts. What did you find inside Ethan's head at the Momus Cafe with that X-ray vision of yours?"

He grinned, showing all his teeth. "You can pick apart birds' brains by glancing into their dumb little eyes. It's not a big talent like mind-reading, but I happen to know that you can look into people's brains, too, kind of like seeing a picture in there."

The comment unnerved Aleta completely because she didn't think anyone knew. She unconsciously twisted her fingers as she stared down at her denim-clad knees.

"Well—"

Kuaray gave her another rude poke in the back. "Well, what?"

"Well, we did this chit-chat, and then Ethan made a Möbius Strip out of a paper napkin and I remember that he told me once how much he loved gravity. I couldn't help it, but he made me think of my father. He was a scientist, too, and he had a narrow way of looking at things."

Kuaray mumbled, "Hmm, maybe scientists on both sides."

Aleta went on, "Ethan really wasn't like my father. He was more thoughtful and he could be funny sometimes, although he was *always* studying."

She suddenly smiled. "But every time I looked at him I saw this Möbius Strip floating around in his head."

Kuaray seemed captivated. "Okay, Mother, that's a good one, Ethan as Professor Möbius. This contest is obviously heating up. Tell me about the other one."

Aleta stood up to leave, looking like a deer caught in the headlights. "I can't do this, Kuaray."

Her swarthy son blocked the aisle. "I think you can. Remember the memorial service?"

Aleta sat down again, but when she continued, she covered her face, mumbling into her shaking fingers.

"I called him by his real name—Sequoyah. He was physically so beautiful that I could hardly bear it, and he couldn't really talk to anybody but me. We hiked down into the redwood grove behind Santa Margarita, and that's where I looked inside him."

She stopped long enough to bring on a vicious poke. "Kuaray, I can't—"

Another poke.

"Well, okay then. What I saw was *nothing*. Only a terrible blackness so huge I started to cry. It was like his soul had been torn out by some awful catastrophe. Later he told me about the residential school and how he lost his people, his Cherokee language, everything that made him who he was."

"Ah," Kuaray chuckled. "So my besotted romantic mother wanted to *save* him, to fill up that big empty void. Kind of a vortex if you think about it. Yeah, I guessed it was something like that."

He looked her boldly up and down. "I'm sure our Sequoyah had a more *exciting* void on his mind, if you know what I mean, and then he got all noble. Just *one time* in the sack, Mother. That's *all*, out of consideration for his best bud Ethan."

He rolled his eyes heavenward toward the ceiling of the bus. "Oh, the longing, the heartbreak—"

Aleta stood up abruptly, her eyes flashing with anger. "I've told you. Let me go."

Kuaray pulled her down again, hurting her wrists. "Not so fast, Mother. You aren't even curious? You don't want to know *why* I asked you?"

Aleta shook her head, weeping now as he gripped her wrists tighter.

His voice rose unpleasantly. "Okay then, I'll *tell* you, Mother. Just this morning the Moon People said I have too many fathers."

He hissed directly into Aleta's ear so that she could feel his moist breath, "So I plan to *kill* the real one, or maybe the other one, I haven't made up my mind which one is which, or—"

Aleta gasped, "You're just playing games, trying to torture me because I abandoned you, but I didn't mean to. I was sick."

Kuaray smiled winningly, showing just how charming he could be. "I know that, Mother, and so I'll put off my final decision. But meanwhile, I'm sure all you nice people really wouldn't object to building me and Yacy a big log house, two stories at least, in a leafy forest glen? No cave for me. Remember how terrified I am of dark places."

He let go of her wrists, still smiling. "'Bye, then. It's been lovely. See you at the funeral, Mother."

Aleta fled, but at the bus door, she turned back. Kuaray had dropped onto the crate of oranges. She could tell from the way his shoulders shook that he was crying, or was close to it. He raised his head to look at her, his amber eyes begging her to stay. The fragrant odor of citrus suddenly reminded her how after his bath she used to kiss his little round baby-tummy, all smooth and sweet from the castile soap and talcum powder. Then he would laugh so hard his eyes filled with tears.

How strange, she thought, that my twins can weep, but the other children can't.

She was overcome by a nagging regret, and at the same time, with new hope for this strange boy, her firstborn son. She even started toward him, but then she reversed her steps. She couldn't face what she saw inside his head. It was far worse than any emptiness. It was a swirling vortex as violent as the one that had yanked him off the Trail of Tears.

Chapter 23 Prairie Dogs

Ariel woke beneath the branches of a pine tree that dripped rain in his face. Water streamed under him and wet needles poked his shoulders through his shirt. He had a headache. No, it was his stomach, too, and his mouth felt like the Mohave Desert.

God, I feel just awful.

And what were those *things* surrounding him and staring at him? Surely not *hundreds of prairie dogs?* He blinked a few times.

What the hell?

Maybe it was the angle lying flat on his back, but these babies looked like the circus freaks of the rodent world. Worse, somehow they'd pinned him down and tied him up way too tight.

Ariel shut his eyes and groaned aloud. *I've been captured. How could I have been this dumb?*

He remembered storming off yelling, so angry with Aleta that he couldn't think straight. After that, he'd headed any old direction, running like a madman.

Suddenly panicking, Ariel twisted, struggling to sit up. But he couldn't move an inch. When he peered the length of his body, he noted that it was fettered from his neck down to his toes with sturdy green ropes made of twisted vines. He was alarmed to see that his fingers looked like black-and-blue balloons, swollen twice their normal size. It was then that he saw and felt eight sharp thorns still stuck between them, piercing the tender webs.

Immediately Ariel understood the sequence of events. First, he'd dropped from exhaustion under this tree. Then, while he slept, the prairie dogs had drugged him by inserting the poisoned thorns as skillfully as any good nurse giving a painless hypodermic. Last of all, the little jerks had tied him up and staked him to the ground.

Strangely, he lost his fear as soon as he figured out what had happened. Indeed, his curiosity to meet the first animals in the new land was now satisfied, which was especially gratifying after Lucy's lament the night before. Besides, he felt no threat coming from them, only their equal curiosity meeting him.

For what seemed like an eternity, Ariel's furry captors stared at him utterly stone-faced without moving a muscle, standing stiffly upright in their dripping wet golden-brown tailcoats with ruffled white shirtfronts, giving him plenty of time to stare back. They held their fists together, fingers clasped inward, perhaps to hide from him their fearsome digging claws. He wondered how these creatures had survived the final war. Most likely they'd huddled deep within their underground burrows, as was their wont.

Sadly, his most vivid memory of them from the old days was seeing thousands of their kind mashed flat on highways throughout the Midwest.

It was true that they still resembled their remote ancestors from millions of years ago. But these prairie dogs had evolved considerably, becoming huge, the size of human toddlers. To construct burrows that would accommodate their current girth would present a formidable engineering feat unless they had adapted to life above ground, say, in cottages, apartment buildings or skyscrapers. A thought ran through his head. Why had they turned down the art-encrusted caves now occupied by the three human families?

Suddenly Ariel noticed that all the prairie dogs' serious expressions changed simultaneously, as if from a single cue. Now, like mischievous children, they were grinning broadly at his discomfort and lost dignity.

Just as Ariel realized that if he were not released soon his bladder would betray him, the yellow-slickered cavalry, Jaroslav, Anichka, Svnoyi, and Lucy, marched over the crest of the hill. The prairie dogs cut him loose immediately with slashing claws that moved lightning-fast in perfect synchronicity. As he bolted behind the trees, it occurred to him that their sole reason for holding him hostage was to bring Lucy, lover of sentient life. The thought made Ariel feel queasy. *They've been spying on us ever since we got here, and who can blame them, really? I thought I felt eyes on the back of my neck.*

When he returned, the entire throng had gathered around Lucy and Svnoyi beneath a protective canopy made of woven leaves that they had somehow managed to suspend high in the pines. The prairie dogs didn't speak aloud, but he could hear them chattering inside his head in a vibrant staccato tongue.

Since it took Lucy a few minutes to recover from whirling in ecstatic circles that momentarily robbed her of her reason, it was Svnoyi who named them Gitli Egodi Anehi, or "prairie dogs" in Cherokee. They liked the name so much that they patted her arm over and over affectionately until she had repeated it three times. Then they presented both girls with handfuls of silky-smooth river stones in vivid colors.

As a final formality, the Gitli Egodi Anehi introduced their queen, hastily named Gitli to accommodate the visitors' new name for them. Queen Gitli was a formidable size, almost as large as a four-year-old child.

Queen Gitli and Ariel bowed gravely as she slipped an unflawed rose quartz crystal into his hand, apparently as recompense for the pain he had endured. Jaroslav and Anichka then presented their own gift:

four sweet Valencia oranges from the box in the Greyhound. The prairie dogs sniffed them politely but put them away for later. Considering how precious the oranges were to the humans, everyone sincerely hoped that their new friends would give them a try. Then the two clans bid each other goodbye with much bowing.

Ariel murmured, "*Dodadagohvi*, see you again," which they seemed to like very much.

***

After the rescue party's departure from the camp, Ethan meandered in the direction of the Greyhound. He was furious, stung by his wife's wholesale condemnation of Kuaray's *three parents, more-or-less*. She'd said it in front of absolutely everyone, except Aleta, who was off feeling sorry for herself, and Ariel, who was conveniently missing. For starters, hadn't he, Ethan Marcus, PhD, mentored Kuaray in physics, working beside him every day on the most advanced theories imaginable while Ariel twiddled his thumbs in Oklahoma? And finally, how could Luz have possibly grouped him with that silly Aleta who had stayed in bed moping the whole time she lived in Frobisher Bay?

But when he caught a glimpse of Aleta sobbing aloud as she fled, he felt a sudden stab of empathy for the woman he had ceased to love, and his heart softened. A few minutes later, he found himself standing in front of the bus door, nervously twisting and untwisting his yellow rain hat.

Kuaray opened the door before Ethan could knock. He didn't smile, and even Ethan, who knew he wasn't the most perceptive guy around, could see that Kuaray had been crying. Kuaray spoke first, his voice catching. "Ethan, I know why you're here. Everyone wants to get me out of this bus."

He added miserably, "I was really mean to Mother just now. I didn't give her a chance. Then when I wanted her to stay with me, she ran off."

Ethan looked up and down the dank aisle for a place to sit down and decided on the stack of cardboard cartons with cans in them. Kuaray followed, sniffling and wiping his sweaty face on his shirtsleeve. He sank down on the familiar orange crate, doubled over with his head on his arms.

Ethan clapped a hand on his slumped shoulder. "Listen, Kuaray, I ...." He stopped because he had no idea what to say.

He tried again. "Kuaray, I think I know how you feel. Two days ago we were successful physicists, and now we're kind of dumb boy scouts trying to camp."

Kuaray lifted his head. "Professor Möbius, don't you ever think of anything besides science?" He raised his voice angrily, "And I'm no boy scout, just some kid Luz wants to drop off a cliff." His head fell onto his arms once more.

Ethan jumped up. "No, no, she didn't mean it that way. She ... oh what the hell, Kuaray, why do you act so fucked up all the time? Just tell me."

He sat down again, awkwardly adjusting his weight on the uneven boxes.

Kuaray straightened up slowly, shaking his head and frowning. "I did try, Ethan, really I did. To fix my life, I mean. I can tell you about it, but some of it's kind of embarrassing."

Ethan beamed the smile of a knowledgeable elder. "I think I can handle it."

"Well ...," Kuaray paused. "Once I started getting horny all the time I realized I'd have to find a girlfriend in town. So I got a job playing violin at the Lazy Daisy. There were all these old women hanging out on the bar stools waiting for Mr. Perfect, but there were also two blond girls and one brunette who worked at the grocery store across the street. They were young and looked okay, although they didn't have too much upstairs."

Ethan broke in, "They probably weren't all that stupid. You just thought so."

On this point, Kuaray was prepared to argue. "No, they were dumb. I could just barely detect a faint whir of brain activity inside their heads, but to their credit, they had a pretty good idea just who had never gotten laid, and they knew that would be me.

"So on my second day there, I heard them giggling their heads off in the bathroom. They came up with a competition to see which one could get me first."

Kuaray turned red. "For the next couple of hours, they sat right in front of me while I was trying to play the violin. I saw more cleavages, thighs and uncovered crotches than you'd find in a strip joint.

"I picked the brunette one, more-or-less at random, for sex that night." His voice dropped. "I was kind of hoping I wouldn't catch the clap."

Ethan was having trouble keeping a straight face, which encouraged Kuaray to continue with gusto.

"Her name was Michelle. After we screwed in the Lazy Daisy's bathroom every night for a week, I thought it was time for her to meet the family."

Kuaray paused so long for dramatic effect that Ethan gave him a gentle prod in the arm.

"And ...?"

"Okay, I'm getting there. I planned out the introductions pretty carefully, kind of like this: 'Michelle, here is my beautiful twin sister Yacy who could model for a *Seventeen Magazine* cover. She's a violin virtuoso like my mother and me and can levitate bowling balls. Here's Oscar. He sees ghosts, and here's Lucy who speaks Maltese.'"

By now, neither of them could stop laughing.

Kuaray gasped, "'Phoenix the horticulturist is going to marry a stick of bamboo, and Ethan, one of my two fathers, is a prize-winning physicist. His wife Luz can shoot down flying saucers.'" He paused to wipe his eyes.

"'And Michelle, my darling, meet Svnoyi and Anichka who are reading your mind as we speak, like most all of us here. There are a few more in my family trying to be Cherokees down in Oklahoma right now, but when they come back, we all plan to leave earth permanently. That is, in a spaceship I helped design. Would you like to come along with us and be my wife?'"

Ethan tried to recover as Kuaray grew solemn.

"Of course she wouldn't have accepted anyway, and besides, the Moon People couldn't stand this girl Michelle. Especially Nessie couldn't, although Sasquatch thought her ass redeemed her."

Ethan registered shock. "I didn't know those freaks still controlled your every move."

Kuaray gave him an odd look before going on. "Those old nutters have been hovering over me *forever*, Ethan."

He turned serious. "Well, at least Nessie had the wit to see there was a problem, so she dug up a bride for me, one of The Skidder's daughters.

"The kid had everything. She was cute as a button, real smart, a mind reader, except she was only *six years old*. I wasn't sure I wanted to wait that long for her to grow up. When I said no, I earned a place on the Moon People's hit list."

Ethan was incredulous. "Why didn't anyone know about this?"

Kuaray answered breezily, "You mean the rest of the family? You think they ever cared all that much about old Kuaray's love-life, until Yacy that is?

"Anyway, The Skidder had a fit when the Moon People talked to him about it. First, there was her age, and he wouldn't let her leave home so young. Also, he hated me because of the way I treated Sequoyah that first day."

Then Kuaray gave Ethan a sideways glance. "And another detail. His brother, the guard at the entrance, was pretty sure I intended to blow up the lab just for fun. He was right, of course, although I never did it."

The last piece of information was too much for Ethan. He got up to leave, his face turning an unhealthy shade of purple. But Kuaray grabbed the sleeve of his slicker.

"Please don't go yet, Ethan. Please, *please* let me tell you about Yacy so you'll be the only one who doesn't hate me."

Ethan sat down again, but he no longer felt an iota of sympathy.

He snarled, "Okay, *what?*"

Kuaray felt tears coming, but he pushed on. "Yacy came to me, actually, after Mother kept yelling at her all the time. I knew she didn't like me very much, but all we had was each other."

He put his head in his hands. "I'm not proud of what happened."

As Ethan stomped down the aisle, he barked over his shoulder, "I don't believe you. Not a word of it, not about what's-her-name, Michelle, not the Moon People, not The Skidder's kid, and especially not about Yacy."

"You considered *blowing up the lab?* Find someone else to care about you."

***

The makeshift kitchen under the tarpaulin was empty by the time the victorious party returned. Luz and Yacy had saved some leftover lunch for them in a covered iron skillet that stayed warm on the dying coals. Four of them anyway, were hungry enough to not complain about the ingredients—baked beans and some kind of noxious root vegetable that Phoenix must have deemed fit for human consumption.

Ariel stared at his tin plate morosely, wondering if his churning stomach was up to it. Maybe he should go see Aleta first, although he was reluctant to face her after last night's argument. No, it was easier to do nothing. He sank down, supporting his throbbing head on an open palm.

Just then Oscar shuffled in, barely able to lift his eyes from the remains of the pine box that he cradled in his arms. Everyone stood up and turned toward Ariel, aware of what the boy carried. In the unnatural silence that followed, Ariel stood up, too, his hands shaking so violently that he dropped his plate.

Oscar hesitated, finally walking the required ten feet to reach Ariel. Then he turned his head away as he thrust forward the sticks and splinters that had once contained Mohe's ashes.

Making the bravest speech of his life, Oscar mumbled, "Oh, please forgive me, sir. I took Kuaray his lunch, and found these lying on the ground by the bus door."

When he finally dared to look up, his luminous saucer eyes reflected the despair written on Ariel's face.

Oscar extended his arms to transfer the bits of wood. "So I-I brought them to you."

Ariel clasped them, his eyes filling. He didn't want to break down in front of the others, so he turned, making his way toward the hilltop where he had kissed the earth only three days before. Weeping, he stumbled on the rain-slicked stones, letting go of the pieces one by one. They meant nothing to him now that their precious cargo was gone.

But he never reached his destination. About half way there, his legs simply refused to cooperate any longer. He lay down by the new path so recently forged by human feet and closed his swollen eyes. His only desire was to block out the hideous white-hot sun that pierced the clouds, its rays tearing his body to bits.

Then with new terror bordering on delirium, he recalled Mohe's request that could never be realized—*to bury the little casket under a shade tree.* He tried desperately to release the last splinters of wood from his wounded hands, but couldn't open his fingers. At the same time, migrainous flashes at the edge of his vision etched The Skidder's warning onto the surface of his brain: *Do not ... do not forget! Only spirit of father help calm anger!*

***

The saving grace for this little band was that news traveled quickly. Svnoyi ran to fetch her Etsi. Still as fleet-footed on a trail as she had been at Santa Margarita, Aleta reached Ariel first. She cradled her feverish husband in her arms, stroking and kissing him to keep him semi-conscious. Anichka arrived on Aleta's heels. She took one look at Ariel's fingers injured by the thorns and at the bluish color of his limbs, feeling rueful that she hadn't been more attentive at the site of his capture.

Now gypsy-fire flashed from her eyes. "Lucy, find that Queen Gitli, take Svnoyi and Oscar, go now. Ask what is this poison."

Then she fumed under her breath, "Gitli Egodi Anehi think big muscle human has same body as *big fat rodent.*"

The three left at a run, knowing that every second counted.

Everyone except Kuaray arrived soon after. Phoenix came first, grasping the fresh tubers that he'd pulled moments before from the forest floor for that evening's dinner. Yacy struggled up the hill behind him, holding Alexej's and Agali's little hands. When she saw Ariel, she fell to her knees crying aloud.

Luz began barking orders, military style. "Listen up. Jaroslav. You and Ethan carry Ariel to one of the caves."

Aleta jutted out her chin. "Don't even *think* of it. No one's putting my Ariel in a cave." She cradled him tighter, whispering for Luz alone, "If you do, he'll wake up and remember first thing how he can never bury his father's ashes under the shade tree."

Luz gave a curt nod of agreement; certainly, Aleta was right.

Aleta turned to Jaroslav. "I know a place where my Ariel will be happy. Follow me." With reluctance, she relinquished Ariel to the capable forester who had carried him before, twelve years ago. But she refused to take her eyes off his limp form.

Then Luz thoroughly unnerved the handful of children who were left. Crouching to stare hard into Agali's and Alexej's frightened faces, she hissed, "*Jeepers,* guys. For all you know, Queen Gitli's thugs have us surrounded, blowguns at the ready."

She pulled herself to her full height and turned toward the hilltop. Filling her magnificent chest with air, she let loose a mighty bellow, "Kuaray, I know you can hear me. See what you've done, you crazy son-of-a-bitch."

***

Ariel slept for three days straight in the flat-stoned niche behind the twisted juniper tree, the same spot that he and Aleta had discovered the night before when they fought over Kuaray's paternity. Aleta never left her husband's side, clasping him to her breast when he wasn't too hot from the fever.

The nights belonged to Aleta alone. During the sunlit hours, Anichka, who had absorbed ancient Cherokee medicine into her own, tried out some of her newest and most imaginative potions to bring down the fever and rid Ariel's body of the Gitli Egodi Anehi's toxic brew. Her diagnosis was not complicated. Along with the poison, Ariel suffered from exposure brought on by a night and day in the rain without a coat or hat—compounded by shock and grief over the loss of his father's ashes.

Aleta's first glimpse of Ariel lying broken beside the path had filled her with remorse. As she dropped to her knees in the mud, the sun broke free of the clouds, blinding her. Probably there wasn't a connection, but it happened just as she gathered him to her. When it hit her then how much he had loved his father for the short time that was allotted him, she couldn't help weeping when she pried the last few sticks of the pine box out of her husband's fingers.

My God, she thought. Most likely my Sequoyah was still in mourning when I got to Frobisher Bay. How selfish I was, pushing him away over and over again just when he needed me most. I even told him to find some bar floozy in town to sleep with. Then, silly me, I cried so hard when he left for Oklahoma.

Shamed by her own willful ignorance, Aleta went cold suddenly when another revelation hit. *Of course, why didn't I figure it out before? Because obviously Kuaray did or he wouldn't have found the most painful way to hurt my husband. One big reason Sequoyah left the world he knew for this wilderness was out of love for his father — to fulfill Mohe's dying request.*

Not for a moment had she missed her own disagreeable parents when she vanished from Ethan's room at the age of seventeen, although during the first uncertain days in Puerto Seguro she had fantasized once or twice that maybe they would miss *her*. But now she questioned whether she might have grown up stunted by their chilly indifference, unable to love other people as deeply as they loved her.

Aleta bent to kiss Ariel's forehead, thinking, Why am I like this if I love him so much?

She tried to block out Luz's strident ROTC commands so she could renew her wedding vows more fervently than when she'd made them first in Stary Smokovec. She recalled Ariel standing beside her, looking handsome and serious in a suit and tie borrowed from Jaroslav, his hiking boots incongruously polished to a high gloss. But when he bent to kiss her, she found herself worrying how her new dress looked that Anichka had decorated all over with tiny white bows and appliqued flowers.

Now, with her voice catching, Aleta gently pushed aside Ariel's matted hair to whisper in his ear, "I *will* love and cherish you, my darling, as never before, always and always."

She also vowed silently to try harder with Kuaray, because she finally understood how much Ariel wanted to make the three families whole.

***

Lucy, Svnoyi, and Oscar started home at dusk, sliding and occasionally falling flat on the sodden pine needle carpet. They took turns carrying a heavy blanket made of fur, a gift from Queen Gitli and all the prairie dogs. Lucy held it as far from herself as possible, giggling.

"Would you just look. The fur side is crawling with fleas."

Oscar gently ribbed his half-sister, "If you truly love all animals, that includes fleas, doesn't it?"

Then Svnoyi examined the blanket closely in the dying light. She couldn't help shouting, "Just what I thought. Here's bear and rabbit fur. And what's this around the edges? Some kind of icky old owl feathers. So there *are* plenty of animals living here after all."

Lucy's face grew long. "Not exactly *living*. I guess the poor things didn't mind dying for our friends the Gitli Egodi Anehi."

Jaroslav met the children half way, bringing one of the precious flashlights to guide them home. They had quite a tale to tell put together from the eye-rolls and expressive gesticulations the animals practiced, and from Lucy's newly acquired prairie-dog vocabulary that danced playfully in her mind.

They laughed uneasily trying to explain that as far as they could tell the prairie dogs seemed to regret Ariel's poisoning: when they arrived, the Gitli Egodi Anehi subjected the children to an annoying ritual. As precious time flew by, the whole pack hung their heads for a good five minutes. Then as an additional act of contrition, for five more minutes they put on quite a show hammering their breasts with balled fists while baying soundlessly at the emerging sun.

But Svnoyi detected a hint of smugness. After all, the prairie dogs must have been thinking that they still held sway over their larger, perhaps less intelligent competitors with that drawling, leaden speech and no flair for the dramatic.

From the outset, Queen Gitli refused to reveal the potion's ingredients even though the knowledge would have helped Anichka treat her patient. Blinking her eyes and curtsying for five minutes, the queen handed Lucy an antidote—a dose of yellow powder that she herself had measured in pinches with her claws before closing it up in a clamshell.

The queen had plenty to say about the blanket, mainly how much she loved it. She kissed it affectionately for five minutes, obviously showing her extreme reluctance to part with it. Eventually, she got around to demonstrating how it worked. She twirled her claws over it, five minutes per side, to show its dual purpose. Placed over the patient fur-side-up, it would put him to sleep. Fur-side-down, it would wake him up.

The children were amazed by the variety of grotesque masks and physical distortions the prairie dogs had in their repertoire. Oscar smiled, imagining them performing equally well the most pathetic tragedy or the crudest comedy. But as the afternoon wore on, he was no longer so amused. He stood off to the side observing Queen Gitli closely. Soon he noticed something extremely interesting, if disquieting, about her mannerisms. He couldn't put his finger on her exaggerated ceremonial gestures without obtaining more information, but his intuition told him that the prairie dog culture had something to do with death.

Hmm, he thought. Controlling sleep with potions and blankets seems to be on the surface. There's something deeper going on.

When Queen Gitli finally got around to letting Lucy have the blanket, Oscar shivered watching Her Majesty roll her eyes around and around for five minutes as she ran her formidable claws through the fur.

***

Not surprisingly, Jaroslav and the children found Anichka at Ariel's bedside. Beckoning them to follow her to another spot, she sat down on a rock to look over Queen Gitli's cures. She opened the clamshell gingerly as if it might explode, and licked a tiny bit of the powder off the tip of her forefinger. She furrowed her brow thoughtfully.

"Ah, remind me this of something, very strong it reminds."

She shot up in disgust. "Svnoyi, tie clamshell tight closed, take thousand meters from camp away from our pure stream and bury very, very deep."

She sat down again, exclaiming, "Queen Gitli like a joke? Or she think Anichka is stupid? Is this test for medicine license? I not play a game when my patient is Ariel."

At last Jaroslav burst out, "Well, wife?"

Anichka explained angrily, "This is mustard-seed and salt, make my patient vomit, but it not work if patient sleeps. Makes him very sick, maybe he die from the choking."

Anichka eyed the blanket with distrust. Eventually, she sidled closer, but only after arming herself with a stick.

When a few gingerly pokes at the fur side released a cloud of fleas, she announced, "Ah, is clear, *very clear* how works this side. So many fleas bite, wake patient right up."

The other side appeared innocuous until she bent forward to sniff it from six inches away.

Then, puffing with pride, she nodded. "I solve many, many mystery like the famous Sherlock Holmes."

When her audience failed to respond, she tried again.

"I solve many mystery like—"

"Tough crowd, eh, Anichka?"

Kuaray appeared at her elbow as everyone else backed away. He went on smoothly as if he hadn't noticed his *persona non grata* status.

"Don't mind me, Auntie A. You were saying?"

Anichka glowered over losing her moment. She mumbled mostly to herself, "Very sweet, this odor. Is musquash root, the hemlock. This side, patient maybe sleep forever."

Then she marched off in a huff in the direction of her cave with Jaroslav in tow.

Svnoyi, Lucy, and Oscar could not help themselves. The minute her bright red skirt vanished around the bend, they turned to stare expectantly at Kuaray. He may have been in disgrace, but he was an undeniably fascinating outlaw.

Phoenix emerged from the shadows, and like a co-conspirator, stood proudly by Kuaray's side. Even Yacy labored up the path to join in, although she refused to look up at Kuaray. Svnoyi smiled reassuringly as she patted the spot next to her, letting Yacy know that she was saving it for her very best friend.

They all sat down in front of Phoenix and the preening Kuaray.

At last Svnoyi asked with a hint of disapproval in her voice, "So? What do you have to say for yourself?"

Kuaray countered, "Okay, okay, I'm really ashamed. This morning after I deeply wounded all three of my parents, although Sequoyah didn't know the terrible thing I'd done to *him* yet, I was kind of crying." When no one acted in the least sympathetic, he went on.

"But then I looked up. I saw these two screwy faces, no, these ugly *gargoyles*, looking through one of the bus windows. They had fur, and sometimes they stretched their mouths wide with their claws and stuck out their tongues, and other times they smushed their noses on the glass and rolled their eyes."

Svnoyi, Lucy, and Oscar burst out in unison, "*Prairie dogs.*"

Phoenix, too, smirked knowingly. For once, he felt like he was in the spotlight, or at least sharing it.

Kuaray commenced with a nonchalant shrug, "So what could I do? I got off my ass and followed them into the woods."

Yacy asked in an awed whisper, "Weren't you scared?" Kuaray grinned, speaking to his sister for the first time in days.

"Well, sure I was, sweetheart, like my pulse was *racing.*"

With all eyes glued on him, he went on with his story. "There was something awful familiar about the way the gargoyles walked, or rather the way they kept falling down and laughing to themselves, and then I put my finger on it."

Kuaray couldn't help crowing, "They were gargoyle *teenagers*, not grownups, and were they ever wasted. Out of their fucking minds, that's how stoned they were."

Phoenix poked Kuaray in the ribs, whispering, "So get to the good part." Kuaray gave his new friend a playful shove.

"All righty roo, Plant-boy. Suddenly, me and the gargoyles meet Phoenix in the middle of the forest. And is he super-pissed. Rainwater is streaming off of him and he keeps yelling, 'Goddam vacuum cleaners. Eat, eat, eat, that's all they do, breakfast, lunch, dinner, gobble, gobble, gobble, even the grossest crap I dig up.'"

282

Phoenix turned scarlet, which only encouraged Kuaray to go on.

"Or like this, 'Ah me, poor little Phoenix, I'm so goddam nice, I just love grubbing all day in the woods after some goddam sweet potatoes.'"

Phoenix murmured, "Hell, I didn't mean it—"

Kuaray interrupted, "Of course you meant it. Anyway, Phoenix comes along, and we follow the stoned gargoyle kids through the pine trees to the back of their funny town where there are rows and rows of these big fields with stuff growing. And standing right there, the whole youth population of gargoyles is waiting for us."

Phoenix broke in, "Let me tell!" His face lit up as all eyes turned to him at last.

"I don't guess this is much of a turn-on for you guys, but the fields are covered with mats stretched on poles for controlling sun and humidity. And they're irrigated with bamboo pipes along the ground with holes drilled in 'em that can spout water."

Kuaray laughed good-naturedly, his amber eyes shining. "My buddy Phoenix looked like he was having heart failure, he was so excited by the irrigation system and all."

He relinquished the floor a second time. "Now, Phoenix, you tell what was poppin' outta Mother Earth's broad bosom."

"Well," Phoenix swelled with importance, "I ID'd everything from marijuana to opium to curare to musquash, you know, that hemlock stuff on the fur blanket. And there was a whole bunch more I didn't know."

Then he sprang up waving his arms and shrieking with pleasure, "Hot damn, you all. Me and Kuaray got stoned just sniffing the air."

Svnoyi twisted her head around uneasily. "Pipe down, Phoenix. Does the word 'parents' mean anything to you?"

Without missing a beat Kuaray remarked suavely, "If they gave a flying fuck about us, at least one of 'em would've read our minds, already.

"And believe you me, if the narcs were still around in the twenty-millionth century, they'd have shit bricks then and there."

Lucy spoke up, and she sounded chagrined having to share the glory of first contact.

"We didn't see you guys—"

Kuaray interrupted, "Of course you didn't, but we saw all of *you* guys and Sequoyah at the top of the hill having a diplomatic palaver with that tub o' lard, Queen Gitli and her nutcase minions. Why'd you think the gargoyles felt safe, Lucy? Because there weren't any adults in the fields to boss 'em around."

Phoenix added, "But the poor kids were nervous, you could tell. About a dozen of 'em were playing lookout, keeping an eye on the summit meeting to see that the grownups stayed occupied."

Turning to Lucy, Kuaray commented, "I couldn't *talk* to the gargoyles, of course. I'll leave that to you, sweetheart. But are they ever smart. Their brains whir faster than propellers with that tk, tk, tk language of theirs."

Oscar spoke gravely, "There's more here than meets the eye."

Kuaray hardly needed encouragement to expand further. He raised a finger, jabbing it toward his audience.

"Damned right there is. Much more! And I saved the best part, or the *very worst part*, depending how you look at it, for last. So gather close."

Everyone huddled in a clump as even the damp air around them seemed to sweat with apprehension.

"Me and Phoenix have proof positive that all that shit ain't just for the Gitli Egodi Anehi. Because we saw ten or fifteen polar bears and a big gang of rabbits working in the fields. Right, Plant-boy?"

Phoenix nodded, sounding grave for the first time. "Right. The bears were clawing out shallow trenches for putting in seeds and the rabbits were pulling weeds with their long white buck teeth. The bears look a lot like polar bears from the old days, a grungy white, except they've grown these weird bendable fingers. And they're small, kind of dog-sized."

Lucy let out a gasp of horror that interrupted the flow of Phoenix's story. He reached out a hand to rough up her blond curls.

"Hold on, Lucy, let me finish. The rabbits are almost as big as the bears with blotchy fur and hideous stringy hair sprouting about a foot out of their ears. Someone, maybe their wives or husbands, made all these rows of ponytails to keep most of it out of their squinty pink eyes."

Then the miserable girl asked in a barely audible whisper, "But do the animals look happy?"

Both boys shrugged. Kuaray frowned, shuffling his feet.

Phoenix threw open his hands, murmuring without daring to look at her, "No, not really."

Kuaray broke in, "Okay, I gotta say it, here's the freaky part. After about ten or fifteen minutes, these huge owls with busted-up feathers sticking out every-which-way flew down from the tops of those poles that hold up the mats. I hadn't seen 'em before, they'd been sitting up there as still as statues. They were carrying a bunch of different-sized packages wrapped in leaves in their little hooked beaks and gave the right one to every rabbit and bear. Then the owls kept the last ones for themselves."

He paused for effect with an eye on Lucy's crumbling features.

"God, these critters were so addicted, they couldn't tear the leaves off fast enough. Then sniff, gulp, snort, and the whole bunch of cute teddy bears 'n bunnies 'n birdies stumbled and nose-dived home—real, real out-of-it."

Phoenix added, "And guess what? Way at the back of the farm another line of animals that looked like ravens and wolves and some kind of big cats waited their turn."

As the somber party rose to leave, Kuaray concluded, "If you ask me, it's a bartering system. The animals work their butts off a few hours a day keeping the prairie dogs comfy, and then they get paid in fun weeds and powders. Maybe they get free food. Or a guarantee that no one will eat them into extinction. And that shoot-off high, of course."

Lucy let out a few heartbreaking wails as Svnoyi put an arm around her shoulder and gave it a squeeze.

"Lucy, don't be sad. You didn't think we'd be making a trip to *Eden*, did you?"

Oscar remarked philosophically, "Who's to say they're wrong? To us, it looks all too human in its ugliness, but you can't correlate the behavior patterns—"

Yacy interrupted, shivering in the night air. "We do have to *tell*, you know. Especially if it'll help Daddy Sequoyah take care of us when he gets well."

As Kuaray glared at her, she wilted visibly, causing the ever valiant Oscar to give her hand a reassuring pat.

Yacy's remark was hardly what Kuaray wanted to hear just then, and he let loose a blast of petty irritation. "Hey, everyone. Don't thank me all at once for cutting out half a year of coy Spy vs. Spy games to find the hidden truth."

He stamped his foot. "And Sis, why are you so damned sweet on Sequoyah all of a sudden?"

Kuaray's easy-going friendliness that had captured even Svnoyi's rational heart just moments ago vanished in a flash, and his new buddy Phoenix stepped a few paces back, out of the line of fire.

With his lips twisting in a scowl, Kuaray barked, "Let Big Chief Sequoyah find out for himself, *if* he's smart enough, which I doubt. *Or else cut the crap and let me take over right now like the Moon People promised me all along.*"

Chapter 24 Babloons

Light too glaringly bright to be the setting sun hit Ariel full in the face. But he was not in the same spot as before. The last thing he remembered was lying flat on a rutted path, his sick limbs sprawled and sinking into the rain-pocked mud. Now he found himself floating, his shoulders lacerated by razor-sharp stalactites that lined the roof of a limestone cave. But the strange thing was, he had no shoulders.

"It's happening all over again. I am in my past, and I'm nothing but Thought, jammed against the ceiling of the Yellow Moon." His whisper echoed against the cave walls.

Then he looked down and saw himself lying far below on a stainless steel hospital gurney, pale, drained of blood, as stone-cold as Miriam had been when he wept by her coffin.

No, no, it's much worse than that. Wasn't drowning in Lake Tenkiller enough? How can I possibly be dead—yet again?

By now, this haunted man had had enough experience to realize that he was inside one of his own visions, but he couldn't wake himself up. He recalled his father's dying words, *Uwetsi, I'm deep inside a laid-stone well an' everything's cool an' dark. I don't see no way out.*

But what were those things? Prairie dogs? Hundreds of horrid little creatures bustled about enveloped in surgical gowns and masks that could not completely hide their furry faces. Their unlovely mugs resembled the fantastical stone gargoyles that protruded from the roof drains of Ariel's most nightmarish gothic conception of Father Xavier's La Iglesia de la Paz.

A woman far too radiant to lie with him in death occupied the gurney next to his. She had long black hair streaked with gray that hung to the floor from the height of the bed, and when he peered closer, she had Luz's face.

But suddenly something repulsive started going wrong with his corpse. He watched enthralled as the entire front of his muscled abdomen pulsated and bulged until his blue work-shirt ripped right through, buttons popping right and left. Then the great hemisphere of his bare belly began to strain, to tear, to bleed. It split open lengthwise, spewing forth a tangled profusion of wild white roses.

God, I recognize those flowers. They have a name. It is the Cherokee rose, and I saw them everywhere in the Ozarks, all along the Trail of Tears.

Responding to an unheard cue, the throng of hospital-clad gargoyles parted like the Red Sea to let the arrogant Queen Gitli stride forth. She seemed in a hurry to begin, so she dispensed with the usual pre-performance bowing and eye-rolling. Tying on her mask, she plunged her stubby forelimbs right into him through the mass of flowers. Then she raked her formidable claws that she loved to clack and brandish all around the thorny stems.

At last, she extracted from his belly a tiny embryo no larger than his own thumb and without further ado, she stuffed it whole into Luz's slack jaws.

***

Ariel clambered his way back to consciousness. After such a horrific string of revelations, he could easily have punctuated his awakening with writhing, sweating, and screaming. But he didn't have a chance to start in. As soon as his eyelids creaked open, his blurred vision came into focus on his sunshine child, Agali. She sat cross-legged by his side staring at him in wonder, her own eyes round like an owl's. Then pure delight flooded her face as a tinkling laugh burst out of purple lips stained by blackberries she'd eaten straight off the bush.

She remarked incongruously, "Me and Alexej, we had a huge adventure when we sneaked inside a secret door. 'Cause we saw the Gitli Egodi Anehi, and they took a whole bunch of itty bitty baby rabbits out of a big babloon."

Ariel was about to say, "Alexej and I, not me and Alexej," and, as an afterthought, "What kind of bab-balloon?"

But she had already run off yelling at the top of her lungs, "Yay, yay, yay, everybody. Daddy waked up, *Daddy waked up.*"

That evening at dinner, the entire clan celebrated Ariel's recovery. Following the tiresome baked-bean entree, Anichka swooshed into the so-called dining room, her bright red skirt swirling about her knees. In her raised arms she proudly bore her own creation scraped together from the ingredients on hand: a resplendent dessert made of whipped sweet potatoes and honey, topped with the first blackberries to ripen on the wild bushes.

Soon her pride would give way to chagrin. Earlier that afternoon she had accepted with alacrity a gourd filled with honey that the Gitli Egodi Anehi had harvested from their beehives behind the opium fields. In no time, almost the entire party fell down, rolling on the ground in a drug-induced stupor.

Only Jaroslav seemed unaffected. Perhaps his year on the bottle had raised his tolerance. As he stored away a mental reminder to inspect such gift-horse offerings in the future, the prairie dogs showed up, creeping among the hapless immigrants who still sprawled under the makeshift tables. The uninvited guests stayed for the rest of the evening, smirking and splaying out their claws in a bizarre attempt to show their camaraderie.

The narcotic effect of the sweet potato pudding lowered Kuaray's and Ariel's defenses. As soon as they could pull themselves upright, they made a wobbly escape, winking at each other like conspirators. Laughing, they tottered toward the beach, their arms linked to keep from tumbling backward onto the shell-strewn path.

Suddenly Kuaray sobered up. He stared at his feet, concentrating on each step to avoid treading on the clumps of succulents that pushed blue-green rosettes through the sand. After five minutes of silence, he couldn't contain himself any longer.

He blurted out, "Daddy Sequoyah, why can't you just say it? That I'm your son, and you love me."

Ariel's stomach lurched alarmingly. *Oh my Lord, how did this come up, straight out of the blue?* He would have wrung his hands if they weren't supporting Kuaray, and he began panting from anxiety, certain that the fishy salt air would suffocate him.

Then he struggled to make sense of the meaning behind Kuaray's words, knowing full well that the dimple-faced youth who mere moments ago had stumbled alongside him laughing helplessly was also a wily competitor, and most likely reading his every thought.

Was Kuaray's question a ruse, a challenge, a game? Or a serious declaration of affection, of need, a cry for help?

To add to Ariel's uncertainty, Kuaray looked up at him, his eyes pleading. The boy seemed younger than he had five minutes earlier. Even his defenseless posture begged for a positive reply from his Daddy Sequoyah. It flashed through Ariel's mind that Kuaray might feel just as torn as he had, wondering if Mohe was his own father.

But then cautious reason took over. To begin with, Ariel didn't know for sure that Kuaray *was* his son. Indeed, he had steadfastly rejected the notion for years. But more to the point, how could he possibly love the monster who had killed Lucy's cat and attempted to murder him two days later by blowing up an airliner full of people? After that, the monster had coerced his own twin sister to join him in his bed, stomped his mother's beloved violin into splinters, and had wantonly thrown away Mohe's ashes. Ariel was absolutely certain of one thing. No matter what answer he came up with, it would fall short.

The two of them dropped to the sand as Kuaray began to sift handfuls of the salt-and-pepper grains through his nervous fingers. Meanwhile, Ariel tried to clear his thick head of the opium, and not slur his words. He forced himself to stand, denying his watery knees.

"Once Aleta told me she hated me because she had seen my people die. You know, on the Trail of Tears. And I wasn't sure what she meant."

Even though Kuaray squirmed uncomfortably at the mention of his mother, Ariel forged on, marveling at his own evasiveness.

"Well, now I *do* understand what she meant, and I know it's the same for you, only much worse. She had seen too much, suffered too much, just like you. As a result, I don't expect you'll ever be quite sane. But as long as you live among us, you have to try to curb your hatred. And try to stop the voices of the Moon People inside your head. Can you do that much for us? For the community?"

With a stern edge to his voice, he frowned down at Kuaray. "Then, and *only* then, we can look into your other question, whether you are my son."

His speech over, all Ariel could think of was the time his cruel words had devastated little Svnoyi.

Kuaray sprang up. He started to cry, not even bothering to hide it and Ariel knew that for once his tears were genuine.

He sobbed, the muscles in his face twitching every which way. "Jesus, Sequoyah, couldn't you just of answered like a real dad? You could've said you were pissed as hell for what I did to Mohe, and Yacy, and all the rest of the things I did. You could've yelled at me, punched me in the gut with your fist real hard to make me a better person — like you loved me enough to care."

***

At next morning's breakfast of johnnycake and coffee, Aleta hung by Ariel's side, draping her arms around him at every opportunity. She acted so solicitous that he could almost picture her feeding him cake crumbs from her mouth like a nesting bird. Her show of motherly affection touched him, but it made him feel uncomfortable in front of the others. Granted he hadn't seen her for days, not since their argument at the juniper-covered niche. Last night he didn't go home at all. After the opium party and the debacle with Kuaray, he'd walked along the beach until sunup, wringing his hands from a despair born of guilt and regret.

Anichka was hardly her usual confident self. She tearfully begged everyone to forgive her for endangering the youngest ones with the toxic dessert.

"More careful I must learn to be. Now two times I make terrible mistake. Prairie dogs dangerous, we must watch for double nature. They are like … are like … what is right word?" She paused before nodding with satisfaction, *Mafioso*."

She need not have upset herself, for after a good night's sleep, Agali and Alexej appeared to be unharmed. They kicked each other affectionately and gave way to fits of giggles every time anyone mentioned the prairie dogs.

Then the two piped up in a singsong unison, "We have a *secret*, and no one gets to *hear* it! Only Daddy Sequoyah. Nah-nah, Nah-nah."

Ariel thought, The sooner I find out what they saw, the better. He had been worrying about Agali's babloons ever since his little daughter had breathlessly related her story, dazed as he still was from his gruesome waking vision.

As he rose to leave, Luz took his arm, steering him clear of Aleta. "Kuaray's missing, but he's okay, I just checked. He's hiding out, trying not to let anyone see what he's thinking."

Then she fidgeted, moving from one foot to the other, wishing she could leap into action. "But I'm worried. He's wandered deep in the forest where we haven't been before. Shouldn't we go after him? I'll put together a reconnaissance team."

Ariel shook his head. "No, only if he's not back by tomorrow morning. Give him some time."

But Luz wasn't finished. With hands on her hips, she glared at Ariel without sympathy, and what she had to tell him was so personal that she spoke into his head.

I heard what you said to Kuaray last night, and it pretty much broke his heart. You had to do it, I guess, since you don't like him. And God knows, he isn't likable.

Sudden anger distorted her usually pleasant moon-face. *If you'd done your job properly, Ariel, and checked in on him occasionally, you'd have known that he loved you. He thought you were his dad. Would that have made any difference to how you felt ... any difference at all?*

Ariel dropped his face into his hands. He wanted to respond to Luz's accusatory question, but could only hear Svnoyi's almost identical words from months ago, uttered on a freezing night in Frobisher Bay in the back of the stripped-down Greyhound bus. *You have to keep track of everybody's feelings, you just have to.*

Yes, he would have made an effort to love Kuaray if he'd known, but now it could well be too late.

Ariel needed to get away to think. He sank down against the trunk of a Ponderosa pine, drinking in its sweet vanilla scent. He closed his eyes to shut out the sun's morning rays and dozed off immediately.

His moment of solitude was short-lived. Svnoyi dropped beside him, jostling his arm to wake him up, and from the corner of one eye, he noticed Aleta looking on miserably, craving his attention. But he didn't want her to overhear.

He spoke into Svnoyi's brain, *Do I still have a chance with Kuaray, or have I ruined everything?*

Gravely, she shook her head. *I don't know, Daddy, you were really, really mean to him. I won't rub it in, but you should have known you were*

Kuaray's last hope and the only parent he wanted. But why not tell Etsi what happened? Why the secrets? She was dreadfully worried when you were sick. She wants to be a part of things now.

Svnoyi hesitated as she began picking apart an old pinecone, one scale at a time. When she went on, a hint of fear jabbed at tender spots in Ariel's head.

And something else, Daddy. It wasn't your fault you got sick, but we've gotten off to a rocky start. You have to figure out how to lead us right away, or we'll fall apart. On that awful rainy day, Phoenix said something like, "We'll all starve come winter, and it will be the Donner Party all over again."

Svnoyi .... He hesitated, watching her pull another scale off the dwindling pinecone. *Svnoyi, what if I can't ever pry like you and Luz want, even though I know I should, to stop trouble before it starts? What then? Will I fail?*

Svnoyi put down the pinecone. Grasping his two hands tightly, she stared directly into his frightened eyes.

No, you won't fail, exactly. But you'll have to find another way. You already rule us with love, and it's what you do best. But as long as you use your heart first and your head second you could hurt us and yourself, too, Daddy. Think about it.

***

Ariel spent the rest of the morning with Aleta inside their cave. Once he started talking, he could hardly stop. He told her everything about the last few days in vivid, heart-rending detail, except when they paused to make love, which they did often and with abandon. But he kept his vision to himself; it was still too terrifying to utter out loud, even to his wife. Aleta didn't speak much, although he sensed new courage deep within her along with an abundance of affection that she hadn't shown him for a long time.

However, even the purest bliss had its distractions. Ariel couldn't help counting the passage of precious minutes when he knew he should be elsewhere—his unease punctuated by the nervous pattering of Agali's and Alexej's bare feet just outside the cave's entrance. They were clearly waiting with growing impatience to show him the babloons.

***

To his surprise, the eager children rushed into his family's cave where he and Aleta had just spent the morning. They headed for a dark corner beyond the animal sculptures, so well hidden by huge crystal-coated boulders that Ariel had never thought to look back there. They poked their feet along the ground next to the wall, obviously searching for something.

Suddenly they ducked into a child-sized archway that made Ariel chuckle because it resembled the quintessential arch-shaped mouse hole from children's books. His next challenge was to make himself as small as possible. Even with the mountaineering skills he'd practiced for rescues in tight places, he barely managed to squeeze through the opening by wriggling like a snake. The children hadn't brought a flashlight or candle, but hugged the wall, feeling along it with sensitive hands. In self-imposed silence, they made their way up a staircase carved along the bottom of a limestone shaft.

Ariel could now stand in a crouched position, although occasionally his head and shoulders brushed the top of the passage. After what seemed like hours creeping up the stairs, he spotted a far-away light that grew brighter with every step. They reached a narrow ledge set high above an immense cavern open to the sun at one end.

What Ariel saw could only be a laboratory decked out with row upon row of stone biers. Swarms of prairie dogs bustled about in matching robes made of some kind of woven fiber, and the bulbous animal-skin bladders they carried must be Agali and Alexej's babloons. But something else disturbed him far more.

His mind recoiled. *The rows of stone beds. God help me, they look like the beds from my school dormitory, but with little creatures lying on them — rabbits, miniature polar bears, bobcats.*

Then he almost cried out, managing to stop himself just in time. On the sloping ceiling directly behind him, he felt the stalactites of his vision cutting into his shoulders.

***

As soon as Ariel managed to squeeze back out of the mouse hole, he shook out his cramped and bruised limbs before racing at top speed to find Anichka. As he ran, he tried to make sense of what he'd seen. He had stayed on the ledge long enough to witness a prairie dog dressed in a flowing blue robe make an incision with a thin flint knife through the abdomen of a comatose polar bear. When the green-clad assistant reached its great claws into the mouth of the babloon to extract Agali's aptly named *itty bitty babies*, Ariel turned away, clamping his eyes tight shut. Not so Agali and Alexej; they stared wide-eyed at the whole procedure until Ariel shooed them back the way they had come, down the stone stairway.

He started. The word babloon made perfect sense. *Such clever children! What else could a babloon be but a baby-filled balloon?*

Still panting from the exertion, Ariel caught up with Anichka and Jaroslav taking a stroll on the beach. Their original intention must have been to gather driftwood for the lunchtime cooking fire, but their roving hands indicated that they were more interested in each other than their task. Ariel blurted out his story nonetheless, giving a description detailed enough for Anichka to come up with an explanation.

"I believe prairie dogs make bear copies." She continued with a mischievous glint in her eye. "Sometimes gypsies try to make twins, even triplet babies. They wave the magic besom over virgin girl's tummy during the new moon, but it not work."

Ariel wrinkled his brow. Her last statement was hardly enlightening.

Anichka lay down her puny bundle of sticks to sit on the warm sand, pulling her voluminous skirt over her knees. She tried another explanation as she covered her mouth to hide a smile.

"Prairie dogs make baby-bear copies, maybe make many, many copies for years, *with no papa bear.*"

Her last remark piqued her husband's interest. He stared down at her with raised eyebrows, his hands on his hips. "No papa bear? He not help make the baby bears?"

Jaroslav shook his head looking bewildered, but then nodded sagely. "Not fun anymore, maybe, or maybe he can't do it after World War III. Very, very bad for making babies, the radiation."

Meanwhile, Anichka leaned her chin on her open hand, staring intently into space. "Now what is word I look for?" She jumped up. "Ah, yes. *Clone.*"

Jaroslav stepped back, frowning, now thoroughly disgusted with the whole conversation. "Ptah, what kind of new world is this? Is not what God wanted."

Ariel remained silent, his stomach churning and twisting. What he'd witnessed had been ghastly, almost as terrifying as his vision. Like Oscar, he was not willing to jump to conclusions about an alien race, but why were the prairie dogs cloning on such a massive scale? It might have made sense long ago when the world was still charred and nearly empty, but surely the animals' reproductive powers had made a comeback by now. *Why keep it going?*

While gingerly inspecting the bruises he'd gotten exiting the mouse hole, another thought struck him. If he and the children had spied on the prairie dogs' daytime activities with such ease, most likely the prairie dogs had already walked the same route in reverse at night since they must have dug the tunnel themselves. Had they observed his intimacies with Aleta? Without a doubt, but in the name of science, of course. And he assumed the other caves were similarly connected to the main laboratory. Ariel shivered in the warm spring sunshine.

Then he shook his head to clear it of morbid thoughts because he had so many things to do. He decided that for now it was better not to tip his hand by blocking the mouse holes. But to discover more, he must locate the laboratory's front door that he assumed lay hidden deep in the forest above the beach.

For this he would need Jaroslav's expertise as forester *par excellence*. They searched a square mile of almost impenetrable stands of old-growth pine and juniper hedges but didn't come across an entrance. Instead, they barely saved themselves from falling into the sinkhole that illuminated the lab's capacious cavern from above—a natural skylight camouflaged by overhanging branches.

***

This unnerving discovery was followed by another. A thousand feet from the sinkhole they stumbled on an enclosed valley with a black whirlpool at one end. The swirling water lay beneath a towering flat-faced rock covered with stunted pines and brambles that jutted higher than the surrounding cliffs. Ariel named the pair Charybdis and Scylla after the whirlpool and rock that almost killed Ulysses and his whole crew on their journey home from Troy.

Indeed, the valley of Charybdis and Scylla seemed to have gone mad. Unnaturally tall pines grew at all angles as foaming rivers ran in ten directions, disappearing and reappearing, slicing deep chasms through the fissured stone. In the middle of all the chaos and glistening like a jewel, there lay an emerald-green meadow overrun with wildflowers that rippled serenely in the breeze.

Without saying a word, the seasoned rangers fled that bewitched place, afraid to look back until they reached the friendly forest near the Greyhound bus. They both began jabbering senselessly, gesticulating, laughing and crying.

Once they had calmed down, they made a joint decision. It was high time to hold a formal meeting modeled on the gatherings that Jaroslav used to chair weekly in the High Tatras. Topping the agenda would be the complete avoidance of the area surrounding Charybdis and Scylla, followed by a cautionary look at the Gitli Egodi Anehi's peculiar animal replication. Then they'd hold an open discussion about the dangerously late planting of crops for the fall harvest.

***

Just as Luz had done four days earlier, Ariel stood atop the galvanized bucket to call the meeting to order, but he did not get far. He had barely opened his mouth to extend a hearty welcome to everyone when Kuaray made an impromptu entrance, marching through the crowd grinning from ear to ear. With the skill of a master band major manipulating two batons, the shameless exhibitionist twirled a homemade bow and arrow above his head. The twirling over, he held aloft a brace of dead rabbits. And at least a dozen drooping pheasants bound together by the feet were slung across his shirtless chest.

The rabbits were as oddly oversized as the ones in the prairie dogs' fields, except these had copious tufts of hair sprouting not from their ears but from their hindquarters, which gave the impression of classical ballet tutus that had seen better days. Blood still oozed from the clean-edged wounds overlying the animals' hearts; Kuaray had always been a crack shot.

Feeling dizzy, Aleta recalled the golden eagle on the Trail of Tears that had plummeted from the sky to crash beside her. Not surprisingly, Yacy made a mad dash for the exit with her hand over her mouth, and Lucy fainted dead away. But the rest of the party couldn't help drooling at the thought of a greasy feast. The more practical among them acknowledged that they could certainly use the pelts and feathers.

***

Only seconds passed before at least twenty prairie dogs led by a livid Queen Gitli stormed in. Luz threw water over Lucy since she was sure her animal-loving daughter's translation skills would soon be needed. For gentle Lucy's most coveted dream was being realized. She and a sweet creature named Tlke, about her age in prairie-dog years, had been sharing their languages daily—the tk, tk, tk tongue of the Gitli Egodi Anehi and the broad drawl of the humans.

Lucy's new friend now helped her to sit up and tenderly wiped the water out of her eyes. As the other prairie dogs angrily clacked their claws together, the two child interpreters began to communicate silently by placing hands and paws just below their respective ears. Lucy translated for the humans as best she could since the sophisticated language of the Gitli Egodi Anehi was constructed in sentences both ornate and adjective-laden. And of course, there had to be a considerable pause between each new thought as the pair conferred together.

Lucy began haltingly. "Queen Mother … Queen Mother, offense find. *High* offense find."

The monarch barred her great white teeth as Lucy continued, "Why make shoe-feet on sacred land? Heavy feet scar green funeral meadow."

With Tlke's help, Lucy tried her best to translate Ariel and Jaroslav's apology, emphasizing that they had no idea that they had been trespassing on a sanctified spot.

Queen Gitli turned to stomp toward Kuaray, clacking both her teeth and claws like a duo of castanets.

In a quaking voice, Lucy translated, "Bad pink boy kill *breed* rabbits. *Meat* rabbits no hair on back ends." And then as an afterthought she added, "Bad no-claw pink boy make murder with curvy point-stick war weapon we call *Azvrkt.*"

Surreptitiously Kuaray smirked for his siblings' benefit before offering his regrets for poaching and using a bow and arrow. He ceremoniously knelt on one knee and bowed his head almost to the ground, which seemed to mollify Her Royal Highness.

Abruptly and seamlessly, Queen Gitli changed her tune. Her rubbery face suddenly drew itself upward into a conciliatory Cheshire-Cat grin as she folded under her dangerous claws.

Looking slightly green, Lucy translated, "Good Queen Gitli put meat rabbits by pink people's door. Every day. *Every day.*"

The queen upped the facial action a notch by rolling her eyes. "Good, *good, good* Queen Gitli show pink people how to plant summer leaf vines and fruits."

Then the queen began to circle the party, bowing low at regular intervals. Everyone stiffened with apprehension waiting for the price.

Lucy went on translating, "Only *very, very tiny favor* from pink people. Pink people die many days away, Gitli Egodi Anehi make nice funeral. Oh, Queen Gitli love, *love, love* nice funeral. Long procession, tall pine branches, white flowers. Much crying Gitli Egodi Anehi send no-claw pink person to *no-end tomorrows.*"

The queen added for emphasis repeatedly thrusting her unfurled claws toward the heavens, "Funeral, beautiful funeral. We make *two* funeral. *Three* funeral. New funeral every day for *seven moons!*"

Everyone stood stock still in silence as Queen Gitli awaited a response from Ariel, giving his yea or nay to the generous terms she had offered.

Only Oscar murmured his favorite platitude, "There's more here than meets the eye."

Suddenly the whole crowd began babbling at once. In a fit of agitation, Ariel stepped off the bucket to walk in circles, wringing his hands. He sensed some kind of catch, but he also knew that his people faced starvation as soon as the cans of baked beans gave out, just about wintertime. And if hunting game was off the table, what would they do for food? They clearly needed help getting seeds into the ground. And what about the fur for winter cloaks and warm blankets? And there were babies on the way. Ariel climbed back onto the bucket. He raised his arms to quiet everyone down.

In a voice with only the slightest quaver, he announced firmly, "I accept."

Luz broke the prolonged silence that followed, laughing until tears rolled down her cheeks. She gasped, "You accept, Ariel, *you accept?*" She wiped her eyes with the back of her hand.

"The Moon People only tanked a week ago and already ... *already* you accept even worse monsters? Slave owners, drug kingpins, torturers of innocent beasts? They're making clones, Ariel. Animals today, people tomorrow. Give 'em a few days, they'll gear up for murder."

She paused for breath to fully replenish the lung capacity behind her trademark stentorian bellow, unconsciously patting her growing belly with both hands. "We only just left the Trail of Tears, Nazi death camps, Communist killers and rapists, World War III. Does the word *totalitarian* mean a thing to you? And you accept?"

Ariel tried to defend himself. "I thought it was for the best. We could starve, there are new babies coming—"

Luz silenced him with a furious "Shhh."

Lowering her voice to a dramatic whisper, she attracted the attention of the entire crowd, including the Gitli Egodi Anehi who had been smirking over Ariel's all too obvious descent into the doghouse.

"True, they don't ask for love. *Not yet, anyway.* But they'll control you someday from cradle to grave. No, make that grave to cradle.

"Grave to cradle, Ariel."

She concluded with scorn adding one of Jaroslav's favorite words, "And you accept. Ptah."

Queen Gitli apparently had picked up far more English than she'd let on. She bypassed her own translator, speaking directly into Lucy's brain.

The terrified girl whispered with her knees quaking inside her blue jeans, "Mama, Queen Gitli says a bargain is a bargain and she's not going to back down. And she says you're high up on her shit list." Then Lucy conferred further with her friend for a less literal rendering.

"Queen Gitli is seeking *revenge* for the things you said!"

Chapter 25 Charybdis and Scylla

During the next few months, the prairie dogs took care of most of the families' food needs as everyone worked on Kuaray and Yacy's log house in the forest. Every morning Phoenix supervised the planting of the crops, and later on, the summer harvest. But every afternoon he left the fields to notch the cut logs. Even Ethan put aside his pet science projects to help out. His main contribution was making sure that the complicated two-story structure with its staircase and multiple rooms would be sound.

To his credit, Kuaray worked as hard as everyone else. Ariel was sure that the estranged youth was making an effort to join in. Daring to imagine a happier future, he persuaded himself that the opium-clouded lecture on the beach was the first step toward the unexpected turnaround. But then Kuaray broke the spell. He imperiously demanded unnecessary flourishes—hand-carved newel posts on the staircase, and Victorian gingerbread under the eaves and around the porch—and to get his way, he threw infantile tantrums. Ariel's hopes for the prodigal's easy return dwindled. The others had less patience. They expected nothing from Kuaray and were secretly relieved that he continued to sleep in the Greyhound bus, apart from them.

All of the builders, with the exception of Ethan, the acting foreman, grew sleek and powerful: most notably the already breathtakingly handsome Ariel, who pushed himself harder than all of them put together. They did it out of love for the pitiable Yacy, who had never rallied throughout the pregnancy.

***

Yacy had been welcomed without question to live with Ariel, Aleta, and Svnoyi. No reconciliation was necessary; she simply slipped into the household as if she had never left it. Even though she had not seen Kuaray since his mean show of megalomania on the day he met the so-called gargoyles, he still preyed on her mind. The morning sickness continued unabated, and her arms and legs grew spindly as her belly swelled to a monstrous size. The bigger she grew, the more she vacillated. One day she'd tell Svnoyi that she couldn't possibly live with Kuaray after the baby's birth and the next day she'd change her mind, declaring that she understood her "duty to the father."

During the hottest weeks of the summer, Aleta sponged off Yacy's dripping forehead with damp leaves just as Unalii's sisters had done for her in the stifling sick wagon on the Trail of Tears. Then she bundled Yacy onto her lap and rocked her, singing every tune she could remember from the *Fireside Book of Folk Songs* that had been stashed in the grand piano's bench in her parents' living room. Yacy's favorite was *The Golden Vanity*, a song about the betrayal and death of the little cabin boy:

> There was a ship came from the north country,
> and the name of the ship was the Golden Vanity,
> and we feared she would be taken by the Turkish enemy ….

***

Luz was hardly better off. Had she been able, she would have squelched Kuaray's extravagant demands in a second, but she was lying in her own cave, almost as prostrated by the heat as Yacy. When Lucy wasn't working on the house, she spent hours by her mother's side, waving a great fan that Ethan and Oscar had woven out of cornhusks from the summer crop.

In early September, only a day after the log house received its final coat of linseed oil, Luz gave birth to a handsome boy who could already smile, a wisp of damp black hair falling across one of his wide-open green saucer eyes. Luz and Ethan named him Lucian. But the attending physicians Anichka and Svnoyi had barely kissed the whole family goodnight amidst general rejoicing when Ariel ran from his cave to fetch them.

Yacy had begun labor weeks too soon. She lay in front of the frieze of stone creatures, her whole body arching in excruciating pain. Hours later, twins were born. A miniature girl-child with gangly translucent limbs and the face of a wizened elf clung doggedly to life, but the boy expired within hours, taking a last gasping breath cupped in his weeping mother's hands. The poor thing never had a chance; he was barely larger than a kitten.

Kuaray could not be approached by anyone. He barred his teeth, yowling like a rabid dog, beating his chest, and yanking out great handfuls of his own hair. But when he started hitting Yacy, Ariel dragged him into the new log house and barred the door from the outside.

The whole clan could hear him yelling at the top of his lungs, "Yacy, you bitch, why didn't you take care of yourself? Did you think I wanted a girl? I wanted a son and heir, not some puny cunt."

This last bit of raving was too much for any of them to take. Ariel and Anichka burst through the door, wrestling Kuaray to the floor in the middle of his madness. Ariel pinned him down while Anichka administered one of the infamous thorn shots, gleefully donated by Queen Gitli herself, for minutes earlier an army of the creatures had arrived to receive their tribute.

Yacy's screams could be heard for miles as they wrenched the tiny corpse out of her arms.

***

Even though Kuaray's door had been unbarred, he stayed closed up in his house in self-imposed exile for two days without making another sound. That evening Luz decided to visit him to see how he was doing. When he didn't respond to her knock, she simply walked through his front door. She brought little Lucian along because she took him everywhere, just as Ariel had once carried the infant Svnoyi to all his classes, snuggled in his arms.

As always, Luz went directly to the point. She put a hand on one of Kuaray's slumped shoulders before announcing too cheerfully, "Listen up, Kuaray, my good man. Sorry for your loss, but you are a dad now and a grown-up. It's time for you to go see Yacy and your little daughter."

Then she smiled winningly. "She's cute, by the way. Just a bit scrawny."

Kuaray stared angrily at Luz's extraordinary milk-filled bosom and her fat infant, murmuring, "They're both scrawny, that *thing*, and Yacy, too. Scrawny!"

"Okay, here's your chance, Kuaray. Fatten them up with a little comfort and love."

Something about Luz's comment, perhaps the mention of the word *love*, set him off.

He exploded, "Fuck it, Luz, I wanted a male heir, not some puny cu—"

"Stop right there, Kuaray," Luz interrupted angrily. "I'm not going to let you say that word again. What's up with this male heir? Just where do you think you are, Mesopotamia in 1000 BC? And you need an heir to rule fifteen people?"

Kuaray shouted even louder than Luz, clenching his fists and stamping his foot. "Queen Gitli *said* I could rule. She said it," and he tapped his skull for emphasis, "right here in my head. And she said I need a *male* heir."

Luz snapped back, "Queen Gitli is in your head now? Gracious, Kuaray, you've forsaken the Moon People so soon. That is far worse than marital infidelity."

But Kuaray had not heard her. Spittle collected at the corners of his mouth and his eyes rolled back in his head for a moment.

He recovered enough to storm, "I'll kill Sequoyah and take over. I'll expand my empire. I'll marry Queen Gitli and find out how she makes those clones. Then I'll kill her and all the other little furry bastards. I'll make human slaves and concubines, farmers, warriors—"

Kuaray bolted upright, pummeling his fists in the air, almost falling over his feet. Once he had straightened himself out, he flexed his arms and puffed out his chest. Clearly, the construction work the muscular youth had put into his house had made a difference. From where Luz was sitting, he looked like the Jolly Green Giant on an unjolly day.

Luz didn't scare easily, but suddenly she was terrified, certainly for herself, but mostly for her infant son. She sent an S.O.S. to Ariel and, clasping Lucian to her chest, she bolted out the front door to run blindly into the deepest part of the forest with Kuaray hard on her heels.

Ariel tore through the ink-black thickets following Luz's panicked cries until they abruptly ceased in the vicinity of Charybdis and Scylla. He had no idea how far she might be from the rock and whirlpool. He wandered about calling her name and wringing his hands in desperation because he had never known her to panic. Tears stung his eyes; he loved Luz. She was his closest friend, his best confidant, and the person most like the mother he'd never had.

***

The rosy-fingered dawn broke just as Ariel climbed onto the crest of Scylla that stood at a dizzying height above Charybdis. He crept to the edge, peering over in fear of what he might see in the whirlpool below. Strangely, the water seemed to have lost its ferocious spin, and floating on the placid sun-streaked surface was a mere speck. No, it was a speck with arms and legs—a human infant who just might be Lucian.

Ariel didn't think about Scylla's height or Charybdis's possibly insufficient depth, or about his near-drowning in the middle of Lake Tenkiller not so long ago. His dive, more an awkward cartwheel that ended in a painful flop onto his back, had enough force to propel the baby onto the stony bank. With his heart in his throat, Ariel carefully turned the little body over. And it was indeed Lucian, unharmed.

In fact, he was sleeping peacefully. Perhaps his excursion on the gently rocking water reminded him of the cozy months in Luz's womb. Inexplicably, the infant had been nicely outfitted with a life jacket cleverly fashioned from hollow reeds bound together with hemp. It was girded around his tiny shoulders and chest with tender young vines that would not cut into his baby flesh.

Ariel snatched Lucian off the shore, and hugging the baby to him, he continued his search for Luz among the valley's twisted pines. But something was radically different about the terrain since he'd visited several months ago. To begin with, the only sound he heard was an occasional bird chirping and the sighing of the wind. Where was the roar of the ten churning rivers? Ariel looked about nonplussed. They had mysteriously vanished from the face of the earth.

Queen Gitli arrived all in a dither, for once, unaccompanied. Although there was a language barrier, she made it obvious by her rolling eyes and grinding teeth that she wanted Lucian returned to her. She moved closer, curling rubbery rodent lips that hung from her hideous plastic face. But as long as Ariel held Lucian, she didn't swipe at them with her scythe-like claws. Suddenly she twisted her head around in alarm and ran off in a hurry on all fours, her sausage-shaped tail switching from side to side. Ariel tried not to laugh; her regal dignity had just been severely compromised.

Nothing could have prepared Ariel for what happened next. The ground trembled, the lanky trees shed handfuls of needles in a sudden blue-green hailstorm, and a few rocks danced around like unruly bowling balls. A family of pheasants burst from the brush to dash about in terrified disarray, heads bobbing and legs twitching. Ariel had a somewhat ridiculous thought considering the circumstances. *They're so stupid, no wonder Kuaray popped off a dozen of 'em.* The earth lurched again. Ariel threw himself over Lucian, almost as panicked as the birds. All he could think of was *earthquake.*

Without further preamble, the great Charybdis and Scylla Funeral Park began gearing up for the day. The ten rivers trickled, then burst forth in all their white-water fury. Ariel didn't see it, but he certainly heard it. The whirlpool began to slurp and churn like a giant flushing toilet.

***

During the next ten minutes, most of the humans arrived at the park, accompanied by prairie-dog escorts, who rhythmically beat their breasts in the usual theatric designed to convey sorrow. For only a half hour earlier, the family members had been shaken from their slumber by Tlke, Lucy's little friend the prairie-dog interpreter, who moved from cave to cave bearing terrible news. Wringing her paws together, she informed them that Luz had perished in a drowning accident and that the funeral was about to commence. In teary disbelief, they shuffled to a designated bench at one side of the emerald-green meadow.

Ethan refused to cooperate. He veered off toward the trees, keening so loudly that he could be heard above the roar of the ten white-water rivers. Then he sank to his knees on the forest floor, clutching his arms over his head. It took six prairie-dog thugs to round him up. Five of them stared ahead with ice-cold eyes, but the sixth retrieved his glasses that had fallen nearby and tucked them safely into his shirt pocket.

Although the rest of the clan sat in stiff silence on a log bench soaked by the early-morning dew, Ethan knelt on the ground with his face thrust against the rough-hewn wood. He wept non-stop, too overwrought to notice that Ariel, Kuaray, Lucy, and his infant son were missing. Oscar sat by Ethan with the lids of his drooping eyes lowered in a crushing grief of his own. As he crooned softly and patted his stepfather's shaking shoulders, the suddenly bereft child knew that his awkward gestures could not begin to soothe a man so broken.

Meanwhile, the entire prairie-dog population gathered silently on the meadow. Although no one from the grieving party noticed, a stone laboratory bed with Luz stretched on it was raised into their midst from some cavernous place below the emerald-green grass.

The prairie dogs held long pine branches and white roses that they waved in graceful arcs to greet their queen. She glided in, decked out in a gown made entirely of clam shells that must have weighed at least fifty pounds. She stood proudly erect on a log platform in the center of the meadow, swishing her hips from side to side to make the shells clatter.

The families realized with sinking hearts that they would have to put up with her funeral oration, but they were relieved to catch sight of Lucy and Tlke. Poor Lucy had just been prodded to the podium by a pair of prairie-dog toughs. She mourned with her tearless eyes tight shut throughout the ceremony, barely able to concentrate on her job.

And there was Ariel, planted on Queen Gitli's other side. He stood with his head averted and his eyes streaming, clutching Lucian to him for dear life. What terrible thing had he done, trading his people's survival for a world like this? Ironically it bore out Luz's prophetic words that had brought the families' first High Tatras-style meeting to a disastrous conclusion. And yet, surely there had been benefits. They were all alive, weren't they, at least most of them. *Ah, dear, dear Luz!*

Fresh tears slid down his face. Just as he had once tried to find Miriam when he walked the long block between La Iglesia de la Paz and the Fork 'n Spoon, he started reaching into Luz's mind. He gasped. Something was still there. The merest blip? Yes, he was sure of it. But not for long. Like a furious bumblebee, Svnoyi dive bombed his brain, hijacking his thoughts. *No, Daddy, stop! It's too dangerous to do that.*

As a hideous introduction to the ceremony, Kuaray was hauled in by four more toughs who dumped him in a heap at Her Majesty's feet. He was gagged and tightly bound by the wiry green vines that Ariel remembered all too well. Kuaray twisted his head from side to side as groans escaped from his stopped mouth, causing Ariel's stomach to knot up with both pity and apprehension.

Gripping little Lucian even tighter, the powerless leader glanced around nervously, half expecting a guillotine to be rolled onto the stage. But Queen Gitli didn't have execution in mind. Instead, she goaded Kuaray with a lightning-fast flurry of toe-jabs made by the claws on her hind feet. The motions awakened a roar of percussive cacophony from the shell dress.

Pointing a single claw at Kuaray's heart, she underscored the gravity of his crime. "Pink beast-monster *mangles all-sacred god-goodness.* He opens great no-claw fingers. Baby-so-pale drops from tall tree-stone mountain."

Not surprisingly with all of her hordes gathered on the meadow, Queen Gitli's words were backed up by a Greek chorus of waving claws.

"Lady-mother Luz loves Baby-so-pale. Lady-mother Luz jumps into black spinning-deep lake. Human lady-mother too big-breast-heavy, sinks below waves. Lady-mother Luz *comes up no more.*"

All the prairie dogs bowed their heads and beat their chests to exhibit overwhelming grief.

Queen Gitli turned the crowd's attention to her next sentence by shaking her shells for at least a minute. "But brave, *brave* Queen Gitli sails Baby-so-pale to stony shore in curvy claws."

Before the applause could begin, she smirked towards Ariel, staring directly into his eyes, her brows twitching. "Good, *good* Queen Gitli-so-happy, she sets Baby-so-pale in Mighty Leader Ariel-Sequoyah's great no-claw fingers."

Then she flaunted her deception with a triumphant grin, reminding him of the debt he could never repay. "Queen Gitli keeps always and *always* her good promise. For many passings of the moons, she gives pink-people delicious meat rabbits and helps grow the fruits."

Almost as if he had heard the queen talking about him, Lucian stirred and kicked his little legs, but he didn't wake up. Ariel nuzzled the baby's downy head and patted his back, wondering how anyone could have left a newborn infant floating alone on Charybdis's waters. Ariel lifted the baby up to listen carefully to his chest. There was no doubt about it. Lucian's breathing was shallow; he had been drugged to keep him docile.

Another thing was obvious to Ariel. The role Queen Gitli had planned for Lucian was ruined by the early-morning rescue. Perhaps she had intended to make an Olympic-style plunge into the whirlpool to save the baby, thereby wowing everyone with her bravery. Or maybe she had planned a baptism into the Holy Order of Charybdis. Or an enactment of the Miraculous Transformation from Death to Life. Anything was possible with these drama-obsessed ritualists.

The last part of Queen Gitli's eulogy was predictably brazen. She knelt at Kuaray's side and cut him loose with her slashing claws.

Extending her stubby forearms sideways like an angel of mercy, she cried out, "Good, *good*, *good* Queen Gitli spares the life of no god-goodness pink beast-monster."

Accompanied by the crowd's waving claws, she bent to kiss his forehead, but he managed to wiggle away, only to roll off the podium and fall on the ground with a thud. He, too, had apparently been drugged almost into unconsciousness by one of the good queen's pharmaceuticals. He promptly drew up his knees to form a tight ball and fell asleep.

And finally, Queen Gitli turned toward Luz's flower-bedecked corpse, rustling and clanking her shells.

She thrust her claws high, announcing as she did so, "Walk round and round, Gitli Egodi Anehi. Walk with white roses, walk with pine branches. Cry-sing Lady-mother Luz, beloved wife of Ethan, beloved mother of Oscar, Lucy, and Lucian. *Cry-sing, cry-sing, cry-sing.*"

And indeed, a grand procession began at that moment. The well-rehearsed crowd of Gitli Egodi Anehi, waving aloft the pine branches and roses, rotated like spokes of a wheel—its hub, the stone laboratory bed with Luz's body lying on it. The procession stopped only momentarily to allow the family to gather closer for a last goodbye. Then it started up again with a relentless monotony, a ritual beautiful to behold, but empty, stripped of warmth.

Svnoyi and Oscar left first. Oscar was in such agony after watching the deceptions of the ceremony that he couldn't help himself. He cried out three times, "But she's not dead. Mama is not dead. I never saw her soul leave her body so I know she's not dead!"

Svnoyi shushed him. "She's dead, and don't play with fire." She hugged him, offering him the only suggestion that might divert him from the horror of his knowledge.

"Sweetie, let's go to the niche."

Ariel knew that she meant the flat rock with the juniper-tree curtain that he and Aleta had discovered, and he also knew how a tryst such as this one would end, eventually.

He shook his head, thinking, *God, I hope those kids know what they're getting into.*

Ethan, too, couldn't believe that Luz was dead. Lying on the stone bed, she looked as fresh as a dewy rose petal—just as he had always imagined her to be even when she was well into middle age.

He thought, Just one kiss, and she'll wake up.

He tried to push his way through the sea of prairie dogs to view his beloved one last time, but Lucy led him away.

Before today, she had never seen her father cry. Nonetheless, she found herself pleading with him, yanking his hand.

"Daddy, do not go back! She's gone. It's over."

But she recalled vividly Queen Gitli's angry words about the *shit list* and seeking revenge. And she would never trust that Luz had drowned like the queen had said. Even numbed by grief, Lucy had noticed that not a hair on her mama's head had been wet.

As the whole departing family collected into little knots, only Phoenix lagged behind because no one could possibly comfort him. His relationship with Luz had been the highlight of his young life and a secret from the others.

Until Lucian was born, on any afternoon that wasn't suffocatingly hot she had met up in the forest with this lonely middle child to help him gather the wild onions, mushrooms, and sweet potatoes for dinner. After they had stashed the dirt-encrusted vegetables in the newly woven Indian baskets that Yacy had made, the two of them would sit down to rest on a flat rock. Then, with her hands quite unintentionally patting her round belly and her voice lowered to a husky whisper, Luz would select from her vast cache of dirty jokes that she'd picked up in the Air Force—five new ones each day. What more pleasure could an isolated youngster approaching adolescence ever hope to find?

***

Jaroslav carried Kuaray home from the funeral, slung over his shoulder. First Ariel put him to bed, then sat patiently well into the evening waiting for him to sleep off the powerful sedative that had kept him nearly unconscious for most of the day. Ariel wiped the sweat off Kuaray's burning forehead, trying to decide what to do.

Surely the boy must be his child. His long, muscular body, dark skin, and high cheekbones had not come from Ethan. In fact, he and Svnoyi could easily be mistaken for the twin pair. But even the father with newly opened eyes could not deny that his son was damaged; the Moon People had made sure of that. Kuaray was cruel, arrogant, destructive, maybe even a killer. Luz had wanted him dead, and for good reason.

But how could I simply throw him away—my son, my child? I would never do that. So I promise—I promise I will learn to trust him, to love him deep down like I love Yacy. I will make him whole again.

***

Ariel held Kuaray close, marveling how he could have denied his son's paternity for so long. Maybe now he could allow himself to recall how the conception had happened.

Aleta, not mine to love, why did she agree to go with me? We walked to the very end of the Cove Crest Trail, and there we lay side-by-side under a redwood tree with low sweeping branches. We could just see patches of sky through the flat needles, so we watched the seagulls circling in the fog that rolled in from the ocean. Then Aleta cried. She said it was because I was sad—sad not to be an Indian anymore. We talked about the Moon People, she clasped my hand, and I thought I knew her fingers from a long time ago when I was four and she was a big girl, fifteen years old.

Who can understand the power of love? She started running her hands up and down my spine, and I forgot about Ethan, my best friend. I did the same to her, and she became music under my touch. My fingers combed the length of her red-gold hair, I kissed her lips, her neck, her breasts. I wound my limbs through hers, and she wound hers through mine. We joined together like twin vines, so interlocked we could not separate the shoots and flowers. The next day, and every day until the Moon People took her away, we talked, we kissed, we fell silent from longing. We wanted each other so much, but I never let it happen again.

***

Kuaray stirred. And as soon as he woke up, he wanted to talk. Sounding groggy and subdued, he explained as best he could what had happened the night before.

"Daddy Sequoyah, I did chase Luz into the forest. She was holding Lucian and screaming at the top of her lungs. I kind of liked the way she was so scared." He paused, looking inward.

He murmured almost inaudibly, "Just before, I was real angry at her. I was screaming and saying crazy things sort of like I was having some kind of fit." He stopped altogether while Ariel waited, and when he went on, tears rolled down his cheeks.

"A few stars were out, but not enough to see by, and we fell into some kind of giant hole. First Luz and Lucian, then me right afterward. Branches hung down everywhere, so even if there was light, I think I would've missed it. I fell hard into a room onto some kind of stone table, and maybe Luz got hurt when she fell. I mean, hit her head on the corner of a table. I don't know for sure, but I heard Lucian crying and I didn't hear her at all.

"It was pitch black, and when I was feeling my way around, I heard some rustling and I'm pretty sure a prairie dog gave me one of those thorn shots.

"I guess I could've thrown Lucian off a cliff like Queen Gitli said I did, but I'm not sure how. I don't even remember being awake."

Then he fumbled for Ariel's hand. "Daddy, I am never going to be okay in the head. But can you help me?"

Chapter 26 Cherokee Rose

Lately Kuaray hardly ever escaped from the polar extremes of narcissism and self-loathing. So naturally, everyone thought that Yacy had made a particularly unwise choice moving into the forest house to be with "the father of her child," as she put it. She brought both of the infants, their tiny daughter, and Ethan's son, Lucian. No one wanted it to be this way. But Ethan was still too distraught to care for Lucian himself, and besides, the babies needed to be breastfed every two or three hours.

Yacy cried when Svnoyi and Oscar carried her clothes and the largely improvised baby supplies from Ariel and Aleta's cave, even though it was only a few minutes away on a sandy path that curved along the crest of the cliffs before veering off.

Yacy knocked on the door diffidently, but as soon as she stepped into the front room hugging the infants to her chest, she made a startling announcement, at least to Kuaray's ears.

"One dead baby is one too many, Kuaray. Besides, you are my brother. I'll never, ever, walk that sinful path with you again." Her unwavering delivery and the way she tossed her head in the style of Aleta at the Frobisher Bay airport revealed painstaking hours of rehearsal.

Predictably, Kuaray didn't adjust well to Yacy's calculated dismissal of him, or to the loss of his solitude. He alternated between trying to force himself on her whenever she put the babies down and punching her when they annoyed him. Then out of the blue, he'd make amends by fulfilling the role of an ideal mate. In the morning Yacy would wake to the sounds of industrious housework, topped off in the evening by a rabbit dish for dinner. On these occasions, she'd rouse herself to look pretty, combing her hair and putting on a fresh dress.

All of the adults except Ethan stood ready to aid Yacy whenever she cried out in fear or pain. Ariel responded most frequently because he had a knack for calming Kuaray down and then gently telling him off. About half the time, the method worked. But when Kuaray found the punishment too harsh, he'd pick up Yacy's violin, which he'd not let her touch, to play Bach's *Partita in D Minor* over and over. He began reasonably enough, but would gradually increase the tempo to a frenzied speed, yelling at the top of his lungs, "I—wish—I—was—dead." When the noise from the ferocious attack on both Bach and himself reached as far as the caves, Anichka or Jaroslav hastened to the forest house with a medicinal tea that seemed to bring him peace for about a half hour.

Every day Yacy brought the babies to Ariel and Aleta's cave. Although she needed her parents' help to bathe them and wash their clothes, she needed comfort more. As the three of them scrubbed the laundry in the galvanized bucket and spread it out on the bushes to dry, Yacy would tell Ariel and Aleta in a frightened whisper that Kuaray talked out loud to the Moon People night and day about ruling the world. She was almost certain that he was trying to lure Queen Gitli with an attractive marriage proposal, which made her throw back her head to laugh hysterically over the ludicrousness of it. But she cried more often out of sheer misery as she watched her brother fall apart.

***

In spite of Kuaray's decline and the continual string of disasters in that household, Ariel was genuinely happy for the first time in his life. He was working on an experiment, an epic poem written in his improving Cherokee. He smiled to himself. *What better way is there to try out something new than for a readership of zero?*

But at the center of his existence was Aleta, who had changed mysteriously after he recovered from his three-day illness. Her chilly reserve had simply melted away. They sought each other out hourly for no particular reason other than to savor the pleasure of being together. They decided to help repopulate the new world, and hardly a month passed before Aleta told him joyfully that she was pregnant.

On a particularly fine morning in early November, the sun's breaking rays slanted into the cave, promising a brilliant Indian summer day. Ariel reluctantly tore himself from Aleta's all-night embrace. He had to get up to do his chores. He'd chop and stack the firewood for the day and then check on the bamboo irrigation system that still watered the late autumn crops: pumpkins, winter squash, and grapes. And something was always in need of repair. With a last caress, he kissed his wife's flushed cheek and whispered an endearment into her ear.

Then he sprang up invigorated, for already ideas flowed through his mind. *A strange combination of words, Indian summer. The last warmth before the onset of bleakness, the long Trail of Tears.*

What a great idea. I'll make Indian summer the subject of my poem for Aleta's birthday, only with a surprise twist. I'll start today as soon as the chores are done.

He stepped into his tattered jeans smiling a little as he began humming one of the few Cherokee tunes he knew, taught to him by his aunties on a rare occasion when they'd felt in a generous mood.

Suddenly his reverie was shattered, pierced through by Svnoyi's cry for help. *But from where? God no, from Kuaray's house. It's my fault if he found her in the forest.*

It had taken Ariel years, but he had finally taught the dear girl, who knew absolutely everything about his intimate life, to understand discretion. Ever since they had reached the new world, she had left the cave's protection at dawn to give her father and stepmother some privacy. Sometimes she helped out the earliest risers Anichka and Jaroslav with preparations for breakfast, but usually, she went to the waterfall to bathe and dress. Then she sat cross-legged on a favorite rock to breathe in the scents of early morning.

Ariel refused to panic because his daughter had seemed more angry than frightened. He sped along the path above the beach, cutting his feet on the sharp stones as a sand-laden wind lashed his bare chest. In a minute he reached Kuaray's house that stood in a clearing surrounded by thickets of juniper bushes, cedars, and ancient drooping pines.

As always, he recoiled involuntarily. The second story was overburdened with ornate cut-outs under the eaves. All of the builders remembered how Kuaray had wangled the scrollwork out of them by throwing childish fits. The same patterns were repeated on the balustrades of the wrap-around porch, now covered with an inch-thick carpet of pine needles. Even after several months, the Victorian look of the place sitting in the dense wilderness annoyed everyone except the proud owner, who called it his Sunbeam Palace.

Ariel flung open the door. The powerfully muscled Kuaray had indeed captured his daughter, his dearly beloved Svnoyi. He had her pinned against the pine-paneled wall, her arms clamped forcibly over her head, and worse yet, he'd flattened himself against her. Kuaray turned his head to gauge the effect he'd created, grinning disarmingly. Then he threw Svnoyi hard against the bare wood of the floor where she curled up into a ball.

"Ha, ha, just kidding. I thought that would bring you, Daddy Sequoyah, 'cause we need to talk. No hard feelings. Honest. She's not my type as long as I have my pretty sister."

Ariel winced as he spied Yacy observing the tableau from the second-floor stairwell, her whimpers mingling with the bronchial screeches of the two infants in her arms. He knelt beside Svnoyi to help her sit up. Although unhurt, she was seething with anger, mostly at herself for failing to fend Kuaray off.

In a fury himself, Ariel yanked Kuaray into the air by his collar and dropped him. Typically, the lithe youth landed as gracefully as a cat. He grinned, showing off his perfect teeth.

"Sequoyah, is that the best you can do? I'm *still* waiting for you to get *really pissed."*

Ariel's rage vanished once he took in Kuaray's clothing. His mad son looked ridiculous. He had decked himself out in the tuxedo and wing-tipped shoes from his performing days, but he had grown so much that the coat sleeves and pant cuffs were three inches too short.

Kuaray seemed chagrined by his failure to impress. Nonetheless, he completed his act by conjuring a high top hat into his hand from its peg on the opposite wall. With a pretentious flourish, he placed it on his head, adjusting it to a raffish angle. Finally, with exquisite coordination, he began to twirl a silver-tipped cane ever faster like a whirring helicopter rotor.

Without warning Kuaray lunged at Ariel, clutching the cane like a sword. With a boxer's dancing feet he closed in, thrusting his jaw forward. But his voice was silky.

"I'm the Sun King, Daddy Sequoyah. The Man in the Moon said so. There's no point waiting for me to grow older, I'm gonna rule *now."* Kuaray moved in closer, his ruddy face suddenly contorting.

Ariel sensed the treachery in Kuaray's lost mind, but refused to play his game; he had talked reason into the boy many times before.

"Kuaray, I'm not going to fight with my own kid. Put down the cane so we can work this out. Tell me, what's really bothering you?"

Ariel managed to grab the blunt weapon in the middle while probing his son's ravaged psyche to locate the last remnants of his humanity. *Don't you remember how we worked together building your house, you and me chopping and carrying the wood, just us two?*

Kuaray tried to wrench the cane free and shut out Ariel's emotionally charged entreaty, but he couldn't begin to match his father's superior physical strength and mental persuasiveness. And so he grew livid, his juvenile voice shooting up an octave.

"Don't try to trick me with that mind-control shit. I am big, *big, Bigger* than you."

Then unexpectedly Kuaray stepped back, releasing his end of the weapon and opening his hands.

"Okay, okay. I give up. I've dropped it. You drop it, too."

Kuaray crinkled up his eyes just as Ariel remembered Nessie doing. "But too bad you don't have *X-ray Vision* like my pal, Superman!"

Just as a blast of Kuaray's venomous poison flooded Ariel's mind, Yacy shrieked, "The hat, Daddy."

Simultaneously Ariel heard the sound of a rabbit screaming deep inside his skull for the third time in his life. It was Svnoyi's most urgent warning cry.

Ariel crouched a split second too late as something metallic flashed. A slender knife appeared in Kuaray's hand from beneath the top hat, and like lightning, it tore through his gut with its bearer's combined mental and physical force. A red wave of agony washed over Ariel. He heard Yacy's and both babies' howls, but not his own high-pitched screams.

Svnoyi swept past him, and next, the floor reverberated with a dull thud. Had he fallen? No, he remained on his feet, but doubled in half, his arms crossed over the fiery gash in his stomach. Another noise pierced the cacophony.

Below him, a frightened little boy's voice cried out, "Daddy, *help me.*" Then came the crunch of cartilage and bone, and a decisive snap.

Ariel collapsed onto the ground inches from Kuaray's vacant face. Through flooded eyes he saw Svnoyi perched high on the dead boy's back like a bird of prey, her fingers transformed into talons. With her mind, and a little help from her hands, Svnoyi had broken Kuaray's neck.

***

Ariel lay on the limestone floor of his own cave, surrounded by most of his clan. Anichka tried her best to suture the stab wound in his abdomen, stitching it expertly with the supple vine tendrils that she had gathered only the day before in the pine forest. But it was too deep and wide, and with every breath he took, the surrounding fibers tore. He didn't suffer. Svnoyi's crystal tears lulled him into a twilight sleep.

The children sat at his side. Some cooled his fevered skin with damp leaves while others caressed his hands and feet. Such a silent flock. Only yesterday they had laughed the afternoon away, tumbling on the sand until the sun sank: Svnoyi, Oscar, Lucy, Phoenix, Agali, and Alexej.

Jaroslav sat close by, but he had turned his back on the others. He was the only one with a tongue, apparently, for with his head bowed he prayed in Latin, resurrecting the long-forgotten Catholic liturgy of his choirboy days. "*Agnus Dei, qui tolis peccata mundi, miserere nobis.*"

***

Anichka insisted that Ethan take Aleta outside the improvised operating theater during the surgery. She whispered wisely into his ear, "Tearing hair and wringing hands ... Ariel does not help."

Aleta, exhausted from crying, sat at the mouth of the cave between Yacy and Ethan. The three of them shivered, for even Nature seemed affected. An icy wind whistled through the forest trees as dense clouds, heavy with snow, began to gather.

Ethan tried his best to comfort Aleta through their feelings that had once been linked, but couldn't manage to do it. Luz's recent death still filled him with such sorrow that he failed to reach beyond himself. He tried to remember the *Kaddish* he'd spoken over Miriam's ashes, but he got no further than the first line, *"Yit'gadal v'yit'kadash sh'mei raba."*

Yacy held the babies, one in each arm, as she cried bitterly. The pale, awkward new mother with neither the time nor the desire to care for herself had long since lost the confidence of childhood. How would she ever feed both of them for maybe two more years—Luz's chubby son Lucian and her own puny, unnamed daughter?

Rocking from side to side, she began an oft-repeated litany that Aleta and Ethan tried to ignore. "I'm so glad Kuaray is dead. I wouldn't take him into my heart, I wouldn't, I wouldn't."

Svnoyi appeared in their midst. She knelt before her stepmother, gently wiping away Aleta's tears with a coveted lace handkerchief, a gift from Ariel that she had saved from her four-year-old frilly days.

Then Svnoyi threw her arms around Aleta's neck. "Etsi, Daddy will wake up soon so you can be with him at the end. We can't save him."

Aleta sprang up, pale with anger. "I knew it. That bastard son of mine was a born killer. And now he's murdered his own father." She added ruefully, "Luz was right. We should have thrown him off a cliff a long time ago." She lowered her voice to a whisper, "When my Ariel dies, I shall die, too."

Aleta wanted to run, but Svnoyi restrained her within the embrace of strong young arms.

Struggling to free herself, Aleta hissed, "Ariel tried to die for Miriam, so I can die for him."

"No, Etsi, stop it! You are the mother of us all, Aleta Gaia, and I won't allow it. I love you too much. We all do."

Aleta fell to her knees weeping, her face buried in the pine needles on the rock ledge. As she beat her fists on the indifferent stone, unrelated thoughts raced through her mind. Only this morning he was standing right here on our doorstep. He was the happiest man in the whole world and humming such a pretty song. I know he was thinking about my birthday poem.

Svnoyi moved to the center of the group, grasping Aleta's elbow to encourage her to sit up. She wrapped an arm around Yacy's waist.

"Once Daddy told me the Cherokee legend about the white rose. It is the very same flower the prairie dogs carried at Luz's funeral with its slender stems lying next to the thick pine branches." Svnoyi mused, thinking about the difference between the two. "The pine is an evergreen that lives a long time, and the rose is fragile and dies right away. But don't be fooled, it is one tough plant, just ask Phoenix. In a way, it is like the pine. The Cherokee rose is still here after millions of years."

When Svnoyi was sure that she had everyone's attention, she began the story.

"So many people died on the Trail of Tears that all the mothers gave up hope and stopped caring for their children. The Elders called on Galvladiehi, Heaven Dweller. He helped them by creating a flower. Anywhere along the Trail where a woman had shed a tear, a baby rose bush sprouted, grew tall, and the flowers burst into bloom in a single day. All this beauty and the strength of the fragile rose gave the mothers new courage."

Afterward, everyone sat in silence. Even the squirming babies in Yacy's arms lay still.

Ethan couldn't help thinking, *How can Svnoyi flow so easily from breaking a neck to offering solace?*

He had completely missed the point of the story thinking about Svnoyi. She had been trying to tell him something important without hurting his feelings: that everyone needed to find the courage to go on. It was high time for him to pull himself together and take charge of his and Luz's baby son.

But not a word of the story had escaped Yacy. Shocked by her own boldness, she handed the babies to Ethan and Svnoyi.

She announced, "I'm going to wash up in the waterfall to get ready to say goodbye to Daddy." She wiped a rush of tears from her cheeks with her grubby fists.

Then she spoke with uncharacteristic firmness, "Ethan, you heard the story, too, and I know you're sad and miss Luz a lot, but Lucian is going to live with you from now on. I'll feed him, of course." The exhausted new mother thought it was past time for Ethan to hold his own son tight to his chest like a proper daddy would, just the way Luz had always done before she died.

Yacy turned to leave but then hesitated, dragging her feet. Ethan, Aleta, and Svnoyi watched as the gangly adolescent grown so pitifully thin turned around with a hint of the liquid grace that they remembered from her childhood. She made a second announcement.

"Ethan, you're not the only bad one. I haven't been such a great mother either. I never named my little girl 'cause Kuaray didn't want her. And ... and at first, I thought she might die like the little boy."

She faced the three of them square on. "I've made up my mind now. I want her to grow up good, so I'm naming her Arielle Luz."

Svnoyi nodded her approval as Ethan grappled awkwardly with Lucian's roly-poly little body, cursing under his breath. It seemed he had forgotten the basics. He was ashamed because no excuses could make up for his neglect. He wished he could say something nice to Yacy, but he was too humiliated to thank her outright.

He mumbled, "Hey, new Mama, don't forget to wash your hair and feet."

***

Standing under the freezing water, Yacy planned out the gift she wanted to give to Sequoyah. She had loved him with the devotion of a besotted child ever since he had knelt to tie the bow of her dress at Mr. Varkonyi's violin shop on Ontario Street.

Although she had no idea why it mattered to her, she thought, When my daddy dies he might need some things for his journey. I don't know what kind of journey or anything like that, but he has to be ready. She hoped the prairie dogs would put her gift beside him on his stone bed at the funeral. She would ask Lucy to talk to her little friend Tlke.

The gift was an Indian basket she had woven out of the local reeds, tree bark, and vines. She had made many of them by now for all their domestic needs, improving with each one. This basket was her finest work with a diamond and chain pattern in green and red against a beige background.

She slipped into a clean white dress as she called to the others to meet her by the stream where the reeds grew. That was where the new basket lay waiting. All of the children met her there. No one spoke as they put their offerings into the basket.

Lucy put in a draft of her story about the origin of the cave sculptures that by pure chance she'd finished only the day before. Svnoyi had helped her get started, using Sequoyah's own words, "I am touching you at last, Mother Earth, but I shall never own you, and I shall never knowingly hurt you." With shaking fingers, Lucy rolled the manuscript up tight and tied it with her very own hair ribbon.

Oscar put in a cornhusk doll that he had originally made for Yacy's baby to have when she got older. It is a strange gift, he thought. Maybe Ariel's soul can live inside it.

Then Yacy added Andersen's *Fairy Tales* from Svnoyi and also from Luz, indirectly.

Alexej put in a treasured pink shell that he had found on the beach, and Agali dropped to her knees to add a bright red cardinal's feather from the forest floor.

Phoenix put a perfect bunch of his hand-tended purple autumn grapes on the top that he had picked yesterday at sundown to save them from the frost.

All of the children were of one mind. *The basket seems ancient Egyptian, probably not old-time Cherokee. But we know he will love it wherever he goes.*

***

When the presentation was over, Oscar led Yacy to the same sweet-smelling Ponderosa Pine where Ariel and Svnoyi had talked last spring just after he recovered from his illness. Yacy cried into Oscar's neck. He held her hand as he gently patted her back, hoping he wasn't being unfaithful to Svnoyi.

"Yacy, I can tell that you miss Kuaray, too. I don't hold that against you. We all thought he was pretty amazing."

Yacy spoke to herself although she knew Oscar could hear her, and not surprisingly, her inner thoughts bristled with poetry.

He was as brilliant as a meteor that burned up in the atmosphere too soon, destroying everything around it. But he was beautiful. I loved him passionately until I found out how dangerous he was—and cruel. But the craziness wasn't his fault, just another part of the saga of the Trail of Tears.

Oscar added directly into her head, *Yacy, I've wanted to tell you this for a long time. He was never better than you at the things he did, just different. You should not think it because it was simply not true.*

Now Oscar was sure that he was being unfaithful. He whispered, *Kuaray was bright like the sun, but you, Yacy, you are glowing like the moon.*

***

Svnoyi had just said a last goodbye to her father, kissing his forehead as her crystal tears still flowed. She held out his granddaughter to him, little Arielle Luz, who touched his face with dainty fingers hardly an inch long.

Now Svnoyi rejoined Ethan, slumping down beside him. She bowed her head over the sleeping infant because her tired neck wouldn't support its oppressive weight.

Ethan usually had to remind himself that his extraordinary little half-sister was only fourteen. But then, he had never seen her in total despair. Svnoyi, capable and wise, was also gorgeous with their mother's wavy black hair and Ariel's majestic features, long limbs and warm, dark skin. She looked suddenly vulnerable, like the child she really was.

She mumbled into Arielle Luz's peach fuzz of blond hair, "How will I live without Daddy? I've never loved anyone more, and I've tried to keep him safe since the day I was born. When he dies, half of me will die, too. And Etsi, will she survive at all?"

She continued more to herself, "He was too pure of heart to see danger because he really didn't understand evil."

She wiped her eyes on the much-used handkerchief. "My tears always fell for Daddy alone. I tried so hard, but even *they* couldn't bring him back."

***

From the rocky outcrop where they were sitting, Ethan and Svnoyi peeked between the dangling juniper branches to watch the Gitli Egodi Anehi congregate on the seashore down below. By late afternoon there were hundreds of them. Decked out in their naturally sleek brown tailcoats and ruffled white shirtfronts, their plumpness and fine attire trumpeted their self-satisfied pomposity. Waving aloft the roses and pine branches, the prairie dogs processed rather than walked. Apparently, choreography was required as a prelude to the double funeral about to take place on the emerald-green meadow. Their stubby-legged pavane was headed by Queen Gitli, belle of the ball, whose slithery hula agitated her clamshells to a percussive roar.

Ethan turned away feeling sick to his stomach. In fact, bile rose into his throat and he came close to gagging.

"Damn it, Svnoyi, I can't stand it anymore. What can we do?"

To regain his composure, he jiggled his son Lucian, who waved his arms about like a fledgling bird. As Ethan looked into the radiant green saucer eyes, he remembered trying to mother little Svnoyi after Ariel had deserted her. And he also recalled Luz saying impatiently as if she were instructing a child, *You don't hold her enough.* He freed up one hand to slide his glasses off his nose and stick them into his pocket, something he always did when he wanted to think.

Suddenly a new idea came to him. "I have to be a real dad to my children … and save all of you. We could make a run for it. It doesn't take a genius to design a boat."

His voice warmed as he contemplated a new engineering project. "We'll use wood, and we'll salvage metal from the bus. We'll make a sail out of those goddam rabbit skins that keep stacking up behind the toolshed. Come springtime, we can sail south across the strait …."

Noticing Svnoyi's reticence, he trailed off. She shifted Arielle Luz to the curve of her other arm so she could put a hand on Ethan's shoulder.

"Ethan, we can't just leave. At least not for a long, long time." She lowered her eyes. "I know this will be tough for you to take, but the prairie dogs are ... they're our only hope."

Svnoyi shivered as heavy gray clouds socked in the entire sky down to the horizon. Everyone was pretty sure that by tomorrow they would be blanketed under a foot of snow. The wind was bitter; before going on, she paused to tuck Arielle Luz's head beneath her windbreaker.

"Ethan, we've never talked about it much, but you must know it's true. You're a scientist; there just aren't enough of us to survive even for a few more generations. The prairie dogs know it, too." She added under her breath, "Especially if we keep killing each other."

Sudden agitation stirred her voice. "Ethan, that's why they're making human copies, or at least they've started doing experiments. They took cells from Yacy's little boy-twin who died."

She found herself trembling all over. "Don't hate me for telling you this. Luz is still alive, but she's in a deep coma. She'll be the host for those cells."

Ethan gripped her arm with his free hand. "The little kids went back then, to the ledge? They saw her on one of those tables?"

Svnoyi nodded miserably.

Ethan sat absolutely still, holding his breath. Then he silently mouthed the word *no* as tears began to slide from his shuttered eyes.

He sobbed out, "Did *they* do this to her, Svnoyi?"

She shook her head. "I-I don't think so. She was injured in a fall the night Kuaray chased her."

Then Ethan doubled over, pressing his face into Lucian's sweater that Yacy had knit from her precious cache of yarn—one for each of the babies. As if they understood, they let out piercing wails, waving their arms and kicking their ineffectual legs inside the rabbit-skin buntings expertly stitched together by Luz.

Svnoyi yelled above the din, "Ethan, you have to listen to me. This is our new world. Not the one we expected, but the one we have."

As the babies quieted down, she took his hand. "And it's not *all* bad. Maybe before too long, we'll get my Daddy Sequoyah back 'cause they *will* be making a copy of him."

She went on carefully as if reminding herself, "But the new Sequoyah won't be the same person, I know that. He'll be a pretty good copy, though ... like the bears. And-and he'll be a newborn baby." After a long pause punctuated by more sobs from Ethan, she revealed the rest of her dream.

"Just think. He'll have lots of people to love him, Etsi and me, all of us, not like the first time when he had no mother and got stuck in that hideous residential school. And when he gets bigger, he can play all day long and run on the beach."

She whispered to Arielle Luz clasped against her chest, "My new Sequoyah will never, never have to walk the Trail of Tears."

She suddenly thrust the baby into Ethan's already full arms, forcing him to abandon his misery and grasp the two of them at once.

Right in front of her on an endless stretch of sun-glazed sand, she saw an exquisite black-eyed child, aged four. Surely she could reach out and touch him.

She didn't know it then, but this would be the first of many visions. And the boy was also her father's parting gift, coming straight from the remnants of his dying imagination.

The black-eyed child was her daddy, the little Cherokee boy. For the rest of her life, she would always remember him best like this. With his sturdy brown limbs flying and a mass of tangled black hair streaming behind him, the boy's feet barely touched the earth. He passed by her only to return, circling around her again and again, his head thrust back in joyous abandon. Did she really need a copy when he had already given her half of himself at the moment of her conception in the lake full of lilies? Her eyes clung to him with a hunger she had never felt before.

But the little Cherokee boy could not last. He was about to vanish, and when that happened, her heart would break.

***

As Svnoyi had promised, Ariel regained consciousness before he died. To be alone with him, Aleta sent everyone away. He had never looked more beautiful to her, even serene, but in his pain-filled eyes she could see Death haunting his thoughts.

She held him close and murmured into his ear, "My dear one, what does '*diquenvsv aquenvdi aquadulia*' mean? You said it to me, over and over, when you were standing in front of the orphanage. And you were such a little boy, crying so hard. Did you know I recognized you the first time I saw you at Santa Margarita?"

"Yes, and I recognized you." Ariel paused for breath, closing his leaden eyes.

"Oh, that mysterious night. Suddenly there you were, the most beautiful princess a child could ever imagine, and I thought you would save me. When you left, I ran down the road trying to catch up."

Ariel's voice was fading. "*Diquenvsv aquenvsdi aquadulia* means 'I want to go home.'"

Weeping, Aleta dropped her head onto his chest even as she stretched forth a tender hand to both soothe and absorb the physical agony of his pulsating wound. *How can I bear to lose this man—husband, lover, best friend, father of my newly conceived twins?*

Ariel's remaining strength waned as he drew near the end of his Trail. Yet he inched closer to Aleta within her already tight embrace because he knew her thoughts.

"When Miriam died, I had nothing to live for, not even my daughter. I withered. I tried to kill myself. With you, I've opened like a flower in the sun. If you take me into your heart, you will sustain my spirit, for when I'm dead, it will nestle deep within the bud of a Cherokee rose."

He lay quiet for a long time, and when he continued, Aleta saw that his eyes had clouded over. "You'll need to take my adopted spirits, too: Miriam, Mohe, and Kuaray, but they won't bother you."

Aleta was stunned. "Kuaray? Your murderer? Why him?"

"He had nowhere to go. Even his sister turned him away. Aleta, he's our son."

After a while, Ariel went on in his softest whisper. "Maybe forgiveness is all that makes us human. You know, the Moon People were hateful, and they didn't want us to love each other. But I forgave them because they joined our hands, made us one forever when I was four and you were fifteen."

He smiled, and for the first and last time, he spoke directly into her brain. *Please take me now. Love of my life, let me die in you.* Diquenvsv aquenvsdi aquadulia."

Afterword

History in *The Last Shade Tree*

Aleta and her children Kuaray and Yacy find themselves thrust into the midst of historical atrocities from the past, and most of *The Last Shade Tree's* mid-20th-century characters also live through bad times. As the years go by and the worst offenses fade from memory, it doesn't hurt to recall when and where the novel's more catastrophic events took place.

The devastating forced relocation of the Cherokee Indians from the American South to Oklahoma in seventeen detachments, the Cherokee Trail of Tears, occurred during the summer of 1838 through 1839. Residential schools designed to "Kill the Indian—Save the Man" were established after the Civil War and lasted almost to the end of the 20th Century. The Warsaw Ghetto, created in 1940 during the German WW II occupation of Poland, ended abruptly in May, 1943. The death toll of the Jewish population herded within and imprisoned behind its walls exceeded 100,000. The forced internment of Japanese Americans in camps throughout the U.S. and Hawaii began a few months after Pearl Harbor, December 7, 1941, and did not end until early 1945. The Drancy internment camp for Jews—a halfway point on the journey to the extermination camps—operated in a suburb near Paris from 1942 to 1944 during the German occupation of France. It is now a Shoah memorial museum. A brief episode in the novel is based on the 1944 liquidation of the "gypsy family camp" at Auschwitz when some Romani prisoners were shipped off to provide slave labor in German factories. The repressive Communist era in Czechoslovakia lasted from 1948 to 1989.

For authenticity's sake, I use period slang, expletives, and also terms referring to race that were commonly heard from 1958 to 1976, the time period during which most of the book is set. But times have changed, and some of the racial terms may not seem acceptable today. They are certainly not meant to offend. For example, people now prefer the word Inuit over Eskimo.

Places: Real and Imaginary

The Last Shade Tree begins in the California I knew as a child—surrounded by live oaks, dusky green, with severed limbs poking from the golden mounds of wild-oat grass. In the spring, apricot orchards bloomed pink against an emerald carpet spiky with yellow mustard flowers. The ocean and the coastal redwoods were close by—and not too far away were the towns, cities, and parks: Monterey, Berkeley, San Francisco, Point Reyes, Lassen, and Yosemite. The rolling summer-yellow hills are still there, but the apricot orchards lost out long ago to the gridlock of Silicon Valley.

The characters from *The Last Shade Tree* tell you about the places they knew. Some of those places have disappeared while others continue to flourish, even if renamed. Santa's Village on Highway 17 near Santa Cruz, CA; Agnews Insane Asylum in Santa Clara, CA; and the Sequoyah Orphan Training School near Tahlequah, OK, all came to an end during the last century. However, Sequoyah Orphan Training School is now Sequoyah High School, run by the Cherokee Nation of Tahlequah. Baffin Island's chilly town Frobisher Bay is still there; it was renamed Iqaluit (place of many fish) in 1987. The High Tatras have not moved an inch but are no longer in Czechoslovakia. In 1992 the country was divided in two and renamed, and the High Tatras became the northern border of Slovakia. Cosmopolitan and bilingual Montreal still reigns in Quebec, Canada. Two important California locales in *The Last Shade Tree* never existed. Do not send a college application to Santa Margarita or try to visit the scruffy seaside town of Puerto Seguro. Puerto Seguro has the feel of old Monterey, CA; and Santa Margarita is reminiscent of UC Santa Cruz, and UC Santa Barbara.

Tsalagi Language

At age four, Ariel (Sequoyah) is sent to a residential school, which robs him of the only language he knows, Tsalagi, or Cherokee. He learns English, but doesn't entirely forget his childhood tongue. Consequently, *The Last Shade Tree* contains transliterated Cherokee words (many of them proper names) and a few complete sentences that are vital to the story. I extend special thanks to Harry Oosahwee, retired professor and a member of Northeastern State University's Cherokee Language Program team. A citizen of the Cherokee Nation and a foremost Cherokee language expert, Professor Oosahwee provided the transliterations in this book.

A note on the pronunciation of the Cherokee transliteration for the letter "v": the "v" is actually a soft vowel sound as found in the word, "sun." Thus the character Svnoyi's name would be pronounced in three syllables: "Su-no-ye."

Mythology

I have written new myths that tie together the more fantastic elements in *The Last Shade Tree*. To mention three, there are the tales of the magical violin, the mysterious cave art, and the unlucky pair of golden eagles. Alongside the new myths nestle bits and pieces of old Greek myths, Cherokee tales, an Aché myth, and a reference to a Norse god. Some of the Greek myths mentioned, such as Prometheus bringing fire to mankind or Ulysses' run-in with the sea monsters Charybdis and Scylla, are well known. Other myths, especially those set outside the ancient world, are less familiar.

Aleta chooses the names Kuaray and Yacy for her newborn twins in the chapter "Losing the Dream." The names come from the old Aché mythology of South American indigenous peoples, who identified the twin gods Kuaray and Yacy directly with the sun and moon. Mythology abounds with powerful twins, and some of them, such as Zeus's twin children Apollo and Diana, were also personifications of those heavenly bodies.

In the chapter "Luna's Fork 'n Spoon," I liken Ariel's outpouring of poetry to Hera's abundant milk. Hera, Zeus's unhappy wife, was a victim of his constant philandering. Her jealous rages turned her into a laughingstock even though she was the all-powerful queen of the heavens. Zeus conspired to bestow immortality on his half-human son, the illegitimate Hercules, by duping Hera into suckling the infant. Hercules was placed at Hera's breast while she slept, but she woke up and pushed him away. Her milk squirted across the sky to form the many stars of the Milky Way.

The sphinx was a composite mythical creature that varied in appearance and personality depending upon its place of origin. What both the Egyptian and Greek sphinxes had in common were feline characteristics, although their sex and natures were opposites. The Greek female sphinx who asked Oedipus the famous riddle was as heartless as her Egyptian male counterpart was benign. Ethan's sphinx that "fell into a pink cupcake" in "The Kidnapping of Svnoyi" is of the Greek variety.

At the end of "The Kidnapping of Svnoyi" Ariel is compared to a number of mythological heroes, including Baldr. This Norse god was known for his purity, his wealth, his wisdom, and his glowing good looks. His doting and fearful mother Frigg entreated every object in the world, except the insignificant mistletoe plant, to vow never to hurt her son. Unfortunately, an enemy of Baldr discovered his vulnerability. The most perfect of the Norse gods was slain by a spear fashioned from a mistletoe branch.

Nessie's snide comment in the "Drancy" chapter about "Zeus zipped up in a swan suit" refers to the Greek myth of Leda and the Swan. As a swan, Zeus seduced Leda in an unlikely coupling that produced four children hatched from eggs with contested parentage: Helen of Troy, Castor, Pollux, and Clytemnestra.

I compare the mourning Aleta in "Departure" to the Greek noblewoman Niobe who made the mistake of bragging about her fourteen children. To punish Niobe for her hubris, Apollo and Diana shot them dead with bows and arrows. The bereaved mother fasted and wept for nine days before returning home to her native Sipylus. There she was turned into a rock that still weeps as rainwater seeps through the porous limestone.

The last chapter, "Cherokee Rose," takes its name from the moving legend that Svnoyi relates. It reflects the horrors of the Trail of Tears that quite sapped the Cherokees of their will to survive. To renew hope, a God-given gift turned the tears shed by mothers no longer caring for their children into rosebushes that burst into bloom in a single day.

Ariel's inspiration for his vision of the whirlpool in "Departure" comes from a tale of the Eastern Cherokee that was collected by the ethnographer James Mooney. Here is most of the myth in Mooney's own captivating story-telling style.

At the mouth of Suck creek, on the Tennessee, about 8 miles below Chattanooga, is a series of dangerous whirlpools, known as "The Suck" .... It happened once that two men, going down the river in a canoe, as they came near this place saw the water circling rapidly ahead of them. They pulled up to the bank to wait until it became smooth again, but the whirlpool seemed to approach with wider and wider circles, until they were drawn into the vortex. They were thrown out of the canoe and carried down under the water, where one man was seized by a great fish and was never seen again. The other was taken round and round down to the very lowest center of the whirlpool, when another circle caught him and bore him outward and upward until he was finally thrown up again to the surface and floated out into the shallow water, whence he made his escape to shore. He told afterwards that when he reached the narrowest circle of the maelstrom the water seemed to open below him and he could look down as through the roof beams of a house, and there on the bottom of the river he had seen a great company of people, who looked up and beckoned to him to join them, but as they put up their hands to seize him the swift current caught him and took him out of their reach.

(James Mooney, "Myths of the Cherokee" Item 85, in the Nineteenth Annual Report of the Bureau of American Ethnology 1897-98, Part I, 1900.)

About the Author

Margaret Panofsky grew up surrounded by Northern California's live oak trees and golden wild-oat grass, but abandoned what's left of that idyllic beauty to live in New York City. She is a musician who plays the viola da gamba and is founder and director of New York University's The Teares of the Muses, a consort of viols. After years of playing Renaissance and Baroque music, she believes that her first novel has a definite musical lilt. Visit: www.lastshadetree.com

ALL THINGS THAT MATTER PRESS

FOR MORE INFORMATION ON TITLES AVAILABLE FROM
ALL THINGS THAT MATTER PRESS, GO TO
http://allthingsthatmatterpress.com
or contact us at
allthingsthatmatterpress@gmail.com

If you enjoyed this book, please post a review on Amazon.com and
your favorite social media sites.
Thank you!

Made in the USA
Middletown, DE
19 August 2017